To Rita

Where There's A Will, There's A Woman

with warm wishes

from

Mary Mae Lewis

Mary Mae Lewis

05/05/18

Copyright © Mary Mae Lewis 2016

The Author asserts her moral right under the Copyright, Designs and Patents Act, 1988, to be identified as the author of this work.

All rights reserved, including the right to reproduce this book, or portions thereof, in any form. No part of this text may be reproduced, transmitted, downloaded, decompiled, reverse engineered, or stored in or introduced into any information storage and retrieval system, in any form and by any means, whether electronic or mechanical without the express written permission of the publisher and author. The scanning, uploading, and distribution of this book via the Internet or via any other means without the permission of the publisher is illegal and punishable by law. Please purchase only authorised electronic/print editions, and do not participate in or encourage electronic/print piracy of copyrighted materials. This book is presented solely for entertainment purposes. No account of any persons living or dead that may be seen to be defamatory are intended as fact. The author and publisher make no representations or warranties of any kind and assume no liabilities of any kind with respect to the accuracy of the contents. Neither the author nor the publisher shall be held liable or responsible to any person or entity with respect to any loss of respect or incidental or consequential damages caused, or alleged to have been caused, directly or indirectly, by the text contained herein.This is a work of fiction. Any names or characters, businesses or places, events or incidents, are fictitious. Any resemblance to actual persons, living or dead, or actual events, is purely coincidental.

www.author-marymaelewis.co.uk

Dedication

To Christopher Stanley Lewis, my devoted and loving husband, my rock for nearly fifty years.

-1-

March 1st 1968

There was never much peace in the little house, and that night was no exception. Kathleen Tyler frowned, lamenting there had just been another family row and blamed it on her parents' poorly paid jobs. Still, her discomfort was tempered as she admired herself in the dressing table mirror and fantasised about living somewhere else. That was, until Mother shouted up the stairs, "It's gone seven, yer conna be late for your date."

Kath's nerves jangled as Nelly's words channelled up the steep staircase and echoed into the darkness.

"Her's still bloody preening hersen," Father barked from the comfort of his armchair in front of the coal fire; three feet from the staircase door.

"You conna be late," Mother repeated. "Mr. and Mrs. Bowley wouldn't like it. Ye said the film started at eight, din't ye?"

"Stop fretting." Kathleen snapped. "If we miss the trailers, well so ..." She was going to say 'so what' but instead, breathed deeply and said, slowly, "Well, it really won't matter."

"Her knows bloody everything, 'er beats me!" Father's words rumbled over his wife's head and up into Kath's ears.

The eighteen-year-old continued applying her pink lipstick in silence; resigned to the 'harping on.' Then, she replaced the lipstick top and put the tube back in the drawer, before pouting like a starlet, winking at the mirror and dashing out of her room; giving a final twirl before she bounced down the stairs.

Moving swiftly past her parents into the parlour, Kath left a trail of Apple Blossom perfume. "And don't wait up for me, I've got me key," she yelled, as she yanked the front door open.

As the door slammed shut, fifty-four-year-old Arthur banged his fist on the arm of his armchair and shouted. "The sooner 'er goes, the better."

"It's just a phase, Arthur; she'll come round one day. All the young ones are like that today, no time for parents, especially old ones like us; it's all this permissive stuff: Princess Margaret carrying on with a divorced man, Rock and Roll and now... mini skirts."

"Well her's getting so sharp, says she can't stand our terraced house! Her'll cut her own bloody tongue off, she will, and it'll be the death of her - and us."

"Arthur, she's a clever girl and she has been Confirmed, so don't worry. He seems a nice man, this Robert. Mrs. Bowley wouldn't have asked our Kath to go on a blind date with someone who wasn't a good 'un, would she?"

"Well, you might be right, hope thee at, but her's too bloody wrapped up in them big ideas of hers, leaving home, going abroad, all that. Her'll end upon her arse, that's all."

"Now stop going on about her grand schemes. It's only natural to have ambition and to want to better yourself. And she 'asn't done too bad so far, has she? Look, she's working and she's going to College in September. I'm proud of my daughter, Arthur, so don't you go undermining her confidence with your bloody this and that."

"Well, her's got 'er head in the clouds. Thinks 'er's better than us. Wants 'ouses with swimming pools and 'osses."

Nelly smiled as she imagined horses swimming around in a swimming pool. "Well, what's wrong with that? You wouldn't say no to those things if you could 'ave 'em, would you? But, you never wanted anything better!" Nelly's voice turned sour. "You wouldn't leave your ruddy mother and that's why we've been stuck in this hole for thirty years. Thirty years living in the same street as your ruddy mother - and sister."

"Now, Nelly, I don't like you swearing where my mother is concerned. And, at least this house is paid for, not like some buggers, where everything's on the never-never."

"Well, why don't we move then, get an 'ouse with a garden and a nice view? What have I got? A damn big chimney stuck outside the back, a brick wall in front of me kitchen window and black terraces facing me front door."

"Well, you've got more than most in this street. How many people 'as got a new telly and a share in a caravan?" Arthur's chest puffed up with pride talking about the caravan. After pausing, he went on, "…and how many have got as many frocks in the wardrobe as you and… salmon sandwiches for tea on Sundays?"

Nelly hung her head as Arthur continued. "And what about my roses at the front? Nobody in this street has got a forecourt better." Arthur banged both fists this time, on the arms of his armchair.

"Well, you're right, Arthur," Nelly finally conceded. "I should 'na complain. You are a good man Arthur, and all these DIY jobs you do, I could ne do without ye. But, let Kath have her dreams. If she wants to make something of her life, get on and be somebody, well, good luck to her." Nelly picked up her paperback, slouched down into the armchair next to Arthur's and, with one leg tucked under her bottom and a Woodbine dangling from her mouth, carried on reading where she had left off...

'Their eyes met across the crowded ship's cocktail bar, the young captain in full uniform stood erect, his thick blond hair magnificently coiffured...'

Arthur disappeared into the parlour where he listened to his records: Mario Lanza, Perry Como and songs from the *The King and I.* It was Arthur's sacred place where he practised his Old Time Dancing steps, for classes held in the Church Hall.

He and Nelly had acquired a large circle of friends because of their dancing. Nearly every night, someone would knock on the front door for a chat and a cup of tea. Kath was always an exemplary hostess, pouring out freshly brewed *Black Boy tea* from a bone china teapot into fine china tea cups. It would have been unthinkable to have such luxury in a humble home like this, had it not been for Nelly and her friends, who worked in the pottery factories, called Pot Banks. There was always somebody who had 'acquired' a bit of crockery from work and passed it on for a shilling or two; behind closed doors. From these gatherings, Kathleen learned something of the world that existed way beyond the grimy six towns of the Potteries, officially called Stoke-on-Trent.

Aunty May, a chiropodist's receptionist, made telephone appointments and opened the door to "well-healed" patients, she liked to quip. May's job was posh compared to Nelly's: aero graphing. Harry, the local cobbler, had an exotic Belgian wife. Jim, the Italian miner, told tales of his youth in the Dolomites, Ravenna and the Po Valley. Teachers at Kath's Grammar School had shed some light on what could be achieved through study and hard work.

The popular press was talking about class barriers disintegrating, thanks to post-war Labour governments, and new opportunities opening up for the workers.

Kath longed for adventure and to escape the burden of her working class existence, which always seemed to be mired in tragedy. Nelly's own father, having survived being a soldier in WWI, had died tragically soon after at thirty-six with bowel cancer, leaving four small children. Nelly was eleven at the time. She had suffered with Arthur too as he witnessed his own mother's decline into dementia.

Nelly told Kath to *laugh-off the bad things in life*. But that was easier said than done. Billy, Kath's brother, had just left home, after a shotgun wedding to a woman who didn't like work, and now had a baby to raise. As Kath rushed off for her blind date, Nelly worried that Kath might do something 'silly' too.

On the dry, pre-spring evening, Kath walked quickly, checked her watch, then slowed down. She didn't want to be late, nor early, but just right. She liked precision and had a natural flair for time management. On the chilly street she felt energized; full of confidence. Her new, steel-tipped stilettos clicked a pleasing rhythm on the granite pavement. At each strike, she felt the drumming up of excitement. *Would he be handsome?* she dreamed. It was all down-bank to the Bowley's flat, a quarter of a mile away. The rows of houses, with grey slate roofs, squat chimneys, sash windows, brown clay brick walls, solid wood front doors painted black and cardinal red tiled front door steps, all looked the same.

It was a Friday night and the streets were deserted. The men were in the pubs, the housewives bolted up indoors with their sleeping children. Kath didn't want a life like theirs.

By the time she reached her destination, her imagination was in a state of euphoria. The chance to be meeting Robert, a gentleman from Wales, who had grown up in a Georgian mansion in Glamorgan, but now lived in London, was intoxicating. She hoped he didn't like going to pubs every night, though. All she knew was that he was a reserved twenty-seven-year-old technical teacher who hadn't had a steady girlfriend for some time… and who wasn't fat. Kath baulked slightly at the idea of going out with an introvert, but then they were going out as a foursome and it was only for one night. It shouldn't matter what he was like or if she fancied him or not. *But not many girlfriends,* Kath pondered, *might he be queer? But surely Mrs Bowley wouldn't have organised this date if he was. She didn't seem that kind of person. Mrs Bowley was an honest, good-hearted type, a regular blood donor.* Kath forced negative thoughts out of her mind. *Mr and Mrs Bowley must think he would suit me,* Kath rationalised.

Keith Bowley gave Kath a lift to work every day. He and Jill had met Robert when they were in Birmingham University doing teacher training. Jill had taken a shine to the posh gentleman, who had visited the couple several times over the years and who had fallen in love with the canals, steel works and pot banks of Stoke. Kathleen couldn't imagine anyone normal, let alone someone of his class, liking the area where she was born and had spent all her life. She mused at how she, a PE student teacher, would relate to a man who liked factories!

-2-

Tilly, sipping a hot mug of cocoa, sat nursing her chilblains, ensconced in a pink velvet buttoned-back armchair. Pet poodle, Peaches, sat at her feet in front of a feeble log fire.

"Better go to bed now, Tiger," bleated Samuel Llewellyn, as he poked his head round the living room door." It's no use… that wood is damp."

"You know I don't like you calling me, Tiger; it makes me sound ferocious," Tilly reprimanded her husband.

The old man frowned and stepped towards his wife. "Better put your coat on Tiger, if you are going to sit there all night."

"Sam! You didn't hear a word of what I said."

Sam jumped back.

"I said," Tilly raised her voice further." Don't call me, Tiger." Then added. "And, I am not ready for bed either."

"Oh dear, oh dear, Matilda," Sam spluttered, as he hastily retreated from the room.

Tilly fixed her attention on the noise upstairs, then put down her mug, threw her head back and shut her eyes, as the pounding got louder. Their 'midnight monster' youngest son, was prowling around again. *Another sleepless night in store,* she thought, shuddering.

Sam returned and threw some dry sticks and a cup of paraffin on the fire. *Woof*! Flames shot across the hearth ."You great fool," Tilly screamed as she scuttled the Victorian chair away from the heat. Peaches ran to safety up a corner. "You could have burned us all alive with that stuff - and we are not even insured!"

The odd couple had only just moved into the Old Parsonage. It had taken six removal vans to relocate their belongings from Glamorgan to Somerset; boxes were still stacked up in the storeroom at the back of the large house.

Moving there had been a snap decision, after Tilly had rowed with the neighbours at their last house, a riverside cottage, which she had built without planning consent. She had seen the advert for their new home, which was once a Jacobean coaching inn, in *The Times*. She was so impressed with the fact that Isaac Williams, author of *The Complete Philosopher* had stayed there once, (there was a plaque in one-bedroom to prove it), that she bought the house after only a twenty-minute viewing.

Samuel, two years off retirement, still had to commute to work, though. Fortunately, as director of an art school, he could get away with being present at the college for only part of the week, claiming he was working from home the rest of the time. Tilly needed him in the new house. Living only five miles from Bath, she had designs on opening an antique shop, but she hadn't bargained on how hard it would be. Neither, had she bargained on having their son - who enjoyed pounding away upstairs on the old piano - living in with her. "Oh God, Sam, go and tell Leonard to stop that plonking."

"What plonking?"

"He's banging on the piano. Can't you hear it?"

"No!"

"Well, that's it; you are off to the optician tomorrow to get a hearing aid."

"Don't be daft, opticians don't give you hearing aids."

"There you are, you heard exactly what I said, so you can't be that deaf. You just hear what you want to hear. You can't fool me."

"Oh dear, oh dear", Sam mumbled and obediently went off to stop the racket.

Leonard, on hearing footsteps on the stairs, stopped playing. He slipped off the piano stool and hid behind the heavy oak door, waiting.

As unsuspecting Sam peeped into the room, Leonard yelled "*aaarrrggghhh.*"

The blood curdling voice blasted Sam's senses; he swayed, rolled his eyes, clutched his chest and staggered down the stairs. "I nearly had a heart attack," he complained to his wife. "What can we do with him?" Sam's eyes filled with tears.

"Look out of the window," instructed Tilly. "I bet there's a full moon tonight. You know how he is when it's a full moon!"

Sam parted the curtains and looked up.

The full moon was out. He turned to his wife and they stared at each other in silence with air of fatalistic resignation.

Leo had been expelled from Goldsmiths Art College the year previously, after going on a rampage and throwing a *Dansette* through the common room window. After police questioning, he was referred to a psychiatrist, then spent five months in a mental institution in Kent, before being sent home. Tilly and Sam told everyone that their son had had a minor nervous breakdown, but Tilly didn't believe that. She believed her Leo was mad; this menace was in his blood, in every fibre of his being. *But weren't all geniuses insane?*

"Oh Lord, it's nearly midnight and do you know its March 1st today? Saint David's Day," Sam said, wanting to take his mind off his wayward son.

"I don't feel like celebrating and I don't feel like being Welsh any more, not after those nasty neighbours in Wales forced us out," Tilly pulled her shawl more tightly round her shoulders.

"You can't let them bother you; we are here now, and by god we will show them! Sam raised his fist in defiance. Tilly smiled, then changed tack. "I wonder what Robert is doing tonight? I don't think he knows we've moved house. I did write to him at Christmas, but he hasn't replied." Tilly picked up a magazine from the floor and flicked the pages in an attempt to hide her disappointment; her first-born hadn't been in contact.

"Well, you know how it is, got his own problems, I suppose," Sam tried to sound sensible.

"Yes, and he still hasn't got a wife," Tilly sighed, as she threw the magazine onto the settee.

"Good Lord, why should he want a wife now? I didn't marry 'til I was thirty-five."

"Don't remind me, I married an old man; 'live to regret it', Mother said."

Samuel didn't want to hear recriminations. He took the empty mug, that Tilly had left on the hearth, and crept into the kitchen to wash the dishes. Peaches, who hadn't stopped shaking since the paraffin blast, followed him.

"Leave the dishes till the morning," Tilly ordered, as she ascended the stairs to her 'boudoir' bedroom, where she slept on a genuine antique four-poster bed.

Ignoring the last command of the day, Sam finished washing-up at midnight, then, for fear of disturbing his wife, he tiptoed his way to his ground floor bolthole. Originally a washroom, the tiny space, with a single bed squeezed in, was now Sam's bedroom.

Leonard laughed himself to sleep over the little trick he played on his father, but then stayed silent for the rest of the moonlit night, far away from his parents; in his attic domain, among the great oak rafters.

–3–

Kath took a deep breath as she knocked on the front door of the terraced house, where the Bowley's lived in the top flat. The sound of footsteps rang down the stairs and across the lino covered hall, then Kath 'froze' momentarily before the door finally opened. Sighing with relief, the young girl smiled as she saw a friendly looking, Jill Bowley. "Come in duck. You look lovely. I love this..." she said, stroking Kath's three-quarter length, bottle-green coat.

"I knit it meself," Kath purred with appreciation, running a hand through her chestnut-coloured ponytail, then pulling down the hem of her black pencil skirt - one inch above the knee.

"You go up first," Jill stepped aside and let Kath through.

After pausing at the living room door, and following a nudge from Jill, Kath - with heart pounding - entered the room. Her date was kneeling on the hearthrug, bending over a radio! Kath chuckled for a second but then focused on the manly back before her. Robert was clothed in a tight-fitting cream polo neck sweater; his light-brown hair brushed the roll neck collar. Feeling that he was being watched, Robert swung round and stood up. His face was only inches from Kath's; their eyes met, his clear sky blue, hers a rich brown. Kath felt a frisson; a flutter in her stomach. Robert's olive skin, high cheekbones and aquiline nose sent a shiver through her. Nodding to Robert, Jill marshalled everyone out of the flat.

"We had better get going. The film starts at eight. It's quarter to now. Better get your skates on. " Jill sounded jolly as she grabbed her coat.

Keith eased himself out of his armchair and followed her downstairs. Kath and Robert were already waiting outside, and then, giggling like nursery school children, the four set off.

Robert placed his hands on Kath's hips, as they proceeded in single file past a little park, where the pavements were narrow. Kath warmed to his touch; she turned and smiled. Robert smiled back and instinctively they made their way to the picturehouse and their destination: the back row.

"Phew…" Kath said, trying to catch her breath.

Robert and Kath flopped into their seats, not noticing that they had lost Jill and Keith in the dark.

"Bloody Hell," Keith said as he reached the back row too and sat next to Robert." Can't wait to get at it, ye buggers!"

Kath drew in a sharp breath. She'd had no inkling that Keith could be so vulgar. There was never a hint of coarseness when she went to school with him in his car, every day.

"By the way, what are we going to see?" Kath asked.

"Poor Cow."

"About farms then?" Kath blushed when an awkward silence followed, but at least no one could see her embarrassment in the pitch darkness.

"No, it's about poor people, crime and prostitutes. One woman has a baby by a criminal. You know… real life drama. Like *Cathy Come Home!"*

Kathleen hadn't heard of this either and squirmed at her ignorance, and at the thought of people getting involved with the police, and living on the streets. She clutched Robert's hand for comfort.

Although she was from a working class home, and would perhaps have been regarded as poor by Robert's parents, she was not *that* poor and was very proud. It had been drummed into her from birth to get a good job: *if you don't work, you don't eat - then it's the workhouse for you*. Kath had therefore always been a good worker; though not always careful with what she earned; she liked fashionable clothes and going out, but at least she was never in debt. She'd had little jobs like a Saturday job in *Boots*, stacking shelves in a supermarket, selling *Avon* and babysitting the neighbours' toddlers. Then, six-months previously, she had seized the opportunity to be a student teacher for a year, before going to teacher training college. With the money, she had learned to drive and passed her test, just a week before. She was still so excited about that, she told Robert, as the film was about to start. Her voice was so loud that five people in the row in front, turned round to complain. Kath blushed again and wondered if Robert disapproved of her already.

She needn't have worried as Robert acknowledged her joy by hugging her, and Kath responded, cuddling in closer. She was enamoured; she could hardly follow the story line until the film showed a woman giving birth. Kathleen sat rigid, mouth agape, stunned by the brutality of it all. Never before had she seen so much blood and gunge – she just had never imagined birth to be like that! Although she was studying Biology 'A' Level, it was all learned from textbooks and there was not a drop of blood in sight. Robert looked away, but Kath, ever curious, stayed glued to the screen. Once the baby was out, and put to the breast, the whole audience fell silent. Kath felt as exhausted as the mother, and slumped back into her seat, sweating as though she herself had given birth.

It wasn't until after the show and they were in the pub, next door, that the subject was mentioned again. "So when are you going to start a family, Jill," Robert enquired, playfully.

"After seeing that film tonight, well, I don't bloody want to see a dick ever again!"

Jill, Kath reckoned, had obviously drunk too much port and lemon. Robert laughed, but noticeably, Keith didn't.

"Too bloody bad, ye bitch, you're getting a big one tonight!"

Kathleen could hardly believe her ears. She still called Keith, Mr Bowley. She had thought of him as a middle-class paragon of virtue! Strangely enough though, it made Kath feel at ease. She supposed it was because everyone in her family swore… and she had previously been taught that only ill-educated people swore. She pondered what the old dears would think of Mr. Bowley now?

Last orders!

"Let's get some fish and chips..." suggested Keith on leaving the pub, and they all followed suit by crossing the road towards a fish and chip shop.

"I only like the ones from the chippy in High Lane, and I am too tipsy to drive. So are you, Keith!" Jill said, looking straight at Rob who immediately took the bait.

"I'll drive up there in the van, with Kath. Come on," he said, as he steered Kath along the road towards his vehicle, which was parked outside the Bowley's flat.

"Fish chips and mushy peas for all, eh? " Rob asked as he started the engine. "It's all on me."

"Bring a bottle of *Tizer*, and one of Dandelion and Burdock, too," Jill shouted from their front door. "I need to sober up or I'll be getting a big dick tonight!"

Kath blushed again.

Robert was oblivious, he was checking his wing mirrors, then he sped down the street. He knew the way to the allotted chip shop and told Kath how much he loved the city's heritage. Kath was ashamed that she didn't know more. Her family didn't *do* local history or geography and neither had it been on her school curriculum.

She had been educated along with hundreds and thousands of other youngsters to get out of Stoke. *Change your accent* they said, and encouraged parents to get private elocution lessons for their sons and daughters. Kath only escaped such classes because Mother wanted a new fur coat. Kath was pleased, at that time, that she didn't have to spend hours reciting: 'how now brown cow', but she regretted that now.

As they drove along, Robert regaled Kath on his love of reading. He had read books by Arnold Bennett, he knew about Henry Doulton - the founder of the pottery dynasty of the same name - and he had studied the work of Josiah Wedgwood. He admired Thomas Telford and James Brindley, the great canal engineers, and had spent one October half-term holiday on a narrow boat, plying up and down the Trent and Mersey canal. Kath was very impressed.

Having bought the suppers, Kath offered to drive, so Robert handed her the van keys. He was pleased that Kath had resisted drinking alcohol that evening and settled on lemonade, instead. Kath pulled out of the car park into the main road. "I'll go a different way back," she said, decisively. As the *Ford Transit* passed the maternity hospital, Kathy shouted out: *Poor Cow!* Going on to explain to a puzzled Robert, "My sister-in-law, Pauline, Billy's wife, has just had a baby boy in there... so, I am an Aunty! Whoopee!"

Robert smiled, but Kath was caught off-guard when she felt a warm hand slip onto the bare flesh of her upper left leg. *Thought he hadn't had much luck with women*, she thought to herself as they stopped at traffic lights. *Well he thinks he's in luck with me!*

Robert squeezed Kath's thigh just enough to make her sigh and him drop the fish and chip packet from his lap onto the van floor.

"Just as well it's wrapped up tight," Kath quipped.

"You wearing a chastity belt then?" Robert joked.

Kath liked his sense of humour.

"I meant the chip packet, not my, er... well, I am not going to say the word."

"Go on – say fanny – that's what you meant wasn't it?"

Kath blushed and flustered about with the gears as they sped off again.

"Well, you two rabbits have been a bloody long time!" Keith swore again as he opened the flat front door.

"She took me on a guided tour of Tunstall," Rob explained. "Told me all about Arnold Bennett and Henry Doulton," he lied, but it did make Kath feel good.

"Well, are the chips still warm?" Jill asked.

"Damn right they are," assured Rob.

Even gentleman Rob was using strong language, Kath noticed.

"Damn well ought to be, he's been keeping them hot on his lap, well... higher up than that!" Kath giggled, adding. " On his bloody crotch. He's damned hot tonight." Kath thought it only right that as everybody else was bloodying, buggering, damning and mentioning private parts, she would join in.

"Well, I am not eating them, if that's where they have been," said Jill, smirking.

"Only kidding," Kath interjected, convincingly, and with that they all tucked in.

Kath felt pleased the Bowlers had taken her word about the chips, she reasoned it was because she commanded a certain amount of authority.

After all, she had been sent on leadership courses and obtained the Silver Level Award in the Duke of Edinburgh Scheme. She'd even been Form Captain three times and School Swimming Captain one year. Coming down-to-earth again, Kath realised that they really had all been so hungry, they would have eaten anything.

It was nearly midnight when Kath let herself into her house in Bluegates Street, her childhood home. Robert had eagerly walked her back from the Bowley's and tenderly kissed her goodnight on the lips, promising to write the following week.

Nelly was still up when Kath turned the key. "I told you I had a key, Mum."

"But you know I can't sleep 'til I know you are in safe and sound. How was it? " Nelly probed.

"Okay, but let's get to bed, I'm tired," Kath didn't mean to be hard on her mother, but she didn't want to invest time and effort on telling her mother about a man she might never see again. London was a long way away and she was going to South Wales to study soon. "I'll tell you another day."

Kath had more things on her mind now than romantic dates. She had to umpire a netball match at eleven the next morning at a school three miles away. She would have to get the bus, because although she could drive, she didn't have a car! And, *damn it*, she had forgotten to get the latest bus timetable and... *damn it* her stopwatch had ended up mangled and useless after mother had thrown her tracksuit into the washing machine, without first checking the pockets.

True to form that Saturday, Kath got up early, called on a school mate, who lived two streets away, borrowed a stopwatch and raced to the bus stop an hour before she needed to - just to be sure she didn't miss the bus.

You never know, Kath thought at the school, *this Robert might come back* - and she wanted to make sure she was in good shape, if he did. She started running round the playground in ever faster circles, smiling as she ran.

-4-

Robert's first letter to Kath arrived ten days after their blind date. Even though his news was a little dreary: *too much marking, troublesome boys, road works from his flat in SE9 through the Blackwall Tunnel to his school in Stepney*... his last sentence left Kath in no doubt that he wanted to see her again, *You are gorgeous - come soon - I'll meet you at Euston Station.*

Kath had only been to the Metropolis once, the previous year, when she had been on a week-long trip for youngsters from a 'deprived' background who would most likely benefit from such a cultural experience. She could hardly wait to wait to return.

Kath wrote a long letter back to Rob, whilst humming along to the pop tunes on Radio Luxemburg. She too summarised her activities since their blind date: getting to know her baby nephew, Matthew; going to a cousin's wedding; visiting Mr and Mrs Bowley (Kath still felt uncomfortable calling them by their first names); seeing *Romeo and Juliet* at the theatre - and helping her brother Billy to move her bedroom furniture into his new house.

Kath bemoaned the fact she now only had a single bed and a mirror left, but reconciled that Billy's need was greater than hers. Besides, soon she would share the double bed with her mother, because her dad was going to have surgery on his knee.

Kath accepted Rob's invitation to the capital and suggested the last weekend of March; train fares would be cheaper before Easter and she had an old school friend living in North London, with whom she could stay. At Easter she was going to Blackpool for a residential educational gymnastic course.

It was after midnight and The Supremes' *You Can't Hurry Love* was playing on her radio, when Kath finally checked over what she had written. When she was happy with the letter, she signed off: *Love....... Love...... Love from Kath XXXX.*

Sticking down the envelope, she realised she hadn't written anything about her job – mainly because she detested it. Mal, Head of PE, was a bully. She had called Kath a blind twit when she missed an offside in a hockey match once, and she forced her to do a five-mile cross country run when she had a bad cold. Furthermore, Kath was struggling to control the thirteen-year-olds in her English classes. Thirty 'C' streamers even once a week for a one-hour was an ordeal. She could just about cope with the eleven-year-old 'B' group but was beginning to realise, with only seven 'O' Levels, how inadequately educated she was to be a teacher.

As she had been a thirteen plus grammar school entry she, along with twenty-one other lucky, (or perhaps unlucky girls), had sat the 'O' Levels a year later than the eleven plus girls. Kath reached eighteen - the minimum age to be a student teacher - soon after sitting the exams and was offered the student teacher post by a well-meaning director of Physical Education. He had thought that the money would help Kath through college. However, Kath was now beginning to regret her decision not to stay on in the sixth form.

The steam train, (one of the last ever to be used for a passenger service in England) puffed to a halt exactly on time at Euston Station at 8.30 pm that Friday night.

Kath had dressed perfectly for the occasion and buttoned up her fitted black, pure wool overcoat, as she prepared to leave the carriage. Then she put on her Russian fur hat and picked up her muff: frost had been forecast. A designer black leather shoulder bag and knee-high black leather boots completed the outfit. Descending the steps on to the platform and peering through the last of the train's steam vapour, she saw her consort waiting a few yards away.

In his black leather trench coat he looked even more handsome than she had remembered. Kath's spine tingled. His hair had grown longer and he looked like John Lennon. Looking into her eyes, he took Kath's weekend case and set it down with a flourish, almost a bow, then rising, put his arms round her and kissed her.

"You look better than Julie Christie in *Doctor Zhivago,"* he said.

Kath trembled. "I thought I was more like Diana Rigg?"

"Better... in fact." Rob kissed Kath again. "So, tell me, where's your friend's flat ?"

"Oh, change of plan. I forgot to tell you. Susan didn't reply to my letters..." Kath voiced only minor irritation. "So, I have booked myself into a youth hotel in Baker Street. But we can go for a drink first, if you like, before I check in."

"How about seeing a film too? We could just make it for the last showing," Rob suggested.

"Okay. But, only if it's something funny. I was traumatised for a week after seeing *Poor Cow*… all that depravity and blood."

"And sex." Robert, with his arm round Kath's shoulder, pulled her closer. "Well let's see a funny film with sex in it then!"

Kath didn't resist. "What's on?"

"Don't know yet, let's just drive down to Leicester Square and see. I had thought about strolling along the Embankment, but it's too bleedin' parky tonight."

"I suppose *parky* means freezing cold?"

"Yes, its Cockney slang."

Having lived in Kent, where he had studied for four years, then London, where he had been working for seven years, Robert had acquired a Southern accent. Gone were the days as a freshman, when he had been labelled Taffy because of his strong South Wales twang.

"Aren't you proud of being Welsh, then?" Kathleen enquired.

"No."

"Well… *my* great grandparents were Owens and emigrated from the countryside in mid-Wales, late 1800s, to work in the pot banks. My great-grandfather, Philomon Tyler, was from North Wales. My ancestors had mines up there. So, my heritage is one reason I am going to Barry - I want to learn about *The Land of my Fathers.*"

"And what's another reason then? It's a long way from Stoke."

Kath confessed, she had applied to Coventry, Didsbury and Matlock teacher training colleges, all within ninety minutes driving distance from home, but had been rejected. "But, it's all turned out well – I am glad to be going to Barry and what a coincidence I met you? But if you won't tell me about Wales, then perhaps your parents will, one day?" Kath stopped herself short; here she was again jumping the gun!

Thankfully, Robert avoided the question and said, "Come on, must get a move on, I am on a ten-minute parking space."

The couple were out of breath when they reached the van and headed into the night, towards the cinemas of the West End.

After cider for Kath and half a bitter for Rob in a pub, they agreed that *Carry On Up The Khyber* was just the thing for a Friday night.

After the hilarious film, Rob drove Kath slowly to the hotel while they chatted; he knew that he wouldn't be allowed into Kath's hotel room.

They went round Trafalgar Square, down Whitehall, passed The Houses of Parliament, Westminster Abbey and Buckingham Palace. On their journey, they discussed school holidays and how they both 'survived' the term times. Teaching had been the last career option for Robert when he left art college, after completing a Degree in furniture design; he would get another year's grant if he agreed to go onto art teachers' training for a year. He confided that he had in fact failed that year, but because he had promised to re-sit within six-months – and there was a shortage of technical teachers willing to teach in the East End - he landed a full-time teaching post in Stepney Green Boys' School.

Standing at the entrance to the youth hotel, Kath threw her arms round Rob's neck and kissed him on the lips, until she ran out of breath.

It was one minute to midnight, when feeling like Cinderella about to be turned into a rat, she ran up the steps and into the building. "Thanks for a lovely evening!" she shouted from reception. "Be back here at half past nine in the morning." She added, blowing kisses.

The night porter booked Kath a morning call for 8.30 a.m., then Kath got in to the lift.

Ascending to her room, Kath reflected that Robert was quite wonderful. She fell asleep under the feather duvet, glowing.

Kath surveyed the frosty Saturday morning through the window of her room on the sixth floor. The city was beginning to stir, but she feared Robert would have difficulty finding a parking spot, or even might not turn up at all! She bit her nails as she waited downstairs in the lobby, flicking through a magazine. At nine-forty he had still not arrived, but Kath breathed out a sigh of relief when he turned up ten minutes later; he had taken the Tube.

Rob looked just as smart in the day as at night, and Kath soon forgave his late arrival. They set off, arm-in-arm, towards the Underground in Baker Street to go to the British Museum and then the National Gallery.

It was 4 o'clock before Kath decided they should go shopping in Oxford Street. She wanted a glamorous swimsuit; she had only owned sporty *Speedo* racing costumes before. She told Rob he could choose one for her and then they would go swimming together in the morning. Rob spluttered and said he couldn't swim.

"Not even doggy paddle?" Kath asked, shocked. "And to think you lived by the sea for twelve years. Well, if you can't swim, I'll teach you."

Robert winced. "Kath… how come you know about where I have lived…?"

"Mrs. Bowley talks, you know! Even if you don't!" Kath joked.

"Anyway… I don't know where there is a swimming baths open tomorrow, and I haven't got any swimming trunks," Rob was trying to wriggle out of the inevitable.

"You can buy some today and we'll check out the pools later," Kath was not to be deterred.

Kath chose a black, pink and green flowery patterned swimsuit after she dismissed Rob's suggestion to buy a white bikini, like the one Ursula Andress wore in the James Bond Film *Dr. No*. Kath wasn't ready for dressing like a Bond Girl!

"Plain black *Lycra* shorts, for you, you can't go wrong with these," Kath held up the trunks. Rob sighed, resigned to his fate, as he paid for both items.

"Let's go back to your hotel for a cuddle now," Rob said, as the shops closed.

"That's not allowed. You already know that. Girls only."

"Run by nuns, I presume," Rob sneered.

"Well, I haven't seen any nuns. Anyway, I am starving. Let's go for a Chinese, eh? I'll go Dutch; after all, you bought me that costume."

Rob agreed. It was up to him now to think of a suitable place. Chinatown was the obvious answer and they walked hand-in-hand all the way.

Sitting in a window seat in The Peking Palace Restaurant, they tucked into their delicious three-course special: dim sum soup, stir fry prawns and fried rice, then a honey cake dessert, all washed down with rice wine. It was as if they had never seen food before! It was 10.30 p.m. when they had finished and started on their way back to the 'crap hotel', as Rob was calling it.

"Damn! We haven't checked out about swimming," Kath reminded him.

"Too late now, we'll have to give it a miss," Rob said, with a look of triumph on his face.

"No..." retorted Kath. "The night porter will know where we can go."

Rob had done his best to fend off having to go swimming, but it was no use. *Kath is very persistent,* he thought.

Just as she had judged, the night porter knew the whereabouts of public swimming pools and Greenwich Public Pool was only a mile from where Robert lived. It was decided that Robert would pick Kath up in the van the next morning.

"But be sure to be waiting for me outside the front door at 10 o'clock," he said. "And... we'll go to my flat after swimming."

Rob panicked as he climbed into his bedsit bed. The prospect of having Kath to his humble room - the box-room of a terraced house in Humber Road - was crippling, so much so that he got up unusually at seven to clean up. The landlady, Elaine, who lived in the house, was not amused to hear the vacuum on so early; waking her three-year-old daughter. She resented having Rob living there anyway, it was only a matter of expediency; they wanted an extra income to pay off the mortgage

At least the box-room had been big enough to partition a section off at the far end, so Rob had his own kitchen, but there was only one bathroom in the whole house, which had to be used on a rota basis. Rob was allocated Saturday nights for a bath and, *damn Elaine*, he had missed his bath slot that night and made do with a flannel wipe down in the kitchen sink!

Still, Robert arrived at the hotel in Baker Street on time and they drove to the swimming pool in Greenwich.

"You are sure that you have got your trunks?" enquired Kathleen, cautiously.

"Of course," Robert said tersely.

"I don't think you are very keen on water, are you?" she probed.

"No, it's not really my thing, nobody in our family can swim," He shrugged, noticing that Kath was plainly shocked. "Anyway, we'll go for a pint and a pub snack after."

Rob and Kath's experience in the pool wasn't as bad as he had anticipated. The water was comfortably warm and there were few other bathers that day. Robert squeezed Kath's thighs furtively under the water. "You are like an Italian model," he enthused, until she reminded him in her self-deprecating, no-nonsense manner that she was only five-foot four inches tall and too broad shouldered and slim hipped to be any kind of model.

"At eight stone and 36-26-34. I'm hardly a model," she said. "But so long as you think I am good-looking, clever and fun, well, that's all that matters." Kath looked at Robert for reassurance.

"And... you are strong." He looked at Kath admiringly. "I wish I was." Although Rob was slim and handsome, he was not muscular. He loathed sport with a passion, especially ball games, and blamed it on having to wear glasses for short-sightedness. As a schoolboy he had been good at gymnastics, but then as he reached puberty, he found the pleasures of drinking, smoking, playing billiards and dating pretty girls. Thankfully, Rob had given up smoking, some years ago, after a menacing bout of pneumonia, but he still drank beer and played the occasional game of snooker. "All in moderation..." he said.

Rob's lack of sporting ability didn't deter Kath. She loved his gentlemanly figure, of which she got a full view in the pool. At five-foot eleven and weighing eleven stones, he was a perfect match for her. Not too tall (she hated anyone towering above her) and not too broad - she loathed those images of weightlifting men with bulging triceps and biceps. Rob, with his smooth skin, was just right.

Before going to Rob's flat, they stopped off at a Thames-side bar and bistro near the *Cutty Sark* in Greenwich. Sitting at a table for two in the conservatory overlooking the river, Rob ordered a half pint of bitter, half of shandy for Kath and two small pork pies. If it had crossed Kath's mind that Robert might be rather stingy and unromantic, the disillusionment was short-lived: Kath listened to Rob's account of the Cutty Sark's history and tales of the London docks, marvelling at his great knowledge. The sound of his educated voice was seducing her already. She relaxed into the basket armchair of the establishment and opened up a conversation about how exciting it would be to have a sailing boat and sail around the world. She imagined herself, bikini clad, sunbathing on deck - while cruising the Caribbean.

An arrogant waiter, who must have heard Kath, and noticed the couple had finished their drinks, soon destroyed the fantasy. He yanked their empty glasses from the table and said, with the air of a Mountbatten,"Sir, if you are going to get this young lady back to Liverpool tonight, I think she should go now!" He was obviously irritated that this pair were spending so little money and taking up precious riverside space, that more affluent customers could be using. But there was no mistaking the attack on Kath's Northern accent. Kath cringed at the insult, but said nothing. Instead, she got straight up and made for the exit. Rob followed.

Kath was still silently seething and chiding herself for not reprimanding the waiter, as she knew her father would have done, when they arrived at Rob's flat. She was going to challenge Rob about his silence over the ordeal but thought it might spoil the weekend, and, in any case, she was so taken aback by the size and state of the flat that her indignation at the waiter's remarks dissolved into nothing. She never imagined a flat being so small and dark. The tiny windows faced north and east and overlooked similar depressing rows of terraces with no gardens and only minute back yards. The bed, jammed into one corner, almost filled the room. It was obvious too that the place hadn't been tidied up before her arrival. "I tried to vacuum, but Elaine stopped me," Robert shrugged.

"But she didn't stop you making the bed properly, did she ?" Kath looked at Rob like a teacher to a child. "And... the bedclothes could do with a good wash!" Rob's glib excuse was that he used the launderette down the road, but it had been out of action that week. Kath didn't argue, but wondered why he hadn't found another launderette - after all, he did have a van.

Rob sensed her dismay, and whipped out a blood-red plaid blanket from the clothes closet in the corner. "That's better," Kath said, flopping onto the newly spread out bed cover. "Smells brand new," she rolled over and buried her nose into the fresh fabric.

"It is... I bought it last week, for you," then Robert changed the subject so quickly, Kath wondered if that was a white lie." Let's have some dinner, shall we ?"

Kath wedged herself into the space, eight-foot by four-foot, referred to as the kitchen, while Robert tuned into the Grand Prix on TV.

Half an hour later, after scraping together ingredients, Kath had produced a pasta and sardine sauce dinner. She offered Rob a glass of

Lambrusco, as he turned off the telly.

"Salute to us," Kath said, as they chinked their glasses together for a refill of wine and sat down on the bed to eat.

"That's Italian for cheers, isn't it ? Robert said.

"Yes."

"How come you know Italian?"

"Well, I only know a few words, but I like the sound of it, and we *are* eating spaghetti so..."

Kath told Rob about the old Italian miner who had been a neighbour and how he had inspired her thirst for travel. Rob told her how he had missed the chance of going to France on his motorbike for a summer holiday with his art college friends, when his bike had been stolen.

"Rotten luck..." Kath sympathised. "But there'll be other opportunities, I am sure."

Elaine banged on the bedsit door. "Just wondering who you have got in there with you?"

"It's my girlfriend," Rob said, without opening the door.

"You should have told me before, you know. I should know who is coming and going in my house."

"Sorry." Robert didn't sound repentant, but at least Elaine disappeared.

"We have only met twice and you are calling me your *girlfriend*!" exclaimed Kath.

"But, you are now, aren't you?" Robert kissed Kath again. "That was a delicious meal, better than that Chinese stuff we had last night," Kath beamed as she put the dirty dishes in the sink and sat next to Robert again.

"Come here, gorgeous," Rob pulled Kath down onto the bed for more snogging.

It was nine o' clock when Kath finally jumped up.

"I'll miss me train if you don't give over!" Kath's cheeks reddened at the sound of her own accent and bad English, but Robert didn't correct her. She loved him for that.

"And don't forget these..." Rob shouted as they rushed through the front door with him shoving Kath's muffler and hat into her hands.

"Keep your suitcase in the cab with you. I'll drop you off right by the station entrance and you can dash from there. There won't be time for me to park up and see you off properly."

Kath prayed she wouldn't miss the train. It was the last one that night and she had to be at work the next day at nine. She couldn't afford to miss yet another day.

Because Kath hated the job so much, she had taken to having two days off at a time, migraines she said, or stomach cramps. She wasn't enjoying her one day a week at technical college either and was skipping lectures there, too. She had only got a place at teacher training college because she had agreed to do 'A' Level Biology. She didn't need to pass the exam, just to study the subject and enter the exam would be enough. However, she found the work difficult and she just couldn't find the time to master it. She had found studying in a mixed group - males and females - intimidating too. She had truly bitten off more than she could chew and now she was getting involved with a man in London!

Kath felt a strange mixture of elation and deflation as she settled into her seat on the express train. She wanted to laugh and cry at the same time and pondered if this were really possible. Still, she reckoned, she must be really happy. After all, she had found Rob.

-5-

"Jeannie is coming for Easter," Tilly smiled in surprise as she looked up from a letter from her daughter, Jean.

"When's Easter?" Sam asked, clearing away the breakfast dishes.

"This weekend. This Friday is Good Friday!"

"Good Lord! I haven't told my students yet."

Samuel was never sure when one term ended and another began, or even what day it was. Although he was an excellent teacher, his administrative duties were wanting. He often missed appointments, ordered the wrong supplies and lost files.

"Well, don't fret, they will all know, somebody else will have told them, and you'll have two weeks here with me to get the last of the boxes unpacked."

Samuel groaned at the thought of lugging yet more tea chests up the stairs and then having to bring the contents down again, when it was discovered stock for the shop was inside.

"Can't I unload them downstairs?" Sam asked, tutting.

"No, I don't know what's in them; and if it's our stock, then better it says out of the way 'til we get the shop set up. We can't afford any breakages!!"

"Pity we didn't label the boxes when we packed..."

"Never have, never will," Tilly was curt. This was the ninth time in their married life of nearly thirty years that they had moved house and, each time, Samuel had sworn it would be his last.

I'll end my days here, mused Sam to himself. That wasn't because he thought he was about to expire soon, on the contrary, he was extremely fit and agile; he was just tired of moving and this time he was determined to stay put.

He loved the 17th Century building they now called home; the quality of the wood carvings on the staircase balustrades, the oak panelling, the generous proportions of the rooms, the high ceilings and, most of all, the wonderful walled garden. Sam had already dug over the top-soil and tidied up the rose beds and was now revelling in the springtime midday sun, which struck to the heart of his vegetable plot and was bringing on his seedlings fast. *There will be an enviable crop of green runner beans, carrots, broccoli and even tomatoes this summer... if m'lady lets me get on with tending to the young plants,* Sam pondered.

When he was home, Tilly had him on the go from morning 'til dusk. He even had to fetch bread from the village baker's every day. No wonder he weighed only eight stone! He had never been a big man, and at five-foot-five he probably wasn't too skinny for someone born before the WW1. But, he was getting thinner by the week.

"Get the double bed ready, Sam," Tilly was giving orders again. "Jeannie's bringing the boyfriend."

"Not the two single rooms ?" Samuel queried.

"No, one bed will do, less bed clothes to wash," Tilly snapped.

"But... what will this boy's mother think?" Sam wrinkled his nose.

"She won't know, of course."

Fait accompli. Sam made up the double bed, which he had hauled in from the garage. It wasn't anything grand like her Ladyship's, as Sam often called his wife; in fact it was a cast off from Tilly's sister, Blodwyn who had bought it to accommodate her eighty-five-year-old mother. The old dame had died on that bed and Samuel and his wife were there when it happened, some ten years ago. Sam squirmed at the thought of how Tilly could be so off-hand about the bed her own mother had died on, but reckoned, after all the years he had known her, she just could be so cold.

"Who's this boyfriend?" Sam asked, as he took a break from his furniture-moving duties and sat down in the Spartan kitchen, waiting for an answer. Tilly was studying the latest electricity bill.

"Bloody bills!" Tilly slapped the paper down and pushed it across the table. "How can we afford this?!" She looked menacingly at Sam, then remembered to answer his question. "Martin Willis. He's twenty-four. They met at the art school in Cardiff in September, when they both started that Art Teachers Diploma course. I'm just glad she's got a man at last!

"So, how do you know his mother?"

"We were at school together, the same form. She was too prissy for me, a nervous little creature; nondescript. She sat at the front and I was at the back."

"Matilda, really!" Sam only called his wife Matilda when she was being really unkind, which was just about every other day.

Tilly had been sent as a day pupil to the exclusive all girls' school, Hill Top in Chepstow, not far from where she was born and reared. Being the youngest - by eight years - of the six children, and being one of only two girls from a hard working family, she was spoilt rotten. Her blonde, thick crop of hair and blue eyes - the ones she had passed on to Robert - and her devil-may-care spirit, had ensured her place as the family tartar. Her academic achievements at the top class school had been negligible and her only claim to success was being class tennis champion five years running; the house she lived in had its own lawn tennis court at the bottom of the garden. However, she did like drawing and after leaving school, not knowing what on earth to do with herself, she was dispatched to the local art school. She resisted being like her sister, who was ridiculed by her siblings for being a hairdresser and marrying a mechanic. Blodwyn, ten years older than Tilly, gave up work after marrying and had lived ever since in a terraced house in the Rhonda Valley. Tilly described the childless couple as dull, and she had little time for them once she had decided on a career in art.

"Hola, encantada de veros!" Jeannie's voice echoed through the hall of the old house, after entering via the patio door from the garden "We are here! That's Spanish for, *hello so pleased to see you*," Jeannie said.

Tilly screamed with delight as Jeannie shoved a three-foot tall stuffed *Jemima Puddle Duck* into Tilly's arms and then put a chocolate Easter Egg - as big a rugby ball - and a bottle of Bordeaux, down on the hall table. "Got *Jemima* from *Harrods* last week," Jeannie lied. (Martin's mother had given it to her for Christmas). "I know you just love Beatrix Potter."

Jeannie stood stroking the soft toy's head, showering it with endearments in Spanish, while Martin struggled into the house with their two suitcases.

Tilly would have shown more interest in Jeannie's linguistic abilities had she not been distracted by the size of the suitcases.

"Presents for Sam, new paint brushes and a box of oils, a new pair of red wellies and rain coat, *Tom Thumb* cigars, and piles of food." Jeannie slashed her hand through the air, then added, " Of course, I am not giving Leo anything. Everything here is for you two."

Although Sam was her dad and Tilly her mother, she called them by their first names, just as her two brothers did. It was at Tilly's insistence on the birth of Robert that she should not be called Mother. Something to do with her disliking her own mother; Sam therefore had no choice but to forgo being called Dad. Most people, on being acquainted with the peculiar couple, commented on this strange custom, but quickly accepted the arrangement and, although they felt sorry for the children, simply thought of the Llewellyns as being eccentric Celtic artists.

After tea in the kitchen, as Jeannie was about to put the rubbish out and Martin was filing his fingernails, Leonard appeared from upstairs, dressed up for an outing.

"Well, well, well, skinny Martin going out with my big sister!" Leo laughed out loud. The two youths had met briefly at Chepstow Art School two years previously when they were both doing the Foundation Course. Martin completed the year successfully, Leo didn't. He had left in a huff, citing boredom.

"Nice to see you again, Leo." Martin was not one to take jibes seriously. "Heard you had more bad luck at College."

"Don't want to talk about that, just let's go for a pint now."

"That's a good idea," Tilly encouraged." You two go. Jeannie can stay with me to cook the dinner." Tilly dragged Jeannie towards the cracked kitchen sink, but neither Tilly nor Jeannie mentioned Leo as they stood peeling potatoes in silence.

"He's not that ill," Jeannie grumbled to Martin in bed that night. "He's just bloody lazy. Thinks if he carries on ranting and raving, he'll get what he wants. He's always had more than me and Rob," she hesitated to include Rob. "He's just a bully. Got Tilly over a barrel, wheedles money out of her right, left and centre. Lies in bed all morning, gets his dinner cooked, goes down the pub in the afternoons, and sits up all night watching TV. Tilly even takes him up a hot chocolate. Pah!"

"And, what about Robert?" Martin changed the subject.

"Well... what about him?" Jeannie wasn't interested in her elder brother.

"What's he up to - when will we meet him?"

"He's another selfish one, not heard a word since Christmas, only came home then 'cause he had broken his collar bone and he couldn't look after himself."

"How did he break that?"

"Riding a motorbike round the school playground and driving into a goal post!"

"A bit mad is he?"

"Well, aren't all the Llewellyns?"

"I jolly well hope you are not."

"No, you're safe there, but, Rob is really mad over motorbikes. Sam can't stand them, still goes on about when we lived in Rose Mansion and Rob and Leo churned his front lawn to bits, zooming round on their monster 500CC machines."

"BSA'S or what?"

"Shall we take Tilly for a ride in the *Mini* tomorrow?" Jeannie changed the subject. Martin was showing too much interest in her brother's activities for her liking.

"Okay, and Sam, too?"

"Oh no, Tiger wouldn't like that. Sam will have to stay here to guard the house."

"Couldn't Leo do that?"

"Afraid not, Tilly wouldn't trust him. No, that's Sam's job, he must stay here."

"Doesn't he ever go out in the car?"

"No, never."

"Poor man," Martin whispered to himself and hoped it wasn't going to be a case of 'like mother, like daughter', after all, he and Jeannie were getting married once they had secured teaching posts and found a country cottage to rent. He pressed for more family details.

Sam's father had had a nervous breakdown and had been institutionalised just after the Great War, when Sam was nineteen. Poverty forced them to move from their tenanted farm in Monmouthshire to a dilapidated cottage. Sam had always felt he'd had to replace his dad as the breadwinner and had felt miserable when he'd found himself as a poor art student in London and couldn't help. Sam's sister, Margaret - a spinster primary teacher - had died after being horrifically burned when her long skirt had caught fire as she raked up the autumn leaves in her mother's garden. One of Sam's four siblings, three years younger than Sam, was only his half-brother. The young girl who had come to live with them, as a domestic servant, was his mother! It seemed Sam's father had been an adulterer!

No wonder Sam is a depressive and Leo, it seems, is too. What a tragic family, thought Martin, as he turned his bedside light out and struggled to get to sleep.

–6–

'*I'm surprised you're not going to visit your parents at Easter,*' wrote Kath, when she finally replied to Rob's letter, after her birthday weekend in London. She had been too preoccupied to write before. Her father's knee operation had gone badly and he was sent on to a specialist hospital twenty miles from home. Kath was taking Nelly to see him every day, as her mother couldn't drive. Billy was working shifts at the *Michelin* factory, so he couldn't help.

"He can't be working all hours just to keep the baby. He's got something else going on!" Nelly sounded worried. "Another woman… do you think?"

"Nahh, not our Billy." Kath couldn't imagine that.

"He wants a motorboat?" Nelly speculated.

"No, that's *my* dream, not his," Kath's eyes flickered with excitement as she accelerated up to seventy miles an hour, heading out of the city.

Mother sighed. "He's not like our son anymore. Plus, there's you and your big ideas, motorboats! Just you be careful, and slow down now. Ye dad might be right. You and your big ideas, you might just end up on ye arse!"

Kath threw her head back defiantly. She had heard it all before, *castles in the air, ending up in the gutter.* Kath determined to prove them wrong.

"Billy will have to help you when I am away at Easter," Kath stated as they parked up. She was more concerned about how Nelly would manage on her own. Arthur was her rock. He had never been in hospital before. "You will just have to rope in Uncle Ken and Aunty Phyllis. After all, look how much running about you and Dad have done for them. It's about time they gave something back!" Kath detested the way everybody took advantage of her parents' generous nature.

Robert didn't explain why he wasn't going to Somerset during the school holidays, but begged Kath to change her plans and spend the time with him in London. Kath reminded him why she couldn't. "I'm helping Mum and you know I've got work at a play centre for five mornings. I just don't like letting people down. Besides… I need the money."

Kath mused how destiny had arranged for her single bed to be in the best room of the house, the parlour, ready for Arthur's discharge. But now it was ready for her and Robert, who was going to stay in Stoke to be with her. Sunshine sparkled through the lace curtains of the west facing window and warmed the room; it was the perfect place for the couple's tête-à-têtes and body talk.

Trying to keep abreast of current affairs, as Robert liked to do, Kath talked about the recent assassination of Martin Luther King. Rob mentioned Jim Clarke, the motor racing driver, who had just been killed, but mainly they talked about themselves and how they would spend the summer holidays together. First working in Stoke, or London, and then going on holiday by the sea. Robert didn't open up about his family but said she would meet the Llewellyns soon enough.

He didn't press to know more about her relatives, but nonetheless, Kath told him. Kath said although she couldn't wait to get away from Stoke, her family was still all-important, and if she was going up in the world, she wanted that for them too!

Rob snorted and urged Kath to just think about herself, but she couldn't, of course; she introduced Rob to most of her aunties, uncles and cousins. Evelyn, Nelly's sister, was still in shock after her son Jimmy's death on a motorbike, but she put on a brave face. She reminded Kath of the holidays they had had together in Arthur's caravan in North Wales. She sang the Kathleen Ferrier song for them, *I Know Where I'm Going* and Kath joined in, just as she had done in Llandulas, looking lovingly into Rob's eyes.

Kathleen was named after the contralto, on Evelyn's suggestion, and fancied she could have been a good singer too, if only she had had the training!

Aunty Brenda and Uncle Alf were revered for giving generous Xmas presents. Cousin Lynne, an Alma Cogan look-alike, and seven years older than Kath, gave her hand-me-down evening gowns and sparkly handbags.

Kath was happy as she started teaching again. Her dad was home, she had more work teaching netball at the local sports stadium for three nights a week and she had been released from teaching English. Student teachers, on teaching practice, had been allocated her groups. Best, she would be seeing her sweetheart in just six weeks.

Rob's love letters arrived every week and Kath agreed to stay with him in his flat during the Whit week holiday. However, just as she was about to book a return train ticket to Euston, she was told that she would have to spend that week in Portsmouth, aboard the HMS training ship, the Foudroyant, with a group of girls from her school.

The teacher who had been expected to accompany the group had been taken ill and Kath was to replace her.

"After all, you have been getting off lightly with no English classes these past few weeks," Bad Mal, as Kath called her boss, enjoyed telling her.

"Scorpio," Kath complained to herself. "...bet she's a bloody Scorpio." But Kath, who was a Libran, couldn't be bothered now to find out. She would soon be out of that damn school forever!

"We can still meet at Euston when I arrive there with the girls and you could come across to Waterloo with us. " Kath suggested to Rob, as she hastily phoned him after their plans had been scuppered. "You could drive to Portsmouth and stay there; we could meet up in the evenings?" The turn of events prompted more phone calls. Kath wasn't sure she could get off the ship at night. "Public phones !" Kath grumbled.

"One day, people will have walkabout phones, maybe? You'll be able to see the other person on a tiny screen, just like on science-fiction TV shows," Robert said.

"Oh, Robert, you and your imagination!" Kath was impressed.

The couple's plans only half worked out. Rob met Kath at Euston and accompanied her and her group through the maze of the Underground system to Waterloo. There, amongst the gaggling and gawping schoolgirls, they snatched a few kisses and tender touches, but Rob didn't go to Portsmouth. Kath had been issued with instructions never to leave the ship alone. She was to stay aboard with the girls, at all times of the day and night. Kath took her duties seriously.

The couple met again on the return journey, as Robert escorted Kath, and her girls, from Waterloo to Euston. She hadn't enjoyed Portsmouth. Her responsibilities crushed her ability to learn things for herself, she confided. She'd been sailing, but couldn't remember the manoeuvres. She had been taught how to tie many different knots, but couldn't remember the names of any. Teaching was an incredibly difficult job, she conceded, and she feared she was not good enough for it!

"It's only practice," Robert said, kissing her hands. "You are brilliant for an eighteen-year-old and, at thirty, you could be a Head Mistress!"

Kath was charmed.

With the week over and the faith of a good man behind her, Kath was in shape for the final sprint to the finishing line of her one-year student teaching contract. She chatted more now to Keith about the Llewellyns. Having known Rob for seven years, Keith knew a great deal about the family.

"Samuel was a student at the Royal College of Art in London in the late ‘20’s and early 30’s. He had also been engaged to a fellow student there, from Stoke.”

“That’s weird, who was she?” Kath asked.

Keith didn’t know, but said she had become a fashion designer and that she and Sam had travelled to Paris together. But then, when Sam had to leave London, the relationship had broken down. Kath learned too that Sam had exhibited annually at the Royal Academy and one year his painting, *The Welsh Rat Catcher* was voted Painting of the Year. Keith said he had even seen a write-up about it in the *Times*, with the Queen Mother on the front cover. Sam had sold the painting to an art gallery in South Wales to fund his marriage to the nineteen-year-old Tilly; thirty-four-year-old Sam had been her art teacher. The relationship was frowned upon by the establishment and Tilly was forced to give up her studies. Sam was then conscripted into the Army.

“He did a lot of war drawings,” Keith elaborated. “He’s got one war painting in an Air Force Museum, *The Attack on...* something or other. On his return from the war, Sam was removed from the College by the old principal, who had engineered Sam’s being called up, and he was sent to be Principal of Neath Art School where he is still working.”

“Poor man.” Kath had empathised.

“Robert was born in 1942, as you must know, and Jean arrived in 1945. Leonard about a year later.”

Tilly, Kath learned, had been a dazzling blonde. She never had a job and apparently spent much of her time dallying, with other men.

“She writes though and had her childrens’ stories published for several years in a South Wales newspaper. A few years ago, she had a book published, which Sam illustrated. It’s all about Dylan Thomas and *Laugharne*. They’ve lived in lots of different houses: 1930s semis; an imposing Georgian manor house; a Victorian three-story townhouse and then a riverside cottage. According to Robert, disagreements with neighbours forced them out. That’s why now they are living in a Cotswold-stone coaching inn in Somerset... as you already know! Jean, the sister, has mystical tendencies...Leo is the dark, brooding, demanding one of the nest. He lived with Rob in London once when he was studying art, but he lost his temper one day and smashed the college common room up. Rob helped him through his testament to the police and his following restraint in a mental hospital. Then he was sent home. He’s still there, I think.”

After Keith's revelations, Kath was in two minds about whether she wanted to know the outrageous lot or not! But it was obvious though she would have to, if she wanted Robert; and she did want him. *Growing up in a family like that he does really need me!* she thought.

July 25th was the end of the school year and the end of Kath's student teacher days, too. Rob drove to Stoke. Kath had secured them both five-week contracts, in a tile factory. Robert had Billy's room and Kath was back in hers. Arthur was again in the double bed with Nelly.

Rob got on well with Kath's parents, especially Arthur. As engineers, they had much in common, but Arthur couldn't make sense of the fact that Rob knew nearly as much as he did about engines and machines, mould making and tool making.

"Now lad, how de ye know so much about motors, when thee'd been to art college?"

"I had to go to art school, my father insisted. I taught myself mechanics. I used to mend all the students' motorbikes."

"They't should e done an apprentice, lad," Arthur went on. "It's bloody obvious ye are a born engineer. Tell thee what, I'll take thee up to the firm one day, before ye go back to London." Arthur was foreman of the pattern shop at one of the largest engineering companies in Hanley - the centre of Stoke city. He had been apprenticed there himself since he was sixteen, after a dismal spell working as a painter for Clarice Cliff Pottery. He had left the 'Bizarre girls', as they were known, due to the debilitating effect of the turps on his skin. Nelly had said he had left because the girls were calling him a cissy. Kath didn't know the real truth!

The couple banked their money, after the backbreaking work at the tile factory, with great satisfaction and a determination never to have to do such work again. They had worked eight-till-five, five days a week and even Saturday mornings - and had only half an hour for lunch break. Rob held the permanent tile packers, mostly woman, in great esteem from then on. He revelled at their dexterity; the speed of their fingers as they sorted and packed the tiles. The fact that they were so skilled they could carry on meaningful conversations with co-workers at the same time as they packed, amazed him.

Not only was Robert in love with Kath, he had fallen for the city and its people too. The down-to-earth folk of the sprawled conurbation of the Five Towns: Tunstall, Burslem, Hanley, Stoke, Fenton and Longton had reached his soul. The generosity of the Pottery folk contrasted bitterly with the self -centred world he had known up to then.

But now, with work and worries behind, it was time for fun. Drives out to the countryside, nights at the pictures and a day at Alton Towers had Robert already talking about them getting engaged.

Kath agreed, but wanted to meet the in-laws-to-be first.

-7-

Robert tried to slip quietly out of the *Cheshire Cheese* pub, after last orders. Arthur was finishing his beer with his friends and Rob wanted to call Tilly from the public phone box across the street.

"I hope thee knows what thee are doing with our Kath, ye know er's a funny bugger, always wants her own road and her's got big ideas." Arthur shouted across the snug, as Rob edged his way to the door. Cringing, Robert dropped his head, pretended he hadn't heard, and dashed outside. The red paint on the telephone box was peeling, the rusty door half off its hinges; inside smelled of cigarette smoke and bad breath, but, at least, the phone was in order.

"Where are you? And why haven't you written? We thought you were dead," Tilly said in one breath, chuckling as she waited for a response.

"I'm in Stoke. I've been working up here with my girlfriend, Kathleen Tyler."

"She's lives in Stoke, then?" Tilly's voice faltered.

"Yes."

"Oh," Tilly said, as if she had stepped on a cockroach.

"And... I am bringing her down to meet you this weekend! You'll be in, won't you? We'll be there on Saturday at two o'clock, for lunch. I want to show Kath a bit of Bath first, she hasn't been before. We'll leave on Sunday. I know you are busy with the business, though... " Robert's change ran out and the phone line went dead.

“Well, well, well,” Tilly reported to Sam. “Robert’s coming with his girlfriend, on Saturday, and, just like him, never even asked how we were.”
“Doesn’t want to waste money on phone calls and I don’t blame him.” Sam was sympathetic.

Kath felt excited to be meeting the accomplished, clever and colourful Llewellyns, but worried she wouldn’t be good enough for them. Still, she was determined to improve herself; she convinced herself that she hadn’t done too badly, so far.
The young couple arrived on the outskirts of Bath at ten o'clock that bright, sunny Saturday, parked the van and headed into town. Already, the tourists were swarming around the Georgian city, taking photographs. Kath lamented that she’d never had a camera and Rob agreed to buy her one for her nineteenth birthday, at the end of September.
Kath wore black cotton bell-bottom jeans and a plain, black sleeveless T-shirt with strappy purple leather sandals. She had accessorised, with a matching purple and black leather shoulder bag. *Sensible clothes,* she thought. *Ideal for travelling, sightseeing and visiting important people.*
Looking like a pilot, Robert looked smart in his pale blue short-sleeved cotton shirt and tailored black slacks. Kath’s long ponytail, tied up on top of her head with a purple ribbon, bobbed merrily as they walked hand-in-hand and chatted. They turned to look at each other now and again, smiling.
“I love your hair pulled back off your face like that,” Robert cupped Kath’s chin, and pushed her head back gently, looking into her made-up eyes. “You are my Egyptian Princess.” He murmured, before he kissed her lips. Kath melted into his arms.
Rob’s tried his best to interest Kath in his guided tour of the city centre, but she couldn’t concentrate, she was too nervous about meeting Tilly and Sam. Robert, however, persisted. He had studied architecture as part of his art course, and wanted to impress. He even threw in the nuggets of information that he had been named after Robert Adam; the great architect of the 18th Century, who was responsible for so many of the great city’s civic buildings. Robert’s parents had had great hope for their first-born. They had aspirations too

for their youngest son Leonard, named after, da Vinci.

"What about Jean? Who was your sister named after, then?" Kath asked as they sat down for a break on a park bench.

Rob looked flummoxed and Kath couldn't immediately think of a famous woman in history called Jean, either. It was only when they were sitting on Pulteney Bridge, watching the River Avon slowly drift by, that Kath thought of the River Seine and suggested that Jean had been named after Joan of Arc. "Joan is Jeanne in French," she said.

Robert looked blank then said he wasn't interested in France and admitted the best he ever did in a French exam at school was to get ten percent.

Kath squeezed Robert's hand in sympathy. "I know you feel bad about your schooling. I feel the same." Kath lifted his fingers to her mouth and gently kissed the tips. "Here we are in the beautiful city famed for Jane Austen and I know hardly anything about her! Schools, eh? And… now we are both teachers. It's a mad world, isn't it?"

"I don't think she's named after a French Woman," Robert, still thinking about Jean, said, "Tilly doesn't like the French, well, since Sam's brother married a French girl."

"Mmm… I expect your sister is clever, though," Kath took up the conversation.

"Well, she does read a lot, mostly horror stories, but no, she's not clever at all. She failed the eleven plus and had to go to secondary school "

"So did I!" Kath wailed in protest at being thought of as a dunce.

"Yes, but that was just bad luck."

Kath had told Robert the story before, about how she had always been near top of her primary school but on the day of the eleven plus, she had been so overawed by having to sit the exam at the grandiose grammar school that she didn't sleep the night before. Plus, she threw up on the landing the next morning. When Kath learned she had failed and another girl in her class had passed, Nelly reckoned that some jiggery-pokery had been going on between the head teacher, the education authority, and the other girl's parents "…and to think our Kath was always top," Nelly complained. "And that Marion was nowhere near." But Nelly only ever said that to the neighbours. Nelly, like her kind, didn't question authority.

"Perhaps we'll meet Jean today? " Kath said, not wanting to dwell on her past vicissitudes.

"Perhaps, but I bet we don't, she told me at Christmas that she wasn't visiting Tilly and Sam again, until they had got the house straight. She was sick of having to sleep in a cold bedroom with bare floors and have to do all the cooking and cleaning for them.

"Maybe the house is all clean and tidy now!"

"No chance! They will never get it right. You just wait and see!"

Bang! The cast-iron doorknocker sent sound waves through the Somerset village like cannon fire from the Civil War. A few moments later, the oak, stagecoach width, Jacobean door opened slowly; its old hinges grinding and grating like a clapped out barrel organ.

Stepping into the sombre interior and down a step onto the uneven flagstones of the hall of the Old Parsonage, Kath automatically stretched out her right hand for a handshake, only to find it being pulled up and down as if it were a bell rope.

"Come in, come in. I've been waiting for you all morning. I 'ave. Up at six I was, digging up new potatoes for dinner, for you. Couldn't sleep a wink last night. I couldn't, not a wink. Do you follow?"

The welcome speech continued, until Kath's arm was released and Sam gave Rob a hearty pat on the back.

"Tilly will be 'ere in a minute but come and have a cup of tea first," the sprightly, jockey-sized septuagenarian beckoned. He then suddenly jumped sideways into a doorway.

His baggy brown tweed trousers, with two-inch turn-ups were held up ignominiously with white string; swung around his skinny legs like a cassock. He left a stink in his trail like that of a Victorian apothecary.

The couple followed him dutifully through the large, dark, dining room into the kitchen.

Two tea bags were already placed in cracked, saucer-less bone china cups and a third cup contained senna pods. Sam muttered something about a bad back, before swallowing four blue, bulbous pills with his brew. Kath smiled as she now believed her boyfriend, when he had said that his father was a hypochondriac.

"And... what do you think of my paintings, then," Sam said as the three of them sat down. He sounded thrilled to have an audience to show off his artwork to. More than ten large gilt-framed oil portraits were nailed up on the walls around the cupboards. The portraits looked flat, non-entities, made even less life like by having suffered the indignities of steam from boiling cabbages and the brewing of Sam's nightly herbal concoctions.

"Grand, really good…" Kath was polite. In truth, she felt reminded of the bleakness of the Van Gough's *Potato Eaters* and recoiled in shame at her reaction.

Rob raised an eyebrow and picked up the *Daily Mail* from the table. Kath sat perplexed as she absorbed more of the spectacle that Sam presented. He wore a threadbare white cotton shirt - one sleeve rolled up, one not. It was in need of a good wash and iron. It was only half tucked into the enormous trousers. A grimy red tartan trilby, with a short, white duck feather sticking up at the side, covered his head and eyebrows. Brown horn-rimmed glasses with thick lenses made his pale grey eyes look like cold glass marbles. But it was his hands that surprised Kath most, very big for such a small man, she thought, and such long, lean, beautiful fingers.

"Mine all mine," Sam resumed his monologue after finishing his drink and removing his cup from the antique pine scrubbed table to the ancient kitchen sink in the corner. Kath instinctively turned her empty cup up to check the maker's stamp, before handing it to Sam. "I am surprised the cup is French, and not one from Stoke?" Sam didn't react to that. Kath assumed he might be deaf.

"This is my cousin, Joan," he said, pointing to the picture of a girl in a red cardigan, holding a doll. Without waiting for a comment, he continued, "And this is our old neighbour in Neath: a pigeon fancier, you see. This one is the vicar in Cwyn Bran. This one the Blacksmith. This is the organist at Llandiloe Church, this one…

Kath couldn't keep track. "Wonderful, wonderful," she said, desperately hoping her insincerity was disguised by the fact that she had buried her face into the coat of poodle, Peaches, who had so conveniently jumped up onto her lap for a fuss and a cuddle.

"Not talking about your paintings again are you, Sam?" Tilly, straining to sound more BBC English than Welsh, was now standing in the doorway, hand on hips like an angry Carmen in a Spanish opera.

Rob had already escaped through the back door.

Tilly moved forward heavily; like a giant lizard. Kath couldn't believe how this large, unkempt, almost fifty-year-old woman had ever been a beauty. Her dyed blonde hair with telltale dark roots of over an inch long was backcombed, gathered up and fastened roughly into a meagre French pleat on top of her head. Her face was caked in pressed powder, the colour reminiscent of the pork pie Kath had eaten in London a few weeks before.

"Well, we only know you are Kathleen and that you come from Stoke-on-Trent. We call it *Smoke*-on-Trent, here. " Tilly who didn't bother with preliminaries smirked at her clever pun and laughed out loud when she saw Kath's mouth drop and mumble her defence.

"Well, some parts are a bit smoky, but I am leaving there to go to Barry College next month."

"Barry Island, good god, another..." Tilly didn't finish her sentence but choked on a muffled laugh, as if she was embarrassed.

Rob had just brought the couple's overnight cases into the hall and was now standing behind his mother. After an uncomfortable silence he said, "Well looks like you have a lot of work on here, Tilly."

"Well, yes, go and look around - see for yourself. I'll talk to Kathleen."

Feeling abandoned in the sultry air, thick with the stench of old furniture, and stuffed toys, Kath felt a migraine coming on.

"I... I need fresh air..." She instinctively moved from the kitchen through the dining room and finally through to the garden, letting herself out. Tilly followed.

Kath didn't look back. She took an aspirin from her bag and swallowed it whole, whilst trying to pretend she hadn't been upset by Tilly's comments. Luckily, Peaches had sidled up to her and was licking her ankle. She picked him up and nuzzled his fur. She was relieved he liked the fuss and she carried him towards the kitchen garden, where kidney beans were ready for picking, enormous cabbages ripe for the pot and rows of carrots and onions were bulging through the earth.

Tilly shouted from the open glass door that Peaches didn't like being petted by strangers, but Kath carried on walking to where Sam was now forking over the compost heap. Kath told him she loved animals, but she had only ever had a pet guinea pig as her parents both worked and they hadn't got a garden. Sam shook his head in disbelief, but he didn't comment, so Kath asked him about his art.

Sam needed no encouraging in this subject. Leading the way into the house again, Peaches at Kath's heels, he held court in the hall where there were paintings of a *Mr. Call who* lived on the next farm to where they had lived in Llansarn. *The Ploughman* from the village where Tilly had grown up. The stunning girl in a black dress with a high lace collar was a *Portrait of Tilly at Twenty-One,* "On the eve of our wedding," Sam enthused.

"She was beautiful. " Kath was in awe.

"Oh don't let Tilly hear you say 'was', she thinks she still is, " Sam chuckled.

"Oh, you are right," Kath conceded.

"Yes, you have got more work on here that you can cope with, Dad," Rob commented as he skipped down the stairs and into the hall, almost bumping into Sam. Kath was astonished that Rob had called his father dad and not Sam, as she had expected him to do.

"Both bathrooms need gutting, looks like dry rot in the big room and if you don't move that old piano, you'll have woodworm everywhere too in no time. " I just wish I could help you more, but you know why I can't. Too busy making a living and surviving in London.

"So, what do you think of this grand house?" Tilly asked, as she dragged Kath away from Sam's paintings.

"I haven't seen it all yet, but, yes, it looks very big.

"What sort of house do *you* live in then?" Tilly went on, as she guided Kath to the sitting room.

"A Victorian terrace."

"A w*orker's* terrace?"

"Yes... but we have got a forecourt where my dad grows roses."

"Terrace..." Tilly repeated, her voice reaching crescendo pitch.

"Mmmm... we'll eat in the kitchen."

Kath was disappointed. She had expected to be led into the dining room, where the table was already set for four with Crown Derby. Trying not to feel slighted Kath, took her seat at the kitchen table, choosing the safest looking chair from the array of old, odd and rickety wooden ones.

"Its fresh roast chicken with homemade stuffing, onion sauce and our very own fresh vegetables from the garden," Tilly said, pulling the fowl out of the oven, then sniffing the aroma.

"My favourite," Kath replied, licking her lips. She stopped when she noticed the label on the poultry packaging, which was on top of the rubbish bin: DEFROST THOUROUGHLY BEFORE USE. An empty packet of *Paxo* Sage and Onion stuffing was by its side.

Why did Tilly lie about the chicken and stuffing… and have them all eating in the kitchen instead of the dining room? Kath's insides curdled. This was an attack on her class. Still, Rob probably hadn't seen the bin and its contents, or the ants trickling around the floor. She would never tell him. *What the eye doesn't see, the heart won't feel,"* At least the vegetables were fresh, even if the chicken and stuffing wasn't. Kath still enjoyed it.

"We've put an offer on a shop down the road," Tilly said as they were having dessert: apple pie and custard. "It's the one on the sharp corner where three roads meet. We'll call it, THREE WAYS ANTIQUES. "

"Can't see you sitting in a shop all day, Tiger," Rob commented.

"No, well, I will be out every day buying and, of course, Sam can mind the shop."

Sam looked at Kath as if he were a lost puppy begging to be given a new home.

"But how can he, if he's going to Wales every week," Rob questioned Tilly, as if Sam wasn't in the room.

"He was retired off in July. He gets a good pension now. Don't you?" Tilly shouted across table at Sam as if she wasn't expecting a reply, and then carried on, "…and Jeannie has promised to come over every weekend to help. They are living in Oxford now, by the way. Martin has got a teaching post in a secondary school in Abingdon. He starts next week. Jeannie hasn't got anything yet, but she doesn't mind for the moment. They are busy setting up home in a lovely country cottage. The rent is only three pounds and ten shillings a week."

Rob looked slightly envious. "I am paying four pounds for my grotty bedsit and that's a bargain. I can't afford to move. But I am very pleased for Jean, perhaps she will invite me and Kath over for a weekend soon?"

"No doubt she will, but not before she comes here, I hope! She's due to be with us next week. I am giving her some antique chairs and a table."

"Thought she might have been here today?" Rob said.

"No, they are in Barcelona this week with Martin's brother and sister-in-law. Martin's mother has paid for all their flights and accommodation, in a five star hotel on the beach."

Rob looked at his mother and bit his lip; she had hardly given him a penny during his student days and even less now.

Tilly must have realised her faux pas as she carried on, “Money isn't everything, you know. And if you earn your own money, work hard; you'll appreciate it all the more. ”

Kath wanted to scream, she was thinking how hard she and Robert had already had to work so far in their lives, especially those last five weeks in the sweatshop of a tile factory.

Tilly changed the subject. “And... what do *your* parents do?”

“My father is an engineering pattern maker and my mother works in a pot bank.”

“Goodness gracious, only factory workers!”

Kath didn't flinch, but turned her attention to Sam.

“Rob told me you had a painting entitled, *The Rat Catcher* in an art gallery? And that it had been featured in the *Times* in 1937.”

“Yes, that's right,” Sam was in his element, talking about his artwork again.

“And you were a war artist and have paintings in the Imperial War Museum. One very famous one, *The Battle...* of the something is in a military academy?”

“Yes, The Fleet Air Army Museum,” Sam corrected, but his pleasure at continuing his talk was short-lived.

“Sam, you know how boring it is if you keep going on about your paintings.” Tilly interrupted. “ Let's all go into the sitting room now. I'll make the coffee.”

Like obedient school children being dismissed from class, the three got up and left the table.

“Robert has told you all this?” Sam whispered to Kath as they sat down in armchairs. “I am amazed, as he rarely talks about us, especially me, to anyone.”

Robert went to switch on the television in the corner.

“Well, Robert has told me a lot about you,” Kath raised her voice and winked across at Rob who, on hearing her shout, had turned round. Robert stood still, in no doubt that what she knew about Sam must have come from Keith and Jill.

“Rob told me too that you had a girlfriend in Stoke once, and that when you visited her, you did a painting of bottle kilns and pot bank workers.”

“Well, I'll be blowed... Rob told you this?”

“Yes,” Kath glanced at Rob, who was enjoying the story.

"He also said that you had that painting on the wall in Rob's bedroom when he was very young and then, suddenly, one day, it disappeared. What happened to the painting, Sam?"

"Oh... Tilly made me sell it. We needed the money you see. We were living in Rose Mansion then and we couldn't afford to. Tilly was to have a B & B there. If she had made a go of that, we would have been all right, but it wasn't her thing, you see. We set up that first summer as *Rose Mansion: The Naples of Wales*. We had an advert in the Rhonda Valley Journal and the West Wales Post, but we only got four visitors. Then, when Tilly met them, rough miners they were, she said she was fully booked. Didn't like the look of 'em, you see. Do you follow?" We didn't get any more then."

"Well, what about the painting and your girlfriend in Stoke?"

" Oh, yes, my Miriam..."

Tilly appeared at the door. "Sam, move those papers off the table, so I can put this tray down, and stop talking about your old girlfriend!"

Sam obeyed.

Kath offered to wash the dishes after coffee, but Tilly said she would see to that, adding, "I've put you in the *Isaac Williams* room, and Robert can have the single room on the top floor next to Leonard. Perhaps you could take your cases up now?"

Kath sensed she was anxious to have a break from the young couple. On the way upstairs, Rob questioned Kath about what she had said to Sam."It was only a white lie. You know I want your father to be proud of you. You said he wasn't, didn't you? Well he might think a bit better of you now. Don't you agree?"

Rob couldn't argue with that logic.

Leo met the couple at the foot of the stairs as he was coming down and they were about to go for a walk. It was four o'clock. Exactly the time Tilly had predicted Leo would appear.

Leo was taller than Rob and at least a good stone lighter. His hair was thicker and darker. It was long, parted in the middle and it reached his shoulders. He had the regal look of his brother, and mother, in her youth, and Kath couldn't imagine how such a handsome fellow had ended up on tranquillisers; living like a monk.

There were no hugs or handshakes, just a nod and hello, plus an invitation to go to a pub in the village.

"I couldn't wear my hair like that," Rob announced as the three strolled to the *Sheep's Head,* a hundred yards down the road. "We teacher's have to have a short back and sides to go with our *Burton* suits.

"I wouldn't want you with hair like that anyway." Kath told Rob. "It's too hippy for my tastes." Then, turning to Leo, she said. " But it does suit you, Leo. You being an artist."

"Well, I don't know *what* I am at the moment. Living here is hell. Tilly always moaning about money and how much I am costing her, and Sam depressed about leaving Wales and having to commute there every week."

"Well, he won't be travelling up and down, anymore. Don't you know? Sam was pensioned off at the end of term - in July," Rob said.

"Oh, how do you know that?"

"Tilly said."

"That's news to me. They never tell me anything. They just get doctors in to give me pills and more bloody pills."

"So, what are you doing about going back to college?" Kath asked.

"Well, can't go back to London, don't want to anyway, shit hole. I've got a place on a photography course in Bristol, if I want it, but will have to drive there every day."

"In Tilly's *Escort* ?"

"No. I'll have my own car."

"And, where are you getting the money from?" asked Rob incredulously. By his admission, even after five years teaching in London, he hadn't got two half pennies to rub together.

"Mind your own bloody business!" Leo was not one to get into an argument with.

After a couple of shandies in the pub's beer garden, the trio wandered round the village. "Poxy place," Leonard opinionated. "Boring old farts the lot of 'em, living hell."

"Well, I think it looks pretty. Come on, can't you just enjoy the sun, the sky, the earth; it's a lovely sunny day. I think it's a great village." Kath tried to make light of Leo's situation.

Beckton had been listed in the Doomsday Book and had prospered in the Middle Ages from the wool trade. Hence the name of the old pub, *Sheep's Head.* Kath noticed on the village hall notice board that there was an array of activities going on for pensioners: British Legion meetings, aerobic exercises, bus day trips to Longleat and Stour Head. There was even a monthly Old Time Musical concert on offer. She noticed too that there was a new council housing estate going up on a field only three hundred yards north of the Old Parsonage.

"It seems a jolly place," Kath commented to Tilly on their return to the Old House.

"Does it?"

Kath mentioned the publicity she had seen at the village hall for the various activities, but they were of no interest to Robert's parents.

"We are not the kind of people who join clubs," Tilly said. "Or go on bus trips, or do old time dancing and the like. We are different to other people, we are artists. We are not like the buffleheads around here."

"I don't suppose you are very pleased with the housing estate going up near here, then?" After her intake of alcohol, Kath was being bold and delightfully provocative!

"No, utter disgrace. Shouldn't be allowed. We've signed a petition to get it stopped."

"Doesn't look as if it has worked though, does it?" Kath was getting deliciously rebellious and continued, "Well haven't you been involved with any village civic activities since you arrived?"

"Sam has illustrated a new church handbook." Tilly said, handing Kath a copy from the bookcase.

Sam's drawings are a lot better than his oils, Kath thought.

"Ah, talking about books, Tilly," Kath went on. "Can I see your book about Dylan Thomas, and all those children's stories you have written, that I have heard so much about? "

"Here you are," Tilly had a copy of the Laugharne book to hand. "But, I can't think where my stories are at the moment. You'll just have to see them another time, perhaps. Tilly strung out the word perhaps so long, eyeing Kath up so menacingly, that Kath felt she wouldn't be welcome in their house again. She tried hard to not let her pain show.

Kath carefully fingered through the pages of the plain beige dust-covered book and heaped praise on its contents, asking if she could take the copy to bed for a closer look. In truth, the black pen and ink drawings looked flat on the pages. The subjects, mostly of public buildings, were uninspiring to the young girl, but she felt obliged to be positive.

“Don’t worry about tea or supper for us.” Kath told Tilly around seven o’clock. “We had a bite in the pub, and, in any case, I need to cut down on the calories. ”

“Why did you tell another fib about us eating in the pub? "Rob asked, as soon as Tilly left the couple alone. "I’m starving.”

“You can help yourself to something from the fridge. I just don’t feel like anything.” Kathy couldn’t face sitting in the ant-infested kitchen again with Tilly, but was reluctant to confide this to Rob.

“I’ve got a headache. I’ll go for a walk on my own. Go and talk to your parents in the garden and I’ll join you later.”

Tilly and Rob, ensconced in patio sofas, were drinking champagne under the apple tree when Kath finally came back. Leonard had already disappeared to his lofty chambers. It was a balmy summer evening and the roses’ perfume filled the air. Sam was still digging and Peaches sat contented in the evening shade.

“Thought you had run off with a gypsy,” Tilly roared, chuckling to herself.

“Got a glass for me?” Kath asked, not acknowledging the cutting remark.

“Thought you were watching the calories?

“One glass won’t hurt, will it?”

“Well, you’ll have to get one from the kitchen. Perhaps you could wash up too now. I haven’t had chance.”

Kathleen was pleased she had been relegated to doing the dishes. Doing something practical calmed her nerves and she was genuinely pleased that Rob would have more time in conversation with his mother. Half the problem with this family she decided was that they didn’t talk to each other, enough. There was no real communication, no honesty; they were like strangers with each other. Kathleen compared her family with theirs. Her’s swore and pushed and shoved each other, slapped each other on the back, laughed in each other’s faces, talked and shouted all at the same time; called each other silly names.

This household was still; stale like the bread left on the kitchen table. As Tilly sat down, Sam got up and left. As Sam got up, Tilly left. Leo appeared, then disappeared like a shadow. There were no knocks at the door, no phone calls.

"Well, all done," Kath exclaimed. "And, I have even cleaned the cooker and wiped around the kitchen."

"You'll have to come again," Tilly enthused, much to Kath's surprise.

"Shall I put the irises you have left in the basket in a vase?" Kath offered.

"That's a trug," Tilly corrected. "Not a basket."

"Oh, well now I know," Kath tried to sound unaffected. "I think I'll have my well-earned glass of champagne now. I expect you two have had a lot of catching up to do. You haven't seen much of each other since Christmas, I believe?"

Tilly looked happy to have been chatting to Rob. *Maybe it's the drink,* Kath thought, but that didn't matter. Rob seemed relaxed too. Kath hoped Tilly was proud of him now that he was an established teacher and had just had a pay rise for being in charge of organising the new CSE exam for motor mechanics.

"Won't Sam stop work now and have a drink with us?" Kath pleaded.

"No, won't touch the stuff, says it gives him a sore throat and wind. He's a real hypochondriac. Leave him be."

"Okay," Kath agreed.

Tilly glowered. She wasn't used to not having the last word.

At ten o'clock, Kath was the first to head up to bed. "I'm taking ye book to me bedroom now," Kath informed Tilly.

"I'm taking ye book to me bedroom! " Tilly mocked. "You sound like Cilla Black!"

Kath blushed, but laughed the comment off, not even bothering to explain that her Stoke accent was nothing like a Liverpudlian one. She quelled her indignance though enough to wink at Rob, the cue for a midnight rendezvous. After picking up The *Dylan Thomas* book from the sitting room, Kath made her way to the stairs, but as she stepped onto the first step of the oak staircase, the wood creaked loudly. Tilly, who by now was also in the hall, shouted, "Mind the ghosts, oooh."

The drink must have had gone to her head, thought Kath as she heard Tilly chortling, but shouted back, "Don't worry, I don't believe in them," but, nonetheless, Kath dashed up the stairs as quickly as she could.

The old house was certainly eerie. Branches of tall trees were tapping at the upstairs windowpanes as the wind got up in the dark night. The dim lights inside flickered and made her skin creep. Goose pimples crept all over her body as she stepped down a high step, from the landing, into *The Isaac Williams Room*. A nightlight glimmered from the far corner of the huge space. Heavy gold braid curtains were drawn across the room's only window. The dark oak floorboards smelled of bees wax. An ancient simple wooden double bed with a horsehair mattress and bolster, made up with white sheets and brown blankets sat stark in the middle of the square room. There was a Victorian washstand in one corner on which sat: an old ceramic bowl, a matching ewer full of clean water, a towel and a bar of *Pears* soap.

Kath instinctively lifted the bowl and smiled to find it labelled, 'Made in Staffordshire'. She glanced up at the large plaster moulded wall plaque, put up centuries before to commemorate the famous 17th Century writer Isaac Williams, who had stayed at the old house when it was a coaching inn. She glanced around the pure white plastered walls, as dull as the unpolished white marble on the washstand and wondered how the room had been laid out when Mr Williams *the Complete Philosopher* had stayed there in 1675?

She had only just finished getting warm under the blankets, when Rob slipped into the room and into her bed. It was almost midnight. "Can't believe this house is so chilly." Robert pushed up against Kath.

"And, it's still summer…" Kath turned over and snuggled herself round Rob.

"Never mind, come on, it's hot down here," Rob enthused as he slipped his hand between Kath's legs and cupped her Venus mound.

"Boiling down here, too," Kath quipped as she held his penis.

"Let's do it tonight…" Rob was ready. Kath too.

Up to now they had only kissed and fondled. They had held off having full intercourse, as although Rob had declared his undying love, Kath feared getting pregnant. There had been enough traumas in Kath's family when Billy had announced Pauline was pregnant and everybody had tutted when she walked down the aisle of the Catholic Church, in pink, six-months along with Matthew. But, Billy was twenty-six and Pauline twenty-five. Kath was still a teenager.

However, Rob's deep throat kisses got longer and wetter, his fingers probed deeper and deeper, he revelled in her neat, round breasts and nubile, wholesome nipples. Kath was lost.

When Robert said, "I just love you so much," – she responded, " I love you too." They lay in each other arms all night.

A crack of light streaming through the slim gap between the heavy curtains alerted them to the break of dawn. Rob crept cautiously back to his own bed and they didn't get up until a respectable nine o'clock for breakfast.

Tilly, who had already told the couple the night before, to help themselves to food, was not around. Sam was busy sorting out some of his pencil drawing portfolios in the hall. There seemed to be hundreds of the dusty files everywhere: on top of the pine dresser, up by the side of the gramophone, a pile on the sideboard, even a stack behind the downstairs toilet door.

As Kath sat down in the kitchen, after making tea, Rob produced a gold ring. "It's for our friendship."

"Friendship?" Kath wailed. "Lover's ring, don't you mean? You remember that you fucked me last night?"

"Oh, Kathleen, keep your voice down."

"Oooooo… I am awful, but you like it. " Kath did a take on Dick Emery, the comedian they enjoyed watching on TV and they were laughing heartily when Tilly opened the back door. She had just been to buy milk.

"Well… did you two sleep well last night?" Tilly smirked.

"Oh, very well, snug as a bug in a rug," Kath sounded satisfied.

"*We* don't say it like that."

Kathleen's hard northern vowels displeased Tilly. "We say, *As snag as a BAG in A Rag*. But that's even too common for us. We would say that one slept like a queen, or slept with the angels."

"Oh well, *we* wouldn't," retorted Kath. "By the way, I like the pottery jug and bowl that was in my room. Spode, made in Stoke-on-Trent it was."

"Hmm." Tilly wasn't interested. Her attention had turned to the gold band on Kath's finger.

"Where did you get that?" she asked.

"Rob gave it to me this morning. It's a lov… friendship ring."

"Do you know where it came from?"

"No, should I?" Kath looked at Tilly, quizzically.

"That ring belonged to my youngest brother, John. He died fourteen years ago of alcoholic poisoning. Gladys, his widow, gave it to Robert."

"That's very nice," Kath exclaimed. "Err… I mean it's nice that Rob was given the ring; it's awful that your brother died the way he did."

"Well, I am telling you that ring is a bad omen for you and I wouldn't wear it, if I were you."

"But, it fits me perfectly. It would be shame not to wear it." Kath fingered the shiny black jet stone that was inset into the gold band, held out her hand and said, "There, it just looks so pretty. And, don't worry, I don't believe in things being bad luck. It's all in the mind, like those ghosts you say live here."

Tilly didn't reply but asked the couple when they were expecting to leave. Rob said they would be off after breakfast, as he had important business to do. Kath wondered what that was, as she thought they were going to stay all day with the Llewellyns and then go back to Stoke that night. Kath was glad now though that they weren't staying there any longer.

"By the way, I like your dress," Tilly said.

Kath smiled, until Tilly went on, "It suits you better than that black and purple outfit you wore yesterday. You looked like you were going to a funeral! " Tilly laughed at her own joke - Kath simply ignored it.

"I made it myself two years ago," Kath explained. "When I was still at school. It must be out of fashion now, but I really don't have that many summer frocks... *dresses*." Kath was acutely aware of her perceived shortcomings. "I can't afford new ones; I have been saving up to go to college. I won't get a full grant, my parents have to contribute."

That set Tilly on a new tack. "Well *you* had a full grant, didn't you, Rob? I never remember having to subsidise you at college?"

"No, to be honest, Tiger, I didn't get a full grant. You should have helped me out, but the fact is you didn't. And, I didn't ask for help. You should have *known* I needed help. Instead, I had to work my way through college. Weekends serving coffees in *Lyons Café* in Trafalgar Square, summer holidays mending roads, pea picking in Lincolnshire. Don't you remember?"

"Well, it's done you no harm... and don't call me, Tiger, please."

It was Kath's turn to change the subject this time. "Well, must be off then, if Robbie says so." Kath ruffled her boyfriend's hair and kissed him on the cheek.

"Yes, let's go," Rob affirmed.

The couple shouted cheerio to Sam from the patio doors, as he was busy raking round his potato plants, and asked Tilly to say their goodbyes to Leo. Tilly showed them to the front door. Kath thanked her and gave her a hug, Rob merely said *bye*.

"Oh, by the way, I've left your book in the bedroom. It looks great. I'll get a copy from the library soon and let you know what I think when I have read it properly."

As Kath and Robert stepped out onto the pavement and into the fresh air, the piano upstairs started to plonk. Leo was at it again!

"Well, what important business is it then that means we have to leave so early?" Kath tugged at Robert's sleeve as they walked to the van. She was bursting with curiosity.

"We are off to Cornwall! That's what!" Rob put his arm around his girlfriend.

"Robert Samuel Llewellyn, you are amazing! Why didn't you tell me you had planned a few days in Cornwall? Where are we staying? I haven't got enough clean clothes and I haven't got a bikini either. What about your trunks? How can you afford this? "

"Steady on, one thing at a time. I haven't booked anywhere, yet. I thought I would wait to see how the weekend went. "

"You mean… see if you got me laid?" Kath laughed out loud.

"Well, yes, and also you said you loved me and that you wanted my ring."

"It's August, you know? Do you think there will be vacancies anywhere? " Kath glanced at the gold ring on her finger.

"Must be. Let's see!"

Kath, realising Robert wasn't going to offer more information, slumped back into her seat and sang along to the van's radio: Mary Hopkins' hit of the year, *Those Were the Days*, Cliff Richard's *Congratulations,* and Nina Simone's, *Ain't Got No Life*.

-8-

Kath was so elated, she had to remind herself not to forget to get a message to her parents, who had expected them home that evening.

It was late afternoon when they parked up by Polperro's petite harbour next to a phone box.

Kath got through to the only people in Arthur and Nelly's street who had a phone, the Bossons'. They promised to pass a message on.

While Kath was busy, Rob spotted a vacancy sign for Bed and Breakfast in the window of a fisherman's cottage on the quayside and knocked at the door. They had a cancellation that very day! The best double room in the house was available and they could have it for half the normal price for the next three nights.

Robert ran upstairs with both their bags, dropped them on the floor, then bounced onto the feather mattress of the four-poster bed. "Wow, it's better than Tilly's bed. Good place to get your knickers off, doll."

"I'll have to wash some first," Kath had run out of clean clothes.

"I'll buy some new ones for you, tomorrow."

"And, a bikini too?"

"Yes, but only if you screw me now!"

"That's bribery and extortion, but of course I like it!" Kath retorted. Then they both burst out laughing.

Kath loved the little fishing port with its narrow streets, tiny shops and intimate bars and cafes. They watched the Morris dancing and listened to the fishermen's choir in an open-air concert that night. They went to Looe and Fowley the next day. The rocky wild shore with its smugglers coves and caves was the perfect backdrop to their romance. *As romantic as Daphne Du Maurier's, Rebecca,* Kath fantasised.

Three whole days of loving had exhausted Kath, but she felt free to be herself. Rob was her man. *He's my everything,* she told herself and felt a wrench when they left their love nest for the Midlands.

The temperature dropped dramatically by the time the van had passed Birmingham, and there was heavy rain as they arrived in Tunstall late that night.

"Way bin werriting to death," Arthur greeted the couple as they tumbled through the front door. "Ye mother 'asn't slept a wink, didn't know where the lad 'ad taken thee."

"Didn't you get the message from the Bossons'?" Kath frowned.

"Well, we got some gabbled rubbish about thee goin' off ter Cornwar."

"Yes, and we've had a great time."

"Bet thee bloody 'ave, but yer only eighteen and ye're going to college. What the bloody hell do ye think you playing at?" Arthur turned to Rob. "Sorry youth, but 'ers my daughter and er and er. Well, get thee in and get warm by the fire and I'll put kettle on. "

"It's not that we don't trust ye, Rob," Nelly took over. "Well we just don't want anything, you know..." Nelly focused on Rob's crotch, "...well anything to happen to our Kath."

"I'm eighteen, Mother - and I have been working for a whole year! I can look after myself."

"Well, eighteen is not twenty-one and you 'aven't got the key of the door yet! Remember, young lady, we are forking out for your college education and we don't want you letting us down!"

"Promise I won't if you promise to give over giving me the Spanish Inquisition."

"Ha's heard her, bloody Spanish Inquisition, where does she get these bloody ideas from! "

"I've made the bed up for you Rob, back bedroom - Billy's old bed again." Nelly looked Robert straight in the eye.

"But, Mum," Kath flashed her ring at Nelly, "Rob's my, errr... best friend now. "

"Well, best friend or not, what you do outside these walls is different, but under my roof, it's separate beds." Nelly fixed Rob with a dark stare, her black eyes straining to impose authority on the young man.

"Don't suppose you want any supper?" Arthur enquired perfunctorily. "Cause if they dust ye'll ave to get thee own, I'm off ter bed. I've 'ad enough worries fer one day!

Rob dutifully disappeared upstairs.

Summer was over and the autumn storms had begun. The night was chilly. Rob reflected as he lay awake under the blankets waiting for Kath to get to bed; he had promised to marry her.

Kath sat on the sofa, her arms wrapped around Nelly's neck.

"Tell me again," Kath insisted. "About the day I was born."

"Whatever for now?" Nelly had related the story a thousand times!

"I just like the story, I like my birthday, I like it was a sunny day and you were so hot you were naked when you delivered me."

"Well, you are a funny girl, how can you like your birthday!

"Dunno, but 28th September is a good date and I like the fact that I was conceived on New Year's Eve."

"Well, how do you know that then?"

"Well, it's true isn't it?"

"Reckon it is, but who told you? "

"Elle - and Hilda told her."

"Well, no need to tell you anymore, reckon the whole blinking street knows too. Your Aunty Hilda can't keep anything to her sen'."

"And… I know all the details of how you and dad were at a party at Hilda's and you left just after midnight, half-dressed! "

"Now, that's enough, but yeh, it was wonderful!"

Although Kath was almost sure she couldn't be pregnant, she had taken a calculated risk that their lovemaking had been in the safe period, there was still a nagging possibility she was. The urge to hold tight to her mother and just talk, overwhelmed her. Her period was due in two days' time.

"Tell me again that I am not adopted and, hand on heart, again this time," Kath begged.

"How many times have I got to tell you that, no, you were not adopted, you are mine and your Dads' and that's that. Look at you, you look just like me and there's no getting away from the fact your Dad is your Dad. Look, you've got his freckles and racehorse legs!"

"Don't you think I have good legs then?"

"Now, I didn't say that did I, don't go reading things into things. You have lovely, slim legs, good for dancing.

"And kicking." Kath punched the air with her right leg.

"Yes, but why do want to go around kicking?"

"Well I don't, unless maybe I have to."

"Always got to have the last word, haven't you? Think it's time for bed, don't you?"

"Yes, about the last word and yes about time for bed. See you in the morning Mum and thanks for everything." Kath squeezed her mother even tighter, then slowly released her.

"How's the house hunting going, by the way?" Kath asked, as she opened the stairs door.

"Oh, you know your Father won't move from here, not 'til they take 'im out in a box!"

"Yeh, see what you mean, still, things could be worse."

Nelly lit a Woodbine and picked up *The Sentinel*. She scoured the property pages and fantasised about moving to a three-bed semi with a garden and upstairs bathroom.

The fire had burned out by the time she had devoured the adverts and dreamed about the little house overlooking a village green she had spotted. If only she could get Arthur to go and see it. It wouldn't be beyond their means. Their terrace was already paid for and they were both working full-time. They could easily get a mortgage. It would mean less of the beer for Arthur, fewer new clothes and holidays. She wouldn't mind, but Arthur did love his holidays. Besides, having a half share in a caravan, they had had family breaks for weeks at a time at *Butlins* in Skegness and Clacton, stayed in a boarding house in Bournemouth and a chalet in Morecambe. They lived well for a working class couple.

It was after 2am when Nelly finally went to bed, the cue for Rob's passage to Kath's bedroom. They both knew their midnight trysts were not a secret, but Nelly and Arthur were just too good-natured to object. Rob was careful not to make any noise as he moved in and cuddled beside Kath.

"I'm shagged out, aren't you?" Kath whispered.

"Yes," Robert was facing yet another four hours on the road the next day and this was no time for sex romps!

Rob returned to Billy's old bed at dawn, just seconds before the alarm rang and Arthur got up to make a pot of tea in the kitchen.

"Wake up," he called at Kath's door, "...got ye a cuppa "

"Just leave it on the landing, I'll get it in a minute."

"And what about your youth?"

"Well, what about him?"

"He'd better get up and get cracking, got a long way to go today, and tell him there's tea brewing in the kitchen.

"Well, just bang on his door and tell him yourself."

Arthur and Rob sat opposite each other, eating toast and dripping, when Kath passed them on her way to the bathroom.

The men were talking "shop", as Arthur called discussing the engineering work carried out at his works.

"When thee come up again, I'll take thee in see fer yourself what they're doing."

"I'll look forward to that, Arthur. Thank you. More than likely that will be half-term in October."

Arthur went off to work looking like a half-happy man.

Kath spoke with Robert outside the front door, before he drove off.

"I promise, if you are pregnant I will stand by you," Rob assured Kath. But let me know as soon as you come on. Oh god, *if* you come on."

"Ring me from your school, you know I can't ring you. Ring Monday morning 11 a.m., during your break. I'll be at the phone box - the one we always use by the church. You've got the number, haven't you?"

"Give it me again. "

Kath reeled the number off to him.

"Your memory is bloody good," Rob patted her on the head. "Love you," Rob said, giving Kath a hug, then a kiss.

"Love you too," Kath echoed.

And, as Rob revved up and the van tore down the street, Kath covered her face with her two hands and cried.

Mrs Parks, the nosey neighbour, stood peeping through the lace curtains of her parlour. The whiter than white material twitched again, as Kath slipped back in to her house.

Nelly coaxed her daughter to lie down on the settee in front of the fire and brought her a cup of tea.

"Ye've got ter much on ye plate duck. It's all too much for ye. Just settle down will ye. Settle down." Nelly was a good mother, didn't interfere and didn't judge. She was just there. Kath could ask no more.

"I am so glad you are my Mum, and not that nosey parker next door. I feel sorry for Sandra!"

"Now, what makes you say that right now, Kath?"

"Well, Aida was nosing at me and Rob when he drove off and she bullies Sandra. Won't let her have a boyfriend and she's twenty-two! Has to be in at 10 p.m. Can't wear miniskirts or go out with the girls."

"Yes, you don't know you are born with us, Kath - just you remember that!"

It rained, on and off all day, and Kath didn't feel too bad about staying home. She *fiddled about*, according to Nelly, not getting down to her packing, but she scrutinised the list again of what she had to take to Barry. She had already bought second hand hockey boots and stick, new trainers, leotards for gym and dance, a tracksuit and books on Educational Psychology, Sociology, Educational Gymnastics and Child Development, Poetry and EM Fosters' *A Room With a View.* Kath planned on buying the other books required once she was away. *Damn it,* she thought, all those books in the attic at Rob's parents, surely they would have copies of some of the books she needed? *Hamlet* and Thomas Hardy's *Mill on the Floss,* for example. She had forgotten to ask. The thought of having to study English Literature filled her with dread. She had struggled with the subject at 'O' Level. Her spelling was atrocious and the influence of her dialect on her writing, dire! Still Tilly was a writer and presumably well read, with all those books to prove it; surely *she would help her with her assignments?*

Kath was sniffling when Arthur got home at teatime.

"What's her bloody blarting for now?" Arthur banged his fist on the table.

"Love struck and leaving home, have a bit of sympathy, will ye."

"Well, her wants too much, wants it all, and ye just can't do it. Burning the candle at both ends, 'er'll get her fingers burned, and all these castles in the air, 'er'll end up on her a…"

"Just shut it will ye," Kath snapped. "If you ever tell me again that I will end up on my arse, I will strangle you, personally, and without compassion. Just… shut it."

Kath had never spoken so violently to her father before and feared reprisals, but, to her complete surprise, Arthur acquiesced.

"Well, play it your own way, but dunna come here blartin'. So you make your bed now, and you lie on it."

"Good."

"Always, bloody right," Arthur conceded before slumping into his armchair, taking his shoes off and putting his feet up on the wooden footstool he had made in his spare time at work.

"May's been this afternoon and asked if you can make a jewellery box for Bernice's sister in Italy." Nelly changed the subject.

"Hope she's not in a hurry, you know how busy we are at work and then I am having a few days off to take our Kath to Barry "

"Well, you know May; she always wants everything done yesterday. She's like our Kath, ambitious." Nelly wanted to bite her lip, mentioning Kath again had inflamed Arthur.

"Yes, ambitious, big ideas, bloody big ideas, her's too bloody big for her boots. Her'll come a cropper. " Arthur's voice penetrated the ceiling into Kath's bedroom above.

"Leave her be, you'll be putting your blood pressure up and be giving yourself a heart attack."

Kath banged on her bedroom floor in protest and didn't stop until the shouting did downstairs.

"There," said Nelly. "Told you, she'll have the last word."

"Last word eh, er'll set the bloody world afire," exclaimed Arthur wiping the sweat off his forehead with the back of his hand.

-9-

Kath was sobbing silently into her pillow when she woke up the next day. Only Nelly's Danish bacon, duck egg and Staffordshire oatcake breakfast, and then getting stuck into packing for college, took her mind off her possible pregnancy.

The brand new, red leatherette trunk - which would double up as a coffee table - sat regally in the middle of the parlour. Even when half full, Arthur complained about the weight and how the 'bloody hell' was he going to lift it onto the roof rack of his dearly loved, shined to perfection, *Corsair,* without scratching the paintwork? Kath said he was belly aching over nothing and continued to pack. Before folding up her duck down continental quit and squashing it down into the trunk, she held it up to her face and smelled the lingering scent of Rob. Shuddering, she wondered when, if ever, she would see him again. She had heard about boyfriends who ditched their pregnant girlfriends!

"Blessed be the ties that bind our hearts in kindred love," Kath suddenly blurted out.

"You sound like you are rehearsing for a play, Kath," Nelly chuckled. "Now, where have I heard those words before?"

Kath pretended she didn't know Mellor's words in DH Lawrence's novel, *Lady Chatterley's Lover*. They had struck a chord with her when she was thirteen.

Nelly had a copy of the book hidden in her wardrobe after it had been declassified as obscene, and was freely published in Britain from 1961.

But Kath had found it and devoured the chapters of the love story, one-by-one after school. She couldn't wait to have her own share of passion.

Nelly didn't think much of the list of English books chosen for Kath's first year English course. Kath recoiled too, but playing Beatles records and singing along to *And I Love Her, Girl, All My Loving, and The Long and Winding Road*, took her mind off that.

"Can't I take the record player with me?" Kath begged.

"No, you can't, and don't ask again," Nelly was sharp. "You know that it's Billy's and it's only here until they get some shelves to put it on."

"Well, you know they will never get round to that!" Kath argued.

Nelly sighed. Billy and Pauline never got round to anything.

"Reckon ye Father'll put shelves up for them over the Christmas holidays." Nelly went on.

It was two o'clock before the trunk was sealed and the three of them sat down. Kath savoured the thick beef stew - the Potteries speciality - and dipped her crusty bread into her bowl with relish." I won't be having this again, Mum, for some time... will I ?"

Kath would be living in the students' residence on college campus, in one of the three girls' blocks. There was only one block for men. The letter from the college stated that she had to report to matron in the reception of Block B between 2-5 pm Wednesday Sept. 6th.

Handing the letter to Arthur, worry gripped her senses and spread doubt in her mind; *I'm not clever enough for this. I may never see Robert again. I might be pregnant!* Still, Kath known for her guts, was not one to give up easily, so she didn't go to bed and sulk, but welcomed those who came to wish her well.

Aunty May was first. She sat down in Arthur's chair by the fire and wouldn't budge, until she had tea and scones. The officious lady combined the well-wishing visit with business and asked if Arthur had made the jewellery box she had ordered. Arthur said he hadn't as he had been helping Billy in his new house. May was unforgiving, told Arthur he was a waste of time and urged Nelly to divorce him! Nelly only smiled and told May that Arthur was a good man, the best, and if everybody was like him, there would be no wars!

But If only Dad had married someone like May, Kath thought, someone *to keep accounts, have a diary, someone to organise everybody, motivate them, be efficient, just think they would have three detached houses, not just even one semi, and her dad wouldn't have to bear the shame of being the street's Mr Packet of Fags Man.*

It was well known that Arthur was regarded as a bit of a pushover. He was a skilled, clever man, but he wasn't adept at business. He made window frames and doors, for half the neighbours in the street, but when they asked what they owed him, he'd say, "Well, mate, since thee at me friend, just give us a packet of fags." Kath was furious that the neighbours actually did give him only cigarettes and it was she who dubbed him the Packet of Fags Man. Arthur took the insult as he did with all other life's knocks, he laughed and carried on dancing!

After May, came Aunty Evelyn and Uncle Dan. "Let's get the photos out," Kath said as she lugged the suitcase, full to the brim with the family photos, from upstairs, and plonked it on the kitchen hearth in front of the coal fire. "We really ought to classify them," she said, taking out some of the black-and-white and sepia photographs.

"Classify, is it, *oh very posh,"* Arthur chided.

"Well you know what I mean, we need a filing cabinet."

"And where would we put a bloody filing cabinet?" Arthur flung his arms wide. "Filing cabinets are not for the likes of us !"

Nelly protested at Arthur's swearing again, even though she agreed with his sentiments. Aunty Evelyn burst into a rendering of *Jesus, Joy of Man's Desiring* and Kath joined in the chorus.

"Who's this, then?" Kath handed a photo to Evelyn.

"Arthur, with Billy, of course. He's in his fireman's uniform with baby Billy in front of your house, summer 1943".

Arthur had been exempt from the Army. Judging from the flowers in the front garden - a patch of soil two metres square - Arthur loved tending his roses even then. Goldy, their pet spaniel sat by the front door. Arthur and Nelly had never had another dog after she died. Kath was annoyed about Billy having been a bully. The two cousins, who lived across the back entry from them, were not that friendly with Kath either; their mother saw to that. Then, when they moved house - when Kath was eleven - she became even more lonely. She would have loved a sister.

Kath dug out more photos, carefully choosing the ones that made her happy, like those of the wonderful holidays that she had had with her

Aunt Evelyn and Uncle Dan over the years in Wales. Evelyn shed a tear as they reminisced about Jimmy, their son, one year older than Kath; killed on a motorbike, some three years before. Their grief was raw and unremitting. *Life was just so unfair.* Kath felt their pain.

Arthur's brother arrived, just as Evelyn and Dan were leaving, and the conversation turned to their mother, Ada. Kath dutifully fished out a photograph of her on her wedding day. She had been a good mother; hardworking and loving. "Why did she go insane?" Kath asked her father.

"A broken heart when Stanley died." Arthur was eighteen when his eight-year-old brother had succumbed to diphtheria. Kath speculated about her grandmother ranting and raving, running round the streets at night, half-naked with an axe. She had also tried to poison the surviving children by putting magic mushroom powder in their porridge. When she left the gas oven on and nearly blew the house to smithereens, she was committed to the Victorian asylum. Kath was only eight when Ada died, but she still had painful memories of her grandmother's decline. Poorly Ada had called her a "Black eyed bugger" and spat in her face. *And if I am pregnant now,* Kath cringed at the thought. *Maybe I don't deserve better !*

Only Uncle Alf and Aunty Brenda's visit took Kath's mind off the worst. Five minutes they said, and they would have to be on their way as it was Brenda's mother's birthday, but Kath managed to get them to stay for two hours. She loved their company. They were glamorous: Brenda was tall, slim and strikingly good-looking with jet-black hair half way down her back. Alf was an Omar Sharif look-alike. They made heads turn. Kath thought of Lynne, their daughter, like a big sister. They had been on summer holidays together several times. Kath won a sandcastle building competition in Bournemouth once. It says much about Nelly and Arthur that they didn't even buy a copy of the newspaper, the nine-year-old was mentioned in. Years later, when the family were on a caravan holiday in Tenby, Kath realised how much then she didn't want to be like her parents.

She had badgered Arthur and Nelly all week to let her have her portrait sketched by one of the local artists working on the sea front. After repeatedly refusing, saying it was 'too expensive' and 'what did she want one for... portraits are not for the likes of us,' Kath's parents relented, on the condition the drawing was in profile. Those were half the price of a full face. Kath duly sat, the money was paid and Kath took charge of the work. Unfortunately, the portrait must have been left in the caravan when the family departed, as it was never seen again. Mother blamed father, father blamed Kath. Kath just cried. The lesson was a bitter one. "If you don't look after yourself and your own things, nobody else will," Nelly chastised Kath. It was a lesson in life and stood Kath in good stead.

It was nine o'clock when the visitors left and Kath told Nelly about meeting Tilly and Sam, then they watched Brian Rix in a Whitehall farce on TV. Kath needed distraction and was in dire need of a good belly laugh.

Nelly intuitively knew that Rob's family wouldn't concord with theirs. "I've made you a nice *Ovaltine*," she said as she set the hot drink down on the mantelpiece next to where Kath was sat in front of the TV. Nelly and Arthur said that they had seen that particular play, so they went into the parlour. Kath only half-heartedly listened to the TV, as she couldn't help but overhear her parent's conversation.

"He seems a nice lad, but I conna see him with our Kath," Arthur went on.

"She's do better with David Noakes, he's been asking about her, and he's got a steady job now, been made up to supervisor."

David - three years older than Kath - lived ten doors away. He worked for the Parks and Cemeteries Department of the Council, had a car and, more importantly, a good family. "Solid working class, as honest as the day they were born." Kath heard Nelly say. Kath got up. She took a deep breath, then barged into the parlour. "Now... don't go trying to fix me up with boyfriends, I'll choose my own. And, just why couldn't you see Rob with me?"

Nelly's eyes averted from Kath's as she held Arthur's hands tight.

"Well, from what Rob says about his mother and father, and calling them by their first names. Their not speaking to anyone, the brother being in and out of mental hospitals, plus all that business about the grandmother dying and his uncle getting all the inheritance... it's all bad blood, Kath. There's no love lost amongst them is there? We are not used to that sort of thing that's all."

"Rob is different, you'll see, let's leave it at that - shall we? " Kath made her way to the stairs.

"And, by the way, your mother was in a mental hospital," she shouted to Arthur from the bottom step.

Kath wished she hadn't said that, she could have slapped her own face for doing so, it was below the belt and it left Arthur floored like he'd been knocked out in a boxing match. Nelly was right, Kath should learn to hold her tongue, but then, *play with fire you expect to get burnt.* Kath wouldn't tolerate any hint of criticism of Rob.

Kath drew the bedroom curtains tight to shut out the drizzly Potteries' night. Then, she buried herself down under the bedclothes, and, shamefaced, contemplated her fate. She could hear the hiss of the traffic as wet wheels passed along the road just outside her parents' bedroom. The stream of cars and even buses was never-ending. *Must have been a wedding or two... oh god... maybe I'll be having one soon.*

She felt her bloated stomach, and had all the symptoms of being ready to menstruate: hot, tetchy, lacking concentration - she couldn't even enjoy the comedy on TV that night. That was a sure sign. *But if I am pregnant aren't I supposed to feel light-headed, faint and sick?*

Kath slept fitfully. She dreamed a baby was born and then dragged horrifically from its mother's womb - just like she had seen on the film she had watched with Rob on their first date. The baby was revealed to be a bloody wet slimy thing with a green nose and blue forehead.

It was a blessing when Nelly banged on Kath's bedroom door at a quarter past ten in the morning.

"My, you really have had a good, long sleep." Nelly mothered as she felt Kath's feverish brow. "Here's your tea, I wonder if you are sickening for something?"

Kath began to cry bitterly. Nelly gave her a hug and soothingly patted her on the back. "Now, tell me what the matter is?"

"I feel so bad that I am going away and will not see you very much again ever, and yet I haven't even said thank you for everything you have ever done for me. Oh Mum ..." Kath sobbed again. "I am so selfish and pig-headed, how can you ever love me, how can anybody love me?"

Nelly didn't answer directly, it wasn't her way. She stood by the side of the bed holding Kath in her arms and rocking her like a baby. "It will be all right, Kathy." Being called Kathy made the young girl feel totally loved. Nelly's love was pure and unconditional.

"Better get to the lavatory, Kathy," Nelly continued, as Kath got out of bed and stood up. Blood was trickling down her calves.

Kath's tears of angst became tears of joy as she screamed all the way to the toilet.

It was already half past ten when Kath realised Rob was to phone her at the box outside the church at eleven. She dashed upstairs again, threw on some clothes and ran out into the pavement. It was five to eleven. Kath raced along the street, praying that the phone wouldn't be out of order.

"Bingo!" Kath shouted as she got to the cabin to find the phone was already ringing. Kath pushed the heavy door open and grabbed the black receiver." Yes… it's me," she cried, then laughed and sank to her knees, dragging the phone down with her. " It's all right, Rob… I am NOT pregnant!" Rob sank to his knees too (*or so he told Kath*) and whispered that he was not alone in the office at the school and could not speak freely. He'd have to be quick too, break was only fifteen minutes. Even though they vowed their undying love for each other, the conversation had been so short and so sanitised, Kath worried that Rob didn't want her after all and that would be that. She cried again and only stopped when she got back home.

"Now will you tell me more about the Llewellyns?"

Kath kept the description of her first meeting with Tilly, Sam and Leo short. Her motives were honourable: first she truly wanted to see the good in these people. Secondly, she knew it would upset Nelly if she knew what a devil Tilly had been to her daughter and then, after all, this love affair might come to nothing!

Nelly now believed that the Llewellyns were a highly educated, sophisticated family with good artistic and literary talents, slightly eccentric, a little egocentric and nothing more… but she couldn't believe how solid Robert was one of them!

With new vigour, Kath cleaned her bedroom, and sorted stuff out for the scout group jumble sale. Then, she went shopping and bought tripe for lunch - a family favourite. They ate it cold with lots of salt and vinegar, bread and butter.

More visitors arrived that afternoon, bearing gifts and good luck cards; single parent Irene next door for whom Kath had been her regular Saturday night babysitter, gave her a pen-set. Mrs. Parson, who had been Kath's childminder, brought chocolates (Kath had forgiven her unkindness but she had not forgotten the slaps, the sitting on a cold, hard floor, instead of a comfortable chair and… the harsh words). School friends Marion and Gemma said they wished t*hey* were going to college, instead of working.

Arthur returned at five and drove Nelly and Kath to see Billy, Pauline and the baby. Six-months-old Matthew had learned to blow. Pauline howled with laughter as she watched him blowing his supper off the high chair tray and onto the floor. Nelly was concerned about the mess on the carpet and although Kath wasn't impressed either, she pretended she hadn't noticed and chatted about her forthcoming move to Wales. Billy went out into the garden - which was still piled with builders' rubble - with Arthur, who measured up for new fencing. That would be his next job, along with clearing the rubbish. Work on Billy's new house would be never-ending.

When the family arrived home, Arthur worked out the quickest route to Barry from the AA map. Nelly and Kath sat together in front of the telly, on the two-seater, brown-winged leatherette settee.

"Tell me again about when Uncle Jack dived into the River Severn and saved a man from drowning." Kath snuggled up to her mother. Nelly's sister had married a paratrooper from Bridgenorth, during the war, when she was working in Shropshire on ammunitions; Uncle Jack was a handsome soldier. It was important for Kath to know she had some honourable people in her family.

"Tell me about my great-grandfather, Tom Brereton, too," Kath was proud he had owned a pottery factory and was very well off. "And how your Aunty Violet tricked Grandma out of her inheritance and left your mum and you all in poverty." It was also important for Kath to know that there were some ignoble people in the family.

"Such is life," Kath sighed, as mother related the details. Then she fell asleep on Nelly's lap.

It was past midnight when she woke and she and Nelly climbed the stairs for bed.

-10-

Arthur struggled for half an hour to lift Kath's lovingly packed trunk onto the roof rack of the *Corsair,* before reluctantly calling his daughter to help him. Nelly watched discreetly from behind the net curtains of the front room.

It was noon when the three of them set off. Sweeping down Tunstall High Street towards the M6, the bright red trunk, with its shiny brass padlock, looked like a treasure chest. Kath dozed in the back seat. Nightmares from the night before, where she had seen herself breaking her neck in the gym, drowning in the sea and being run over by a bus, lingered in her mind. Arthur drove in silence, except to cuss at the traffic now and again, saying it was the poor signposting that made him take a wrong turn. Nelly read and by the time they crossed the Welsh border, she had finished her paperback *Murder in the Abbey*. Kath marvelled at her mother's ability to read under any circumstances. Billy and Arthur would have been at daggers drawn, engaged in open warfare, shouting and thumping each other over wrong turns, but Nelly just sat still like a statue, with one leg curled under her bottom, book in one hand and a lit cigarette in the other.

Their house was as noisy as a railway station; double-deckers hooted as they passed their front door, nearby factory machinery banged and blew, neighbours rowed, dogs barked. Kath fantasised about her own little room in Barry, a sanctuary where she could breathe easily and shut out trouble completely.

It hardly seemed that three hours had passed since leaving Stoke when they passed a large sign sporting a red dragon symbol and the words, *CREOSO I CYMRY*, (*Welcome to Wales*). A few minutes later they drove into the College car park, next to the entrance of the girls' block where Kath was to stay.

The half-empty car park left Kath with a feeling that she may have arrived on the wrong day, but, undaunted, she entered the austere building and rang the bell at the unmanned reception. A stern, large middle-aged lady appeared from an office behind the counter. Matron - Miss Olivetti - spoke perfect, standard, RP English and hearing her clipped tones, the Tyler's stood to attention. After an efficient, almost brutal, reception, Kath's name was ticked off the New Arrivals list and she was given a key to Room 69, and a list of 'House Rules'. Then, the red trunk was hauled into the reception. Matron studied the trio through her horn-rimmed spectacles, as Arthur grunted, trying to squeeze the luggage into the lift. "Eh up duck what dust thee thin' they 'at, shift the legs will yee," he yelled at Kath, who was doing her best to follow his instructions. The old Matron sighed, then smiled. *Perhaps she is not that bad after all,* thought Kath.

Room 69 was on the sixth floor and Kath didn't like its location. It was the furthest room away from the lift - about fifty yards. The kitchen, bathrooms and toilets were just as far away too. I'*ll be up and down like a yo-yo,* thought Kath!

The too distant room was just the first of the disappointments; the canteen was five hundred yards away in another building.

Meals were tightly scheduled: Breakfast 8-9am, Lunch 1-2pm and Dinner 6-7.

She was to find out too that eating on mass meant the ordeal of endless queuing and by the time you got your food, you only had ten minutes to eat it.
Kath soon started skipping meals.

Alone that first night, after her parents had left, Kath read and re-read the House Rules. Trunks were not allowed in the students' rooms. Hers would have to be put in the storeroom on the ground floor. *My precious red trunk relegated to the storeroom, and I have bought it specifically to use in my room.* Kath banged her fists on the desk. *The absurdity of it! And kettles not allowed in the rooms either, so a trek to the kitchen every time I want a hot drink. And we can't cook in there either!*

The list went on. Kath shivered as she read, *No individual electric fires allowed in the rooms* - and contemplated the insignificant little radiator on the wall under the pokey window. It was an Indian summer outside, but like the Arctic inside. *What would it be like in December?* Kath shuddered again. *No posters to be put on the walls. No men in the rooms. All visitors to rooms must be signed in and out at reception. Visitors only allowed 7-9pm Monday to Friday and 5-10pm Saturday and Sundays.*

She sat desolate for a moment, head in hands. She hadn't even got a record player to cheer herself up. She had a little transistor radio, but the reception was so bad it wasn't worth listening to. She gathered it was something to do with the steel building and the fact that her room was not facing the right way.

She burst into tears when she heard the Righteous Brothers' song, *What Becomes of the Brokenhearted* coming from a room down the corridor; Robert was so far away. Kath wandered slowly down the corridor and popped her head into the room of a girl who looked to be the same age as her. Charlotte smiled, although it looked to Kath as though she too had been crying. It turned out that she was doing a PE Course.

Kath returned to her room and, in the tiny mirror over the desk, pulled a face at her reflection; damning fate that she should feel so wretched!

She shook her head and forced a smile, resolving to make the most of life at college, if only to please her parents. Then she thumbed through the books that she would read for pleasure: *The Secret Garden, Jane Eyre, The Virgin and the Gypsy, Women in Love, The Rainbow, The Doll's House...* and put them nearest to her bed, placing the awful books - those compulsory on her English course - as far away as possible. The books prompted a memory of Tilly's attic hoard: Kath still had to write a thank you for the weekend in August; but first she would write to Robert. She put pen to paper, informing him that she had discovered a public pay phone on the ground floor - by Miss Olivetti's office - and instructing him to ring from school on the following Monday morning at 11am.

She had discovered that lectures never started on Mondays 'til after lunch; the authorities had learned by experience that after students' boozy weekends, it was not a good idea to start classes early. After all, this was the swinging Sixties, a little late arriving in Wales, but nonetheless they were here.

It was midnight, when she finished writing to Robert and regretted that she hadn't even got a photograph of him; neither of them had cameras. Still, Rob had promised to buy her one for her nineteenth birthday and she wasn't going to have to wait long. Kath fell asleep, contemplating her new life and wondering just how she would manage a boyfriend in London – plus all of the other changes in her life.

That weekend only a swim would calm her nerves. It felt like ages since she had felt the cool, silky water caressing her body, so finding the College pool open for a general swim that Sunday morning was a godsend. She invited Charlotte to join her, but when she said no, Kath decided to find some more friends.

Christine, was more Kath's type and she met her whilst waiting in line for Sunday dinner. Kath was grimacing about the long wait when the short girl with a fat face and long straggly hair, said, “How goes it, Bach?” Kath laughed. It was the first Welsh she had heard spoken in Barry and she knew from her holidays in North Wales - and also from Rob - that 'Bach' meant small one. Before Kath could answer, Christine said, “I bet you know some good, dirty jokes.” Kath laughed again and admitted she did, proceeding to tell one of Dave Allen's:

> *1st Irishman: What is the first thing you are going to do when you get home?*
>
> *2nd Irishman: Take me wife's knickers off.*
>
> *1st Irishman: That's a bit sexy isn't it?*
>
> *2nd Irishman: No, the elastic is killing me.*

As she laughed aloud, Christine's belly shook. A mature twenty-two-year-old student from Welshpool, she was engaged to a Shropshire farmer. She had worked in a bank, got bored and then decided to become a teacher, “To get good holidays,” she said. “…and have time for kids, if we ever have any.” What's more, she was studying English as her main subject. *Manna from heaven,* Kath breathed deeply. *Perhaps Christine could help her with her English assignments?* Christine couldn't swim and Kath would teach her. *Fair exchange*, they said, and they shook on it.

Rob phoned Kath as arranged that Monday morning: he complained he couldn't sleep, as he was missing her so much - he wasn't eating properly either, his old stomach ulcer had flared up. He begged to see her that weekend. Kath was firm: they had to wait two more weeks. She had so much to do in Barry and she couldn't stand the strain. Kath had planned go to London for her birthday weekend, but how she was going to get there! The train was expensive and coaches took too long. Hitchhiking was an option, but she wouldn't dare do that alone. Rob offered to fetch her in his van but that would be ludicrous. “Just leave it to me, I will find a way,” she said, as she rang off with love and kisses.

It was when the Third Years started pouring into College at the end of that week, and the halls were filling up fast, Kath learned that one of the girls in their Modern Dance class had a boyfriend in Lewisham and she often went up to the Capital to see him. *Lewisham* was only two miles from Rob in Blackheath! Lesley, it turned out, not only had a boyfriend in London but also her family lived in Stoke. So, not only could they both hitch together to London, but to North Staffs as well! Kath was ecstatic. They made plans to leave college early, on the Friday of Kath's birthday weekend. They would be dodging lectures: Kath, Welsh studies and, Lesley, Religious Education, but reckoned a weekend in London with boyfriends was worth it!

In the meantime, Kath worked hard. She got up early to practice dance routines in the studio and do gymnastics in the gym; cartwheeling from one end of the room to the other before breakfast made her fit. She excelled at netball too and was chosen to play for the College once a month, fortunately on a Monday evening; the match was at home one week and away another. A mini-bus transported the team and they always went for a drink after the match in the Park Pub, where all the students met for a knees-up and a 'sauce pan fach' sing song.

Swimming lectures were once a week, but as the pool was open from 7am everyday, Kath swam most mornings too. She was shocked however to learn at her first official class that she had not got the correct regulation black swimsuit. Hers was too high in the leg and too low at the front! She would have to conform; the swimming mistress was strict. Kath complied, but not without complaint: she was already spending too much money on what she termed 'just breathing'. She had already spent half her grant and all the money her family had given on her departure from Stoke! Still, it was her birthday soon and mum and dad would give her money, also, she would get a job at Xmas. *Perhaps a shop assistant again in Boots, or a postwoman.* But Kath had no time to worry about money now. It was nearly the end of the month and she still hadn't written to Tilly! Rob said it didn't matter, Tilly wouldn't mind, after all, Tilly hardly wrote to him from one year to the next. Kath was horrified and just couldn't understand how families could be like that as she exchanged letters with her parents every week. They wrote about mundane news and sometimes there was a bit of scandal like when the fifteen-year-old vicar's daughter got pregnant. The baby's father was still at school and she was sent to the unmarried mother's home to have her baby, then it was adopted. *Poor Janet! That could have been me!* Kath chastised herself and promptly sought contraceptive advice at the doctors, but was refused the 'pill'. It was prescribed only for married women. Robert suggested she see a doctor in London; as far as he knew there were no restrictions there. Kath baulked at the idea of going to the doctor's on her birthday and joked that if he didn't get some decent condoms, they would abstain!

Kath wrote to Tilly, saying she was going to London for her birthday and they had already got tickets for the musical, *Hair*. She then listed the books she needed for her English course: *If you have any of them, I can collect them at half-term, late October.*

-11-

Kath's relief on locking her room at two o'clock on that Friday afternoon manifested itself in a display of singing and dancing in the street, with her hitchhiking companion, Lesley. After their jig, it was thumbs-up for a lift along the A40 to London.

After just three weeks in Halls, Kath felt trapped. She imagined the white gloss painted walls of her room had metamorphosed into oyster shells, the floor tiles, molasses. Flouting the rules, Kath had put up some posters, one for a *Ban the Bomb*, The Beatles in *A Hard Day's Night* and a portrait photograph of Martin Luther King.

But, with Lesley - an experienced traveller - in charge, Kath forgot about College, followed her mate's instructions and prayed they would arrive on time.

And they did. At five minutes past six, Robert was waiting for them at the Hampstead flyover. Zipping in and out of traffic, the van crossed London in record time. Lesley got out at Lewisham and then Robert ardently embraced Kath. "Madam landlady, Elaine, is going to be away all weekend," Robert beamed. "We can make as much noise as we like…" Kath knew then Robert was going to be hers forever and… she relished making a lot of noise!

Naturally boisterous Kath was still smarting after being suspended for a week from the College library for clattering about wearing *Dr. Scholl* wooden-soled sandals!

Rob had tried to make his bedsit more cosy. He had swapped the single bed for a double and had put fresh curtains up to match the new bedspread. The pale-green candlewick bed cover, with its white and yellow daisies, didn't quite match Kath's taste, but at least it was an improvement on the red plaid blanket. A telephone had been installed in the hall; a pay machine. Elaine wouldn't have trusted otherwise, but at least it was better than having to rely on Rob phoning from school or a public phone box.

That Friday night didn't disappoint. Rob had secretly been attending circuit-training classes and had enrolled for swimming lessons twice a week at Greenwich Baths. He had taken Kath's warning, I *won't marry anyone who can't swim,* to heart. His stomach ulcer was under control, and should be cured within two months… if he stayed off fatty, spicy food and alcohol (which he was doing).

On the Saturday morning, during their long lie-in, Kath was wondering if Rob had forgotten her birthday. But, just as she was about to remind him, he plonked a plastic carrier bag on the bed. "Your birthday present. I haven't had chance to wrap it up." Kath's jaw dropped at the sight of the bag from *WH Smiths* and her bottom lip quivered in disbelief as she discovered a dictionary and a *Parker* pen inside.

"You said you were buying me a camera!?"

"Did I?

"Yes, you did!" Kath was firm. "When we were in Bath, sitting on that bridge that I can't remember the name of."

"Pulteney."

"There, then. You do remember." Kath was stunned.

"Well, cameras are expensive and I couldn't afford one. Anyway, you said you were having trouble with your spelling and you needed a new pen as your old one was blotting."

Rob was right, so full of common sense.

"Look - it's not just an ordinary dictionary. It's a dictionary and thesaurus combined."

Kath pondered, *Rob is sensible. I can have a camera another time. For now it really is important that I should write essays properly! Robert just has the knack of doing what he wants - but making me think it is what I want. How does he do it!*

Kath linked Rob's arm as they strolled out into the Indian summer sun at midday. "It's just like the day I was born." Kath surveyed the blue sky.

"How do you know ?" Rob stroked Kath's cheek.

"My Mum told me. I expect, as you were a January baby, it was snowing when you came into the world?"

"I have no idea."

"Didn't you ask?"

"Nope."

"Well, I know you were born in Chepstow, but was it in a hospital or at home?"

"I don't know. You'll have to ask Tilly if you really want to know.

Talking about Rob's mother prompted Kath to say that she had finally written to her and addressed the letter to Sam and Leo as well, but had had no response.

Rob said he wasn't surprised, as Tilly hardly wrote to him and was not known anyway for her letter writing skills.

Strange… thought Kath *Tilly is a writer, an authoress with children's stories and also a book on Dylan Thomas to her name.* She started to say something to Rob about this but then her stomach rumbled and she thought about food.

The couple had been invited to lunch with one of Rob's art school friends; a half-mile walk away. Living alone, and not interested in cooking, Robert always seemed in need of a good feed.

Charlie's chilli con carne with boiled white rice was a sensation, a new experience for Kath. She was in awe of Robert's avant-garde art school pals. Alun, described playing strip poker, Jack naked with a Greek student once, who ended up riding around Eltham at four in the morning on a motorbike, with only his long black beard covering his 'John Thomas'!

Rob, told the story of being chased on his motorbike by a police car for speeding. Having no tax or insurance, Robert had revved up even more and slipped into a side road. He finally dodged the police by skedaddling over a footbridge and hiding his bike in an alleyway, only returning when it was dark to collect it.

Kath was glad though when the party broke up and they went back to Robert's flat. It was her birthday after all, and she wanted a cuddle before going to see the West End smash hit musical, *Hair*.

Rob filled the bath, big enough for two. "Well you know, when the cat's away!" Kath shouted, as she slithered over the side and sank down into the bubbling, piping hot water. Rob followed. Wallowing like playful young seals, they took turns scrubbing each other's backs 'til the phone rang.

"Damn it!" Rob yelled, still dripping wet. He had stubbed his toe on the bottom stair as he was about to ascend again. It had been a missed call. When Rob slipped back into the bath shivering, Kath kissed him on the neck and whispered, "I still love you. You, stark bollock naked, you."

Kath begged to go to the West End in the van. She hated the impersonal, crowded Tube. But Robert insisted; it would be almost impossible to find a parking space there on a Saturday night. Still it was worth it for a good show and Kath found herself singing, *Let the Sunshine In, The Age of Aquarius, and Good Morning Starshine,* all the way back to Blackheath.

After Sunday's lie-in, Kath was more in love than ever. Robert's gentleness and creativity complimented her athleticism and stamina. But, Kath wanted to see how Robert's swimming had progressed too, so they drove to Greenwich Baths. Rob completed a length for the first time. Kath said that was the best birthday present he could have given her. They celebrated his achievement with friends that afternoon at the Jazz Club, sang a quick *Happy Birthday* for Kath, but flats were the main topic of conversation. Rob was serious about moving to a bigger place, now that he had Kath to consider. The problem was he couldn't pay more than four pounds-fifty a week, which was nearly a third of his weekly teacher's pay. Rob sounded out his mate, Tom, who'd just received compensation for a nasty motorcycle accident and was talking about buying a big house, consisting of two or more flats, one of which he was certain to rent to Rob. The prospect looked promising and the couple were happy as they sped over to Lewisham to pick up Lesley. The plan was to get to Hampstead flyover for their hitching journey back to Barry.

As they settled down into the leather seats at the back seat of a hyped up *Jag*. Kath was bubbling over about her birthday weekend, but when she sensed Lesley's visit hadn't gone so well, she shut up. She had said enough about boyfriends and dirty weekends! Fantasising about Robert getting a bigger flat was a safer topic.

-12-

Kath picked up more birthday cards at the reception as she scrambled into her Hall of Residence at midnight.

First, she opened the card from Arthur and Nelly, knowing there would be a cheque inside, and skimmed the accompanying letter. *Great Aunty Polly was giving her a gold bracelet, to be collected at half-term. Matthew had cut his first tooth*. Kath threw a punch in the air*! Billy was going to give her his record player. Cousin Elle was to marry her sweetheart, car salesman, Derek.*

Kath wrote back that night, she didn't mention the wedding, thinking how unthoughtful is was to hold it when she would be sitting exams! Kath assured her mother she was coping; she couldn't bear to tell her she wasn't! Finally, she asked Nelly to order Tilly's, Dylan Thomas book, from the library and as a P.S. wrote: *Robert and I want* to *buy pottery in Stoke and sell it in London and Wales. Can you speak to Uncle Alf about supplying us with some mugs from his warehouse?*

It was only when Magariad knocked on Kath's door, at two in the morning, complaining about the radio still being on, that Kath realised that she hadn't had a birthday card from Tilly; she still didn't know if the eccentric woman would lend her any of the books she needed. *And it will be four weeks before I see her again!* Kath felt agitated and forced herself to sleep.

College work was punctuated by Robert's letters and phone calls. He worried that Kath would tire of him; she swore she wouldn't.

Once the Mexican Olympics had started, Kath couldn't get access to the TV in the common room so gave up and listened to her radio instead, but Matron complained it was always on too loud. *That Magariad must have grumbled,* Kath surmised. She found herself in a strop too with a tartar from Pembroke Dock when she lost her dinner pass and was refused entry to the canteen. Plus, College work was grinding.

Half-term loomed: Kath wrote home again, she said she was flagging and feared she might not stay the course. Already, three girls in her year, had dropped out. One had been drinking heavily and shooting drugs, another was pregnant and the third was a mystery. But her news wasn't all bad. She had been approached to be a contender in the Barry College Beauty Contest, but refused. The feminists took Kath to be one of them, until she flashed her Friendship ring and said she was going steady.

Arthur replied straightaway : "WE TYLER'S DON'T GIVE UP" was written in bold capitals on the top of his letter. Kath stopped complaining, and, in the words of Winston Churchill, '*...kept buggering on*'.

That weekend break back home in October was a blessing; Kath got the gold bracelet, Arthur had acquired several boxes of pottery from Uncle Alf's pot bank to save Rob the trouble, and had packed up Billy's record player and records, ready to be taken to Barry. Nelly had acquired a copy of Tilly's *Laugharne* book from the library and stocked up with oatcakes. *Love is what you do, not what you say,* thought Kath and it made her think of Robert.

"Our Kath, dunna ferget yer' 'at!" Dad shouted, waving her fur bonnet madly as she and Rob were about to leave Stoke in the van that Sunday night.

"And don't forget to read Tilly's book, neither," Kath shouted back, grabbing her hat from Arthur as he pushed it through the open side window of the moving van. It was already snowing slightly.

"And dunna ye werret about all this studying. It'll addle thee brain lass," Arthur shouted into the darkness.

Arthur's pottery dialect seemed stronger than Kath had ever noticed before. Having been away for six weeks, she realised how much her own accent had neutralised. Kath hoped Tilly would approve. Although she had picked up the Welsh intonation somewhat, she felt she was veering towards sounding like Rob. After living in the South East so long, he had only the merest trace of a Welsh accent.

-13-

Samuel was alone in the kitchen when the lovers arrived at the Old Parsonage. It was half past eleven. The journey had taken five hours, instead of three, due to the snow and hold-ups. Samuel only shrugged when the couple slipped through the back door and Kath apologised for keeping him up late. He carried on mixing up something that smelled like Sulphur, then drank the concoction with two Ginkgo biloba tablets. Kath prickled with guilt and humiliation. Only the thought of the drive that evening, alone with Rob, winding their way through the night as the tall, black tree-lined lanes slipped by serenely, revived her spirit. Watching the snowflakes drifting down, she had leaned against Rob's shoulder and her world was at peace. Lulled by the swish of the blades, she reflected. Life was challenging, perhaps it always would be, but with Rob she knew she would thrive.

Kath stood by the *Rayburn* savouring her time with Rob when Sam, still wearing his threadbare red tartan trilby, put his cup down and spoke. "Tilly's put you two in the *Isaac Williams* room. She reckoned you could manage in one bed." He then checked the back door was locked and disappeared into his little room, next to the downstairs toilet. Sam's brief 'welcome' left a chill in Kath's veins. *Was Sam annoyed with them, or was he ill?* Rob, unperturbed went straight to bed.

Kath lingered downstairs. The ancient house felt cold; exposed. The autumn rain and north winds had tentacles that inveigled their way through every nook and cranny, and the electric storage heating system was no bulkhead against the vagaries of the British weather. Kath made herself a cup of tea and casually picked up a copy of the *Daily Mail*, 'Sam's opium', from the kitchen table. Two black American athletes made headlines: Tommie Smith and John Carlos, stood on the Olympic podium. Wearing a black glove each, they demonstrated the black salute: a protest for racial equality. Kath felt solidarity for the men, but failed to read more of the cover story - she felt uncomfortable, like an intruder, in this strange house. But then, Peaches, who had been in his dog basket, begged to be picked up. She wrinkled her nose in distaste at his bad breath, but she still cradled him gently. He responded with a sigh and lay limp as she carried him quietly around the ground floor of the rambling house. Only the old oak grandfather clock ticking in the entrance hall, broke the heavy silence. The dining table was no longer set for dinner with the Crown Derby, as it had been before on her first visit, but was piled high with small antiques: brass candle sticks, a silver candelabra, a pile of dusty brown leather-backed books with titles such as, *Great County Houses*.

Stock for the new shop, Kath assumed. A pile of new Dylan Thomas books stood in the middle of a pile of pewter ware. Kath opened the top book to see Tilly's and Sam's signatures on the first page, then flicked through the chapters, stopping, merely by chance at page eighty. *The hospitality of the Welsh is famous and nowhere on earth could you be sure of a better welcome. A meal is provided almost instantly, with the best china and tablecloth in honour of your visit.* Kath winced at the off-hand way Tilly had provided their last meal, and how unlike it was of the Welsh hospitality she had written about.

Kath crossed the hall to the stairs, stopping to view Sam's paintings again. A portrait of Tilly, done in oils, sat next to a Gainsborough print of a Mrs Fitzherbert portrait. The likeness of the two women was striking. The bellowing blonde hair, the aquiline noses, the rosy cheeks. Sam's portraits of a Spanish looking girl in a red dress and grey shawl and a little boy in a Tam o' Shanter looked quizzically at each other across the stairwell. Several pen and ink drawings of animals dressed as humans and a large oil still life of a Welsh dresser and sides of hams filled one wall. An enormous canvas, a seaside village landscape, filled another. Kath hadn't warmed to Sam's work when she had first seen it a few months before, but now she saw its merits and was thrilled to think her boyfriend had such talent in his blood. But how the vibrancy of the paintings contrasted with the grime and decay of the Old Parsonage: the overflowing rubbish bin, dirty dish cloths, rank toilets and the rotten window frames.

Rob was still reading a car magazine when Kath joined him in the horsehair bed.

"Thought you were never coming..." Rob complained. "Come on, get me warm, it's bloody freezing in here."

"I'll do my best." Kath wasn't enthusiastic." I just don't feel welcome here. I can't believe your mother didn't wait up for us, mine would have; and there was no food left out for us, either. Remember the last time I came? We had to eat in the kitchen with old plates and dirty glasses - yet the dining room table was laid with Crown Derby."

"No, I can't remember that, but don't go on about it now."

"Your mother doesn't like me." Kath confided.

"Now, I wouldn't say that. She just doesn't think. Anyway, you are just too sensitive, got a chip on the old shoulder if you ask me."

Kath's hackles rose, but she simply said, "Well, if that's what you think, you can have your ring back, Mr Llewellyn! I know what I feel and if you don't believe me, then what is the point of our relationship?"

Rob was more interested in keeping Kath's voice down, than home truths, so conceded. "Okay, okay, I believe you. But, just let's talk about that when we are out of here. I love you, isn't that enough? Just settle down now and give me a big kiss – then it will be all right."

Kath warmed to his touch and let the day's events slip by into the night.

It was eleven o 'clock when the couple descended to the kitchen for breakfast. Sam was sketching Peaches on the blank back page of a brand new art textbook entitled, *Giotto.*

"Let me see," Kath asked as she leaned over his bony shoulders, visible through his thin cotton white shirt. "Well, you are a wonderful artist, Sam. I was admiring your paintings on the walls last night. I so wish I could draw." Sam only grunted, then exclaimed what a fine Italian Renaissance painter Giotto was and how he had seen his famous Scrovegni Chapel frescoes in Padua when he had travelled to Italy as a student.

"You must study art," Sam went on, looking up at Kath. "Look at it and you will learn." Kath confessed she had not the slightest talent for art and preferred science.

"I do like looking at paintings, though," Kath hoped for some kind of acceptance in Sam's face, but there wasn't any. She turned away and helped herself to a bowl of cornflakes. "Where's Tilly?" she asked.

"Oh, I dunno, out buying antiques I 'spect. Always out."

Just then, Peaches coughed; he was choking on a chocolate drop, Sam had thrown him. Kath rushed to the dog, only to find Sam was choking too. "Damn things stick in your throat," he spluttered; his bottom false teeth fell out as he wretched. Robert slapped his newspaper down on the table. "What's all this hullabaloo ?

"Oh, it's nothing, nothing at all." Sam regained his composure and put

his dentures back. Peaches, quietly slipped under the table.
"What a lot!" Kath raised her arms then sighed as she cleared the table and started washing the dishes.
"I see the piano has gone, Sam," Rob restarted the conversation.
"Sold, I suppose," Sam wasn't sure. "No more plonking now, do you follow? Leo spends more time in bed now."
"We were going to ask him to come with us to Bovington Tank Museum this afternoon. Do you think he would like that?" Kath said.
"Yeh, why not. I fancy a spin out today." Leo had appeared at the kitchen door, and stood with one arm leaning against the doorjamb, the other on his hip.
"Good to see you, Leo, you're looking a lot better," Kath said. "How is your course going?"
"So-so, but I have been having trouble getting to Bristol. That bloody *Triumph* I bought is no bloody good, keeps breaking down on me."
"*You* bought?" Robert stuttered? "Don't you mean, *Tilly bought?*"
"Ah, don't let's go down that road now. You know I can't do anything here in this god-forsaken village without a car. I have to be able to drive".
"An expensive car, too? Do you realise that car cost twenty times my weekly salary? Just think how hard I would have to work to get a car like that - and you get one on a plate. Just put your hand out and you get. I bet you're paying a fortune to get it fixed, a specialist mechanic is needed for a collectable car like that."
Sam's eyes watered and he shook his head." Just think yourself lucky you can work, Rob."
"Lucky?" Kath questioned and added under her breath." Poor Rob."
"What's going on here then?" Tilly demanded to know as she strode into the mêlée.
"Nothing." The three men replied in chorus.
"Nothing…" Kath confirmed.
"Hmm…" Tilly was not convinced but decided whatever had gone on was better left unsaid.
From the kitchen windowsill, Robert picked up a recent invoice for replacement brake pads, "Twenty pounds including parts and labour!" Robert scowled at Leo and turned pale." That's four times the weekly rent on my bedsit!" Leo pretended not to hear and Tilly didn't respond either, but, after a pause, she said, "You will help me unload the car

won't you, Robert?"

"And what about Leo? He's got two arms and legs, why can't he help?"

"You are stronger. Leo is unwell and you know you like hard work!"

Kath bit her lip.

"Oh, Tilly, did you get my letter a few weeks ago? I asked you about some books?"

"Did we get a letter from Barry, Sam?"

"Can't remember."

"You remember, don't you, Leo? " Kath questioned him.

"Who me? No."

"Well, I addressed the letter to all three of you. Surely your mother would have shown you the letter?"

"Likely she wouldn't. The fact of the matter is nobody tells me anything!"

"I listed a few books I need for my English course, like *Hamlet* and *Mill on the Floss.*"

"Oh, I don't think I have any of them," Tilly answered.

"But... you have many books in the attic, I'm sure you must have a copy of *Hamlet* at least?

"Well, go and have a look yourself, I don't have the time."

Kath needed no prompting. She raced up the stairs two at a time as Robert went to help his mother unload the car.

Boxes and several piles of books tied up with string, littered the dusty attic floor. Kath methodically sorted through the eclectic collection: books about the human body, French history, fashion and beauty, gardening, Greek Mythology - but no sign of any of the books she needed.

Ten large cardboard portfolios of sketches and some paintings were stacked against one wall. Kath was curious. The work was Sam's: pencil drawings of toys and dolls, antique statues, bowls of fruit, a pair of shoes, and even a man copulating with a duck! Kath recoiled in shock.

"Nothing I need," she exclaimed as she entered the drawing room, still shaken, adding, " Oh well, it was worth a try. Anyway, we're going to Bovington Tank Museum today and taking Leo. Perhaps we should take a picnic?"

"Well, you can't take food from here, I haven't got much food in. Just

get a snack out and I'll cook a chicken dinner for tonight."
"That would be nice."
Robert rolled his eyes.

The three set off in Rob's van, with Kath squashed in the middle of the front seat and Chris Montez's, *The More I See You*, you playing on the radio. Kath mouthed the words and looked longingly at Rob as he drove.

"I won't come in with you two: I am not really up for tanks and war, besides I need to do some serious reading," Kath said, halfway to the museum.

"We'll skip lunch too," Rob said." But Leo, you can buy us a pint at the next pub."

"I haven't got any money. Not a bean. Tilly says she keeps me in food, a roof and a car and that's it. I have to buy and sell antiques to make a living and I haven't sold anything yet."

"What about a grant for your course?" Rob wriggled in the driver's seat.

"Only enough for books and materials, mate."

"So, that means you expect me to pay your entrance to the Museum?"

"Sorry, but you invited me!"

"Bloody cheek," Rob growled. "In that case, we'll go without the pints."

"He is your brother, Rob, he would do the same for you if he could, wouldn't you, Leo? And, I can't do without a drink. So go on, Rob, stop at the next pub and I'll buy us all a beer."

"Bloody hell, Kath, you are a sucker, my God you really are!"

"Oh well, better to be kind than cruel. Better to give than receive." Kath smiled at Leo.

"You can take some good photos of Rob driving tanks and send me a few copies. It will be good practice for your photography classes. I want big photos of Rob to put on my wall in College."

"But, you told me you weren't allowed to put stuff on the walls in your room, Kath?"

"Well, *the rules* say we are not allowed… but I have put some posters up, anyway."

"So, you're a rebel, too," Leo looked at Kath with admiration.

"Well, only a little one, I know how far I can push, I'm not that daft!

Got to tow the line sometimes."

Leo mimicked her accent, "*Daft, daft, daft!*"

It was 5pm when the Museum closed for the evening and the two brothers left the building looking as if they had just pissed on the school bully.

"Great day, eh?" Leo laughed for the first time in front of Kath.

"Rob's been riding Big Willy and Little Willy."

Kath looked nonplussed.

"Keep her guessing..." Leo was a torment, but Kath resisted the temptation to lash out. She carried on reading *Room With a View*.

"Finished... " Kath announced with relief as they made their way back home for tea. *Hell of a boring story, though,* she thought. *Still it's made me think about the hypocrisy of the British class system.*

Tilly's chicken dinner that evening was an exact replica of the meal Kath and Rob had had at the Old Parsonage back in August: roast chicken and stuffing, eaten in the same kitchen, on the same rickety chairs. Peaches snoozed in the corner.

"I got an 'A' Grade for a short story I wrote in College this week, Kath announced, after she had drunk a pint of strong, dry cider and built up the courage to speak.

"Did you?" Tilly answered indifferently, before changing the subject. "Robert, I've got some jobs for you to do while you are here."

Catching Rob's eye, then frowning, Kath mouthed, "Got to earn your keep !" Robert didn't flinch.

Tilly's voice crescendoed. "I need some mirrors taking to Lampeter. Two Empire mirrors, they will fit in your van. You could take them tomorrow when you go to Barry with Kathleen."

"Well, actually, I won't be taking Kath back 'til Wednesday."

"But, she said she would have to be back in College on Tuesday."

"When did you tell Tilly that, Kath?" Rob asked.

"In the letter I sent to Tilly weeks ago. The letter asking about the books?"

"So... you did get Kath's letter, Tilly?" Rob glared at his mother.

"Well, I suppose I must have done," she confessed and avoided all eye contact.

Kath took a deep breath and counted to ten, then breathed out slowly.

"How do you like my new bracelet?" she asked, holding out her arm towards Tilly. Kath had worn it all day and Tilly hadn't commented. "It's all gold, Victorian, a real antique. Must be quite valuable. What do you say, Tilly?"

After only a cursory glance, Tilly said. "It's late Victorian, that is if it is that old, and it's only nine-carat gold. These chain link bracelets are ten a penny. I wouldn't buy one at any price. Too common."

Kath had expected her to at least touch the piece, feel the weight, assess the quality in her fingers, like a real lover of antiques would, but she didn't.

Rob broke the ensuing silence. "We're going to Longleat tomorrow, just Kath and I."

Leo looked disappointed.

"Marvellous Hall," enthused Sam. "Wonderful architecture. The Elizabethan Great Hall is the finest in the country. Oh, the Grinling Gibbons carvings, John Wootton's hunting scenes, second to none... Van Dyke portraits," Sam writhed in ecstasy at the thought.

"And the exquisite Ming vases, the Louis XV1 cabinets, the marble fireplaces." Tilly commented.

"Tilly has been many times," Sam seemed sad about that. "I have only read about it, seen the photographs, you know what I mean,." confessed Sam. "On first name terms with Lord Bath, *she* is."

"Hmm, yes." Kath said. "I'm sure we will enjoy it. But what happened to Jeannie and Martin this weekend? They were supposed to be coming here to meet me."

"Were they?" asked Tilly

"Yes. Rob said Jeannie had written to him saying she would be here mid half-term. Didn't you know?"

"No."

"And they haven't got a phone in the new cottage?"

"No, not yet."

"Oh well, we'll just have to meet them some other time."

"By the way, Rob says you like sewing?" Tilly didn't seem concerned about her daughter.

Robert nodded at Kath as he looked up from a car magazine, hoping Tilly had forgotten about the mirrors!

"Well, I have made a few things. I have an old hand sewing machine in Barry, but I can't say I like sewing that much. I do it to save money. I was never very good at…'

"Well… can you make a dress and some knickerbockers for this doll?" Tilly interrupted, as she brought a bisque-headed, soft-bodied, twelve-inch doll to the table.

"Here is some cambric fabric and lace. You can look up a suitable design for the dress," she said, in a way that implied it wouldn't take a minute and would be no effort at all. "And, mind you look after my doll, she's genuine Victorian!"

"I'll try my best, but I told you I'm not that good. Don't *you* sew, Tilly?"

No, absolutely not. I hate it.

"Oh dear, not even a button?"

"No."

"*Got to earn your keep*," Rob jibed in a whisper behind a cupped hand, but his mood changed when his mother started speaking again.

"Oh, and what about my mirrors ? You can take them to Wales on Wednesday, then? "

Robert stopped laughing and meekly said, "All right."

Sam sat reading an old newspaper in the kitchen, smoking a *Tom Thumb* cigar and drinking a cup of strong, sweet tea when Rob and Kath returned to the house to say goodbye, after loading the van with the heavy mirrors that Wednesday.

"What do you think of the Black Salute at the Olympics then, Sam?" Kath asked as she glanced over Sam's shoulder and noticed a photo of the controversial Olympic black athletes making the news.

"Shouldn't be allowed," Sam retorted.

"What shouldn't be allowed?" Kath asked, not sure what Sam was getting at. "Too many immigrants in the country, too many blacks!" Kath steered the conversation away from the fiery issue.

"Don't you ever sit in your sitting room?" Kath went on.

"No."

"Well, you should, at least now you have got some decent chairs and a chaise longue."

Sam didn't respond. "Enoch Powell is right, 'Rivers of Blood' - that's what we will see if we aren't careful. Those damn trade unions, strikes and more strikes. No hope, no hope," he shook his head, oblivious to Kath and her concern that he should relax more in his own home.

"When are you going to set up a studio and start painting again?"

"Oh, dear, oh, dear, I don't know; no time you see, all these great antiques to clean and sell.." He waved his hands about like a desperate hitchhiker.

"Don't ask him about his painting, Kath, he will just go on and on about it. He'll do it when he's ready. He does exaggerate, likes to play the martyr," Rob put his arm round Kath. "Come on, we had better get going"

"But, he isn't happy, is he?" Kath mouthed to Rob.

"Happy being a sop."

"Shush, shush…" Kath put her hand across Robert's mouth.

"What really happened to the piano, Sam?" she asked.

"Oh… that. Well, an Irish dealer took it away. Full of worm. We just let it go, for nothing."

"What did you pay for it in the first place?" Robert couldn't resist a dig.

"Oh, a lot of money. You know Tilly when she fancies something, there's no stopping her, and she's been swindled a few times already."

"Do you think it's wise to be setting up an antique shop, if she keeps buying things and selling them at a loss?"

"Ssshhh… don't let Tilly hear you say that. It's our business anyway."

But Robert wouldn't leave go. "Actually, I was told that the piano had been left upstairs by the previous owners of this house?"

"Oh well, I dunno," Sam confessed.

Rob looked up to the ceiling in wonder, bit his lip, then got back to the matter of the mirrors. "Oh, I nearly forgot. Where exactly are we taking the mirrors?"

"Tilly left the address here on this slip of paper; and here's a pound for petrol."

"A pound! That won't get us to the Severn Bridge!" protested Rob,

"But you were going that way anyway, the pound is just a little extra."

Rob shrugged his shoulders.

"But you are coming back here after dropping me off, aren't you, Rob? And you'll be staying 'til the weekend, won't you?" Kath reminded him. "You've got to earn your keep…"

Tilly scowled as she crossed the threshold and caught Kath jeering.

"Well, we'll be on our way now." Rob was serious. "See you tonight, late. Give me a back door key and you needn't wait up."

"That's fine, here you are," Tilly said, as she handed Rob the key.

"I've had a good look at your book, Tilly."

Robert looked at Kath and frowned impatiently.

"Very impressive," Kath went on. She liked to please. "But I can't understand why it has just a plain paper dust jacket? Why isn't there one of Sam's drawings on the cover?"

Sam merely sucked hard on his false teeth, stamped his feet under the table and breathed in deeply through his nostrils. Kath ignored the tantrum and continued. "A portrait of Dylan Thomas on the front would have been apt, but then the text concentrates on the town and its history, rather than Dylan's life. The drawings are what really make it."

Tilly glowered and Kath realised her faux pas, but it was too late to make amends; Tilly had already turned her back on the pair. "Thanks for everything, Tilly," Kath said as she patted the woman gently on the shoulder. "Bye, Sam," she shouted as she waved from the door. "And bye, bye lovely Peaches. Do say goodbye to Leo for us, too."

The piano gone, Leo was now plaguing the household with loud music emanating from his record player. The couple left to the sounds of Manfred Mann's, *Ha Ha Said The Clown.*

Finding the place in Lampeter where the mirrors were to be delivered, was traumatic, as they hadn't got a map. Tilly's hurriedly scribbled down directions made no sense, and no one seemed to know where Dai Jones' establishment was anyway. After over an hour of cruising around the town and almost on the brink of aborting the task, they finally stumbled on the modest establishment, a mile from the town centre.

"Genuine antique, gold leaf mirrors for a chip shop, of all places," Kath laughed out loud as Rob and the short Welsh proprietor struggled to lift the treasures from the rear of the van and around a hole in the pavement. New gas pipes to the premises were being fitted and an area of pavement in front of the shop was cordoned off. Two attempts were needed to get the tall objects through the front door, but then, having been paid in cash, Kath and Robert were also rewarded with two free packets of fish and chips. They ate their supper off their laps as they set off back to Barry.

"I'm on good terms with the new supervisor in the canteen." Kath told Rob as they pulled up on the College car park. "She'll let you in. That old bag from Pembroke's gone now. Let's go and have a drink and I'll sneak you up to my room for a bit after." Kath shot Robert a smile.

"Yeh, right on, babe. Let's get the party going."

Their little tryst ended at nine and, when Robert left, Kath read her mail, and took stock of her situation once again. First, there was a formal notice from Matron: during half-term there had been a room inspection and Kath was being reprimanded for having posters and photographs on the walls. These had to be removed immediately. She was also in trouble for having her trunk and kettle in the room. The punishment was going to be having her name read out at the next monthly House meeting. Having your name read three times in a year could mean an expulsion! Kath decided rules were rules and reluctantly she would have to obey them. Right now, though, she would simply enjoy her music. Paul Anka's, *Oh Diana.* Helen Shapiro's, *Walking back to Happiness,* Jackie Trent's, *Where Are You Now My Love, Oh La La* by Elvis and The Beatles, *Rubber Sole* album. Kath danced round the room till midnight, then she drew up a list of things to do.

Please God give me strength, she thought as she dropped off to sleep.

Kath decided to stay in College for the next few weeks to get on top of her workload and urged Robert to make the most of his time with his parents. He would be at Tilly's until the end of the following weekend. Kath would meet her love again at the Old Parsonage, late November. Rob and Kath had spoken about getting engaged at Christmas engagement, but not until Arthur had given his approval. It was expected that Rob would get a job and move to South Wales. *Surely Sam would help, he knew important people in education, surely he could use his contacts?* Rob would just have to ask.

Kath perused estate agents windows. Respectable three-bedroom semis were from two thousand pounds. They had a hundred pounds saved up from selling pottery and doing furniture removals during their weekends together in London. They also had begun collecting pre-1947 silver coins in a dimpled whisky bottle. Already, it was an inch deep in sixpences, shillings, florins and half-crowns. However, Rob didn't seem overly enthusiastic about moving to Barry. It wasn't the prettiest of towns and now with the summer over and the Bristol Channel winds blasting in from the sea, battering the coast, it was drab and foreboding. A hurricane had destroyed much of the docks and the shipping industry in 1955 and, when *Butlins* had opened in the early 60's, further up the coast, what little tourism Barry had was left in tatters. Kath found solace in solitary walks and the unspoilt beach at Cold Knap, where she sat on Nell's Point and breathed in the brisk sea air.

Not having to rush off on Fridays to hitchhike or to catch a train, she managed to get on with her course work and found time to make Tilly's doll's outfit too. Letters every day and phone calls twice a week from Rob kept her happy and by the time she was due to set off for Somerset again, she was in good form. She had to be, as she would be meeting the elusive Jeannie and Martin.

-14-

Robert met Kath at the railway in Bath at nine that Friday night.

"By, god. What's in this… Lead?" Rob said as he slung Kath's rucksack over his shoulder.

"Books… Tilly's doll, cigars for Sam, wine and chocolates."

"They won't thank you, Kath. You are just too good." Rob shook his head.

It was dark and looked like it was about to snow. Kath pulled her anorak hood up and linked Rob's arm. Being with him dispelled the discomfort of cold feet.

Robert had just sold his racing motorbike leathers, which he used at Brands Hatch. "I've put the fifty quid into our bank account." Kath patted his hand affectionately, but then yawned when he mentioned being the staff room shove halfpenny champion again for that month. She resumed her attention however, when he said he had applied for a job in Chepstow.

"You should get it," Kath enthused. "One word to the Welsh Director of Education from Sam and you'll get an interview." Kath looked hopefully at Rob, but reading his thoughts, she added despondently, "Won't you?" then broached the subject of Christmas jobs.

She said it would be better if they could both do something in Stoke. Rob agreed, at least he wouldn't be having to put up with his landlady being miserable about Kath staying, but he didn't want to think about that now. He was keen to show Kath the new stereo radio in his van, which he had fitted himself. The last one had packed up after their trip to Cornwall. During the twenty-minute drive to Beckton, they sang along to the latest pop songs, including The Beatles', *All my Loving*, Otis Reading's, *Sitting on the Dock of the Bay,* and Frankie Vaughan's *Can't Take My Eyes Off Of You* - and listened to an interview with model Twiggy about the pressures of being in the public eye.

Jeannie and Martin were already in bed, with 'dastardly' colds, as Sam described their state, when Rob and Kath arrived at the Old Parsonage.

"They're sleeping over the shop," Tilly explained. "I've put you down there too. You'll see, in the room before theirs."

"Is the heating on?" Rob rubbed his cold hands together as a silence ensued.

"Well, no, but what does a healthy young couple like you pair need heating for, when you have each other…?" Tilly laughed like a Kookaburra, adding, "…here, have some porridge and honey. That will keep Jack Frost at bay."

Kath sat down at the kitchen table, shivering, still with her coat hood up. Ice crystals lined the inside of the back kitchen window. " Isn't the *Rayburn* working?" Kath put her hand on the cold metal contraption.

"It is, but we've run out of logs, haven't we, Sam?" She looked accusingly at her husband, who was darning a white sock with red wool.

"Oh dear. I will have to chop some more up, tomorrow," Sam whined.

"Perhaps you could help, Rob?" Kath volunteered her boyfriend.

"Well, what about Leo?" Rob protested.

Tilly reacted as quick as a Jack-in-a-Box. "Never wanted that boy. Didn't even know I was expecting, 'til l I was five months gone. Still breast feeding Jeannie when I got caught. Never realised he was on the way. Knew he was mad when he came out: the big black eyes." She looked directly at Kath. "In fact, his eyes are just like yours!"

Kath spluttered on the porridge but managed to hold her temper in. "Here," Tilly said as she pushed a black-and-white photograph of Leo as a six-week-old baby under Kath's nose. "Mad. Plain mad."

"Do you have any photographs of, Rob?" Kath asked, as she put Leo's photo on the table.

"A few," Tilly confessed. "Thought you might ask." She plonked a white studio photo on top of Leo's picture." Here you are." Both photographs must have been taken at the same time. Leo as a tiny baby was lying in front of a three-year-old Robert and an eighteen-month-old Jeannie.

"Lovely blond boy Robert was." Tilly enthused. "Like me... a natural blond." She lifted her chin and drew her fingers through her hair.

"Yes, a beautiful child – and a beautiful man now." Kath glanced at Robert across the table. He smiled. Kath was at a loss about what to say about Jeannie, a skinny child with short, mousy hair, and no front teeth. "Leo really enjoyed his day out at Bovington. He took a lot of photos of the tanks and things. Said he'd get them developed in the College dark room and would send me some copies..."

"Oh, dear, yes, that reminds me," Tilly looked unashamed as she picked up a large brown envelope from under a pile of magazines which were balancing precariously on the edge of the scrubbed pine table. "These are for you." The correspondence was clearly marked with her address in South Wales and was ready for posting.

Kath inspected the contents, four black-and-white prints, of poster dimensions, showing her handsome boyfriend driving tanks and on the back of one was written: *Robert on Big Willy*, and on another: *Robert on Little Willy*. Kath laughed. Now she knew !

"Jolly good photographs," Kath was pleased. "Good for Leo. I hope he can just stick to it. Now what about the new shop? How is that going?"

Sam looked glum. "Oh, dear, I dunno, she leaves me there, never puts a price on things... I sold a chair for two pounds today and she said she paid three pounds for it last week."

Tilly scoffed, "I do price things up, he just doesn't look. Liability 'e is."

Tilly was forgetting her aiches! Kath noticed.

Rob, after finishing his supper, clearly bored with the conversation, stood up.

"Suppose we will need a key for the shop?"

"No, the door's on the latch, just drop it when you get in."

Kath instinctively joined Robert and the two of them moved towards the front door in harmony, like dance partners.

"I've put everyone's presents on the hall table. They are all wrapped up and labelled, so you can see which is whose. Good night."

"Goodnight " said Sam.

"Oh, by the way," Tilly said as the couple were about to shut the front door. "...there's a chamber pot under the bed,"

Kath giggled at the thought of using a pot again. Their bedroom was on the top floor of the shop building. The bathroom and toilet were on the ground floor, but that was now completely separated from the top by a brick wall. They would indeed have to make do with the chamber pot. Kath visualised how the space could be divided up to make a neat apartment. She would tell Tilly her ideas tomorrow, if she got the chance.

Jeannie and Martin were snoring gently in the adjoining bedroom, when Rob and Kath snuggled down under their feather quilt on the brass bed with its sprung mattress and feather pillows. "Luxury for a change," Rob commented.

Yeh, a step in the right direction, thought Kath, remembering her previous visits to the Old Parsonage, when she had slept on a horsehair mattress under rough, woollen blankets.

It was nearly ten o'clock the next morning when Kath woke, feeling breath passing over her cheeks. Jeannie was standing over her, shouting, "Wakey, wakey!" Kath sat up with a jolt.

Jeannie, dressed for the Artic, stood only inches away. Two young fox stoles hung round her neck; their front paws dangled either side of her shoulders. A green tartan jacket, a shiny brown leather skirt to below the knees, red woollen tights, black fur boots and hat completed the bizarre picture.

"Hi, you two." Jeannie's nose twitched like a guinea pig as she introduced herself, then she turned, setting the two fox heads swinging from side-to-side across her back.

"See you later." Kath sat rigid. "Nice to meet you," Kath tried saying, but her words got lost in a heavy sneeze, induced by the scent of moth balls which Jeannie had created as she swept by.

Kath hardly recognised Jeannie as the harridan who had woken her that morning when she and Rob arrived for breakfast in the kitchen of the Old Parsonage. Jeannie, sporting two pigtails and wearing a trim white apron, looked the paragon of domesticity.

"I'll help you..." Kath offered.

"No, I won't hear of it." Jeannie's hazel eyes narrowed and changed colour as she sought to take control. "You just help yourself to cereals." Jeannie pushed the cornflakes across the table.

"Have you seen the film, *Rosemary's Baby*?" Kath asked, startling herself and spilling some milk. Something about Jeannie's eyes had triggered the memory of that scary film. *That's it*, she thought. *The baby devil's eyes.* "We saw it up in London a few weeks ago, didn't we, Rob?" Kath looked at him for support, but Rob was telling Martin about how he was going to have to sell his *Velocette* if he and Kath were going to get married.

"We saw the *Witchfinder General* last night at Jerry's."

Kath looked blank.

"Oh, Jerry is Martin's brother, he lives in Bristol. No washing-up liquid! I'll go and get some from the shop next door," she said, then darted through the back door.

Kath was fussing Peaches, after finishing her cornflakes, when Tilly came into the kitchen, insisting that she, Robert and Martin move to the living room. Tilly wanted everyone to see her latest antique acquisition, some high-backed, winged armchairs. *Perfect for draughty rooms,* thought Kath. Sam was ordered to the shop and Leo was, as always, still in bed.

"Have you been to Jeannie's cottage yet, Tilly?" Kath asked as the four of them settled down in the living room. "Rob hasn't said if you had."

"Well, he never rings us, no letters nothing, so he wouldn't know." She lifted her chin in a 'devil-may-care' attitude, looked at Rob and sniffed the air. "But, no, I haven't been yet. They haven't got a guest bed." Tilly gave Martin a dirty look, then shouted across the room, to the door as Jeannie peeped through in to see what was going on "You haven't got a guest bed yet at your cottage, have you ?"

"Can't afford one," Jeannie sniped. Evidently Jeannie was in no hurry to have her mother stay. She shut the living room door with a bang and went back to the washing-up.

"I've heard it's in the middle of nowhere, apple trees and pear trees, rambling blackberry brambles and roses around the door. It sounds so idyllic. Lucky you," commented Kath to Martin, but couldn't help muttering under her breath, "...and fancy poor Rob in a tiny bedsit."

"Anyway, what's this about you two getting married?" Martin asked.

"Steady on… first my dad has to approve, but I know he will. He loves Rob. I'm hoping Rob will get a job near Barry next year. We could buy a house - we're saving up now for the deposit. Rob has already applied for a job in Chepstow."

"Chepstow!" Tilly repeated, as if she hadn't heard correctly. "I don't think he will get it…" she said with conviction.

Kath rallied. "Well, couldn't Sam help… with all his connections?"

Just then Sam appeared at the door. "I've just cut some winter sprouts for dinner, Tiger."

"Ah good we'll have them with the roast chicken later but weren't you supposed to be at the shop – and *don't* call me Tiger!" Tilly said in one breath.

Sam left quickly before there were more recriminations.

Roast chicken again, thought Kath… o*h well, better the devil you know*.

"Oh by the way, Tilly, do you have a spare copy of *The Miller's Antiques Guide* I could borrow, perhaps one that's a little out of date?" Kath had noticed a few old copies around the house.

"Oh, I don't know - I use all mine."

Kath was taken aback. "It's just that I've been browsing around junk shops. I might be able to buy things you could sell for me in your shop. Try to make a bit of extra cash. You know, we're saving up for a house."

"Oh, you don't want to get a mortgage at your age. Noose round your neck."

Robert got up and left the room. "I've applied for a job in Chepstow." Robert told his father, after finding him in the garden chopping up wood. "I thought you might have a word with the Education Department. Say who I am, put a good word in. At least get me an interview, eh?"

"Oh dear, I don't know anybody now. All changed since I left."

"It's less than six-months since you retired, surely there are people in charge who remember you?" Robert spoke louder.

Sam stepped back and turned away.

"You don't really want to work in Chepstow do you, Rob?" Martin took up the conversation as Robert returned to the living room, feeling defeated. Tilly was still holding court. She had evidently told Martin of Robert's job application. "I wouldn't go back there for anything. It's gone down the drain. Drugs in the schools, no discipline."

"Couldn't be any worse than Stepney."

"Can I help you with anything, Tilly?" Kath offered. "I can clean some of the antiques, carry stuff to the shop, anything you want."

"No, thank you, we can manage.. but you *can* peel the potatoes and carrots for lunch and don't forget the Brussels sprouts."

Kath needed no prompting and buried herself in her culinary duties while Rob discussed the garage opposite with Martin and how they were ripping off Leo for repairs to his *Triumph*.

Later, with the dinner over, the family moved again to the living room. Sam piled wood onto the fire, where spits would once have been used to roast a whole sheep or pig. Robert was reading an article on E-type *Jags* in *Motor Cars* magazine.

"The editor of that, Douglas Brady, is a friend of ours," Tilly announced proudly.

"Not any relation to Ian, I hope?" Kath commented, referring to the Moors Murderer.

"Wouldn't think so!" Tilly said, "...he's from Tasmania. He only came to London three years ago. He loves antiques and he, and his model girlfriend, Tina, buy from me."

"A Brady From Tasmania, eh? Devil's Island!" Rob was curious. "Could be he is related to Matt Brady: bushman, thief, murderer. He was hung in Hobart for horse thieving in1826."

"How do you know that, Rob?" Kath gaped at her boyfriend.

"Tilly, aren't you impressed at the great knowledge your son has?"

Tilly didn't answer as there was a loud knock at the front door.

"Good God, if it isn't Bill Evans," shrieked Tilly as she let a couple in. "We haven't seen you or Ethel for years! Come on in and sit yourselves down! Sam... get the Crown Derby out."

Bill, an old friend from Neath, and his wife, were just passing they said, after a trip to see some relatives near the Shaftsbury Hill Fort.

"See you still like wearing your moustache, Bill," Tilly drooled.

Bill had been a Wing Commander in the War and was proud of his fine, black, handlebar moustache. At six-foot-four inches, he still cut the fine figure of a gentleman, especially now in his Sunday suit and highly-polished new leather brogues. *How dowdy his wife looked in comparison*, thought Kath. *Plain faced, with a down turned mouth she had a boyish look.*

She couldn't have weighed more than seven stone and was as grey as the antique alabaster bust of Shakespeare which sat on the wide windowsill of the room they were now all taking tea in.

It had been some years since the couples had enjoyed each other's company and by the glint in Tilly's eyes, Kath guessed it might have been a case of more than friendship between her and Bill. Leo had talked much of his mother's comings and goings, as he'd called them, especially when they lived on the farm, Rose Mansion, in Llanfarn.

Bill had been the artificial inseminating officer for the Milk Marketing Board after the War and had met the Llewellyns when he had been called upon to attend to their cows. Kath envisaged the man wearing the special inseminating glove, the heavy leather thing reaching up as far as the elbow, then plunging into the depths of the cow's rear end. The imagery sent her queasy.

Tilly, sensing Kath's unease, devilishly sought to prolong it. "Nothing beats getting your hands on those cow's udders and giving 'em a squeeze, Bill?" She laughed like a hyena and slapped her knees.

Rob looked embarrassed, Jeannie jumped up and offered to fetch more cake and Martin sniggered.

It wasn't until the Evans' left that the conversation turned to Leo.

"He's up all night, goes prowling round the village and off for long drives in the car. He says he can't sleep," moaned Tilly.

"Well, what do the doctors say?" Kath asked.

"All quacks the lot of them, no good," Sam said.

Tilly nodded in agreement.

"Well, who can help him?" Rob asked.

"Nobody, nobody," Tilly threw up her arms. "He'll come out of his depression one day - or we'll just have to live with it."

"Perhaps we could take him out tomorrow, a trip to Weston-Super-Mare? Maybe a walk on the beach, some sea air…?" Kath suggested.

"We could *all* go - you and Sam in the *Mini* with Martin and Jeannie and Leo with us in the van.

"Impossible." Tilly was forceful. "Sam can't go very far in a car. His cataracts are making him dizzy and car rides make it worse. Furthermore, we can't leave the house unguarded. So… that's that."

"We'll go with Leo if he wants to come. And, you two will want to?" Kath looked at Jeannie.

“Well, err… we can’t, Martin butted in.” We’re going to visit my mother tomorrow and we said we would be there by one for lunch.”

Just then, Leo appeared at the drawing room door. “Thanks, Kath, yes, I would like to go out with you tomorrow.” He pulled a face at Jeannie. She shrieked like a banshee, uttered the ‘F’ word and ran from the room. The pair had never got on.

“Why did you offer to take Leo out, Kath?” Rob complained, as they walked downhill to the shop for bed that night. “Especially all that way to Weston-Super-Mare. All that petrol and you know we will have to pay for the food and the beer. I am not a bloody Rothschild! You will break the bank of Monte Carlo with your bloody generosity!“

“What *else* can we do?” Kath answered. “Leo is your brother, blood is thicker than water, well, it should be. Remember love is more important than money…” Kath went on. “…but, you are a tight arse, aren’t you? Just like your mother.”

Rob didn’t flinch. “Well it’s a good job I am. Somebody has got to keep a hold on the purse strings!”

“Okay, but he has given us some photos.”

“Let’s just shut up about Leo for now. Tomorrow’s another day.”

Leo was washed, dressed and waiting for the couple in the kitchen when Kath and Robert arrived at the Old Parsonage at ten-thirty the next morning. Jeannie and Martin had left, and Tilly and Sam were not in sight. Holding the photos of Rob taken at the tank museum, Kath thanked Leo and added, “…better late than never.” Leo looked bemused. “I only got them last night,” Kath explained. “ Tilly forgot to post them to us.”

“Bloody Tilly, there you are, now you know what I have to live with! Bah!” Then he went on. “Can’t believe Jeannie is going out with that squirt, Martin. He’s a cissy boy. Can’t draw for toffee. Artist? Call that streak of a wimp an artist?” Leo’s venom knew no bounds. “And that doll’s dress you made for Tilly is a load of rubbish. You can’t sew a stitch.” Kath blushed with both embarrassment and anger, but remained composed. She and Rob were about to take him out, pay for the whole day and here he was with the audacity to start criticising her.

“Are those your words - or Tilly’s?”

“Both. Tilly says the same.”

Kath flipped. Leo might have been lying about Tilly slandering her, but enough was enough. "Well… you are a load of shit yourself, so there. Living off your parents, can't get a job, can't even stay the course in an art school, idling your time away, thinking you are better than you are. Little Lord Leo, eh?"

"And… you are a slut!"

Kath was flabbergasted.

"Come on, Kath, let's go." Robert pulled Kath's arm. "I told you, you can't win with him, bites the hand that feeds him."

"Oh dear, oh dear, what's all this shouting?" Sam asked his sons.

"Leo's being abusive and has insulted my fiancée! We're going now."

"Tell Tilly I will write," Kath cried. "I've left the dirty bed clothes, ready for the washing machine, in a bundle on the wicker chair by the stairs."

"Kath, Kath, don't bother, come on." Rob dragged her to the front door. Kath noticed the presents she had brought them all were still unopened on the hall table.

Kath sobbed as Rob started up the van engine. "What shall we do? What *can* we do?"

"We're off to Weston-Super–Mare, that's what."

"No… what about Leo and your parents…?"

"Well, what about them ?" Rob wasn't fazed. He had seen it all before.

"Aren't you ashamed of me, Rob?" asked Kath.

"No… Leo would make a priest swear."

"But, I shouldn't have lost my temper with him, should I?"

"Don't lose any sleep over it. Next time, just put your hands in your pockets and count to ten. That's what I do and if you are going to teach, well… you will be putting your hands in your pockets a lot, believe me."

Rob was so sensible, so level headed, a gentleman. Kath was so proud of him.

"By the way, Tilly hasn't got a washing machine. She's never had one." Rob said.

"Never?" Kath gasped.

"No, never."

"Well, how do they manage?"

"Easy, they just don't wash their clothes very often, and when they do, they wash by hand."

"And... what about when you were children?"

"We washed our own, by hand. Tilly did have some help in the house when we were small, a German au pair and you know about Rocio the Italian one, already. You were admiring Sam's portrait of her in the hall, weren't you?"

Kath nodded and went on, "...Jeannie is a bit strange. She didn't even mention visiting them in Oxford or ask me anything about Stoke - or Barry."

"Well, I warned you. Now you know why I'm not that bothered about this bloody family."

Kath cried again. She had looked forward to meeting Jeannie, fantasised about having her as a girl friend; the sister she'd never had. Now that would never be!

Only a long walk on the wide, flat sandy beach at Weston-Super-Mare settled her nerves. Kath should have been catching the train to South Wales from Bath, but Robert insisted on driving her. "Must look after my little love," he cooed. "My lovely lady, my gorgeous, lovely woman." Kath revelled in the sentiments and told him she loved him too.

Rob left the College campus at eight p.m. Kath was still sad at the way the weekend had gone, but quickly wrote out a Thank You card for Tilly and Sam, and said how nice it had been to meet Jeannie and Martin - she then put the matter out of her mind. There was an English essay to write before Friday and a much-needed letter to her parents. Arthur had written a few weeks previously, berating her for having been reprimanded for flouting college rules. *I WISH YOU WOULD NOT DISOBEY ORDERS* was emblazoned across the envelope of her father's letter and had caused giggly comments amongst the students, picking up their mail at reception.

-15-

Shall I put photos of Rob at the tank museum on the walls or not? Kath pondered perversely after a few days back in College. But the ignominy of having her name publicly read out, and worse still, having her father sprawl what he had across the envelope, made her think twice. But how bleak her room looked with bare, off-white walls.

Lying flat on her back on her bed, later that week, railing at her situation, she had the brainwave to put the photos on the ceiling! The rules only said no posters on the walls. Forthwith, she pasted up all four photographs. Kath felt chuffed, like Byron in Trinity College Cambridge, she mused; for, when no dogs had been allowed in the Halls of Residence in Great Court… he had installed a bear! With Rob looking down on her every night from an armoured tank, she felt safe and snug. Rob was her hero and, just think, he might even become an officer in the Army. After their visit to Bovington, Rob had come away with all the information and application forms for joining the army. *Officer class*, he had stressed. With his level of education, he would be well in line for a superior position. Kath had asked him several times if he had filled in the forms, but he hadn't. She didn't think too much about that, she was more concerned with him getting a teaching job in South Wales.

There were only four weeks left to the Christmas holidays; she would be in London for a week with Rob, where she had already secured work for a week, delivering the post, then they would be in Stoke for two weeks.

Again the amount of things to do before the end of term was unnerving. She must see the doctor. She desperately wanted to be put on the pill. She had to see the dentist as she was having a gnawing jaw ache. She had a health project to finish and then all those Xmas cards and long-promised letters to old friends to write. Furthermore, Rob insisted she have a weekend with him in London before the festive season to buy presents and get herself some new clothes. "A likely story," Kath joked with him on the phone when Rob had suggested a weekend for shopping! "You are a bloody fibber, Rob. Shopping?" Kath's voice rose a pitch." You mean for a bloody good shag, don't you?" Rob didn't contradict and so Kath continued, "Well… I don't blame you. That's what I want too, so there, that's that. Whether or not I can get to London depends on finding someone to hitch with. Lesley can't come."

Kath did manage to find a hitchhiking partner; she left campus the first weekend of December.

Rob was not in good spirits when he picked her up on the Hammersmith by-pass that Friday night. The house his friend, Tom, and his wife were going to buy, had fallen through. Rob hadn't heard from Chepstow about the job and there were no other jobs on offer in South Wales. He said he would try North Staffordshire and Kath could transfer to Madeley College, near Stoke.

"Well, what about your Army officer application?" ventured Kath as they entered his bedsit, thinking that a job in the Forces may be the answer.

"I haven't applied," Rob admitted, shamefaced.

"Why not?"

"No, bloody time - and you should see how many pages there are on the application form!"

"Well, I'll help you fill them in…" Kath spotted the forms in a muddle by Rob's bed. "Let's look at these now then," Kath scooped up the papers.

"Do we have to *now*?" Rob had other plans.

"No, come on Rob, get your priorities right, will you," Kath said as she pulled his hands off her backside and perused the papers, muttering under her breath how they should not have been so mussed up. "Well…" Kath declared at last. "I'm looking at the list of things you have to do in basic Army training, Rob." She shouted to him from the bed, while he was making coffee in the kitchen, behind the makeshift partition. "A six-mile run every day carrying a ten-kilo rucksack. Scaling a ten-foot wall with full backpack and guns. Swimming a mile. Carrying a man for a hundred yards over rough terrain. Do you think you could manage all that, Rob?" Kath sounded sceptical.

"No…" was the defining answer which fell hard on Kath's ears.

"Now, you really must see a doctor about your stomach ulcer," Kath said as she disposed of the Army papers in the waste paper bin. "It's all those tinned beans, and greasy chips from the café. You must look after yourself… get more fresh fruit down you. If you don't look after yourself, nobody else will."

"But, *you* will look after me, won't you, darling?" Rob said as he hugged Kath and gently kissed her face and hands.

"Yes, I will." Kath vowed as the couple lay together on the bed. Kath was secretly glad her Rob would never be a soldier.

After a while, Robert spoke, " You know I can't live without you, don't you, Kath? You… you must marry me." Robert slowly took Kath's hands in his as they rose, and then he pulled her into him.

Kath melted into his embrace and sighed with each kiss he gently placed on the corners of her mouth. Feeling too emotional, Kath couldn't speak, instead she nodded and let herself lie back on the bed again, willing Rob to carry on explaining his devotion to her.

"I love you oh so much," he said, brushing his fingers over her lips, tapping the tip of her nose playfully and finally cupping her face with his two hands. "Kath Tyler, I just love the feel of your soft skin, and…" he said, slipping his hands down over his lover's breasts, before running the back of his fingers over her smooth thighs.

Kath, breathless and feeling like she would faint from ardour, moaned with delight as Rob's hands continued caressing her in waves.

"Just say you will marry me, please, Kath. Say those words," Robert stopped his caresses and sat bolt upright again, pulling Kath up by her hands so he could look intently into her eyes.

Their gazes locked, before both giving in to the moment and their ardent kisses.

Kath closed her eyes and moaned with pleasure; she felt like she was in the middle of a dream that would never end. She kissed Rob again and then said, "Yes… yes, I will marry you, Rob. You are… my world…"

"Wonderful. I'll buy you an engagement ring tomorrow, then!"

Kath suddenly woke from her stupor. "So soon! But… I don't want to announce it till Christmas. My Dad has to give us his blessing first. That's only right."

"You old romantic, you," Robert laughed, holding his fiancé's hands tightly in his, once more. "Oh, you'll never know how much I love you, Kath. My Kath."

Saturday was spent in frenetic activity, shopping in Oxford Street, where Kath bought a Mrs. Peel *Avengers* outfit: a black cat suit with a broad white belt. She also bought a tan leather mini skirt and new leather boots. Rob winced at the price, but it was Kath's money; her share of the blue band pottery sales, she reasoned. Their little business was going well. They had planned to sell plywood in Stoke, too. Rob had his contacts.

But now there was the ring to buy. If they were to be engaged at Christmas, then they should look for a ring this weekend. Keeping it a secret of course, until Arthur had agreed. Kath thought it was only fair he should approve, but she would get engaged anyway, if he didn't. Oh, it did seem so hypocritical. Still, tradition was tradition and Kath wanted a white wedding. They settled on an eighteen-carat gold band with a large single set black opal. Kath loved the dark, peacock-blue colour of the stone and liked the idea of not having a diamond. After all, everybody had diamonds, and although it would induce the ubiquitous words of her father, "Thee 'at out o' step agin', our Kath, aluss out te step," Kath didn't care. She loved Rob, she wanted his ring and that was all that mattered.

Rob needed new spectacles too. He had been myopic since the age of seven and had worn thick-lensed glasses ever since. It irked him that his bad eyesight had affected his sporting abilities, but true to his character, he rarely complained. Heavy square black-rimmed glasses were becoming the fashion and Rob chose a pair which made him look like Michael Caine.

Half of the Sunday morning was spent having a lie-in and the other half with Rob making hyperboloids for Kath's maths lessons. Lunch was a snack at the Jazz Club with Rob's friends and then a quick dash to drop Kath off for hitching back to Barry.

It wasn't until Dec 21st that Kath realised she hadn't heard from Tilly, or Jeannie. She had already sent them Christmas cards and arranged for their presents were to be delivered to the Old Parsonage the next day when a classmate would be passing the Llewellyn's front door, on her way to Wells for the Xmas break. Kath gauged that when the Llewellyn's received the gifts, she would already be at Rob's in London having hitched a ride again, and she would surely get a phone call from Tilly then. Rob had phoned his mother once since the weekend they had stayed there in November, and relayed his plans for Xmas, telling her he would be in London, with Kath, then with her in Stoke. Tilly had made no comment.

The first day of the Christmas holiday, Rob busied himself with marking and lesson preparation, while Kath went out to deliver the early morning post. He then gave the van a service and clean in the road, in front of the house. Elaine, the landlady, complained about the amount of water he was using. Kath took to creeping about the place and wished she wasn't there. It wasn't ideal. Elaine grumbled too that Rob was consuming too much electricity and gas. She had actually burst into Rob's room one afternoon to glue down the thermostat on the radiator as Rob and Kath were in the middle of a cuddle on the bed. Although Kath had finally been prescribed the pill, it would be two more weeks before she would be regarded as 'safe', so for now they were being careful.

"Damn woman," moaned Rob, as Elaine left the room, leaving the couple crippled with humiliation. "Won't be here much longer," Rob promised his fiancé, feebly.

"But... where can you go?"

Rob was adamant he couldn't afford to pay more than he was paying now for rent and the couple just couldn't find anything else better for the same money. Unless, Rob got a job outside of London.

There was just one other hope in sight; a teaching post in Market Drayton in Shropshire. Only twenty miles from Kath's parents. Market Drayton was a lovely old-world market town with an Elizabethan-style town centre. Kath prayed Rob would get the job: an assistant woodwork, metal work, and technical drawing teacher in a Comprehensive school. Kath was convinced there was no one better for the post.

Driving home to Stoke on Xmas Eve took longer than expected; the van was overloaded. There was plywood for Arthur to sell and presents for all, including a big rocking horse for Matthew. It was pitch dark when the couple pulled up in Bluegates Street. Nelly cried and stayed up 'til two in the morning with Kath. Nelly just shook her head and repeated over and over, "...look at ye, skin and bone, skin and bone."

A few bacon, egg and oatcake breakfasts, Christmas and other dinners over the next two weeks soon put Kath right in her mother's eyes. Arthur and Nelly approved of the Engagement and, even though Mother looked slightly bemused by Kath's choice of ring, she said nothing. When the news got out about the betrothal, visitors came with gifts and good wishes. Nelly complained a little, saying she had got used to the house being empty and couldn't cope with the onslaught. Old boyfriends even turned up. One even dared to say she was making a mistake. Kath showed him to the door; she wasn't having anyone spoil her relationship with Rob.

It niggled her a bit that he wasn't generous with presents for her, but in offering his time and patience, good advice and love, that was enough. What did it matter that she only got records, and a soft back copy of *The Joys of Sex* from him for Christmas. After all, they were saving up for a house together and that didn't come cheap.

Arthur let Kath and Rob use his beloved parlour for their courting, and let them use his record player. "I trust your youth," Arthur said. "I would trust 'im with me life. Rob's a good 'um, our Kath, dunna you ferget that!"

Kath warmed to Arthur like she had never done before. 'Cat and dog' Mother used to call them and was happy that their scrapping was on the wane, when Arthur conceded by saying, "Looks like the cat's got the cream then." Kath merely smiled.

She was more interested in listening to her new records, The Beatles' *White Album*, Manitas de Plata, Herb Albert and the Tijuana Brass and The Righteous Brothers. She also loved Ramsey Lewis's *Wade in the Water* and always sang along to the Beatles', *Ob-La-Di, Ob-La-Da.*

By New Year's Eve, Kath was on the pill and they toasted to the fact they would need no more condoms !

"By the way, Rob, have you heard about what's happening in London tonight? You know... with Vanessa Redgrave, Julie Christie and Mick Jagger?

"No ?"

They've got something going on called, '*Let's Make Love in London Tonight*'. A musical love-in or something. We could see it on the telly."

"I don't care. Just come here, give me a kiss and we'll do our own love-in!"

"Yeh, damn right. Come on, Mr. Llewellyn... 69 eh?"

-16-

Arthur and Nelly welcomed in the New Year MC-ing at the Town Hall dance in Tunstall, blissfully unaware that Rupert Murdoch had taken over the *News Of the World* and Jane Fonda - actress and Vietnam war protester - was being hounded by the USA Government for her perceived anti-American and pro-Communist activities.

Conversation in their house centred on Arthur's uncomfortable situation at work; the family firm had sold out to a multi-national and Arthur was no longer on first name terms with the big bosses. New rules and bitter job losses were to come. Although Arthur's job was fairly secure, he had been with the firm since he was sixteen and he would be costly to make redundant, plus… he no longer enjoyed his work, yet, he had another ten years before his sixty-fifth birthday. *It seems a long time to have to bite the bullet,* Kath thought. Holding back tears, she poured her dad a cup of tea. "Well, at least you are fit and healthy. If you look after yourself - stop smoking for a start - you should have a good retirement." Turning to Rob, she added, "We will see to that, won't we, Rob?" Rob nodded, as he helped himself to another oatcake, pulled his shoulders back and smiled.

"You are good, our Kath, and your fry ups for breakfast are better than your mother's!" Arthur winked at Robert. He didn't dwell on misfortune, and neither did Nelly.

Billy's announcement that Pauline was pregnant again, the sibling for ten months-old Matthew was due in June, brought calls for shandies and cheers all round. Nelly's liver and onions, spotted dicks, *Wrights'* pies and fish and chips, over the past week had revived Kath's battered soul. Wolfing down *Cadbury's Milk Tray* chocolates and watching her TV favourites, like *Hancock's Half Hour*, *Coronation Street and Panorama,* had completed the therapy. Kath was ready to face the world again; with the exception of Tilly.

Robert wouldn't be visiting Somerset before Kath went back to Barry, for the start of the new term, and so he drove himself to London.

Tilly wasn't perturbed, after all, Rob had been absent from the family home for the past several Christmas' and New Year's.

Rob relayed thanks to Kath from Tilly for the Xmas presents sent over, but she complained that the Wedgwood cameo ring was too small. Rob offered to stretch the band for her the next time he was at the Old Parsonage, but Tilly replied mischievously that had better be quick, as she had an antique jewellery box and a treadle sewing machine for Kath, and a surprise present for Rob – and, if Rob didn't collect them soon, she would sell them!

When Rob dropped off Kath in Birmingham, so that she could get a lift back to College, she was clinging to the hope that Rob would get the job in Chepstow; she just did not want to change college's. Although life at Barry was demanding, she had grown accustomed to it. She had had some success with her work and friendships, although it was a strain having Rob so very far away.

Kath cried alone in her room that night, but rallied by the time Rob phoned the next day. She surprised him with the news that she was going to look for houses for sale in Barry. "You don't seem keen, Rob?"

"Oh… I am." Rob sounded insincere, but nonetheless, Kath set off for Barry town centre.

Williams and Williams Estate Agents were offering a three-bedroom terraced house in good order, near the sea and just one mile from the college for £2,600 and a two-bedroom property for £2,300. Kath had worked out that on Rob's salary they could afford a mortgage of up to £3,000. The money from pottery sales and other odd jobs Rob did in his spare time, was growing nicely in their joint savings account.

Kath galloped up the three steps to the front door of the estate agent's Victorian stone building. The reception was deserted. Kath punched the brass desk-bell, which sat prettily on the heavy oak counter. She rang twice, before a red-bearded fat man appeared from the back room.

"I am interested in the house in the window, the one at £2,600.The three-bed terrace, in the town centre one mile from the college, in good—"

"Yes, yes," the man interrupted, and in his strong Glamorgan accent continued, "…it's now £3,000. It's got a new bathroom and a new kitchen."

Kath gulped. She hadn't reckoned on complications. "Well… I would still like to see it. £3000 is still within our budget."

"Sorry... but it's off the market."

"Why do you still have it advertised in your window, then?" Kath asked.

"Well, it isn't now, said the man, as he tore the advert from the pane of glass where it had been stuck on with Sellotape.

"When will it be on the market again?" Kath was not being deterred.

"Reckon in six weeks, when the work on the bathroom and kitchen is finished."

"Six weeks? Okay, we can wait." Kath pulled her shoulders back and stood tall. "Now... what about the other house in the window, that two-bedroom one at £2,400?"

"Hmmm... it's not for sale, either."

"And, why not, may I ask?"

"The owners have changed their minds about selling." The man again yanked the photo off the window, crumpled it up and threw it in the bin.

"I'm not having much luck, am I? I will just have to go to another agent." Kath wanted the last word, but the agent was not going to let her.

"You're English, aren't you?" His voice grated.

"Yes, I am." Kath proclaimed, loudly turning to the onlookers. By this time, a young receptionist had taken up her position at a desk by the main door. Two other members of staff gathered by the back door, and a customer was just coming over the threshold.

"And... what has being English got to do with buying a house in Barry?" Kath's gaze swept around the room, finally becoming fixed on the estate agents eyes.

"I'm just curious to know how a young thing like you can afford a house anywhere? Bet you are a student up at the College? Where can a student get £3000 to buy a house? They're always moaning about having no money, and how measly the grants are, but they have enough for beer and fags, and... you always see 'em in the pubs at night "

"First of all, aren't you being rather presumptuous about students? Yes, I am a student but I am also engaged, look!" Kath flashed her ring. "And, my fiancé is a teacher. We are getting married soon, so we want a house in Barry. But, Mr Whoever You Are, we won't be buying from you. So there. Good day."

Kath marched out of the building, not knowing whether to laugh or cry, the situation was absurd. She raced back to College, eager to tell her story. She wrote to Rob first and then went to the Common Room, where she embellished the facts so much that students ended up rolling round the floor in hysterics. Everyone had something to say on the subject:

"*Welsh study practice in the raw, eh?*"

"*Greasy Welsh goat's balls for brains.*"

"*Let's lynch him*," suggested one of boys.

Just after her debacle, Kath learned that Robert's application for the job in Chepstow had not been successful. *Perhaps now Rob will find a job in the Potteries,* Kath thought.

Kath accused Robert of being relieved not to have to move to Wales. Rob denied it, but she knew even if he didn't want to live in Wales, he *did* want to live with her: he was making her a coffee table from Himalayan teak, for their home together, and a pair of silver buckles.

She had seen some she fancied in a shop window in Regent Street before Christmas. Rob had snorted at the price and reckoned he could make some the same, if not better. Kath took him at his word. If he promised to do something, he had to do it. He was becoming too fond of saying he would do this and do that and nothing ever came of it.

Kath, cruelly raked up his futile talk about joining the Army. "Officer class, you said!" Kath was beginning to wonder if he would ever move out of London. He had found a niche in Stepney. He was in charge of his Department's tea money, and threatening to double subs for Albert the technician, who had told him that Kath was too good for him. Kath began to wonder if she would ever marry Rob but pushed it to the back of her mind when he told her to arrange a Bed & Breakfast weekend in South West Wales for the end of January. He wanted to show her Neath where Sam had worked, and Llaugharne, the home of Dylan Thomas, Llanfarn and St. Cleeves where he had lived.

Kath rang a guesthouse she had seen advertised in the *Western Mail.* A young lady answered, but she couldn't confirm if there were vacancies for the two nights required or even what the rates would be or… whether dinner could be provided.

Kath persevered. "Well, at least can you tell me what the double room we might have is like?"

After a pause, the Welsh voice, rolling the r's answered, "Well, there is an ironing board in the room." Kath slammed down the receiver, then burst out laughing. It felt better than screaming.

At her second attempt to book a room, she secured a place in Pendine. *Mrs and Mrs Tyler*, she repeated to the landlady.

Kath was excited about her *field trip for Welsh studies* as she put it and took on a renewed interest in the subject. As she had been studying Dylan Thomas poetry, Kath delighted in telling her classmates and tutors about Tilly and Sam's book and how Tilly had known Thomas' wife, Caitlin.

Rob arrived in Barry late afternoon on that Friday. He had spent the night at Tilly's, after calling in sick at school, to collect his and Kath's Christmas presents, including a marquetry jewellery box and sewing machine. Kath noticed a handle missing on the jewellery box and the machine was rather rusty, but she said nothing.

Rob was truly annoyed with his gift. "Another bloody briefcase," he moaned. " I chucked it into a farmer's field on the way up here!" Kath opened her mouth to condemn him, but before she could speak, Robert carried on. "Let's forget the bloody presents, shall we and go and get some ironing done!" With his arm round Kath, he led her to the van and off they drove out of the college Campus.

They reached the B&B late, after stopping at a pub for a pint and listening to the News on the radio in the van. The Beatles had just had their last live concert together, on the roof of their company's *Apple* building, as a climax to their successful *Let it Be* film. Saddam Hussein, the Vice President of the infamous Ba'ath Party in Iraq, had caused outrage after ordering the shootings of nine Jews in Baghdad, and torturing another fifty for spying.

The Beatles' *Honey, You Got a Hold On Me,* Gerry and the Pacemakers' *Don't Let the Sun Catch You Crying*, Shirley Bassey's *Gold Finger*, Petula Clarke's *Down Town* and Tom Jones' *What's New, Pussycat?* were topping the charts.

Kath rocked the van singing so much to the Tom Jones' hit, that Rob switched off the radio, for fear of her rolling the vehicle over. Kath didn't argue.

"I thought you were never coming," the landlady complained as she answered the front door in her slippers, dressing gown and curlers. "Mr and Mrs Tyler, eh?" she said, eyeing them up. "There's a list of rules here on the back of the door and, remember, don't put condoms down the toilet."

Kath blushed, but Rob, as philosophical as ever, rolled his eyes and whispered. " Well it's only for two nights," and he promptly slipped his shoes off as they turned into the bedroom, and slithered onto the bed.

The weather was bright but bitingly cold the next morning; snow had been reported in the mountains just north of the coast. In Pendine the air was bracing. An early morning arm-in-arm walk along the seven mile long stretch of firm sand on the beach dispelled all traces of disappointment at the landlady's reception the night the before. Rob related, in gory detail, the story of Parry Thomas, the famous racing driver, who was killed there while attempting a world land speed record in 1927. The car called, *Babs,* was still buried in the sand they had just walked over.

Kath's teeth still rattled at the thought of the racing driver's decapitation, until the hearty Welsh breakfast back at the guesthouse took her mind off the incident and Robert talked about Laugharne.

On the way to Brown's Hotel later, Rob said if they were lucky, they might bump into some of Dylan Thomas' creations in *Under Milk Wood.* The Welsh poet had evidently based the characters of the play on Llaugharne folk and called his fictitious town, *Llareggub*, which, spelt backwards, read *Buggerall.* Some of the people would still be living. Butcher Benyon, for example, who was more than likely, based on a Mr. Williams, who was still in business.

Kath was sipping a half pint of dry cider at the bar of the hotel, when a voice shouted from the front door of the establishment. "By God, it's Rob Llewellyn!" and a man limped in.

"My god. It's Douglas. You haven't changed a bit... You No Good Boyo!" Robert shouted back.

Douglas grinned and Kath was astounded. Dylan's *No good boyo* was a lazy fisherman who caused shenanigans in the washhouse. This chap certainly fitted the description. The three moved to a table, then Douglas beckoned over the village postman. He was a short, swarthy, fifty-year-old, "This is Willy Nilly," Douglas laughed. "Like Dylan said, he steams letters open and spreads gossip."

Kath sat down in disbelief. The dark-skinned man now sitting opposite her winked twice, and said she looked like a stripper he once knew in Soho. Kath demanded he buy her a drink for his cheek! Four port and lemons followed and, come home time, Kath teetered out of the hotel. Falling across the pavement, she stopped an elderly gentleman getting past and he scoffed as he stepped into the gutter.

"That's Eve Williams," Rob said. "You know, Dylan's *Organ Morgan*." He was my old Latin and Greek teacher at Carmarthen Grammar."

"You didn't tell me you had studied Latin and Greek, Rob?" Kath did sound impressed.

"But, what bloody use was it! Come on, get up and let's get going." Rob helped Kath to her feet and gave her a shake, which sobered her up enough to walk to *The Fishing Reel*. Unfortunately, the restaurant was closed, but the owner was on the premises. Rob tapped on the glass front door.

"Good God… if it isn't, Rob!" A tall woman, about the same age as Robert, pressed her face against the pane.

"It is he," confirmed Rob. "And, how are you these days, Deirdre?" Kath remembered the name. Tilly had told her that Rob had had a girlfriend in Laugharne called Deirdre. This must be her.

"We were just coming to you for lunch, pity you're closed," Rob said, as Deirdre opened the door and joined the couple on the pavement, before turning round to lock the door behind her.

"Ah yes, we only open Friday evenings and Sunday lunch in the winter, why don't you come tomorrow?"

"Sorry, but we can't… we're off to Neath " Kath reminded Rob over his shoulder.

"Oh, never mind. I can't have you in here now, sorry. I'm just on my way to baby-sit my niece."

"Another time, then."

As the three of them walked together into the centre of the village, Deirdre asked, "…by the way, how are your folks? Haven't heard a thing since Bill Evans visited them; he told us you had a new girlfriend though from up North." She glanced at Kath, before disappearing down an entry and waving goodbye.

Kath felt uncomfortable. *New girlfriend* indeed, and *one from Up North*.

Still, Kath felt no remorse when Rob explained, and Kath believed him, that Deirdre hadn't been his girlfriend - just a girl who was at the art school with him. Tilly had obviously lied !

Kath yanked her Astrakhan fur coat up around her ears against the cold, pulled her black fox fur hat down over her eyes and forced Rob's mother out of her mind.

The village was deserted and the couple made their way to the ancient castle where *Lord Cut Glass*, another of Dylan's creations, was a take on the real gentleman, Mr. Stark, who lived there. Circling the high walls, they followed the path up the hillside next to the estuary until they reached the boathouse, where Dylan had lived for several years, with his wife and three children, before his death in 1953. The house, now empty, was closed up to the world; awaiting its fate. The curlews screeched their silhouettes above, stark against the crystal blue of the deep sky.

Robert stopped the van on the bridge over the River in St. Cleeves, so they could see the three-storey villa that Tilly had built over a ruined cottage. The lofty abode still stood proud on the water's edge, even though due to high tides it had been flooded every year. Robert shook his head at the folly of it all. Kath took a photograph and suggested they drive up to the house and have a closer look. Rob baulked. " I'll never get my van up that lane. It's so narrow."

"Well, how did your parents get cars up there, then?"

"With great difficulty… they had to get rid of the *Jag*, when they moved in, and buy a *Mini* instead."

"Well, how did the removal van get in with all that big antique furniture?"

"The men had to carry it all along the lane from the main road."

Kath was both shocked and amused. She knew the house had been built illegally and it was only posthumously, by some grace of God (or, as cynically-minded Leo put it, by bribing Council officials) that the house had been allowed to stay put. Over the four years that the Llewellyns lived there, Tilly had tried to get the road widened. It meant purchasing land off the respective owners, half a dozen in all, and they were having none of it. It had even been said that she tore down fences. In the end, tired of scrapping with the neighbours, she and Sam sold up and moved on.

“Well, let’s just walk up the lane and have a *butcher’s*.” Kath had picked up Cockney rhyming slang after being with Rob so much in London.

“No, there’s nowhere to park and it’s too far to walk now. The lane will be sodden, thick with mud, and I don’t want to spoil my shoes.” Rob’s common sense won and the pair drove off to town, with Rob lecturing on local history.

“I’d like to see the coracles in action one day.” Kath said.

“You will, one day, but first, let’s go and see Neath.

The town was busy on its market day; the van chugged up the hill, trapped in a long line of cars, as they passed the high, dark grey stone walls of the Norman castle’s outer bailey. Half of the castle itself had fallen into ruin after being sacked in 1405 by Llewellyn the Great. Kath said that Rob might have some of the Welsh warrior blood in him. Rob pushed his chest out with pride and carried on with his lecture.

Rob parked the van in the town centre. It was too cold to hang about in the streets and, as neither the castle or the other national monuments were open to the public, Rob and Kath opted for a pub lunch. *The Black Lion* looked jolly and the couple took two seats by the window, overlooking the main street. Kath enjoyed people-watching. She loved ‘taking off’ the Welsh accent, incorporating a few Welsh phrases that she had picked up. Robert wasn’t that enthusiastic however about his Celtic roots and only pointed out the red brick building that was the Art School, where his father had worked.

“Oh, Rob that was a bit quick,” remarked Kath as they sped off again in the van. “Don’t you like being around here.

“No, I don’t… ” Rob was direct.

“But, you loved Llanfran, didn’t you?”

“Yes… and that’s where we’re going now.”

Rob sped along the country road. It was all down-bank to the sea, but before arriving at the beach, the couple stopped on the road to take a peek through the open wrought iron gates of Rose Mansion, which had been his home for seven years.

Kath was left breathless. She had only seen Sam’s pencil sketches of the house, when it had been in a worse state of repair and beehives were scattered on the front lawn. Since their departure, after a series of owners, the latest residents had spent millionaire money on the property. Even the heavy gates had White Hall quality. Gone was the ubiquitous Virginia Creeper; the brick was now clearly visible and had been cleverly repointed. The Georgian sash windows had been restored to their former glory and the panes sparkled in the frosty air. The lawn swept up smoothly to the wide front steps, guarded either side by carved lion statues. Tall trimmed pine trees lined the side boundary, like soldiers on watch. Kath took photographs.

The River was in full flood as they drove by the village green.

"Played football there," Rob said, as he parked up by the estuary. "That's Jetty Side," he pointed out the hamlet across the water. "As kids we used to walk across the estuary at low tide. Couldn't do it now, we wouldn't be allowed, health and safety, you know, too pussy foot today, no fun in anything, too much regulation."

"But, I think it's a good thing to have banned people from walking across like that, it's too dangerous. You told me yourself how many drownings there were each year. Isn't that good if people are saved?"

"Well, people should have more common sense, they should look after themselves."

Kath, unusually, didn't carry on the debate. The damp had got to her bones and her jaw was aching again. Still, she agreed to walk up to the castle with him.

It was a good pull up the narrow path to the castle walls, but the puff was worth it as the view was magnificent. The castle ruins were deserted and wide open to the elements. Kath climbed around the crumbling outer walls of the castle one way, and Rob circled the from the other direction. It was both exciting and scary. Kath shouted across to Rob to be careful, but the wind took her words out to sea. They reached the western tower together, exhilarated and happy, and hugged each other in triumph. Robert said he felt like a ten year-old kid again.

Kath stretched out her arms to the sky and faced the sun. The sea breeze wind was burning her cheeks as she breathed in the strong salt spray. She felt cured, whole again, her bones no longer painful. Peace surrounded her heart and the magic of Merlin sealed her soul.

Newedd Plas, a white mansion, dazzled below them. Designed by the 18th Century John Nash, it had been built by the Hilsan family and had the largest walled garden in Wales. Rob had enjoyed several Christmas Eve's there, along with other children of the village, when they had sung carols, bobbed for apples and met Santa Claus.

On the other side of the Castle, a solitary white cottage sat in the bay. Clambering over cliffs, Rob and Kath reached it safely. Built as a summer home for a famous Antarctic explorer, the house was closed up for the winter. Rob remembered how he and some school friends had sneaked into the house one January and were frightened out of their lives by what they saw inside: stuffed animals, including a penguin, a puffin, a sea lion, a walrus with three-foot tusks, and even an albatross with a fifteen-foot wing span, filled the rooms. Rob swore he had seen the albatross bat its wings and heard the sea lion screech. The boys had never dared enter the house again.

This was the beach where Rob had enjoyed fishing, cockling, playing hide-and-seek and Cowboys and Indians. Later, it was where he'd had his first attempts at wooing. He told Kath how sad he had felt when finally Rose Mansion was sold and he was forced to move to Laugharne.

Mrs Davies had dinner ready as she had promised at 7pm. Kath didn't eat, though. She was coming down with a cold and asked if she could have a hot bath, instead of a shower. The landlady complained about the extra hot water that would be needed, but relented when Kath grabbed her hand and put it to her forehead and said, " There you are, I'm dying of fever and if you have a bit of *Vicks* or camphor for the water, that will help." Mrs Davies didn't argue. She even offered Robert second helpings and lit the fire in the lounge especially, so they could watch Frankie Howard on TV before going to bed.

Kath was still delicate as they left Pendine the next morning, but insisted on Rob driving along the coast through Amroth, Saudersfoot and then onto Tenby. "I want to see as much as possible," Kath said, putting up a fight when Rob hesitated. "I might never come again!"

"What do you mean? You're already organising a trip in June, aren't you?"

"Yes, but it may never happen," Kath wailed.

"Why ever not?"

"Well, I might die – look how bad I am!"

"Kathleen… you are just so bloody dramatic. Cor blimey!"

"Well, so what if I am, come on, you know I love Tenby!"

"Oh yes, you went on a caravan holiday there once."

Kath fought her aches and pains, she was laughing so much. Along the Black Mountain roads, she took photos of the snowdrops.

It was late when they got back onto the main road. A snowstorm had brewed up and visibility was bad. Rob had the windscreen wipers on full pelt. "Better not stop in Swansea after all. You're too ill, and I'm bloody freezing." Rob was right. Kath knew she was being a fool, trying to do and see too much.

"Yes. Just let's get back to Barry. You are just so very sensible, Rob."

"Damn good job I am - or we would be in shit street."

"Without a paddle," Kath added.

"You're mixing your metaphors again, Kath," Rob laughed.

"Damn right I am, and a bloody good job - or we would be up the creek in shit street!" Kath chirped.

They turned to each other simultaneously - and kissed.

-17-

Kath sat down at the rusty treadle sewing machine, which Rob had oiled and got going, before leaving for Bath that frosty cold night. As she treadled, she thought of Rob braving the icy roads.

She had already cut out the pieces to make a kaftan, in anticipation of the gift. The swathe of black and red taffeta silk slipped easily through the machine. The blur of the needle thrusting up and down, her feet peddling - was therapy. Kath, enthralled by the vibrancy of the cloth, lifted it to her face from time to time to enjoy the feel of the luxurious texture against her cheeks. The material had come from the swirling full skirt of the dress Nelly had worn on her twenty-fifth wedding anniversary; she had danced all night. Kath loved the bold red poppies, the striking green leaves, the rich ebony black background. The kaftan would make a handsome addition to her wardrobe.

Kath sat up nearly half the night to finish the garment, but she would pay for her folly; she was confined to sickbay a few days later. The sore throat had turned to laryngitis, her jaws ached and she had pains in her abdomen *Ovaries,* she thought, "*...it's that pill, shrivelling up my ovaries*! She wished she was dead. She felt ashamed and spoke to no one about her feelings, but merely asked Christine to let Rob know she was indisposed. She would contact him by phone as soon as she felt better.

It was three weeks before she would see Rob again. Impacted wisdom teeth, discovered after an x-ray at the orthodontic clinic in Cardiff, meant she had the four offending teeth removed in one go. Kath left the hospital with a mouth full of stitches, which felt like barbed wire. Kath's self -pity then turned in on itself and she began a period of self-loathing. She wrote home disguising her true state of mind, but she had lost her spark and damned the day she ever went to Barry. Only Rob's letters, pledging his never dying love, kept her going. Kath fought hard to stem the blues. She told Rob she would like a wedding dress with a white fur trim, like Lulu's: the star had just married Maurice Gibb. Kath wanted three bridesmaids and purple flowers in the bouquet. Rob only wrote back about the maiden flight of the *Boeing 747* and the forthcoming *Concorde* tests. Kath didn't know whether this was a good thing or bad. She had already complained to her mother that Rob didn't give her flowers or chocolates. Nelly had concluded that that was definitely a good thing.

"Rob will be true to you," Nelly had said in her letters. "Ye needn't worry about him going off with fancy women." It meant a lot to Kath that she had a man like that. She could live without the flowers and chocolates, if it meant he was faithful. She did listen to Nelly, after all.

It was the last week of February when Kath was finally strong. She went back to her studies and was looking forward to a weekend with Robert. Arthur phoned to say he had sent a pound note in the post and was concerned that Kath had not replied. She had to tell him that the money had never arrived. Arthur took the bad news like he always did, a quick damn blast and then all forgotten. A good man was Arthur. Kath felt sick at the thought that someone in her Hall must be a thief.

Rob finally arranged to stay with Jeannie and Martin in Oxfordshire for a weekend. He would go to his sister's on the Friday and Kath would be picked up at the railway station in Oxford, the next day.

Three weeks in Halls and Kath was beginning to 'claw at the prison bars'. The call of the wild beckoned: the open road - and spring not far away. Kath's spirits soared. She was to leave Cardiff on the 9.15am train. An early night on the Friday before was sensible, but at 11pm she was woken by banging on her bedroom door. Rob was outside! The Halls were locked up for the night.

"What the hell are you doing here now?" Kath shouted down, from a corridor window, as Rob, looking bedraggled and forlorn, stood on the grass verge by the car park.

"Jeannie wasn't in - the bitch!" he shouted back.

"Shush!" Kath didn't want the whole campus to know their business. "Just wait there. I'll come down." Kath raced down the stairs to the ground floor, but the Hall doors were locked. Matron didn't appear to be in her room. Kath banged on other doors, one after another. A dozen dressing-gowned girls piled into the vestibule. Kath explained that her fiancée was outside. It was suggested that Kath made her leave through a window, but none of the windows opened out enough.

"Imagine if there was a fire. It's outrageous ! All these women locked up here and no way of escape! Kath's stark statement caused a hush, then a dishevelled Miss Olivetti appeared.

"Now... back to bed everyone, I will deal with this, no need to miss your beauty sleep, girls." On a more authoritarian note, she turned to Kath and demanded to know the meaning of all this fuss. Kath guiltily explained, then was told to hurry up, pack her bag and go. How humiliated she felt as she crept through the Hall door and slipped into the night and the arms of Rob. Tears followed and didn't stop, until they had gone beyond Cardiff.

"But, where can we go this time of night?" Kath whimpered.

"Gladys will be in," Robert was sure.

Aunty Gladys was the elderly widow of Rob's Uncle John - who had given Robert the Friendship ring. Gladys had met John when he was a soldier in her hometown in Nova Scotia, Canada towards the end of the war and had lived with him since in Rolly, a suburb of Chepstow. Their home was a pre-fab bungalow in the grounds of the in-law's Georgian house. John had died young and Gladys had grown fat, living the life of a lonely widow for twenty years and having only chocolate and cats for company. Still, she was a gentle woman and she always had a spare bed made up.

Gladys smiled as she answered the late night knock on her front door. Rob left nothing to the imagination when he told Gladys of arriving at Jeannie's cottage to find a note on the door saying, *GONE OUT, WAIT*. "What a cheek, all that way from London and then an awful trek down miles of muddy country lanes," Rob was in no doubt that it was a dreadful trick of Jeannie's and that it was living proof she was a witch! Kath made light of it. She didn't want to fall out with anyone in the family, least of all Jeannie. She had her earmarked as her chief bridesmaid, (or Maid of Honour, if she got married first.)

Kath warmed to the short lady with the lilting accent and gentle smile and couldn't understand why Tilly had called her a numbskull with no style or taste. She had even found fault with her dusting skills. Robert relaxed in his auntie's company too. They reminisced about the comings and goings of the old house where Rob's grandmother had lived. Rob related how he loved to go to the pubs with John, where he would play the piano and have all the drinkers singing. Kath finally asked Gladys if Tilly had told her she and Rob were engaged. She hadn't.

"'spect she's too busy with the business these days to write to anyone! But... congratulations anyway. Have you set a date for the wedding?"

"Probably in September, we will finalise the arrangements at Easter, won't we, Rob?"

Robert just nodded and went on about how his Uncle Bill let him play with his army guns from his days as a soldier in the Sahara.

"Still the same little Robbie," Gladys ruffled Rob's hair. "Boys will be boys." A sad look of resignation filled her round, ruddy face. There had been no children between her and John and she only had the nieces and nephews from her husband's side to think about.

Talk inevitably turned to them one-by-one, as they sat before the open coal fire, sipping hot chocolate and devouring Gladys's homemade fruitcake. Kath absorbed it all with interest. Robert hardly spoke about his cousins, but Kath learned that: Mavis, a domestic science teacher, lived nearby; Barbara owned a frozen food shop in Weymouth; Rosemary lived in Canada - and Ian had become a policeman.

Gladys went to work early the next morning, leaving the couple to clear up the breakfast dishes and making it clear that she couldn't put the couple up for another night as she was expecting her gentleman friend.

Robert said they would try Aunty Blodwyn. Blod, as she was affectionately referred to, lived in Blackwood, not far away. She too was childless, but her husband was still alive. Rob was in awe of his

Uncle Tim's achievements. He was a bus mechanic, and as a child, Rob would go to the bus depot with him, where he would ride on the buses up and down the valleys, from morn 'til night!

Aunty Blod was at home, making a Bakewell tart when the pair arrived. "Just in time for elevenses," she said, as she opened the front door. The tiny terrace was spick and span and the aroma of cakes baking in the oven was welcoming. A log fire roared away in the tiny front room. "It's as if you knew we were coming, Blod..." Rob said.

"I knew you were, I just had that feeling; a premonition."

"Like Jeannie," Kath blurted out. "Jeannie sees ghosts and apparitions and believes in magic."

"Well, don't you?" Blodwyn asked, demanding the affirmative.

"Well, no I don't think I do, actually !"

"Tilly loves haunted houses and all that hocus-pocus!" Blodwyn scoffed and Kath steered clear of mentioning Tilly's name again. Instead, she talked about College and the engagement. Old Blod approved of the ring, but suggested wisely that the stone might not stand up to much wear and tear, so it would be best to remove it when washing-up, for example. "But, tell me now what brings you here today ?"

Rob related his story again about Jeannie and having to sleep at Gladys'. Blodwyn was aware the couple might be trying to get a bed in her house for the night and deftly turned to the subject of DIY problems. "You could have stayed here tonight," she said, "...but we've have had our roof leaking and our spare room is upside down. We have to get a plasterer in now and....."

Rob cut in eloquently. "Aunty, no, we really didn't expect you to put us up for the night. Don't worry, we are going to Cwm Bran. Kath's old school friend is teaching there and she has already offered us her sofa for tonight."

Kath's eyes opened wide in disbelief.

"What a porky," Kath remarked as they left Blodwyn's after dinner. "We just can't turn up at Adri's." Kath insisted.

"Well why not ?" Rob stated. "If she arrived on your doorstep, you wouldn't turn her away, would you ?"

"Well, no."

"Well, then! Let's go!"

Adrianna was in, and not completely shocked at seeing them on her doorstep "I knew you would turn up sooner or later, come on in, TROUBLE! So this is Rob. I've heard so much about you, and your father. He is from these parts, isn't he?"

Rob wasn't in the mood for talking about his father, but Adri pressed on, only to be impressed when Kath continued, "Yes, his name is Sam and he was born to tenant farmers, Simon and Elsie in 1905 at Chepstow, but they then moved to a farm in Llanbrechan - just down the road from here. In the 1911 Census, his father was listed as a farm bailiff. Sam was their third child. He had an elder brother and younger sister. After grammar school in Pontypool, he was apprenticed to be an architect, but rejected this in favour of studying art in Chepstow. Eventually, he was awarded a free studentship to the Royal College of Art, where he studied for four years. He's got his most famous painting *The Rat Catcher* in Chepstow Art Gallery, which won painting of the year in 1937 at the Royal Academy. Sam sold it to the gallery to get money, so he and Tilly could marry. Isn't that right, Rob?"

"Yeh, but talk about something else now, please?" Rob got up and went to the bathroom.

"Are you on the pill, Adri ?" Kath asked, after Rob was out of earshot.

"Well, actually, I'm not. Gary is very careful! I don't trust pills - too many side effects!"

Kath was relieved she could talk to someone about the aches and pains in her abdomen and hips that had developed so rapidly after starting the contraceptive pill. Adri told Kath just to get off it. Kath shut up about pills and pain when Gary - the fiancé - arrived. He was an American soldier based in Bridgend and he had met Adri by chance, on a train a few months previously.

Gary was everything Kath had ever learned an American was. Bold, brash and handsome. Sparkling white, even teeth and a heavy sun tan. "Nice to meet you, folks," he said.

He beamed with conviction and had a strong handshake. His conversation didn't disappoint, either and Rob too was enthralled. Gary was an arms expert. His father owned a publishing company specialising in weaponry and ran a gun club. Kath breathed a sigh of relief as the two men got on and offered to make the dinner with her friend, while they chatted. It was a wonderful evening and they all went to bed late.

Kath and Robert managed well enough on the couch and didn't wake the next day, until late. Adrianna and Gary had already left. A note on the front door said, *Nice to see you guys. Enjoy your sweet dreams. Had to go early, train to catch. Just let the latch down when you go and see ya sometime, Adri & Gaz xxxx*

-18-

Kath reminded Rob that March 1st was the anniversary of their first meeting and that she expected some sort of celebration! Rob suggested a weekend at the Old Parsonage with his parents, as he was running short of cash. Two of his evening classes had been cut and Elaine had put the rent up on his flat by ten shillings a week, due to Kath being there so often! Kath said she would prefer to visit Jeannie, but Rob was adamant he wouldn't go, until she had apologised for the last fiasco.

Kath agreed to go to Somerset, but managed to delay the visit for a couple of weeks, so that she could catch up with her College work and enjoy some social life on campus.

Kath was determined that the weekend at Tilly and Sam's would be better than the previous one. She had already written a polite letter with both hers and Rob's news and thanked Tilly for the sewing machine and jewellery box – but she hadn't mentioned Rob's aborted visit to Jeannie's. She phoned Sam too, and left a message to say that she and Robert would arrive on the Friday night, but not to have a meal ready, as they would have a take-away in Bath. Rob would drive her back to Barry on the Sunday.

Tilly immediately rang Robert and bamboozled him into collecting some antiques, which she had bought in Portobello Road and Petticoat Lane during her buying sprees. She also promised to lure Jeannie to Beckton, the same weekend.

The grey stone Old Parsonage appeared even more gloomy in the moonlight when they arrived at the front entrance, but was slightly more welcoming once they were ushered into the hallway. Sam had put up more of his paintings and drawings, "...that's my mother," he said, as he pointed to a sketch of a thin, tiny lady. Her hair was scraped back off her face, and fashioned into a tight bun; half lens spectacles balanced on the end of her nose. The old lady sat deep in concentration, turning the handle of a sewing machine. "She liked sewing then?" Kath enquired.

"Yes, of course, she was a fine seamstress... "

"Rob hasn't told me much about your family," Kath went on. "...but he did say you had a brother, Joe - and a sister called Margaret."

"Aunty Margaret died in a fire," Rob interjected.

Kath gasped.

"Oh aye, poor Margaret. I can't bear it, can't bear it..." Sam wailed. "Just don't let Tilly see me," he said as he stifled a tear and scuttled off towards the kitchen. Kath and Robert followed. "She was sweeping up the autumn leaves in the garden, towards the fire when the wind changed and the flames caught her long skirt. There was nothing anyone could do. She was a fine teacher, too." A tear trickled down his cheek.

"Now... what's all this?" Tilly rushed into the kitchen. "Upsetting Sam with all this talk about Margaret. I heard you asking questions... probing. " She looked Kath straight in the eye.

"I, I ..." Kath choked, feeling helpless. "Sorry."

"Sorry for what!" Rob exclaimed. "Kath has nothing to be sorry for! Anyway, we're tired. I trust we are back in the Isaac Williams room? We can talk in the morning."

Tilly picked up a pile of letters from the table. " I just came down for these," she said as she backed out of the kitchen. " See you in the morning, Kath... sleep well."

Kath entered the kitchen late the next morning, with pangs of anxiety. She hadn't slept well after the upset the previous evening. She picked up Peaches and held him tight to her chest. Sam was washing dishes and Tilly was already unloading antiques from Robert's van with Leo and Rob. Sam poured Kath a mug of tea and offered her some toast and jam. She confided in him that Rob had not been called for an interview for the job in Chepstow and that there were no other job opportunities near Barry in the pipeline. Sam shrugged; Kath bristled at his indifference, then changed the subject. "Rob took me to meet Gladys and Blodwyn a few weeks ago. You know that, don't you?"

"Good God, no! Why should I ?"

"Hmm.. well, I wrote to Tilly about it all, five days ago "

"Tilly never tells me anything. All I ever do is sit in that damn shop." Sam was resigned. "Never go anywhere, I don't."

"Now, that's not altogether true, is it Sam?" Rob was at the door, out of puff, after having helped bring in a sedan chair.

"You chose not to learn to drive, you like being at home, you like being the house boy." Robert was in no mood to listen to his father's cry of martyrdom. " But, I see you're painting again. You have started a mural in the Catherine of Aragon room, too."

Sam's mood changed. "What do you think of it? Pretty good, eh? *Saint James' Park in the 1880's*. Big job that, eh?" Sam waved his arm, as if he were still holding his paintbrush. "And... what do you think of my Beatrix Potter room, too?"

"It's just wonderful, you have Mrs. Tiggy-Winkle just right," Kath enthused. "The Old Parsonage has come to life and it smells good! It's no longer musty and damp."

Samuel frowned at Kath as Leo pulled a face, then pushed past to help himself to a beer from the fridge.

"You can smell the linseed oil and turpentine in the paint," Robert explained, aware of Kath's discomfort.

"By the way, we are officially engaged," Kath flashed the ring. "It's a black opal." Kath announced, as Tilly came in, carrying a framed Rossetti print.

"That's a bad omen," Tilly almost spat. "Opals mean tears and toil."

"Well... I don't believe in all these old wives tales."

"At your peril - so be it." Tilly glared at Kath.

"Tilly has to have the last word," Sam whispered to Kath, as she turned away, before speaking again.

"Well, *I* love it and it goes with my new kaftan!" she said as she gave a twirl. "I just love the green leaves, look! They are the same colour as my black opal."

"You made that yourself, didn't you?" Tilly observed and, without waiting for affirmation, she pulled at a dangling loose black thread. "You haven't tied up all the loose ends!" she said as the side seam stitches unravelled and the front came away from the back.

Kath screamed and Leo giggled as she ran out the room in tears.

Tilly was supping gin when Kath finally came back to the kitchen, wearing a dark-coloured polo neck sweater and black slacks. In her hands was the blighted kaftan.

"I'll stitch it up," Kath said. "Can I have a needle and thread please?"

"We don't have needles and thread in this house!" Tilly unashamedly said. "I wouldn't be seen dead sewing!"

"Well, I saw Sam darning socks the last time I was here - so you must have needles and thread." Kath wasn't to be deterred.

"Darning is one thing, sewing another. I haven't got any needles. Ask Sam, then."

Kath found Sam potting Hollyhock seeds in his potting shed but he said hadn't got any fine needles or black thread, so that was that. Kath returned to the house to find Tilly fingering the red brocade cloth doors and the velvet tiebacks on the sedan chair. "This is part of the sublime period of history: English suburban life of the Eighteenth Century. Life at its best !" she enthused.

"It wasn't so good for the workers and the poor folk who had to carry the sedan chairs, and empty the chamber pots. Slaves – they were no more than slaves. Shame on their masters."

"Now, Kath," Rob came to the rescue. "You can't change history, let bygones be bygones."

"Got a right Communist there, then..." sniggered Leo as he joined the group. "She's a Red in your bed!" Leo poked Robert in the ribs.

Kath didn't retaliate, but picked up the *Daily Mail*.

"John Lennon and Yoko Ono are getting married in Gibraltar and Sandy Shaw is tying the knot too," she said, wanting no more talk of history.

"Weddings on your Red brain," Leo remarked. "Always knew Rob was a romantic. Been on the lookout for a wifey for years. You are about the fifth girl he's proposed to."

Kath glanced at Rob, but he was giving nothing away. "Well... I'm the lucky one then, the other's don't know what they would have been missing." *Kath was so damn loyal*, Robert thought. He loved her for this.

"Aren't we going out today?" Leo was presumptuous.

"Well, I thought we might go for a drive, then a drink at the George Inn at Norton St. Philip," Rob offered. "After lunch, of course."

"Sounds good to me." Kath was looking forward to getting out of the house again. She picked up the *Discovering Somerset* handbook left handily in the fruit bowl on the table. "It says here that the Inn is one of the most famous in the country, first licensed as an ale house in the Fifteenth Century. 'The downstairs rooms are excellently preserved' she read out aloud. "' ...and the Duke of Monmouth stayed here shortly before being defeated at the battle of Sedgemoor in 1685. He narrowly missed being shot–'"

"We don't want a bloody history lesson," Leo interrupted. "Get up and help get the dinner ready."

Kath's patience snapped. "Who the hell do you think you are, Leo? Some lord of the manor or what? I will help with the dinner, but you are not to talk down to me again or–"

"*Talk down, talk down*," Leo mimicked.

"Tell him, Rob, please! " Kath begged.

"It's no use, I've seen it all before. He likes a fight." Rob grabbed Kath by the arm and said, "Just ignore him."

Kath, bit her lip and started to peel the potatoes.

"I'll join you in a minute," Tilly said. " I will now attend to the roast chicken and home made stuffing..."

They all said in chorus, "Oh yeah, oh yeah," and laughed.

The trio's jolly jaunt to the pub passed amiably, except Rob was left fuming after having to pay for the drinks all round, yet again. Leo had pleaded poverty and damned his mother for being so mean. At least it was a nice spring day and the country lane walk that followed set them in good spirits for when they arrived back at the old house - just in time for the Six O' Clock News. Rob sat with his mother, watching the TV and putting the world to rights. Leo vanished to his attic room and Kath joined Sam, who was wearing three jumpers and standing by the *Rayburn* in the kitchen. Sam explained how much he felt the cold and Kath wasn't surprised. He had lost weight since she had last seen him - a good stone or more - and she thought he could only weigh about seven stones now.

"Rob told me about your youngest brother..." Kath couldn't resist asking about the family history; it was important to her.

"Well... he wasn't my *real* brother, but I didn't know that 'til I was twenty. He was, errr... illegitimate. The son of the woman who lived with us, a Mary Levin. She cooked and cleaned for us. She was only sixteen when she had Bun. He was christened, Eric, but nobody ever called him that."

"I suppose he got his nickname, 'cause he was the 'Bun in the oven'!" Kath was pleased with her pun! Sam only grunted.

That night in bed, Rob said he thought that Bun's father was Sam's father; that's why they had taken Mary in. "It happened a lot in those days, I suppose. But it sent old Simon - my grandfather - round the bend, that's when the old fellow ended up in a mental asylum."

"The poor woman," Kath felt an affinity with Grandmother Elsie, the woman at the sewing machine in Sam's drawing. Life was just so cruel.

The next morning, Kath and Robert joined Tilly and Sam in the sitting room, after snatching a bowl of cereal. Rob told the story of how his van had broken down, right in front of Buckingham Palace when he was on his way back from Portobello Road with the sedan chair. Kath warmed to the sound of Rob laughing with his parents, as he told them the police had been called to see to this man with a jacked-up van by the main gates of the Queen's residence and were not convinced that the sedan chair hadn't been stolen. After some debate, they had believed Robert and he went on his way.

Yet more Royal Family tales surfaced. Sam related how Augustus John, as famous for his filthy Welsh temper and bawdy manner as his artistry, had told him about the Queen Mother fancying him.

Tilly told the story of when Prince Philip had visited the Art School and had stepped on her toe!

It was a shame when the conversation ended, as Jeannie called on the phone full of excuses as to why she hadn't been to stay. *The cat was sick, the washing machine had broken down, Martin had to referee a basketball match*!

"And no mention of her not being in after she had invited us that weekend?" Rob enquired.

"No, not a word. She's an odd one." Tilly said.

"Yeh, birds of a feather, her and Leo," commented Rob, as he got up to leave the room, anxious to be on his way with Kath to Barry.

"Yes, Jeannie and Leo, are alike," Kath said, when they were alone in the van. "You wouldn't think they were your brother and sister, would you, Rob? They are nothing like you. Well a bit alike, with your big noses - like your mother's ..."

"Eh! Enough of the big noses… mine's not that bad, is it?"
"Well, not as bad as theirs," Kath answered, and Rob was satisfied.

-19-

Kath sighed, aghast at her seven-pound weight gain, as she pulled her stomach in and stepped off the scales. "That bloody pill!" She swore out loud. "Look at my bloody belly!" The excess pounds seemed to have accumulated around her abdomen and she despaired at the thought of ever wearing the white towelling bikini she had just made on her antique singer machine. Rob had suggested a white one, after mentioning Ursula Andress in the James Bond film, *Dr No,* again. He liked the lean athletic look of a woman. *Bloody hell, what was he going to think of his girlfriend now!*

Kath put on her bathrobe - another of her creations - then settled down to her reading. She enjoyed the Educational Psychology and Sociology classes and quickly gained an insight as to why her own talents hadn't blossomed well enough: a childhood of intellectual neglect couldn't be compensated for so easily. If ever she had children - and she wanted four - she would make sure they were educated properly. But, the Biology lessons were boring, as there was too much botany. She found having to learn the Laban notation for dance, rather a waste of time too. Still, most of the lectures now were geared towards going on teaching practice for six weeks, after Easter. Even the PE girls on the secondary school teacher training course, like her, would have to do their first practice in a junior school. Kath was to share a class with another student in a village school in Llantrisaint; they would have to take the bus every day. It was going to be a one-hour trek there and back, carrying all their visual aids, and the school was a good ten minutes walk from the bus stop! Kath bemoaned her bad luck. Of all the students and all the schools, why did she have to be given the most awkward place to reach? Still, there was a chance next year would be different. She would be with Rob, but it looked like it wasn't going to be in Wales, or Stoke, after all. Sam and Tilly hadn't even tried to pull a few strings and Kath's parents had no connections in Staffordshire either, so that was that. Kath braced herself to accept the fact she would have to go to London. "I will rent a better flat," Rob had repeated a thousand times, as Kath hitched up to London most weekends throughout the rest of March and until Easter. She had no desire to spend a weekend at Tilly's again just yet, not while the trauma of the kaftan and Leo's hurtful comments were still raw.

Weekends with Rob were enough. He was a good draughtsman and he produced posters for Kath to use on TP. He showed her how to make useful aids for the maths and science lessons, too. Kath and Charlotte were to share a class of first year juniors and had decided on using the theme of 'Animals' for their lessons. Rob loved the story, *Wind in the Willows*, so the couple took turns reading it aloud to each other and discussing how it could be used with the little ones. Kath made a Mr Toad puppet with papier mache and a monocle made from fuse wire. She stitched up a little black suit and fashioned out tiny black shoes and a belt made from an old bag she had bought in the Saturday market.

It was two days before Kath was breaking up from Barry for Easter and was planning to hitch home to Stoke, when she finally heard from Tilly. A parcel arrived in the post and, besides an unusually long letter, the packet contained a silk kaftan. Tilly hoped Kath had sewn up the old kaftan satisfactorily, but, in any case, she said the new one would compensate. It was true, the present was magnificent, an antique, heavy, Chinese black silk garment, colourfully embroidered all over with Chinese motifs, including peonies, the willow pattern bridge and bonsai trees. It was delicious. A Victorian import, Tilly said, from *Harrods*. Kath believed it. Tilly pardoned herself for her tardiness in replying to Kath's thank you letter some four weeks previously. Leo had taken a turn for the worse. He had rowed with his tutors again and left Bristol Art School for good. He was sleeping all day and was refusing to see a doctor; they didn't know what to do. Sam was still working on his Saint James' Park mural and refusing to sit in the shop. Tilly was having to pay a neighbour to be there, but it was no use, the profits were nil. 'Three Ways' would have to be sold, but they would carry on the business from the Old Parsonage. Tilly's final whinge was about Jeannie, she wasn't helping out as she had promised to, and hardly phoned, let alone send a letter. Kath wasn't surprised, but hurriedly wrote back with a few words of sympathy and signed off, *See you after Easter, after I have been home.*

Kath was in need of succour and as much as she had chided her upbringing and didn't look up to her own kind, it was from them she got strength and where she only truly felt she belonged. *But how on earth am I going to enjoy being home, when I have three essays to write, as well as working every morning at play centres for ten days with primary school kids?* Kath worried.

Rob was joining her too, in Stoke, he had already signed on for casual work with the *Manpower* Agency. Kath lamented bitterly that she had little time for just *dossing*, which most of her College friends did. They were idling around in their kaftans, smoking pot and wallowing in flower power, listening to Beatles songs and John Lennon anti-war rhetoric, when all she seemed to do was work! She wasn't completely oblivious to contemporary events and she did warm to John more than the other Beatles, but felt bad for his wife Cynthia and their son Julian, when he left her for Yoko.

However, Kath was more worried about getting pregnant or that Rob might leave her for another woman. Her blood ran cold, thinking the worst, 'til she played the latest Beatles Album and sang along to the words of, *Honey Pie*.

Nelly had a pot of *Black Boy* tea ready when Kath arrived home, after dark, at the start of the Easter holidays. "Ye dad's at the Cheshire Cheese with Bill and his other mates from the Scout group committee. Big discussions are happening tonight," Nelly was telling Kath, when Robert arrived a few minutes later.

"Money's gone missing from the Scout group building fund. Said he wouldn't be long, but I don't believe him. He's got a lot on his plate now and he can't stand his own company for a minute, got to have an audience, he has."

"That's cause he doesn't read," remarked Kath.

"No, you're right, only what he has to, for work," went on Nelly. "He'd rather talk. Gift of the gab he has." It was true, Arthur told a good story. Carrots they'd called him, she recalled. Arthur wasn't a ginger top any more though. The flaming locks were all gone and only a shiny bald patch and a ring of silver hair remained.

"There you are, our Kath, that'll put some meat on your bones," Nelly said as she laid a roast ox heart and thick gravy supper on the table for the couple "There's nothing on ye," she said, pinching Kath's arms and thighs.

"But Mum, I have actually put on half a stone since Christmas, but I don't want to talk about that."

"Well, I conna see it! And there's a lot thee dunna want to talk about." Nelly complained that Kath kept her own council and 'ran deep'. "I dunna know," she sighed. "Ye don't look right to me. Doing too much, addling ye brain, all this studying and all this werreting about jobs and getting married."

"Give over, Mum." Kath readily lapsed back into the Potteries dialect. "Talk to Rob while I unpack."

"Elle and Derek are getting married in June." Nelly went on.

"My cousin," Kath shouted down the stairs to Rob.

"They've got ears everywhere, they at," Nelly answered back. "Her dunna miss a thing, does her. I don't know how you put up with her. Ye must be a saint! Anyway, they've bought a cottage on Biddulph Moor. It's a wreck but they are doing it up together."

"What's up with thee?" Arthur asked Kath as he joined the family later in the crowded kitchen, unexpectedly returning early from his 'meeting'. "Ye've got a face like a bosted settee. What's up?"

"Deck it, Dad. It's Eamonn Andrews on TV – doing his *This Is Your Life.*"

"Her's dirty guts, Elle and Derek have bought a house," Nelly said. Kath shrugged her shoulders, pleaded not guilty and forbade Nelly to mention her cousin again that night. It did sting though that she would be getting married too, but would have to live in a rented flat. She tried hard not to feel jealous.

Kath was the first to mention Rob's job rejections. His applications for all jobs had all come to nothing, but Arthur wasn't perturbed. "Ye seem well in down there in London, our youth," he went on. "I would'ne worry thee sen about chucking the job in there. Just ye keep dipping yer bread in the gravy. I see you've got the plywood in the back of the van. Well, I've got folks fer buy it already. Good as money in the bank," he rubbed his hands. Oh, Arthur was good.

"And watch her," Arthur pointed a finger at Kath. "If her dunna get her own road, oo... 'Er pulls 'er face, there's no living with 'er, her chunters, oo there's no living with her. It upsets me just for think about it!"

"Just deck it, will ye," Kath retaliated. "All this talk gets me down. I'm going to bed."

But she still kissed her mother and father goodnight.

The two weeks holiday passed frenetically. Between work and play, the couple managed to visit most of Kath's aunties, uncles, ten cousins and, of course, Billy and his wife. Pauline was expecting… again!

Evelyn and Dan offered to provide the wedding cake. Kath was just to say what colours and design, and they would see to the rest. Danny, their eldest son was living in Toronto, but they would say no more about him. The family had closed ranks when he finally admitted to being homosexual. On the very day in 1967, when the draconian laws against sodomy were repealed, he went to live openly with another man. Eileen, their daughter, was 'at least normal', they said and happily married with Diane, seven, and Neil, two. Diane was to be a bridesmaid at Kath's wedding, along with cousin Lynne's daughter, three-year-old Kay. Kath would get a dressmaker to sew up the dresses, but all in good time!

The Bowley's had finally moved into their new bungalow; Rob and Kath went over for a guided tour. Kath was impressed and announced that one day she and Rob would own their own home of such calibre. Rob winced at the thought.

"So long as you have a van," teased Kath, "…you'll be happy." Rob agreed.

The cosy nights curled up with Rob in front of the TV and the open fire in the kitchen in Kath's home came to an end. Kath was disappointed she wouldn't be following *Coronation Street* for a while and asked Nelly to let her know what 'Elsie Tanner', in particular, was up to next. The *Benny Hill Show* was another of the couple's favourites, along with *Top of the Pops*.

They left Stoke to spend a couple of nights at The Old Parsonage, before term started again. Kath took oatcakes and a dozen blue band mugs for Tilly.

"Much too modern for our taste," Tilly decided, on seeing the pottery. "Martin's mother can have them."

"Well, at least you can keep modern houses warm and clean." Kath stressed the word 'clean', looking in disgust at the filthy kitchen of the Old house. The bin was full to the brim again and there were mice droppings in the kitchen corners. Kath felt like pointing out that the blue and white mugs would be a lot more hygienic than the chipped, cracked and crazed cups in use, but she thought better of it. Although she wanted to expound the virtues of the Bowley's new bungalow, she thought it best to turn the conversation to the wedding plans instead.

"Tilly, do you think Jeannie would like to be a bridesmaid?"

"Ask her yourself !"

"Okay, but who should we invite from your side."

"I'll let you know later," Tilly seemed too preoccupied with Leo and the business to engage, but then suddenly enthused," Your kaftan looks marvellous, first class." Kath had worn it not just to please Tilly, but because she was genuinely thrilled with the garment.

Sam sat with his head in the *Daily Mail,* muttering about students and how ungrateful and disrespectful they were: the Paris mob brewing up for more demonstrations. Then he went on about drugs and foreigners in the country, pop groups earning millions and how disgusting Modern Art was. David Hockney wasn't worth a sou, he said and neither was Andy Warhol.

Rob disagreed and raved about David Hockney's recent *Big Splash* picture, and said he would take Kath to see it in London soon.

Sam scowled.

"I suppose Sam's paintings are out of fashion," Kath said sadly in the privacy of the couple's bedroom that night. "He hasn't had all the recognition as an artist he should have had. He hasn't sold much. Has he? I suppose he's of that generation who are regarded as *academic* artists, too traditional, too classical, not original enough, not rebellious, too romantic. But then… I'm not an artist."

Robert wasn't listening.

Sam was reading about Titian in the kitchen the next morning, when Kath went down for breakfast. "I don't know anything about artists," Kath said. "I didn't even do the subject at 'O' Level."

"Shouldn't be allowed," Sam raised his voice. "Everybody should learn to draw, to paint, to love art, to love history, too."

Kath agreed but explained that, at her grammar school, they'd had to choose between Science, Art, History and Geography.

"My Dad was good at art, though. He went to Art School," Kath mumbled. Sam looked up, then closed his book, but didn't speak. "It's a pity about Leo not going to the College in Bristol any more... what went wrong?" Kath went on.

"I don't want to talk about that... " Sam got up, slowly.

Kath watched him from the kitchen window hurrying towards his rhubarb patch.

"Kath is going to transfer to a training college in London," Rob explained to Tilly as she arrived back from the village shop and plonked milk and bread on the kitchen table.

"Is she?" she said perfunctorily, as if Kath was not in earshot.

"There's no chance of me getting a job in Wales or Stoke now," Rob said.

"Isn't there?"

"She's having an interview at Avery Hill soon."

"Is she?"

"Errr... I'll take Peaches for a walk," said Kath, as the kitchen had gone silent. "Where's his lead, though?" Kath was desperate to get away from the heartless Tilly.

"He doesn't need one," Tilly snapped. "The garden is enough for him, isn't it, my little pet?" She said as she scooped the mite up with one hand and kissed his wet snout. "He's a beauty, isn't he?" she purred.

Kath slipped through the back door, alone, and into the sharp air, turning immediately into the nearest country lane. The half a dozen stone terrace cottages either side soon gave way to the hawthorn hedgerows and the open fields beyond. Primroses nestled at the foot of tall trees, amongst the old leaf mould from the previous autumn, and now the bare branches above were just beginning to sprout again. Birds twittered busily in and out of the undergrowth as they went scratching and searching for material for their nests. Kath filled her lungs with the clean country air and imagined the oxygen feeding her brain, clearing her thoughts and cleansing her soul. The sun broke through the clouds, as if on purpose, to lift her spirits. A single hiker passed by with a nod and "Morning" and a ready smile. After an hour, Kath felt good enough to return to the old House.

Tilly and Rob were ensconced in the two armchairs in the drawing room and were discussing Leo's predicament; he was still in bed. The sofa was piled up with copies of the *Daily Mail* and *Country Life*; books at one end, Peaches asleep on the other. There was nowhere for Kath to sit, so she offered to make coffee for everyone. "No need, we've had one," replied Tilly and so Kath retreated to the kitchen.

Sam was at the sink, mixing up a mêlée of chemicals in two glass jars. The pungent smell made Kath heave and wrench. "Now some strychnine. That'll do it. Kill the moles, I mean…" Sam explained.

"Strychnine? Poison. Kill the moles?" Kath, ignorant of such bucolic practices, repeated his words - then recoiled in horror.

Sam, unperturbed, went on. "Ruthless little creatures, well they can eat these," he said with relish as he scuttled out to the back lawn, Kath following.

Sam then tipped the contents of the two jars - now containing worms - down the holes in the middle of two enormous molehills. "That'll get em," he continued, wiping his hands on an oily cloth just inside the greenhouse door and setting the two jars down on a shelf.

"But, moles are lovely velvety creatures. How can you?" Kath pleaded. "Diggory Diggory Delvet, a little old man in velvet," Kath sang the Beatrix Potter ditty she had sung so often to the little ones in her charge.

Sam disappeared to the far end of the garden to dig over a new bed for cabbages. Talking of moles, reminded Kath of Mole in *Wind in the Willows* and the need to be thinking about her pending teaching practice.

"Kath's going to do her TP in Llantrisaint," Rob was telling Tilly as Kath joined them again in the lounge."

"Is she?" Tilly yawned.

"Yes - starting in three days time."

Kath, who by this time had removed some books from the sofa and sat down, pursued the topic, "I am using the theme of animals in my classes and I thought you might let me use some of your short stories. You know… the ones you wrote for the *Western Mail,* which Sam illustrated. Rob has told me about them. I presume you have copies? Blodwyn showed me copies of your stories and newspaper cuttings, when we visited. She is very proud of you, you know."

"Is she?" Tilly sounded surprised.

"They look very interesting and if I were to read them to my pupils, I think that would be unique." Kath looked at Tilly, hoping she would take the hint.

"Well… " Tilly stalled. "I'll see if I can find them, later, of course. Now… Rob what were you saying about your motorbike? You said you left it here in pieces in a box? A *Matchless,* you say. I can't say as I have seen it. Leo might know something, though."

"So… what is Leo going to do now he's finished at Bristol?" Kath ventured.

Tilly threw her arms into the air "That's anyone's guess." She looked close to tears, but stood up and straightened her clothes, muttering something about having to phone dealers. She left the room as composed as she could.

"He's going to have to pull his weight in the business more." Rob took up the conversation. "Look how much stock Tilly's bought," he said, indicating a high pile of boxes and crates stacked up in the dining room. "She's been buying up old dolls, toys and children's books."

"Yes, I saw an old pram in the back, must be Victorian?" Kath guessed.

"When will she ever find time to write her novel?"

Tilly was writing about riots in Wales after the Napoleonic Wars.

"I will write it eventually." Tilly entered the conversation again, on overhearing Kath.

"I've been learning about the Rebecca Riots at College." Kath's knowledge of Welsh history was sure to impress her in-laws-to-be.

"Riots all over Wales, eh?"

"Mid and North Wales," corrected Tilly.

" Yes, at the end of the 19th Century."

"No, the beginning…" Tilly contradicted.

"Named because of Rebecca in the Old Testament; she was a good leader?"

"No, they were named after what the men wore – oh, never mind…" Tilly couldn't be bothered to explain.

"The men dressed up like women, in cardigans!" Kath finished, triumphantly.

"How goes it, Leo?" Kath asked when she found Leo in the kitchen. She was enjoying speaking in a Welsh dialect; she'd perfected it to entertain her friends in Stoke.

"Don't speak to me in that phoney voice," Leo spat back.

"You deal with Leo," Kath hissed as she slid past Rob in the hall and let herself out into the garden by the incongruous 1950's metal-framed French doors. She had a job to open them.

"Stop, stop..." Sam boomed from behind his wheelbarrow. "You'll have them off their hinges. We don't use those doors any more. They're too rusty."

"Well, I'm surprised you haven't got Rob to fix them while we are here," Kath commented, flippantly. "Or... you could get Leo to mend them?" she added, sarcastically.

"The poor boy is ill. He's on ten pills a day. He can't sleep. Nerves are a terrible thing."

Kath wasn't impressed with Leo, and neither was Jeannie, she discovered.

Tilly waved a letter, and, after making Kath and Robert sit down with her in the garden, she summarised its contents. "Jeannie says she's not coming down here again until Leo learns to get up at a reasonable hour, does some visible household chores, stops swearing at her and Martin, and we stop treating him like a prince!" Tilly was clearly indignant. Kath and Rob said nothing.

"That's a tall order from Jeannie," Kath remarked to Tilly as they went indoors to watch the 6 O'Clock News on TV. " But you can always visit her, I am sure." Kath was always one to find a solution. "I would like to visit her too, sometime. Perhaps we can go together?"

"Impossible!" Tilly blurted out "Have you no idea how much work it takes to run a big business like this?"

Kath nearly cried, but was glad the darkness of the room hid her face, as she tiptoed out into the kitchen.

Sam stopped reading the *Daily Mail* when he saw her and went to the sink to wash some dishes. Kath helped herself to a glass of white wine from the open bottle on the table; the remains of what they had had at lunch, with yet another roast chicken lunch. "Tilly's a good cook," Sam enthused as he scoured the battered roasting pan with a metal pad.

"Yes, she is," Kath agreed. "But that pan needs replacing - chuck it out and get a new one."

"This is an antique! Sacrilege it would be to discard it !"

"And, I suppose these chipped and cracked plates are priceless too?" Kath couldn't resist a dig. *The silly man*, she thought.

"What was that you said? I haven't got my hearing aid in..."

"I just want to say... you are a great artist. And... I'd like to learn about art too…"

Sam heard that all right and warmed a little. "Read and read more," he said and offered up a pile of books he had squirreled away on a tiny shelf above the pots and pans: *Masters in the National Gallery, Van Dyke, The Life and Times of Gainsborough, Picasso and His Mistresses, Le Petite Henri – the life of Toulouse Lautrec* - and *The Best of Rembrandt.*

"I'll show you some of my drawings, now," Sam said, rushing off, then returning to the kitchen a few minutes later with a portfolio of sketches.

Kath looked at Sam's work with awe: first there was a pen and ink sketch of a half-naked Roman woman. "That was a statue in the antique room where I worked in Chepstow, before the Great War…" Then came a pencil sketch of a hay barn and haystack, "Our smalholding after father died… and this is Tilly when she was eighteen. It's the first sketch I did of her."

She was beautiful, like a Greek Goddess, Kath thought. Tilly was caught in the height of her beauty, with her long neck, full lips, almond-shaped eyes, high cheekbones, beguiling forehead and her head a mass of full, loose curls.

"This is another of our farm…" Sam said, as he handed Kath a drawing of the old-fashioned water pump and large metal water jug.

"We had a white-enamel jug like this in our caravan in North Wales. We had to get water from a tap in the field. My Dad built our caravan."

"*We* don't like caravans…" Sam said emphatically and moved to the next picture.

"I love this one," Kath fielded the perceived snub.

Groups of women in long dresses were holding hands, dancing together in a circle.

"I love country dancing, too," Kath gushed. "Wish I had nice hair so I could have a long plaits, like these girls…"

"Augustus John liked this painting, and he looked in admiration at my work, in general. I used to see him a lot at the Royal College. In fact, he was furious about me missing out on the *Prix de Rome* place, by only one point. By God, he was mad about that…"

"Tell me more about your years in London, Sam. You had a scholarship, didn't you ?"

"Yes, that's when I lived with my Aunt Susan. She was a widow and had a three-storey rambling house in Earl's Court; took in lodgers, too.

I met Conan Doyle there. Aunty Susan was into Spiritualism, you know. He bought some of her pictures. She was an artist, but too modern for my taste. Yes… my years there were absolutely marvellous."

"You were engaged, then?"

Sam didn't answer but went on, "These are paintings are of Indian dancers…" He handed Kath a collection of three exquisite watercolours. "I got sick to death of damned life drawing at school, so I absconded to the Imperial Institute, next door. Mind you, I got reprimanded by the principal, Rothstein, for poor attendance, but when I told him that I had been 'living' between the British Museum and the Imperial, well… he was highly impressed. I could do as I pleased from then on!" Sam revelled in the glory of his youth and the associated status of being a Royal College student. He had a box camera he said and recorded everyday life.

"But you don't take photographs now," Kath had observed.

"No, haven't had a camera for years, not since I got married, no time…" he snapped the portfolio shut so unexpectedly it made Kath jump.

"Seems you didn't do much painting after you got married?" Kath speculated.

"No, but I never stopped drawing. I hope I die with a pencil in my hand!"

"I suppose with teaching you were too busy, as well. You must have worked hard to build up the College so much. Rob told me you started with only five students and when you left there were more than two-hundred."

"Yes, but those days are gone now. Gone, forever."

"Oh, by the way Sam, talking about your School of Art. There's a boy in my year, David Pellam… his father taught with you."

"That scoundrel!"

Kath was taken aback.

"Fake, bloody fake he was. Dead now, mind. Set himself up as a master glass blower; stained glass expert, too. Rubbish it was. Got all the churches in Llanfarn and Jetty Side to buy his windows. Scrapped the old glass, they did, and put in his new fandangled stuff…"

"But, David told me he had commissions for cathedral windows in America – he can't have been be that bad?"

"Well, it's a disgrace, that's all I can say. Don't want to talk about it anymore..."

Kath was left in no doubt about Sam's feelings for modern artists and his own disappointment in the commercial art world.

Rob caught the end of Sam's ranting, as he came into the kitchen to fetch himself a beer from the fridge. Later, he told Kath that his father's failures was his own fault. He could have had more commissions, but he wasn't a businessman, and he wouldn't trust anyone else to promote him. "Let the plonker stew," he said.

Kath didn't want to be drawn into a debate about Sam's lack of commercial acumen, but pleaded with Rob to have more sympathy with his father.

"Sam's given me these..." Kath pointed to the pile of books she had placed on top of a red lacquered Chinese cabinet, near the front door.

"Not on there!" Tilly shrieked. "That's eighteenth Century! Pack them in your bag, now and then get to bed. We'll have to be off early in the morning if we are going to Stourhead."

Kath spluttered, "What?!"

Rob had promised that they would return early to Barry the next morning, as she had a lot of preparing to do for her TP.

"Tilly's adamant we take her to Stourhead - just the three of us. She needs a break from Sam and Leo. We have to go, Kath," and before she could get in a word of protest, Rob dragged her up the stairs to bed.

"Well, you are blessed," Rob commented. "Sam giving you those books. Never gave me anything in his life, the old skinflint. 'Scrooge' they called him at the Art School. Wouldn't even buy you a cup of tea. Never had any money. Only ever carried a one-pound note, folded into four and tucked deep into his wallet for emergencies, he said. Still there, I bet." Rob said as he dropped off to sleep.

Kath tossed and turned. She kicked Rob in the back twice because he was keeping her awake snoring, but he never woke up, just turned over, grunted and carried on snoring more softly. Kath felt agonised about the next day, to be spent walking round gardens with Tilly and pretending she was enjoying it. It wasn't so much she wouldn't like seeing the flowers and trees, it was that she knew so little about such grand places and her ignorance was sure to attract Tilly's criticism. All this talk about Palladian design, par-terres, Doric columns, stucco ceilings, the beau monde, William Kent, gazebos, Italianate and Lancelot 'Capability Brown', left her dizzy with migraines. Still that was all going to be tomorrow, she told herself then recited, silently:

I must down to the seas again, to the lonely sea and the sky,
And all I ask is a tall ship and a star to steer her by,
And the wheel's kick and the wind's song and the white sail's shaking,
And a gray mist on the sea's face, and a gray dawn breaking.

I must go down to the seas again, for the call of the running tide
Is a wild call and a clear call that may not be denied;
And all I ask is a windy day with the white clouds flying,
And the flung spray and the blown spume, and the sea-gulls crying.

I must go down to the seas again, to the vagrant gypsy life,
To the gull's way and the whale's way, where the wind's like a whetted knife;
And all I ask is a merry yarn from a laughing fellow-rover,
And quiet sleep and a sweet dream when the long trick's over.

She did feel better.

-20-

In the College's storeroom, Kath carefully placed Sam's books into her red trunk; she wouldn't have time to study Art. Then, dutifully, she wrote to Tilly, thanking her for the weekend. The visit to Stourbridge had gone went well and the weather had been fine; they had picnicked by Apollo's temple.

Kath hoped that her future mother-in-law would remember about the children's stories she had promised to fish out for her. After finishing her letter, she thought to herself, *we are all animals*, and dipped back into Desmond Morris's, *The Human Zoo.*

Kath needn't have worried about Teaching Practice; she was a natural, both her TP supervisor and netball coach said so; but Kath did find it a strain.

Overcoming the limitations of a working class background was not easy for her. Still, she passed, *in spite of not having Tilly's stories,* Kath wrote to her mother!

Now, there were the June exams to prepare for. She had already been interviewed at Avery Hill in London. The College had accepted her application, pending satisfactory exam results at Barry. Kath hated the idea of moving to London, and became even more adverse to the inevitable, after being interviewed. She would only be acceptable for the primary school PE course, and she would have to go on a two-week intensive elocution course, before the autumn term began. Kath's sense of failure intensified. She knew her Northern accent was a bar to her progress, as Tilly never failed to mention, but she wanted it to change naturally, not be forced by some mechanical, heartless training.

Rob was so concerned about Kath, her rancour at his failing to get a job in Wales and her mood swings, that he insisted on a few days holiday for them in Aberaron, near Aberystwyth. Alun's cousin had a cottage near the beach, and it was to be theirs for five days, at Whit - before exams. Kath suggested inviting Jeannie and Martin, but Rob said, "Over my dead body! I want to be with only you."

"Lovebirds eh?" Kath did so want to sound romantic and exciting.

"And… don't forget your bikini," Rob said, during their phone call.

"…and… don't forget your tennis racquet."

They didn't play much tennis there though… their ground floor hideaway was perfect for lovemaking. The patio doors opened out onto a secluded lawn, giving way to a few apple trees and then a high red brick wall, covered in ivy. They put the double bed in front of the glass doors, which caught the morning sun. Caress followed caress and kiss after kiss.

"Love you so much."

"Love you, too."

Give Peace a Chance emanated from the radio; Kath hoped her bond with Rob was as strong as John and Yoko's. *But how could they be so bold and brazen, being photographed in bed? Hers and Rob's affair was private, the best,* she thought, *simple joy*. That was until the third day, when their romps came to an abrupt end. Naked Rob had just rolled over after lovemaking, when Kath saw the village postman, with his red face pressed against the window calling, “Bore Da”. Kath grabbed a sheet, wrapped it around her exposed flesh and fled. Rob tried to preserve his dignity by holding his discarded, black Y- fronts to his private parts. Kath sniggered round the corner from her vantage point as Rob faced the Welshman.

“Just called to say there’s no mail today.”

“Well, was there any yesterday?” Rob did sound silly.

“No... there wasn’t.”

“Well, well.” Rob was stuck for words.

Kath spoke. “Now then, if there’s no mail today and there was no mail yesterday, then there is no need for you to be here then. You came here ‘cause you knew we would be here, you have been spying on us, you have. You are a perv... a Peeping Tom! Just bugger off will you and stop spoiling our holiday.” To Kath’s astonishment, the man disappeared and the couple burst out laughing. “There, I told you Rob, these Welshmen are not right in the head!”

“Well, you are marrying one, so there.”

Although the incident was passed off as a little something to laugh about, Kath wondered about Rob’s ability to look after her as he promised. They had known each other for over a year and she thought she knew her husband-to-be well, but now realised she didn’t. His lack of sportsmanship and self-awareness irked. “*When your elbow is sticking in my back, you should know it is, without looking at the damn elbow and you should know I don’t like it and you should move it away*!” Kath told him more than once. Rob rolled his eyes and took no notice.

Kath pushed her negative thoughts out of her mind and mused again over the wedding plans. She hadn’t asked Jeannie directly yet to be her chief bridesmaid, but Tilly no doubt would have mentioned it. However, Kath thought it would be a good idea to send her, and Martin, a postcard from Wales. Kath agonised over the wording, but thought it best not to say anything about the aborted weekend in January! She was aware too that Jeannie would be feeling disappointed she hadn’t managed to get a teaching post and was having to work in an old folk's care home again, and Martin was spending too much time with his family in Chepstow.

After watching Mary Hopkins singing *Those Were the Days* on TV, Kath finally wrote the card:

Dear Jeannie and Martin,

Wish you were here! It's very hot. By the way, Jeannie you look just like pretty Mary Hopkins. Lots of love and hope to see you soon in your lovely cottage.

Rob huffed and accused Kath of having a fertile imagination, but conceded that perhaps, in a good light, and with blonde rinse on her hair, Jeannie did favour the Welsh singer.

Kath, happy after the holiday, sang Lulu's Eurovision Song Contest hit that year, *Boom Bang a Bang*, on the way back to Barry. Rob was going to spend two nights with Tilly and Sam, before returning to London and Kath had insisted on him buying laver bread, salt marsh lamb, Welsh black beef and Pendawaach cockles for them, before he dropped her off.

Robert phoned Kath from his flat, the following week. He said Tilly had shown no interest in the wedding, or the fact that they were hoping to buy their own house. Now that the business was booming, Tilly thought of nothing else, he said. She had him driving up and down Somerset to take and fetch furniture.

"Got to earn your keep," Kath reminded him jokingly and then steered him off the subject.

Kath had more important things to think about, but at least her exams would all be over by June the twenty-fifth. She had just three weeks to revise. There would be no weekends out of Halls, no shopping trips, no distractions whatsoever. She would only write to her parents and Rob, and phone him once a week.

Kath had left Nelly and Arthur in charge of the wedding arrangements, but Kath was scheduled to buy her wedding dress in London. The ceremony was to take place at Christ Church in Tunstall, on Saturday, the twentieth of September; where Kath had been christened and confirmed. The reception was booked at the Sneyd Arms Hotel, in on the corner of the town square, where about seventy relatives and friends would be offered a buffet tea. Dancing and party games afterwards would be organised by Arthur, of course. Keith Bowley was to be the best man. The couple would have a one night honeymoon in a hotel and then head back to London. Rob would have already started back to work in Stepney, but Kath wouldn't start College till after the wedding. Rob was going to find a one-bedroom unfurnished flat, near the College, over the summer. Already, they were being offered carpets, a fridge, and a three-piece suite! Everything was all going to be all right, she convinced herself.

Only the daily dips in the College pool, and Rob's letters, with SWALKFYLC embarrassingly emblazoned across the back, kept her going.

Rob spent three weeks looking for another flat and a summer job for her in London for July, but was unable to secure either - so when Rob arrived to move her from Barry to London, Kath insisted he take her to Stoke, instead, where she knew she could work. She didn't want to live in his bedsit with Elaine breathing down her neck any longer than she had to.

Kath worked mornings at play centres and did a couple of evenings a week waitressing. The little black dress she had used before, although a little tight, was still serviceable and she talked her way into a job again at a top restaurant in the city. "On my terms," she boasted to Nelly. "You have to be persistent, demand, let 'em know what you want, expect it. After all, it's the crying baby that gets the most milk." Kath stamped her foot.

"...and the most smacks," Nelly wisely counteracted.

Nelly's wisdom made Kath think and reflect. "Yeh, you might be right. Can't be too pushy," she conceded as Billy and his family arrived. Eighteen-month-old Matthew pressed his face to the glass of the front door and hammered to be let in. Pauline followed with four-week-old Kerry in her arms, wrapped in a pink shawl.

"You are just so cute, gorgeous, adorable, lush..." Kath kissed baby Kerry's cheeks, as she took her niece from Pauline.

"Lush?" enquired Pauline.

"Yeh, they say that a lot in Barry. It means lovely," Kath explained.

"I thought it meant green! You know, when you hear about lush grass," Pauline looked puzzled.

"Well... it means lovely too, but don't lose any sleep over that! How's the house going? Dad's put a fence up for you in the back, hasn't he? Rob says he'll give Billy a hand putting the flagstones down in your drive, when he comes up at the end of July for two weeks. Then we'll go down to Somerset again. Tilly has some furniture for us, for our new flat. Well… we haven't exactly got one yet, though… but Rob's trying to secure one. Unfurnished, one-bedroom. Good job Rob's got a van, eh?"

"Glad I don't live in London," Pauline went on. "I don't like pigeons."

"Pigeons!"

"All those pigeons in Trafalgar Square, you know. They are like those birds flying around in that film, *The Birds…* the Hitchcock film."

"Don't be daft. That's only in the centre of London. Where Rob lives, you never see even a sparrow!"

"Now, what's this you calling my Pauline, daft, eh?" Billy shouted at Kath from the back door.

"Well, sorry I didn't mean anything," Kath apologised. but Billy would hear none of it.

"Just because you're going to College, you think you are better than us. Fancy pants, they are calling you."

Kath didn't respond, but she felt ashamed. She didn't want to sound superior, she just wanted to be herself. If it meant leaving one camp and then not being accepted in another, then so be it. She picked up the baby again and sang the *Beatles* song, *While My Guitar Gently Weeps.*

"Wasn't that terrible news about Brian Jones, drowning in the swimming pool?" Kath started the conversation again with Pauline. "Drugs overdose, they say."

"Don't like the Rolling Stones, anyway," Pauline commented.

"Nor me, I prefer the *Beatles* and soul music. Marvin Gaye's great." Kath burst into a rendering of, *How Sweet It Is To Be Loved by You.*

"Yeah, Otis Reading too," and Pauline began singing *Sitting on the Dock of the Bay.*

"And what about Jackie Wilson?"

"Oh yeh – and hey, what about The Supremes? Don't let's forget the women, soul sisters, eh?"

Kath was relieved that she hadn't made Pauline an enemy and was asked to baby-sit.

"Yes, but only if you'll let me use Billy's car sometimes," Kath bartered, and the deal was done.

Billy was working shifts at the *Michelin* factory. He was on good money and was paying his mortgage nicely; even putting money aside, quite a substantial amount, for a rainy day, he said. He didn't mind Kath using his *Morris Minor* to take school friends out and do the rounds of the aunties, uncles and cousins.

It was mid-July before Kath had a letter from Jeannie, via Robert, saying she had written to her in Barry. Kath replied straightaway, saying she hadn't received the letter but, anyway she was pleased now that Jeannie had agreed to be their Chief Bridesmaid and she and Rob would be thrilled to spend a few days with her and Martin at *Bellows Cottage.*

Jeannie was reading about Edward Kennedy, the US senator, who was ignominiously making the news headlines, when Kath and Robert arrived at the isolated, hillside cottage. Tucked away miles down an uneven track, the dwelling faced north and overlooked a woodland on the other side of the valley.

Even in July, there was a chill indoors. The sombre maroon curtains, purple cushions, two antique longcase clocks, and several wall and mantel clocks ticking away out of unison - gave the impression of an old-fashioned Swiss clock shop. Stuffed animals in glass cases and under glass domes sat on windowsills. A fully-grown, stuffed badger stood on its hind legs in the hall. A mole's skull sat on the top of the toilet cistern. Spiky plants grew by the back door. Ivy and thistles sprouted by the front door.

Lunch was rabbit stew with mashed swede, and pumpkin pie for afters. Robert ate only the vegetables. He confided in Kath that night in bed he just couldn't face the meat, after seeing all those taxidermy creatures. Jeannie had put them in a single bed.

If only she had said before that she only had one single bed, Billy would have lent them one of his sleeping bags. He wasn't camping now they had two babies, Kath thought as she too lay awake; listening to the sound of the ticking clocks and the owls twittering in the moonlight. It was past midnight when she overheard the conversation going on in the bigger bedroom, next door.

"Perhaps the doctor can give you some randy pills," Jeannie whispered.

"I've tried them before. Just can't get it ..."

"Shhh..." Jeannie interrupted Martin. " I'll think of something. There must be a cure, an aphrodisiac or something…"

Kath nudged Robert. "Did you hear that?"

Rob, only half-awake and unaware of his sister and husband next door, shouted, "Where am I?"

Shhh," Kath put her fingers to his lips. "I'll tell you in the morning." The couple embraced, kissed, and held onto each other until dawn.

Martin was the first in the cottage to get up. He let the cat out and made a pot of tea.

"Rob loves pig pudding," Kath remarked as she sat down at the table for breakfast.

"*We* call it black pudding," Jeannie's abrupt response left Kath in no doubt that she belonged to a different world.

After breakfast, Jeannie insisted on a long country walk, then a pub lunch.

Bees hovered busily around the flowers and only a slight breeze stirred the trees. Trout wriggled up and down in the shallow stream, which meandered around the hillock by the cottage. Rob took his shoes off, rolled his trouser legs up to his knees and tried trout tickling, like he used to do during his childhood. He looked happy and relaxed, until Jeannie spoke. "Terrible, wasn't it, about Michael Weeks drowning," Rob winced and then closed his eyes. He didn't want to be reminded that his best friend had died in the sea when they were both twelve-years-old.

Jeannie, grinned. She seemed to come alive only when she spoke of tragedies, treachery, dirty deeds, ghouls, ghosts and the inevitability of death. Kath had trouble envisaging her in a peacock-blue shantung bridesmaid's dress with a pretty bow in her hair.

"Jeannie, Rob and I are having a church service with seventy guests. I'll have a white dress and a diamond and gold band ring - but we haven't got the ring yet." Kath wanted to take Robert's mind off his poor friend.

"Well… we are getting married at the Registry in Frome, on August the twenty-ninth." Jeannie dismissed talk of weddings like she was snuffing out a candle.

"But… I must measure you for your Maid of Honour dress, before we leave. I'm having the dresses made up, and…"

"Oh, Kath, you do fuss so much," Jeannie scolded, then added,

"...about nothing at all."

Kath bit her lip, took a deep breath, counted to ten, and feigned indifference.

Back at the cottage, Martin fiddled with the knobs at the back of the black-and-white TV to get a good picture, so they could watch the first ever moon landing, live. Rob was sent up on the roof to adjust the aerial, then there were only two minutes to spare before the four sat down to watch the greatest event of the twentieth Century

Holding Rob's hand, Kath went all goosepimply when Neil Armstrong from the Apollo 11 spacecraft said, 'The Eagle has landed' and later on, when emerging from the craft, 'That's one small step for man; one giant leap for mankind.' Kath hugged Rob frantically and yelled, "...and hope for the future. To *our* future!"

Jeannie had already disappeared from the living room and was calling "Boogy boo, Booby," at the back door. She always did give her cats silly names. Martin at least remained with his guests and carried on polite conversation about how poorly paid teachers were, how hard it must be for Rob, teaching in a deprived area. It was obvious that Martin was having discipline problems with the teenagers in his charge at the local comprehensive school.

"They should never have brought in mixed schools," was Rob's reaction. "Girls are evil in classes with boys," he concluded. He was glad he taught in an all-boys establishment.

Jeannie finally managed to find a measuring tape and Kath duly noted down her vital statistics. At five-foot, five inches, and size ten, Jeannie had an enviable figure.

Kath enthused about the cottage to Tilly and Sam when she and Robert called in at the Old Parsonage after their stay with Jeannie and Martin. "I don't understand why they don't have you over. Sam could help them in the garden," Kath continued.

"You know we can't go anywhere!" Tilly sighed.

Sam looked down at the floor. "I get car sick..."

"Well, what about our wedding? You will *have* to come to that!"

"Oh, we'll come on the train." Tilly had an answer for everything.

"With Leo, of course?"

"Of course."

Leo wasn't home and wouldn't be back until the following evening, Tilly informed them. He was having psychiatric tests in a clinic near Gloucester. "He's got some sort of personality disorder. Ten pills a day they are giving him." Tilly shrugged her shoulders.

"A private clinic?" Kath enquired.

"Good God, no. We couldn't afford that."

"Couldn't you?" Rob narrowed his eyes, but thought better of mentioning the thousands upon thousands of pounds worth of antiques that they had in the house.

"I hope you are insured for this lot," he went on.

Tilly didn't reply. Ever adept at avoiding difficult situations, she dragged Rob off to the garage to look over her new acquisition, a 1960s shooting-brake. She had written the *Ford Escort* off in a motor accident. The new car wasn't starting properly and she wondered if Robert would take a look at it. "...and then we'll go in your van to fetch some pictures I have just bought from Wells." Her word was law.

Kath was pleased to be left alone with Sam. She made him a cup of tea, careful to make it strong and sweet, the way he liked it. They sat down together at the kitchen table, Peaches was curled up on the next chair.

"Why did you never you finish this one?" Kath asked, looking at a half-painted painting of an angel blowing a trumpet. A watercolour on buff-coloured paper, which Sam had dragged out from his portfolio under the table.

"No time, no time. You see... my father was very ill, I had to leave London. Help my mother. Nobody else would do it. Jo was in the Navy and all that. Nobody else, there wasn't."

"I like this one, Sam," Kath picked up a crayon, pencil and watercolour creation from the file. Sam's face brightened.

"Oh, yes, that's the funfair at Chepstow in 1925. It came twice a year. I used to go to capture the excitement, the movement, the hurley–burley music, the happiness of people escaping from reality."

Sam's own unhappiness was so palpable, Kath wanted to cry, but the tears wouldn't flow. He had been so indifferent to her, scathing that she hadn't studied art, not commenting on Tilly's jibes about her accent, her lower class family... she held back and offered neither kind words nor a comforting arm around his shoulder. "I like your painting in the hall, the one with the ham hanging up and the eggs on the dresser." Kath got up and Sam followed. She needed to get out of the kitchen, it was too intimate, too entrapping; she needed space.

"Ah, my Welsh Dresser," Sam explained. "The last painting I did for the Royal Academy Exhibition in 1953. The last... one." Sam's face hardened. "That was the old dresser in Rose Mansion. That is our pet pig, Susan, hanging up there."

Kath squirmed at the thought of slaughtering a pet pig and eating it.

"And you called your pig, Susan ? Your Auntie's name? How could you, Sam?"

"Aunty Susan actually wasn't very kind, after all. She said she was going to leave me money in her will when she died, just before the war, and I didn't get a penny. Not a farthing." Sam was still sore. "Joan got the lot. Jo's daughter."

"Joan? Isn't that your niece? The one who married the Frenchman and now lives in Calais?"

"Yes, she married the heir to the *Citroen* Empire. Devil, little devil."

Kath was dumbfounded. It was all news to her. *Rob must have known all this and he hadn't mentioned a thing!*

"And, this was the composition I prepared for the 1930 Rome Scholarship, before I decided on entering my big mural. I missed out by one point, only one. Tragic, tragic," he muttered.

"But where is your mural now?" Kath murmured.

"Rolled up in the attic. It's in a bad state. Paint peeling, the damp's got in." Sam had tears in his eyes.

"With the others?" Kath had seen a pile of canvases rolled up, when she had been searching for books at the beginning of her College course.

"Yes, they are all there. *Jason and the Argonauts*, *Saint James Park in the 20s*. *Chepstow Wartime: The Home Front*."

"Can't you get them out, put them up, do something?" Kath pleaded.

"No, not now. No time and all the money is going on this." Sam looked defeated and waved his arm around the room. "Antiques," he finally said. "...and Leo."

"How is Tilly's novel coming along, then?" Kath, said, trying to divert the conversation.

"Marvellous, marvellous. She's a natural. Just whisks it off, just like *that,*" and he mimed handwriting in the air.

"She's not typing it, then?" Kath asked.

"No, no - all by hand. She can't type. She can always get a typist, anytime. Ten a penny, typists." He had got onto his high horse again, as Nelly would have said. "Best seller it's going to be. A top TV comedian, says so."

Kath's eyebrows shot up. "What's a comedian got to do with novels?" Kath was intrigued.

"He's got connections and he says he can get the novel made into a film. He's a friend of Tilly's Literary Agent."

"Well, fingers crossed then," Kath cheered, but felt sidelined that that was the first she'd heard of the good news, and then she said, sardonically "Well, let's hope Elizabeth Taylor and Richard Burton get the lead parts."

Sam, even looked hopeful!

"You were quick," Kath remarked, when Tilly and Rob came back with a van full of artwork.

"Well, two hours," Tilly checked her wristwatch.

Kath was astounded that she had been talking to Sam for so long; time had fled. "Sam has told me about a TV comedian coming here to talk to you, Tilly, about your novel. Isn't it exciting, Rob?"

"Yeh, great stuff, " Robert frowned.

"Well *you* never said! But… we must get off now. We'll get some hot pies on the way."

Tilly didn't argue, she had more things to occupy her time than be entertaining her family with tales of meeting celebrities. "Sam, help Rob to unload the van. He's in a hurry."

"Oh, by the way – I've had my exam results," Kath said to Tilly, as they were waving goodbye and setting off in the van. "Only failed one subject. Guess what that was?"

"English?" Tilly didn't hesitate.

Kath grimaced and shouted in retaliation. "No. Welsh Studies, but that doesn't count. Avery Hill aren't bothered about Welsh Studies!" Kath triumphantly brushed the affront to one side.

-21-

"Oh damn. Forgot to ask Tilly who we should invite to the wedding, from your side that is." Kath slapped her forehead as she and Robert left Beckton.

"And, how many times have you reminded her to give you the list with addresses?" Rob gripped the steering wheel harder and Kath noticed his knuckles go white.

"Well, only a few," she lied. "...she has a lot on her plate, what with Leo... and now Sam going blind."

"Blind?" Rob sat up straight in the driver's seat.

"He's got cataracts and he says he will eventually lose his sight. Such a terrible fate for anybody, let alone an artist."

"Putting it on, I bet. He won't go blind, cataracts can be removed easily. He always was a hypochondriac, that Sam."

Kath sighed. "Anyway, you will have to phone Tilly when we get to Stoke and ask her to send me the list. By the way, do you realise my Mum and Dad haven't met your parents? Don't you think they should, before the wedding, I mean?" Kath waited for an answer.

"Well... I suppose so."

Nelly met the couple at her front door. The pantry was stocked with her daughter's favourite foods: *Cadbury's* chocolates, ox tongue, Cheshire cheese and smoked bacon. Roast lamb, and apple pie with custard were on the menu several times during the next few weeks. Kath complained that she was piling on the pounds. She still had a wedding dress to buy, and wanted it to be a size twelve. Only getting off the pill would solve the weight problem, along with curing her cervical ulcers, the doctor in Stoke had said.

Kath flushed the six-month supply of the dreaded pills down the toilet and calculated she would be rendered infertile for at least a month, including the wedding night.

Rob phoned his mother from the phone box, after being reminded.

Tilly's letter arrived two days later. Written on headed notepaper, marked *THREE WAYS ANTIQUES* - with a sketch of an elegant Victorian oil lamp, which Sam had drawn, in the right hand corner:

"My dearest Robert and Kathleen,

Apart from Gladys, Blodwyn and Tim, whose addresses you clearly know, I think you should invite your Uncle Bill and Elsie, Aunty Edith and your cousins, Barbara Ian and Rosemary. None of them will come of course but presents will be forthcoming. There is Mavis, the other cousin, but I can't remember her address - so we will just have to leave her out!

As for Nelly and Arthur visiting us - well yes of course they must. However, I can't accommodate them here, you will understand. I suppose they could find a cheap B & B nearby.

Best wishes, yours sincerely Tilly and Sam.

"Blodwyn knows Mavis' address," Kath said. "But surely your mother would too? She's always talking about Mavis and Don."

"Bah, Tilly!" Robert was disgusted.

"Still, it'll be two less to feed and water, and don't forget my parents are paying for all this," Kath said. "What do you think Tilly will give us?

"Two ha'porth of nothing, if I know her!"

Kath squirmed, but was more preoccupied with her parents visiting the Llewellyns. Arthur looked forward to the occasion.

"It'll give us a chance to try our new caravan. We ana had time te tell ye yet, but we've just bought a touring caravan. Just for the two of us. It's parked up at work."

Kath squealed with delight, but then asked, "So what's happened to our old one in Llandulas?

"Had to get it off the field. It wasn't modern enough. The new owners of the campsite said it was too much of an eye sore. So, we had to get rid of it quick. Cheeky buggers only gave us a fortnight to shift it. What could we do?"

"Well, what *did* you do, Dad?"

"Let the old farmer take it away. Wanted it for a hen coop. Let it go for a fiver." Arthur let out a sigh.

Kath put her arm round his shoulder and led him to the settee. She shed a tear as the memory of those long summer holidays and endless weekends in North Wales flooded her thoughts. Nelly brought them cups of tea. Arthur said "Dunna you fret over that wench. You'll have worse to deal with one day."

Kath dried her eyes and broke into the Kathleen Ferrier song, *Blow the*

Wind Southerly, then said, "Well, new worlds to conquer, Dad, and Somerset won't be a bad place to start, will it?" Kath stood up and took the empty cups back to the kitchen.

"I'll go and get the caravan now." Arthur said. " Give it a checking over, then you can pack it up, Nelly. We'll be off at the weekend. I'll check in my Caravanning Club book and see where the nearest site is".

"By the way, I'm go to London with Rob this weekend - to buy my wedding dress," Kath told Nelly. "We had better get the invitations out, before we all go away."

Nelly took the stiff white embossed cards off the bookshelf. Kath approved the quality and good taste and duly sat down with her best *Parker* fountain pen to write. She wouldn't trust her mother's or father's handwriting.

After two hours, Kath put down her pen, with a flourish. "There... all done. I'll post them tomorrow," then she turned on the TV and settled down with a mug of *Horlicks* to watch Tommy Cooper. Nelly sat reading a Barbara Cartland novel.

"By the way, halfpennies will be obsolete on July the thirty-first," Kath reminded her mother, as she checked her purse for the coins in question, after listening to the news." You'll be able to change them at a bank though for a few months yet, but better get rid of them now, eh?"

Nelly reminded Kath of the time when she thought she had a counterfeit halfpenny in her change and went to the police station to report it. "You could have only been eight-years-old at the time," Nelly laughed, a belly laugh. It was good to hear her so happy. "...and what did the policeman tell ye? That if anybody was daft enough to spend all that time and effort counterfeiting halfpennies, then bloody good luck to 'em! Counterfeit ten pound notes yes - but halfpennies? It did make the policeman laugh."

"Yes, it's the sort of daft thing you see on Tony Hancock's *Half Hour* or Eric Sykes shows," Arthur said, as he heard them talking when he came in after fetching his tourer.

"Yes, great stuff comedy, isn't it?" Kath mused. "You should have been a comedian, Dad, you're a bloody clown, you and your escapades up and down, gallivanting. Look at how you wear your braces, too!"

"I'll brain ye," Arthur joked, as he held a fist to Kath's face. "Thinks

I'm crackers, do ye? Well, it won't wash with me, but I won't be bellyaching over that." Turning to Nelly, he said, "…the van's champion, Nelly. Dry as a bone." The tourer had been bought second hand from a workmate and now finally had Arthur's approval.

"Had a bit of palaver getting out of the works. It's that sharp bend as you go in, bit of a bugger that." Arthur made himself a cup of tea then picked up the Evening Sentinel. "The weather forecast is good for Saturday, Nelly," he said. Nelly nodded. Turning back to Kath, he continued the conversation, regarding comedians. "He's a comedian - that Larry Trubshaw on the telly."

"But Dad, he's a handyman – a DIY expert!" Kath shook with laughter.

"Well, that's what I bloody mean. Calls himself a craftsman, he does and he can't hold a bloody hammer right. Makes me laugh he does. How they get these bloody jobs, I dunna know. Beats me!"

"It's being in the right place at the right time - and being lucky," Kath offered her wisdom. "Plus, being here in Stoke is not the right place to get lucky. Nobody likes Stoke. Except, Rob, of course. Everybody thinks it's a shithole! I'm glad I am going to London."

"Now dunna you run us lot down. We are the salt of the earth, the workers, the backbone of British Industry. Show some respect, lady!"

"Sorry, Dad, but you know yourself there isn't the opportunity here and I want my kids to have opportunities."

"Jumping the gun again, 'er is. Kids talking about kids already. You'll end up on your…"

"Stop. Just stop. Now, Dad you promised not to say *arse* again to me. Remember?"

Arthur went quiet. "You're right, Kath. Just wish you all the best, girl. I just don't want to see you ending up without a pot to piss in." Arthur turned to Nelly. "We should have got out of Stoke years ago. You wouldn't come to Manchester with me when I had the chance on Metropolitan Vickers after the war," Arthur whined.

"Hey up. It was you who wouldn't go, cause of your ruddy mother!" Nelly counteracted.

"Now, don't go using that word ruddy about my mother. How many times have I told ye Nelly? Jesus bloody Christ!"

"Well, I'm off to bed. You can thrash it out between yourselves," Kath said as she made for the stairs.

Arthur shook his fist in her direction. "You started all this, our Kath. All this talk about comedians and opportunities. Ye al'ays bloody causing trouble."

The weekend in Somerset went well. Arthur and Nelly returned flushed with excitement. They had stayed on a campsite in a field at the back of a pub with a Happy Hour, where cider was on tap, along with a game of bowls with the 'Hoi Polloi' as Tilly had described caravanners.

"None of your gin palace motors there," Arthur beamed, handing Kath a glass of the scrumpy he had brought back. Nelly gave Kath a peacock tail feather she had picked up at the tropical bird garden in Rode.

"But... what about meeting Tilly and Sam?" Kath couldn't wait to get a full report.

"Our Kath, bloody hell, getting involved with them, the likes of them, all bonkers they are. Tilly said that peacock feather would bring you all the bad luck in the world. You would die young and you would never be happy!"

"But, Rob is different - he's normal. You'll see." And then she added, "...but you must admit, they *are* clever. Tilly went on too about how my black jet ring was going to bring me tears. Then she said my black opal engagement ring was evil. Now, it's peacock feathers being a bad omen! I know Rob would tell her what to do with the bloody feather. Stick it up her... well, I won't stoop to your language, Father. You know what I mean!"

Arthur nodded, then Nelly took up the story. Tilly had insisted on collecting them from the campsite in her shooting-brake as there was no room to park near the Old Parsonage.

I bet Tilly wouldn't have wanted the neighbours seeing Arthur's beaten-up old Corsair on her posh antique shop car park! Kath cynically thought.

On the way, Tilly had spotted an old pram in a muddy ditch and insisted that they all go back to the Old Parsonage to collect Sam and his Wellington boots, so he could rescue the thing. *Poor Sam,* Kath thought as she imagined him in his Santa Claus rubber boots, which Tilly boasted she had bought for ten pence in a the Red Cross charity shop.

"...and Tilly said Sam wouldn't travel in a car!" Kath was exasperated.

"Well, he had to," Nelly went on. She described how Sam had waded into the ditch until the mud squelched over the tops of his boots and trickled down into his socks. “Up to his knees in mud,” Nelly laughed. “We thought he was going to go down and down, like he was in quicksand.”

“But did he get the pram?” Kath enquired.

“He did indeed!” Nelly rocked with glee.

“We all had to make a human chain to drag him and the pram up the bank. An old farmhand saw us and joined in, and eventually we got the damn thing loaded up on the roof rack. Made a real mess of Tilly’s car, it did, the mud was trickling down the paintwork and all down the windscreen. Oh, it was funny!” Nelly laughed so much the tears rolled down her cheeks.

Arthur continued the saga. “Well we were right mucked up after that, bloody hell. Stank to high heaven. Tilly shoved us down the shop to swill off in the kitchen sink there. No curtain up at the window, the neighbours getting a full view of Nelly’s bloomers. Oh it was a laugh. Any road, she did put on a good dinner.” Arthur licked his lips, as if savouring that meal.

“And, don’t tell me,” Kath interrupted, “…she gave you roast chicken?”

Arthur nodded. but he was more interested in relating the rest of the events that day. “And when she got on that accordion after the champagne, well what a shindig. She played us *Roses from Picardy* and Maurice Chevalier’s *Little Girls.* Even Sam rolled up his trousers and joined in for *a Knees Up, Mother Brown.”*

“Did you meet Leo?” Kath finally enquired.

“Well, he did put in an appearance.” Arthur said. “Stuck his head round the door when we were having tea. Needs a haircut and a good wash. Poor lad, they’ve spoilt him, they have. No discipline. Should have put him in the Army, that would’ve cured him. You should have heard Sam screech when I said that! Never heard a man’s voice so high-pitched before! I thought he was going to belt me! Ooh, our Kath, what are you bloody letting yourself in for? They’re all as mad as hatters and there’s no love in that family.”

Silence followed, so they all went to bed.

In Greenwich, London, Kath found her perfect Empire Line, lace wedding dress, with a Maid Marion style hood. Rob bought his new suit without too much fuss either; an off the peg Beatles-style, black outfit, with a long jacket, high collar and velvet lapels.

Rob stayed on in London looking for a flat, while Kath returned to Stoke by train. Kath took the family to Shrewsbury to see the Flower Show, in Arthur's *Corsair*.

Matthew and Kerry had a double christening later that month for thirty people at the Sneyd Hotel in Tunstall, after church. Nelly commented about how good the spread was, "Ham rolls with plenty of ham on 'em, sherry trifle with real sherry and none of this artificial flavouring," she said. "Hope it's as good for your wedding," Nelly looked at Kath.

Kath smiled as she thought of her wedding, but first she would attend Jeannie's.

The event was a low-key affair at the Registry office in Frome. Female guests were instructed specifically not to wear a hat, and that was just as well, as they were in the middle of a heatwave. The reception, for twenty, was held at the Old Parsonage. Kath had offered to help with the catering and would go to Somerset a couple of days early, if needs be. But as Tilly said her services would not be required, Rob collected her from the Bath railway station the day before the ceremony. She nearly missed the stop! She had been so engrossed reading *The People* newspaper story about the Sharon Tate murder. Heavy drug use had been involved. Kath wondered about Jeannie's strange habits... Leo's problems might have come from drug use too...

She broached the subject with Rob in the van on their way to Beckton, but he only said, "...so be it if that is true. I can't worry about that now. After three weeks without you I just want to love you!" Kath gave him a peck on the cheek.

Jeannie and Martin had been allocated the *Isaac Williams* room and somehow Tim, Blodwyn and Gladys had been squeezed into the attic. Robert and Kath were to sleep in the room over the shop. Kath was relieved she was not to be under the same roof as the rest of the family. She was having migraines again.

"You are overdoing things," Arthur had warned her, thumping the '30's oak veneered dining table in their cramped kitchen, before she left with Billy, in his car, to catch the train to Somerset. "Too much on ye bloody plate lass. Ye'll be the death of us, our Kath."

Kath didn't mention Arthur's outburst or her headaches to Rob as they lay on the double bed underneath the window, where the afternoon sun shone through the white crocheted curtains, Tilly had put up since their last visit. A large, Turkish rug lay over the bare floorboards and there was a colourful bedspread to match. Kath appreciated the thoughtful touch.

Jeannie didn't arrive at the Old Parsonage until after 6pm, when Martin dropped her off on his way to Chepstow. Kath and Robert were in the living room of the old house, by then.

"We've put your present and card with the others in the dining room," Kath said. " It's a Doulton figure, and, by the way, I have left your bridesmaid's dress, for our wedding, wrapped up on the table by the front door, you can pick it up when you leave. Let me know if it fits okay, won't you?"

"Okay," Jeannie turned to speak with Blodwyn, while Gladys arranged flowers around the house. Blodwyn's laugh was just like Tilly's, a cackle, with a sting like acid. Jeannie had been this auntie's darling of the family, staying with her as a schoolgirl every school holiday, while Rob was at his Nana's and Leo stayed at home.

"Did you ever meet up with Rob at your grandmother's when you were at Blodwyn's?" Kath asked Jeannie.

"No, never, Nana didn't like me and, besides, Rob was always working. Either gardening, painting walls for her, or delivering bread on the vans with Bill up the Valleys. Nana was a slave-driver!"

Startled at Jeannie's bitter tone, Kath's conversation shifted to the current heat wave.

On her wedding day, Jeannie looked pretty in her fashionable, cream silk dress. The mini-length dress, with a scooped neckline and long, puffy sleeves, was gathered at the waist. It accentuated her tiny waistline and pendulous breasts. With her long, blonde streaked straight hair hanging freely over her shoulders and down her back, she epitomised the decade: the Zeitgeist of the Sixties, the individuality, the unconventional, the emerging modern woman and sexual liberation.

Martin, by contrast, appeared the archetypical, middle-class '50's male. He sported short back and sides, Brylcreemed hair and a flannel suit with turn-ups. Still, they seemed a happy couple. He kissed his new wife gently on the cheek after the solemn oaths of the marriage ritual and gave her a small pinch on the bottom. She reciprocated with a kiss on his forehead.

The afternoon reception, in the *Catherine of Aragon Room*, at the Old Parsonage, spilled into the garden as the temperatures soared. Kath was amused that Blodwyn still wore her hat: a yellow, a woolly affair with a red flower on top. Having also donned dark-rimmed, cat's eye glasses and glossy lipstick, she looked like Barry Humphries as his Dame Edna persona - but Kath kept her thoughts to herself.

With the guests in two main camps, strictly *his and hers,* Kath flitted from one group to another to escape from trivial conversations, like the price of butter going up, and having to defend her Potteries accent. She overheard Blodwyn saying how much she dreaded going up North to Rob's wedding and having to stay overnight in a ghastly hotel in the city. Even benign Gladys admitted to never having been up North before and Martin's parents said Birmingham was far enough for them.

Kath tried telling Tilly about her recent visit to Shugbourough Hall, as they all sat nibbling the food, but she was brushed aside with orders to hurry Sam along, with, more bottles of wine, from the cellar. Kath observed it was he and Gladys doing all the to-ing and fro-ing, upstairs and downstairs. As Sam came in with a tray, still wearing his purple velvet dickey bow he had worn at the Registry, rosy-cheeked Gladys went out with one, just like a pair of Austrian carved wooden figurines in and out of an alpine barometer. Kath gorged herself on smoked salmon, which she had never tasted before, filo pastry vol-au-vents with French mushroom fillings, canapés, *fois de gras* delicacies and quails eggs. But when she got tipsy, and said the Asti spumante was like Babycham, she received looks of disapproval, and slunk off for a country walk. Kath only got back in time to wave the couple good luck on their departure and a honeymoon in Tenerife.

Kath was a little envious of Jeannie's travelling. Neither she nor Rob had been on a plane.

With the newly married couple and the grooms' guests gone, Kath found herself clearing up in the kitchen again with Gladys. Tilly was holding court with Blodwyn, Tim, Rob and Leo. It was only when Kath was passing through the hall with a tray of drinks, for the 'court', that she noticed Jeannie hadn't taken her bridesmaid's dress!

“Jeannie’s forgotten her bridesmaid’s dress,” Kath said as she set down the tray on the dumbwaiter in the drawing room.

“Got more on her mind tonight than being your bridesmaid,” quipped Tilly with a salacious look in her eye. “Mind you, you wouldn’t think he had it in him, that Martin. Skinny as a rake, no go in him,” and she tightened her fist and pulled her forearm up towards her chin in the unmistakable gesture of meaning fornication. Kath blushed as the rest of the company collapsed in alcoholic-induced laughter. Kath scowled at Rob.

“You’ll have to post it on to Jeannie,” Tilly resumed the topic of the dress.

“It’s a Maid of Honour dress, not a bridesmaids’,” and that concluded the matter.

Kath swallowed her indignation and joined Gladys and Sam in the kitchen. Gladys didn’t think Jeannie forgetting to take the parcel was a problem either. After all, Kath could send on. Jeannie was a busy lady, she had a house to run and a new job; teaching art in a private junior school. She was due to start after the week’s honeymoon.

Sam returned to his favourite subject, the war, “…we couldn’t afford honeymoons when Tilly and I got married. War was looming. Three days after our wedding, Hitler invaded Poland.” Kath consoled herself that her hardships were nothing compared to those days, ‘the olden days’, as her parents naively referred to anything to do with the past.

“But… you had a white wedding,” Kath went on, to Sam. “I saw your wedding photograph. Tilly with a lovely big bouquet of white roses, she looked beautiful. Just like Jeannie today. Well, apart from the hair. Tilly had hers scraped back then, just like she does now.”

“Oh yes, but that was a long time ago,” Sam said.

“You were rather handsome too, about the same height as each other, weren’t you then?” Kath was curious, noticing now how much shorter than Tilly, Sam was.

“No…” Sam explained. “Tilly was two inches taller than me. Back then, I wore Cuban heels. It didn’t do for small men to be marrying big women in those days.”

Kath smiled to herself as she recalled the many holiday postcards her parents had sent, and received, depicting scrawny little men in predicaments - with big-breasted, fat-bellied wives.

“By the way, Sam. What happened with the old pram you got from the ditch with my mum and dad, that day?" Kath asked.

"I nearly drowned in that ditch," he said. "I can't swim, you follow. Up to my chest in water, I was, pullin' and shoving, good lord, never seen anything like it. Good job the farmer came. I would never have got out alive."

Kath sniggered. "But what happened to the pram?"

"Oh, no good, too far gone you see, rotten inside and out, and too modern for Tilly anyway. She's after the *real* old ones, with wooden wheels. I don't know anything about prams. I just draw 'em. I draw what she wants. Good God, I'm up till all hours drawing for her. " With that, he disappeared in a flash, only to return again with a folder full of sketches.

"This is me, a self-portrait I did when I was twenty and at the Royal College, and me again in my soldiers' uniform in 1941, just as I was called up." Sam beamed when Kath said she found him good-looking, then he turned to a different sketch. "...and this is my cousin, Joan." Kath admired the way he had painted the white daisies in the detail on the dress.

"The one who inherited all your Aunt Susan's money?", Kath remembered.

Sam grimaced, but carried on. "...and this is Gladys in '39, sitting in Tilly's mother's front room."

Kath remarked on the Spanish, flamenco-like black leather shoes, which had been the height of fashion at the time; the likes of which her grandmother had also worn in the Thirties.

Kath's conversation with Sam was short-lived, as Leo barged into the kitchen. "That pukey spumante has gone to my head," he said as he grabbed a glass from the draining board. "Look at this bloody filth," he went on as he examined the glass. "Lipstick still on the damned rim! Who's been washing the dishes?" He accusingly eyed first Sam, then Kath. "Come on, own up, you two, who was it?"

"Now, come off it, Leo," Kath dared to challenge him. "If you were so concerned about dirty dishes, then why don't you wash some yourself? I've never seen you lift a finger in this house. Lazy, you are, just plain lazy."

Sam annoyingly wagged a finger at Kath and pleaded with her to stop attacking Leo. "He's ill, the poor boy is ill."

Kath was nonplussed and angry that Sam could so blatantly accept such appallingly bad behaviour from his son, even if he was ill. "No wonder he treats you like dirt, Sam. If you let him get away with it, he will."

Sam scuttled away and took his drawings with him.

"Leo, you are a lout," Kath shouted, as he gulped his water from another glass and she slammed the kitchen door.

"What's that banging?" Tilly shouted from her 'throne' in the sitting room.

"Nothing much," Kath tried to make light of the incident.

"She's badmouthing again," Leo shouted over Kath's shoulder, "...and Sam's had enough, he's gone to bed."

Kath felt choked and misunderstood. "It's not true," Kath wailed. Rob jumped up, took Kath by the arm, told everyone he thought she was drunk and guided her out of the room and off to their bedroom over the shop.

Kath tried to explain about the dirty glass and the ensuing spat, but Rob didn't want to know.

The next morning, desperate to be with her own kind again after the trauma of the weekend, Kath begged Rob to take her back to Stoke. She picked up the bridesmaid's dress, thanked Tilly and waved goodbye.

Kath sat dourly in the van as they headed up the A-roads towards the Midlands. She was beginning to doubt if she really wanted to marry Rob. Arthur's words, *they are all bonkers* bounced around in her thoughts. The trickery Leo had played on her, all this talk about the black North and her being unpolished – her 'lack of breeding', *her lack of taste*, as Tilly had stated, when she'd said she liked tripe better than truffles and would like a modern bungalow better than a Victorian town house.

"That's it, the wedding is off. London is off, Avery Hill is off, you're off and that's it. We're finished," Kath blurted out. Rob didn't flinch. He said nothing, but calmly pulled into the next lay-by and turned the ignition off.

"Now... you don't mean that. I know you don't. It's just that you are tired and stressed, overworked."

It was true. Kath still had a week of work left on the play centres before the kids went back to school; she still had to chase up non-payment of work done since June and she still had to fill out forms for her grant. In addition, she had to visit relatives and see friends. "And... being on, then off the pill, it makes you irrational; you're worried about getting caught. It's only natural."

Rob was right to a point, but not about being irrational. Kath felt perfectly rational and right about telling Leo off and about being angry that his father was such a sop.

Rob was so calm and cool about her feelings, so patronising and so laid back, it rankled. "You are too boring for me, Rob. You won't stand up for yourself; you let people walk all over you! Look how your Landlady bosses you around! Plus, I remember how you didn't stand up for me that day the waiter insulted me in that pub by the *Cutty Sark,* when we only ordered pork pies!"

Rob looked blank and said he couldn't remember anything about pork pies and waiters. "There you are," Kath yelled. "And a bloody bad memory!"

"But, it's pointless remembering things like that. Insults are not worth thinking about, it's best to forget them. You're too sensitive, you've got a chip on your–"

"Stop, just stop," Kath butted in. "You are cold, just like the rest of your bloody lot. No, it won't work, you and me, no, no, no." Kath broke down into hysterical crying and got out of the van. Before she knew what she was doing, she was striding along the grass verge, away from him. Rob ran to catch her up. He grabbed her by the arm, but she shrugged him off.

"There! I hate you. That's what I think of you and your lot! I just don't want any of you, do you hear? Let me go, leave me alone, I hate you! You can stuff the wedding, stuff your bedsit, stuff the bloody lot! Go to hell, all of you. Go f... yourself, shove it, do you understand? We're finished." Kath's screams disappeared into the roar of the passing traffic. No one heard her heart tearing to shreds as she contemplated throwing herself under a passing lorry. Rob took hold of her firmly, both arms encircling her torso, like never before. He began to cry himself. He shook her, first harshly, then more gently. "No, you don't mean that. You can't mean it. You know how much I love you and you love me. You can't leave me. I won't let you. I would die without you."

He kissed Kath so passionately and ran his hands all over her body, that she believed him and she let herself surrender. Weak at the knees and trembling all over, Rob led her back to the van.

Kath felt ashamed that she had even dared to think about calling off the wedding, so much down the drain, so much disappointment and passing up such a good man as Rob.

No, he was her rock, her mainstay, her everything.

She did love him.

-22-

Mothers' instinctively know when their own are in pain and Nelly was no exception. "You've been crying." Nelly said, as Kath stepped through the front door at 92. "I've made your bed up." Nelly hugged her daughter." Go and get a good night's sleep in now before you completely burn yourself out, girl."

Nelly turned to Rob as she ushered him in. "...and yours is made up as well, in the back room, as usual. But perhaps you'd better go and have a pint with Arthur up at the *Cheshire Cheese* before you turn in. He wants a word with you, before you get off in the morning." Rob was concerned that Arthur needed 'a word' with him and even more taken aback that he was expected to leave in the morning: he wasn't due back at school for another week. He had planned on staying in Stoke for a few days. Still, Rob didn't argue.

Arthur told Rob how troubled they were over Kath. Although they trusted him, they felt he was putting a lot of pressure on Kath, insisting on her having to go to London. The problem of getting a new flat was upsetting Kath; Rob had to promise solemnly to find a suitable one before the wedding. Robert said he would. He drove to London the next day, after picking up a vanload of Blue Band Pottery, from *Staffordshire Potteries.*

The sun was out, Kath was home. She posted the dress to Jeannie. There were just three weeks left before the wedding; if it didn't fit, then there would still be time for adjustment.

"Colonel Gaddafi has just headed a coup and ousted King Idris in

Libya." Arthur read out aloud from his newspaper, after breakfast. "Blood thirsty lot, them Arabs."

Kath didn't answer, she was listening to Van Morrison's, *Brown Eyed Girl*, which Rob had dedicated to her.

The wedding invitation acceptances arrived steadily. Kath filled her days with friends: Marion was working, but she took a few days off work so they could go Trentham Gardens, Hanley Park and shopping in Manchester; where Kath bought a chestnut-coloured ringlet hair piece for her big day. She spent the nights at home with Nelly and together they entertained visitors who brought nuptial gifts. Other times, they watched TV, Kath's favourites were: *Stanley Baxter, Morecombe and Wise and Top of the Pops.*

Arthur spent his evenings in his parlour, listening to his music: Alma Cogan's *Never do a Tango with an Eskimo,* Perry Como's *Some Enchanted Evening,* Doris Day's *Sugar Bush* and Eddie Fisher's *Lady of Spain.*

Kath eventually sorted out her bedroom and boxed up some keepsakes for storage in the cockloft, for the time when she and Rob would have their own house. She reluctantly had given up on trying to achieve the Gold standard of the *Duke of Edinburgh's Award.* She reconciled herself that marriage would be enough. Piles of folders and paper went into the bin; bags of clothes, books and knickknacks were stacked up by the front door, ready for the Scout Group jumble sale. After eighteen years in that house, she had only one box of possessions left. D. of E. and swimming Certificates, sports medals, school reports, letters from old boyfriends and pen friends, postcards and photographs. There were also two miniature Doulton china pottery figures, *Pearly Boy and Pearly Girl*, which her maternal Grandma had bequeathed to her some three years before, and a wooden music box, in the form of a miniature grand piano, which Arthur had made for her seventh birthday.

Even the red trunk Kath had so cherished in Barry, had been sold off. Kath felt poor - and old. The past two years had been manic. Girls she had been at school with in her 'O' Level year had now only just finished their 'A' Levels and were still wearing white ankle socks. Kath felt bereft. 'Always out of step,' as Arthur was fond of saying. He was right!

Still, Rob wrote every day and Kath wrote back, mainly with a list of things he had to do before the wedding. Jeannie hadn't acknowledged delivery of her dress, so Kath asked Robert to phone his sister and check. Also, could he make sure that his art college friend would take the wedding photographs. It had been Rob's suggestion to call on Chas, who had three new cameras. Would Rob also collect the buttonhole carnations from Covent Garden the day before the wedding, on his way up to Stoke.

Kath didn't dare tell Arthur about Rob not securing a new flat. He only learned that on the day before the wedding, from Tilly, when he had to ferry her and Sam to the hotel from Stoke Station. Arthur muttered on about Rob's failure to provide a decent home for his new wife to Blodwyn, Tim and Gladys too - when he collected them later from Crewe. He then let the matter drop, for Kath's sake !

True to wedding tradition, and oblivious to her father's concern, Kath wore something old: her mother's gold stud earrings. Something new: shoes. Something borrowed: Nelly's eternity ring strung round her neck on a gold chain, tucked away behind the high neckline of her modest dress. Something blue... her knickers! Her perfectly matched ringlet hairpiece had been pinned in at the hairdressers that morning, but Kath had put on her own make-up. She had perfected the art of the Sixties fashion of painting eyeliner right around the rims of the eyelids.

Squeezing past wedding presents assembled in the parlour, she stepped out of the front door into a sunny day and the waiting wedding car, feeling like a nervous kitten but, she took her courage in both hands, determined to march down the aisle on Arthur's arm, looking the picture of happiness.

Well-wishers gathered outside the church, and she blew kisses as she got out of the car. Kath felt humbled. She hadn't invited some of the people in the crowd, like Mrs Parsons, her cold-hearted childminder. She shuddered even now at the sight of her.

Boys she had been at primary school with and whose ears she had boxed, gave her the thumbs-up. The vicar's wife commented on how lovely she looked.

The guests were in the pews, fifty-nine on the bride's side and eleven on the groom's, as Kath strode down the aisle to the strains of Mendelssohn's Wedding March.

Jeannie looked stunning, her dress fitted perfectly, as she trailed Kath and Arthur with the two little bridesmaids, in pink, beside her.

Blodwyn, sporting the same squashy hat as she had worn to Jeannie's wedding three weeks before, sat in the front pew next to Keith, the best man.

Tilly and Sam were on the row behind. Leo, Alun, Silvia and Jill sat three rows back. Wearing an enormous, white, wide-brimmed hat and a fur stole, Tilly stood out from the crowd. Sam, in his best Sunday suit, minus his trilby, and with a recent haircut, appeared as ever the obedient consort, but Kath noticed none of the men were wearing carnation buttonholes! Rob obviously hadn't been to Covent Garden !

The ceremony was short and to the point, at Kath's request. She was only having a white church wedding to please her mother. Nelly had bemoaned the fact that she herself had got married in a mustard-coloured wool suit and only had one flower, a white carnation, which had looked lost amongst the bouquet of feathery fern leaves. It had been wartime then. Kath kept her parents wedding photo in her handbag and, one carnation or not, her parents had looked happy.

Kath wanted to make Nelly happy again and was taken aback, when, on leaving the church, she found Chas standing on the steps, fiddling with his cameras and cursing that none of them worked! Kath yanked Rob's arm, alerted him to the situation, and shrieked, "Oh my God!"

She was a stickler for duties and promises not to be broken. She had been a Girl Guide and her brother, Billy, a Scout, like nearly everyone she knew. *To do one's duty to God and the Queen,* was engraved on their pottery workers' souls. She shouted at Chas, but his response was drowned out as the guests stampeded out of the church like a herd of bison. Kath tripped and lost a shoe. When she bent down to rescue the slipper, somebody's elbow knocked her head and her curly hairpiece went askew. Luckily, Rob stopped it from falling to the floor and managed to clip it back into place. In the mêlée, no one seemed to notice.

Chas, having got a camera fixed, clicked away aimlessly, taking photos of the rabble, until Kath, having resumed composure, summoned order and said she thought it was about time Chas told people where to stand. Childlike, he confessed he had never taken photographs at a wedding before – so Kath found herself orchestrating.

"First Rob and me," she tugged Rob's arm and shooed the other people away from the church steps. Next, she shut the two heavy church doors and ordered clueless Chas to shoot her alone. Then, Kath shouted for the two sets of parents and bridesmaids to step forward, but Jeannie had lost her little charges: in the hullabaloo, they had taken fright and disappeared into their mother's arms, sobbing.

"Press on," barked Kath, scowling at Rob for not taking charge himself. He shrugged, told Kath she was doing a fine job and to carry on. Tilly looked smug, stood back and smiled as required. Sam smiled too, but it was a blessing when the last confetti was used up and the vicar appeared, ready for the next ceremony.

Kath ordered a double gin and tonic before the guests arrived at the reception, trusting her nerves would then settle. The bar was on the house. She ordered another. Poor Arthur, he was footing the bill again!

Tipsy, on an empty stomach, she wobbled as the guests arrived, then there were more drinks.

With Arthur's choice of music playing, Kath flitted from one table to another, thanking everyone for their presents. Kath was well aware that presents hadn't been forthcoming from Rob's aunties and uncles who had been invited, but who declined to attend and neither had Tilly given the couple a wedding present, yet. Kath avoided their table and was relieved to sit down, when Arthur announced it was time for the games.

Teams of willing contestants ran up and down with sausage-shaped balloons between their legs, and passed oranges tucked under their chins, along a line of alternate men and women. Pass the parcel, which one of the seven-year-old bridesmaids won, caused a scene when she held up her prize, a giant sized pair of men's underpants with *A Present for Willy* emblazoned across the bottom; she went screaming into her mother's arms for comfort.

Musical chairs ended in a fight when Billy and cousin Danny both claimed the empty chair. Arthur intervened and saved further bloodshed when he disqualified both contestants - and triumphantly carried on with the game.

Tilly looked on disapprovingly, she left half the ham and Branston pickle sandwich she had put on her plate, along with half a sausage roll, but Sam was doing his best to entertain the guests with his wartime stories. He had previously been seen dancing about like a champion fencer, then took to prancing about like Charles Hawtrey wielding a bayonet, in *Carry On Up the Khyber*.

Kath's inclination to order another gin was overwhelming; she left the reception quite drunk.

Luckily, the couple were not going far that evening, and they were travelling light. A change of clothes, ablutions bag and an enormous packet of condoms - a present from Billy and Pauline - compliments of the *Michelin* tyre company! "We'll have to share these with Jeannie," quipped Kath. "Twenty dozen, we'll never get through that lot!"

Rob only grinned wolfishly, and said, "Want to bet?"

They were going to stay one night in the *Post House Hotel*, in Newcastle, just five miles from Tunstall. Rob was in charge now and resigned himself to his wife's dishevelled state. When Kath threw up in the ensuite, Rob promptly put on the TV and stuffed the condoms back in his suitcase.

Rob woke Kath the next morning with the news that he had a big surprise in store for her, when they got to Blackheath.

"A new flat? "Kath questioned, but Rob wouldn't let on.

Kath's spirits sank as they entered the Greater London Zone and the traffic gathered momentum. She hadn't found the city very welcoming as a visitor, so how would she find it as a resident? Facing Elaine, Rob's' landlady, again everyday was going to be worse than the severe pain she had experienced in her jaws for weeks on end, before having her wisdom teeth out.

At midday, the old van screeched to a halt outside the house where Robert's flat was and Kath prayed the surprise would be a new flat, but, as Robert stopped in the forecourt, he said: "This for you." Then he whipped off the tarpaulin from a shiny red motor scooter. "It will be cheaper than bus fares!"

Kath didn't know whether to laugh or cry. She had just two days to adjust to married life in the bedsit before College started !

The trendy, *Triumph Tina*, although second hand, looked brand new and it was true using this would save her at least an hour in travel time. She laughed at the number plate MOO 1 but took to riding the machine like a duck to water. Rob showed her the best route to College through the back streets. When not in use, she was to cover it up and park it in the forecourt. Elaine had approved of her living there, but only after hiking the rent to a massive five pounds per week.

Kath had her instructions and some modicum of independence. Her first task was to stock up with food, the second was to look for a better flat and the third was to get ready for the new term. Her tools of the trade filled the little room; hockey stick and boots, tracksuit, trainers and books.

However, Kath's first day at the new College was a disaster. She had arrived late, after failing to kick-start the scooter in the morning and had had to take the bus. Rob had long gone to work.

She entered the anatomy classroom, twenty minutes into the lesson, where eighteen PE girls sat, in silence, scribbling answers to a test set on work covered in the first year. Next, she was ushered to an empty desk at the back of the room. No one noticed how flummoxed she was. It was all double Dutch to her, she hadn't learned all this stuff and she wished she could just disappear. She wrote her name on the paper, attempted about a quarter of the questions, wrote an apology and explanation to the teacher for her obvious lack of knowledge and sighed with relief when finally the group were told to put their pens down and hand in the papers. Kath was the last to leave the room; the teacher taking no notice of her, as she followed her new "friends" to the cafeteria. The girls soon dispersed into the crowds and Kath found herself alone, sipping an orange juice, until a tall, blonde woman struck up a conversation and sat down. Pat had been a nurse but didn't like shifts and so she had decided to become a teacher. The twenty-six-year-old was engaged to a farmer and teaching would fit in with their plans for a large family, she explained. Too bad she wasn't in any of Kath's classes. She was on the English course for secondary school teachers - but at least they might be able to meet up for chats at break times. *Any port in a storm*, thought Kath.

Pat was the epitome of good breeding. She had been privately educated, had a smart sense of humour, and she had been a champion swimmer who had represented Hampshire in the backstroke. Kath, in turn, told her about her recent marriage and strange in-laws. She hoped they would stay friends.

Over the coming weeks, only the break times with Pat sustained Kath's will to live. The PE girls were a clique. They had their loyalties and set partners for gym, for dance - for everything. Kath was the odd number and, when partner work was required, she either had to make do in a group of three - wherever the lecturer chose to place her - or had to partner up with the lecturer. It was messy and Kath was punished for it. Being married didn't help either. Most of the girls were on the Feminist bandwagon and thought Kath an imbecile for marrying in the first place. They were burning bras and reading Germaine Greer's, *The Female Eunuch*. The personal had become the political. Men were sapping women's energy, *oh the villainy of men,* the PE girls said.

Kath was too busy trying to be the good wife and making money, to be worrying about male oppression. After all, they were saving up to buy a house.

The girls' gave her a wide birth and, in turn, she left them to wear the purple and green boiler suits - the colours of which had been adopted from the early twentieth Century suffragettes. Gender aggression and sisterhood cartels were not for Kath. She didn't think it right that married women with children should leave their husbands to find fulfilment. It hadn't happened in Wales; her colleagues there all had boyfriends and were planning white weddings. But, this was London and the new wave of Feminism had taken root.

Kath's frustration at not being able to kick-start her scooter at will was beginning to show. Having to call Rob out to collect her from wherever she was, or having to get the bus home, was wearing. Also, the situation with their landlady was getting worse. One day, just before the October half-term, Kath had a row with Elaine, who had denied stealing the scooter cover. She was also forbidding Kath to take out their household rubbish through the kitchen to the backyard, like Rob had done previously. Kath was expected to walk around the block, some two-hundred yards there and back, in the cold. This was unacceptable.

Rob begged her to comply with Elaine's orders, as it wouldn't be long before they found another flat. Kath then turned on Rob, accusing him of not doing enough to get them out of the dump, but she calmed down when Rob said he had bought her a car. He had traded the troublesome MOO 1 in for an Austin A35 and it was taxed and insured - all ready to go. Kath drove to Stoke, while Rob stayed in London, with orders to secure a flat.

The little grey car did the journey in less than three hours and Kath prided herself on having picked up two hitchhikers, who were told they must contribute towards the petrol. She arrived at Number 92 with money in her pocket and a less heavy heart. She made light of her difficulties with her studies, the lack of new friends and the awful situation with Elaine. She felt better when Aunty May, who knew about these things, told her to report Elaine to the local council's harassment officer.

It was good to be home. Nelly's earthy smell - baking clay - imbued her very being and complemented Arthur's scent of fresh wood shavings and sawdust. Theirs was a clean, wholesome house. Since Kath's departure the year before, Kath had watched her parents growing closeness with joy. Holidays in the new touring caravan: Scotland, Wales, Norfolk, Cornwall – all corners of the Kingdom – had put colour in their cheeks and broadened their outlook. Kath spent a night with them that weekend on a camping site near Consall Forge, bordering on the Moorlands, from where they visited Caverswall. This village was famous for the burning of a local witch called Agnes, who, at the time of the Black Death in 1349, was burned at the stake for failing to stop the plague. Kath thought Tilly would find this place interesting, but Kath hadn't heard from Rob's mother or sister since the wedding. Rob hadn't found this particularly disturbing, but Kath did, and insisted they go to the Old Parsonage on the next weekend.

Tilly requested that Rob take his van; she had plans for him. He was to collect a grandfather clock from an auction room in Bath, and deliver two prams and a doll to a manor house near the *Cheddar Gorge*. Robert didn't mind. Whilst in Cheddar he would take the opportunity to make enquiries at the motor museum there about housing his AJS vintage racing motorbike. He had restored it and it was now languishing in a storeroom at his school. It was worth quite a few hundred pounds, Rob informed Kath. He baulked when Kath said he ought to sell it, so they could get money towards their house purchase. No, Kath wasn't allowed to interfere with his motorbike. They would get their house one day, and a place for the bike, Rob said.

Kath's and Rob's arrival in Beckton, early on the Saturday morning, found Sam consulting Mr Middleton's 1947 revered publication, *All the Year Gardening*.

Kath left wine and *Tom Thumb* cigars, on the hall table and Robert made tea, before Sam declared it was time to prune the gooseberry bushes and dig manure into the now fallow vegetable plot. Kath joined him. After the arduous journey up the A40, she needed fresh air. They stood enchanted, watching two robins chirruping, flapping their wings and flashing their red breasts at each other in defence of their territories.

Tilly was upstairs getting made up. Since becoming a reputable dealer, Rob's mother had taken to having her hair dyed strawberry blonde, more regularly, so there were no more black roots. She also powdered her face, giving herself the tanned look - and wore bright red lipstick.

She descended the stairs in good humour as she helped herself to tea, then sat with Rob. Kath caught them laughing as she came in from the garden. Tilly had lost weight since their last meeting and now she was excited about having acquired a set of first edition Beatrix Potter books, the most valuable one being the *Tale of Peter Rabbit,* dated 1902. She said that they were in pristine condition and most surely she could sell them on at a good profit. "Best to put them in Sotheby's," Rob advised, but Tilly wasn't so sure. She had tried putting other things with the big auction house but they were 'sniffy'; it wasn't easy to meet their standard. She didn't trust them either; she related stories of dealer friends having put clocks up for auction there in good working order, only to be told at the point of sale that, the pendulum was missing or a hinge had come loose because of a missing screw, and that the item therefore was not going to reach it potential price. All too often the seller was faced with either withdrawing the item and incurring carriage expenses or leaving the item where it was and meekly accepting the lower price, knocked down to someone in the know, who would have a suitable pendulum or odd screw to make the clock as right as rain again.

"Bloody scams," Leo appeared at the door. "Bloody rogues, the lot of 'em." I wouldn't trust any of 'em. Dirty dogs they are."

Kath admitted to no knowledge of the auction scene, after all she had nothing to sell and no money to buy anything, but nonetheless hoped that would change one day. "We're saving for a house," she told the present company.

"Yes, we know. How many more times do you have to say that? You're like a bloody gramophone needle got stuck, *buy a house, buy a house, buy a house*," Leo mimicked.

Kath bit her lip, picked Peaches up and forced herself to ask Leo how he was getting on in the art school in Yeovil. "None of your business, and if I told you, you wouldn't understand."

Kath looked for support, but Rob had gone to the toilet, Tilly had gone back upstairs and Sam, who was just about to come into the kitchen, double-tracked and went back to his digging. Kath's migraine kicked in again, as she followed Sam into the garden.

"Perhaps Leo's a queer?" Kath approached Sam as he started to harvest some potatoes. "He can't accept it, that's what's getting to him? It wouldn't bother me of course, it's legal now, in this the modern age, the age of liberation." Kath began to sound like the Feminists she was at odds with in her college.

"Well I'll be damned," Sam was aghast. He stood agape. "No, no, you've got it all wrong, you see, it's not that at all." His fingers were stretched out in front of him, like a pianist about to play the piano, but then his hands shook. "No, the boy's a genius," his arms began to flap, "He doesn't think like you. Remember *Van Gough*?"

Kath was not impressed.

"You'll see one day, you will..."

Kath felt her weekend was already ruined. Leo was no more than a sad soul who needed love and understanding. He was of high intelligence, no doubt, but to be dubbed a genius, that was insane. What had he done to prove himself? A handful of mediocre paintings and sketches, a few passable photographs. It was all beyond comprehension.

Her Rob was the genius, the epitome of grace, with good manners and a talent for engineering.

Kath's mind was taken off the *silly situation*, as she referred to the family's unpleasantness, by the arrival of Douglas Brady, the Australian chancer who had won Tilly over so much, she had parted with some of Sam's sketches for a pittance.

"I've come to try out your new *Aston Martin*," Douglas told Leo, who had bought the car from a friend of this charismatic car magazine editor.

"*Aston Martin*?" Rob sounded incredulous.

"Yep." Leo was nonchalant. "All mine. Leather seats, does a hundred-and-fifty miles an hour. Trade's good in antique clocks!" and he smirked right into Rob's face.

Kath only sighed and patted Rob on the back, resigning herself to such injustice.

"How on earth can he afford such a car?" Rob couldn't help but question his mother.

"Trade's good, like he said," she echoed, Leo.

After Rob, Leo and Douglas roared off in the new car, Kath looked around the shop and the house." I like this table." She pointed to a round, Regency walnut-veneered breakfast table. It had a carved tripod leg on brass casters and a one-hundred-pound price tag.

"It will be sold before you get somewhere to put it," Tilly smirked.

"I'm telling you now, so you know what kind of things we like," Kath pulled her shoulders back and looked her mother-in-law in the eye.

"Well, just don't count your chickens," Tilly turned, leaving Kath wondering just what she meant.

"Don't count your chickens, indeed!" Kath's mouth felt sour. She wondered if Tilly was thinking that she and Rob would never be able to buy their own house, would always have to rent, and might even not stay married that long? Kath was not happy.

Rob returned from a test drive with Leo and Douglas, convinced that Leo had overpaid for the car. "The engine is rough and the gear box is grinding." Rob knew his engines.

Leo scoffed. "That's just sour grapes," he said, and went off to his bedroom.

"He sleeps a lot," noted Kath, but Tilly didn't answer.

That night, Kath went to bed early, leaving Rob with Tilly.

Later on, Kath was still awake, reading *The Secret Garden,* when Rob got into bed with her. Tilly had confided in him that she hadn't heard from Jeannie since seeing her in Stoke in September. Her excuse for not visiting during that half-term had been that there was too much work to do in their garden. Tilly had concerns though about Martin and his "extracurricular activities." Was he having an affair, Tilly wondered, but then said if he was, it would probably be with a man! Kath hoped all this wasn't true, even though she had heard with her own ears, that night in Oxfordshire in Jeannie's cottage, when Jeannie suggested Martin go the doctor for pills to make him randy. Kath felt sorry for Jeannie. It would be a pity if she never had children; cousins for the children that Kath hoped she and Robert would have one day.

Sam was the first up again the next morning and Kath was second. She had a good hour with him in the kitchen before the others intruded on their convivial conversation.

Sam relished talking about his boyhood on the farm where he had grown up, just north of Chepstow on the English/South Wales border. He'd been born in 1905, he told her, and he was nine when World War One had broken out. The Ministry of Defence arrived on the family's farm to take two of their ploughing horses for moving heavy guns and wagons in France. 'A Samson of horses,' Sam said, and explained how they'd had army numbers carved on their hooves, before being taken away in a huge, closed lorry. Tears filled his eyes as he recalled Bailey coming home at the end of the war and how he had hugged his beloved Shire horse, but cried bitterly when he learned that Elgar, the other, had died on the Somme.

He dug out some sketches from that period and explained their significance: Mother Elsie plucking a chicken, plenty of pony and traps with brothers and sisters in the back. Cart horses pulling carts, and not a motor car in sight.

Tilly broke up the twosome, Rob already having been dispatched to fetch a large suitcase full of vintage children's clothes from a house ten doors away.

"I have to study children's literature now at College," Kath informed Tilly, citing some of the titles required. I need copies of *Swallows and Amazons and Treasure Island* for a start. I also need *Gulliver's Travels, Robinson Crusoe* and *Lord of the Flies*. Have you got any of these?" she asked, hopefully.

"No!"

Kath could have slapped herself for allowing the putdown so brusquely yet again but she retaliated by not even mentioning Tilly's own stories again.

Tilly obviously had more important things on her mind. *Was the shop, Three Ways losing money ?* Kath wondered. It was probably a lie when she professed business to be good when confronted with Leo's *Aston Martin* purchase.

Kath mentioned Tilly's contradictions to Rob, but was met with only a, "Well yes, you never know where you are with her!"

"No you certainly don't. We won't be able to depend on her for anything !"

It was true, Tilly confessed that night, that the shop would have to be sold and business would be conducted from the *Old Parsonage*, unless, and Tilly's face lit up at the thought, she could secure a mortgage on the shop next door, which could easily be changed from a sweet shop to antiques.

"I could knock a doorway through from this house to that. There's a flat upstairs that I could let out." Tilly was never happier than when she was negotiating buying a new property. She was addicted to bricks and mortar and there was no sign of the affliction abating.

"I'll let you know when we move," were Tilly's parting words that weekend, "...and you can come and help us."

Kath was furious, but waited until the van had left the village to express her anguish. "We do all the work and Leo gets the payment! Bloody cheek, I won't let you, Rob, you dare."

Rob knew the score; Kath was getting tough.

Returning to College after the break, Kath was pleased to find out that one girl from the nineteen in her PE group had dropped out. Pregnancy was reported. It meant not having to work as a trio, or cause friction by splitting up established pairs. The only downside was that the girl, who had dropped out, had been the partner of the most cantankerous girl in the group, Jenny Prado. The pair had been seen in Pimlico at the weekends, and it was rumoured they were working as prostitutes. Kath pushed Jenny's supposed activities to the back of her mind but it was hard, especially in gym when Jenny's backside, albeit covered amply by a black leotard, was only inches from her face! Kath would have forgiven Jenny her sexual exploits, if she had at least shown one ounce of human kindness, but she didn't. She deliberately let go of Kath at compromising times in the gym. Jenny only smiled – still, it was Jenny or no partner. Kath just had to put up with it for now.

She found solace in listening to Leonard Cohen songs, going to the Deptford Jazz Club with Rob and watching TV programmes like the fabulous *Whicker's World*. She spent Sunday mornings at the swimming pool in Greenwich, sometimes with, but mostly without Rob - after he finally admitted he hated swimming.

Kath was not impressed with her new College and their wacky ideas.

One English lecturer had handed her a movie camera and said, 'go out and film people's feet'! Kath decided she'd prefer to go to Brighton and film people on the beach, but when she handed the film in, it was never mentioned again.

More pressing, these days, was the desire to get a better flat. Kath spent most of her free time scouring the *Evening Standard* and looking at the adverts in the local paper shops. It was the week after Bonfire Night when she spotted something that might be just right. The advertisement read, *To Let. Three large furnished rooms on the ground floor of Edwardian semi, in Lewisham. Shared bathroom. Five pounds per week. Apply in person to view.*

Kath flew round to the address, then arranged to visit again with Rob. Anything to get away from Elaine, and the rent was the same as they were paying, but the rooms were twice as big. Kath's patience had paid off. The couple moved within a week, on the day John Lennon made headlines after he returned his MBE in protest at the Vietnam War.

Kath spent the first day cleaning, but felt miserable when she realised that the old furniture she had asked to be removed, had to stay. And what about the wooden conservatory on the back, which was accessed from the flat's bedsit, but which was locked up and out of bounds for the couple? It would have been lovely to have used it as a through route to the garden. No, that too would remain as it was, locked. Mrs Litchken, the landlady, would not bend!

-23-

With colour in her cheeks and a sparkle in her eye, Kath turned the new flat into their home : the extra room, with a proper dining table and four chairs, meant room for guests.

It wasn't 'til the winter frosts, at the end of November, that the flat's heating arrangements, a one-bar electric fire and electric storage heater, took the smile off her face. As the temperatures plummeted, mould grew on the dining room and kitchen walls. The geyser, in the kitchen broke down. Getting hot water upstairs, meant putting pennies in a metre and cranking a lever to fill the bath. It was easier to boil water on the gas stove and deal with ablutions downstairs in the kitchen. The other residents in the house, three single woman - each in their own bedsit apartments - kept themselves to themselves. A Jewish furrier, and his four machinists used the basement. The smell of the furs permeated the house and made Kath feel sick, but the couple had signed a six-month lease on their flat, and paid a heavy deposit. Kath said she couldn't suffer that long, but Rob promised that within the six-months they would buy a house. Kath believed him and just got on with living and saving up. Being near to the town centre, she shopped at the markets. She scoured the stalls late Saturday afternoons when stallholders were packing up and selling off perishables at half price. She would be back home by six with: joints of lamb, bacon, slabs of cheese, bags of potatoes and hot pot root vegetables. She would cook the dinner and then they would go out again to the pictures for the eight o'clock show, where they always got seats on the back row.

Kath gasped as two grown men wrestled each other naked in *Women in Love* and cried during Nell Dunn's working class drama, *Up the Junction*. *Easy Rider* made her laugh, though.

With the prospect of buying their first house, Kath began to enjoy married life. Although careful not to neglect her studies, she expanded her Staffordshire pottery sales to the *Avery Hill* College students, teachers and cleaners. Rob took on more evening classes and repaired motorbikes. Kath acquired furniture for restoration in their dining room and sold it on. The landlord complained, but left Robert to deal with that. Kath kept her mouth shut, until their first electricity bill came!

Mr Litchken appeared at the couple's flat just before Xmas, waving a bill and demanding fifteen pounds, the couple's share of the quarterly statement. Kath protested and asked for time to check the bill with the reading on their slave meter.

Mr Litchken returned the next day. On Rob's calculations, their contribution should have been seven pounds and forty-two pence. The landlord insisted on his fifteen pounds. Kath put up a fight and shamefully called him miserly! Rob told Kath to shut up, and handed over fifteen pounds.

"You are a gentleman, Mr. Llewellyn, but your wife is no lady!" Mr Litchken said as he counted the pound notes.

Kath gave Rob a grilling all week, scolding him for being a pushover and doubting now if they would ever save up enough to buy a house! Rob simply stayed on at school and did a few more 'jobs'. He reminded her that they were, after all, pushing their luck by using the dining room as a workshop and could be evicted for that, so it was best to pay up and shut up. Kath didn't argue again.

Christmas was looming and Kath would be delivering the post again. They would drive to Stoke on Christmas Eve. Tilly hadn't said anything about the festive season.

"We should really make an effort to see your parents," Kath said. "They can't come here, obviously..."

"They don't make the effort with me or us."

Kath sighed. It was true. Tilly hadn't even given them a wedding present yet. The last they had heard from her was a card acknowledging their new address.

Jeannie had still to reply to Kath's correspondence too. It was a pity they had no phone in the new flat.

Kath was wrestling with her conscience about not taking the initiative to organise a visit to Somerset over the holiday, and possibly a visit to Jeannie in Oxford, when, just two days before Christmas Eve, a card, letter and cheque arrived from Tilly. She apologised for the delay. Leo was troublesome and the antiques trade hard going. The ten pound cheque was their combined wedding and Christmas present. As they didn't have the room to put any furniture, Tilly wrote, she wasn't going to give them any!

Rob simply shrugged and said the cheque wasn't even worth cashing. Kath agreed, tore it up and ditched it in the dustbin! A card, but no letter, from Jeannie, arrived on Christmas Eve. It took all Christmas and a good dose of home life in Stoke, before Kath resumed her composure.

However, Kath's Christmas was not like it used to be. Since cousin Jimmy's death, Aunty Evelyn and Uncle Dan no longer hosted the family Christmas Day party. No longer did they play party games like they had enjoyed so much before: *My Old Stage Coach* had been hilarious. Participants ended up saying silly things like, 'My greased nipples need scrubbing,' or, '...my rear end needs a good stripping'. *Blind Man's Buff* was another favourite, together with *Pass the Parcel*, and

Chinese Whispers. Kath and Nelly nearly fell off their seats laughing as they relived the family's antics from previous years. Nelly and Arthur still put on their family Boxing Day tea though and held a raffle, where every guest won a prize. Kath chose the presents and wrapped them up, like she always did, but not until she hurriedly set up the old, artificial Xmas tree after admonishing Nelly for not having done so before. Nelly confessed she was depressed and worried about Kath living in London. She pointed to the bruises on Kath's arms and legs. Kath laughed, as she realised Nelly thought Rob was knocking her about.

"No, not my Rob, you never need worry about that, Mum," Kath went on. "He's a gentleman, never lays a finger on me. It's that girl, Jenny, the ugly girl I told you about at College. She drops me in the gym, on purpose! Still, she won't have a chance next term, we're on teaching practice." Kath's exuberance deflated for a second at the thought of the tasks ahead, but she managed to rally and concentrate on the joy of parcelling up the raffle tit-bits. There was the usual toilet roll, a bottle of constipation relief tablets, a tube of ointment to cure piles... they were sure to get a laugh.

Homemade mince pies would still have to be baked and fresh salmon sandwiches made with de-crusted, thin-sliced white bread and butter. The sherry trifle needed topping with fresh cream and silver balls.

Nelly and Arthur would be going to the big New Year's dance in the Town Hall, but this year, they wouldn't be acting as the MCs. The couple had finally stepped down. Nelly's feet were not up to it anymore. She had suffered with bunions and corns for years, but now it was too much to ask to be dancing every dance of the evening. It bought a tear to Arthur's eye as Kath brought the subject up, but Kath was just glad she didn't have to go to any more of those dances. Up to the age of fourteen, she had no choice and cousin Elle had always been a dead loss to dance with. Kath remembered how she had been left alone on the floor, gyrating to Chubby Checker's, *Twisting the Night Away* at midnight, and being at the mercy of every drunken, middle-aged man wanting more than a New Year's kiss! Kath had pushed them off like flies, disgusted at the bad breath and wet mouths of their sloppy kisses. No, this New Year's Eve, Kath and her Rob would be tucked up in bed - in their own flat.

It was on the day after Boxing Day that Rob phoned Tilly from Stoke.

She didn't mention the cheque or her letter. Rob didn't either, but it was decided that the couple would pay a visit on the thirtieth of December, before going back to London for the New Year. Kath took the receiver and asked politely about Leo and, more importantly, if Jeannie and Martin would be there.

"Jeannie was here Xmas morning, she won't come again 'til the New Year. You two come for lunch, I would like to see you. I've got you a little present."

Kath felt a strange mixture of fear and flight, but, with a strong yearning to be friends with her husband's family, she accepted the arrangements.

Kath took wine and chocolate for Tilly, and miniature cigars for Sam. "Leave them on the hall table. I want Rob to fetch some stuff for me, before lunch." Tilly said as they arrived at the Old Parsonage.

Kath did as she was told, but later added, "Robert can't use the van to fetch your things Tilly. It's full with blue band crockery, bedding, new curtains and a rug for the new flat. Also, we've got a Christmas tree that my Mum gave us. "But, maybe Leo will help?" She looked the younger brother directly in his eyes as they ate the usual roast chicken lunch, in the kitchen. "Rob could fetch the things you want, in Leo's car. But, you know, Christmas has been exhausting. I've been working on the post, then babysitting for Billy and Pauline, then all this travelling, and I still have all the preparation to come for College."

"You don't know what work is, girl " Tilly wagged her finger at Kath "One little flat to keep; think of us and this big house!"

Kath wisely said nothing, then Robert left the room with Leo. Sam went out to his potting shed.

Tilly and Kath moved to sit in front of the big roaring fire of the 'withdrawing room', as they now were obliged to call the living room. Holly was draped across the deer antlers, which hung over the great stone fireplace. How gorgeous the little real fir tree looked, potted up in the corner and smothered in delicate gold and silver filigree antique baubles. Tilly ordered Kath to be careful not to disturb the display.

The two women ensconced in royal gold velvet, wing-backed armchairs, faced each other. "So, how are Jeannie and Martin?" Kath asked.

Turning her nose up, Tilly didn't answer, but went on, "We have a buyer for *Three Ways* and contracts should be exchanged by the end of February. I'm getting a mortgage on the property next door and our business will continue from there."

Kath cringed at the thought of the move. "That will be a big job," she said.

"We expect that Rob will help."

"I expect he will," Kath said, unconvincingly. *Not on your Nelly,* she thought to herself.

Luckily, Tilly didn't detect the ire and went on excitedly, "We will move into the flat above the shop. Leo can stay put in the attic and then we're going to open a pram museum here. We will need all the rooms for display."

Kath could believe that. Old prams, dolls and nursery paraphernalia were already piled up in all the other main rooms of the house. Boxes of unpacked Victorian toys, purchased at auction, were stacked in nearly every room. Tilly was going to have the biggest collection of prams and toys to be held in private hands in the whole of England!

Sam joined the pair and told Kath about how a cultured gentleman, a retired director of the Royal Ballet, had visited them just a month before. Listed in Debrett's *Who's Who,* he was an avid collector of infant memorabilia: silver rattles, ceramic feeding bottles, silk and cotton christening gowns. The man, Archibald Pasqual, had fallen in love with Sam's mural, *Saint James's Park in the 1880's* and the Beatrix images, which Sam had just painted in the room dedicated to the children's writer. "He adores Sam's work and has commissioned some sketches of things from his own collection," Tilly explained, as Sam opened his sketchbook and showed Kath his latest creations.

A beautiful, curly-haired, little girl sat up in a brass and iron bedstead, in large bedroom with a fire blazing in the Victorian fireplace, a patchwork quilt on the bed. The girl, with large, round, dark eyes, was holding an enormous baby doll. "That's Tilly when she was eight," Sam enthused. "She loved dolls, even then."

"Did you draw that from a photograph?" Kath's simple query struck the wrong note.

"Of course not!" came the acerbic reply. "I did it from Tilly's description and my own imagination." He said, quickly turning to another page.

"We're going to write a book together," Tilly went on. "Called,

Nursery Needs. Sam will do the illustrations."

Kath was intrigued, but couldn't get a word in.

"Lobsons will publish it, they've already said so."

"Lobsons? Oh yes, they published your Laugharne book, didn't they? And what about your novel, then? When will you get that published?"

"Well, when do you think I have time to be writing novels! You have no idea how hard it is to write a novel."

"No, I don't suppose I do," Kath said glumly. She turned to Peaches for comfort, lifting him up. "He doesn't seem his usual self," she said.

"He got mauled last week by an Alsatian," Tilly explained.

Sam shuddered, remembering the scene. "Next doors' dog got into our garden and gave him the run around, before knocking him over with his great nozzle and rolling him up and down the lawn. I had a job to get him off our Peaches. In the end, I threw a bucket of water over the bugger and he ran off."

"Well, YOU left the gate open, Sam. None of this would have happened if you hadn't. Now you are crying about it. All your fault, Sam, so don't go on sniffling about it around me." Tilly said.

Sam scuttled off like a naughty schoolboy and Tilly took Peaches from Kath, saying, "Come to your Mummy then, come to me, my love."

Kath went to the toilet and was glad that, on her return, Rob and Leo were crossing the threshold. Shivering, they sat in front of the fire. Kath got up to make them a brew, she didn't talk again until it was seven and time to leave.

Tilly promised to visit the couple in London, for a few days, but not until the frost had passed. "That won't be until just before Easter, and then the mould on the walls will be gone." Kath said.

"Of course not."

Rob's description of the green, slimy mould, black spots, yellow streaks and brown mould, of their dining room wall had been graphic; designed especially to deter a visit.

Tilly handed Kath a parcel as she left the Old Parsonage and stepped out onto the pavement. The packet had obviously hurriedly been wrapped up with cheap *Woolworth's* gift-wrap and stuck up with thin, clear Sellotape. "This is for both of you!" Tilly said.

"Thank you. I'll open it in the van," Kath shouted, as the couple waved goodbye and headed off up the road towards their vehicle. "I bet it's a jewellery box - another one." Robert drew a death breath but didn't comment. "It's beautiful," she said fingering the foot tall Japanese, black-lacquered, octagonal shaped cupboard. Standing on exquisitely turned bun feet with two tiny drawers at the bottom it was decorated with mother-of-pearl flowers and hand-painted leaves. "But, of course, the thing needs mending !"

"Bah, say no more, I've told you, okay? "Rob turned up the radio. "You should know Tilly by now, so let's just forget it, okay!"

Hearing the warning in his tone, Kath lay back in the front seat and slept.

New Years Eve, in Lewisham, was a couple of hours and few drinks in the local pub in the High Street, with Alun and Silvia, then back to their own flat, alone. It's what they both wanted. To the couple's relief, they were the only people in the whole house that night. Even Mrs. Smith, the old lady upstairs was out. She had been knocking on their door on the pretext of borrowing a little bit of this and that, when all she wanted was some company.

Kath, consulted her diary and gauged she was in the safe period of her monthly cycle. They wouldn't need condoms.

They had the best sex ever, they both agreed, before falling into slumber at four. When they woke at ten, the record player turntable was still spinning and needle still whirring round the last of the LP's, which Kath had piled up a few hours before, to play the night away.

Kath made the tea, then pulled back the French window curtains, which normally they kept closed, on account of the landlord always poking around in the conservatory. But, today was New Year's Day; surely he would not be around?

The crystal-clear, blue sky and freezing fresh air over London hailed in the Seventies. Kath's spirits rose to the occasion. She felt the urge to step out into the tiny garden that they were banned from. Anticipating frost, Kath pulled on her knee-high, fur-lined boots and a thick overcoat. Venturing past the dustbins, and taking the opportunity to dispose of the *Babycham* bottles and beer cans they had drunk from the night before, Kath defiantly pulled up the gate latch and let herself into the garden. Water lay frozen solid in the birdbath and the Italian-style fountain remained out of action. A wrought iron park bench sat angled in one corner. Snowdrops sprouted from below a chestnut tree. *How wonderful it would be*, Kath thought, *to spend an hour a two here in the summer*. She was still savouring an imaginary sun, when along the south-facing garden fence, she saw hundreds of animal pelts staked out across a wide canvas. *Squirrel furs,* Kath reckoned, and retched. She flew back to the safety of her flat and sobbed on Rob's shoulder. "Can you believe it! On New Year's Day, of all days - and the old sod is still working!" The couple listened hard to the whir of the industrial sewing machines, only slowing now and then when a titter of voices was heard, followed by the sound of laughter.

-24-

It was the last day of the Christmas holidays and Kath trotted around the town's estate agents, looking for houses for sale, for less than five thousand pounds. She detested the flat, with animal skins staked out within sight of the bedroom window and still having no proper hot water supply. Rob said, prudently, it was too soon to go house hunting, predicting they would need another six-months at least to get the deposit together. Kath dutifully forced herself to concentrate on College work henceforth, and went on a food shopping spree. She stuffed the little fridge-freezer with ready-made meals. Being on Teaching Practice for the next ten weeks, she wouldn't have time for cooking.

She had been assigned to a primary school in Woolwich, with a student from her English group. The pair were to team-teach sixty eleven year-olds between them. This didn't appeal to Kath, she had a sleepless night worrying about the situation.

Feeling weak and light-headed the second day in the school, Kath crossed the snow-filled playground, heaving with woolly-hatted, snowball throwing children, and climbed the twenty-five stone steps to the front entrance of the Victorian schoolhouse; her leather briefcase was bursting at the seams. Sheila, her team-teaching mate, got caught in the snowball crossfire and a splosh right on her nose took off all her lipstick. The incident earned her enough sympathy to be allowed to sit in the staff room to recover all morning.

Kath faced their charges alone. So much for another day of observation, as she had expected! One of the two teachers, in overall charge of the children, and who should have been teaching that morning, had rung in, saying his car had got stuck in the snow and he would be late. The other teacher was tied up in a meeting with the headmaster.

Someone hurriedly shoved a class register into Kath's hands and told her to go to the hall; her classroom now. Kath faced the gaggle of Cockney children, sitting in groups around tables, shivering to death in their wet shoes and socks - after not being able to find their PE pumps in the cloakroom. Kath thought quickly. Luckily there was paper and coloured card piled up on the teachers' desk, along with new boxes of crayons. She read out the first six girls' names on the register and recruited them as monitors for the day. Then, she wrote their names on the blackboard and asked them to distribute paper and crayons .If there was another system in place, it wasn't obvious. One of the boys shouted out, "We don't need no monitors, we get what we want usselves." Several children stampeded to the desk, where Kath sat, feeling like a shipwrecked sailor. Her head twirled, her temperature rose - but she still stood up and moved to the blackboard. She felt her knees buckle, but she pressed on and wrote on the board, *A Christmas holiday to remember*.

"Now children, we are going to think about your very own Christmas experiences, the Christmas you have just had, and maybe some better, or even worse ones. Let's share our experiences with each other. First of all, tell the person next to you about your Christmas this year. Take turns. Then we'll write."

Kath's voice was lost in the din of the kids shouting and laughing. They hushed momentarily, when teachers in the adjoining classrooms poked their heads out and complained. It was obvious these children were not used to lessons like this. She had made a big mistake. These kids were feral, predatory, like the kids in *Lord of the Flies*. Kath was within a horse's breath of fainting, when a whistle blew.

The six-foot-four - Mr Short – at last entered the fray. Kath smiled at the incongruity of his name. Bony and bald as a bat, Kath judged him to be about fifty-five-years-old. He controlled his charges like a referee in a football match and had averted her fainting attack; she thankfully made way for him. Miss Long, who had been with the Head all morning, arrived later. Kath smiled again; Miss Long was only five-feet tall. Mr Short and Miss Long relied on work sheets and the children doing what they wanted and just asking for help when they needed it!

Kath and Sheila were ordered to follow suit. They were to produce work sheets on the theme of Water: for English sea stories, for Maths capacity, for Geography oceans and rivers, for History old boats, for PE playing pirates and swimming once a week at Greenwich Public Baths.

Kath survived the first week, but not before vomiting twice. Team-teaching was not for her. She would say 'No' to one child, for example, if they wanted to open a window at an inappropriate time. Then the child would ask the other teacher and get a 'Yes'. It was both unnerving and depressing.

Kath slept more than usual during the next month and Mrs Litchken complained about the state of their flat. A Victorian set of double bed brass and iron bedsteads were waiting for a coat of paint in the dining room. Kath had painstakingly pulled the sheet brass off the iron rods with pliers and a piece of the brass had ripped through the nail of her middle finger, turning septic. She had it lanced, then stitched up at the doctor's surgery; it was still healing when Kath started TP. One day, she passed out at the supermarket, dropping a box of eggs.

The doctor put the fainting down to the effects of the antibiotics for the septic finger and the strain of teaching. She was ordered to take time off to rest, but Tilly was due to visit, at half-term, and they had to get the dining room cleared, enough, at least to fit in a blow-up mattress and a sleeping bag.

Tilly would be coming by train and staying four nights. Kath was to collect her from Paddington, and then take her to South Kensington to deliver a French bisque-headed doll to an ex-Miss Britain, now married to a wealthy Jewish businessman. The Jumeau doll was too valuable to be sent by post. Tilly said it was a pity Pasqual Archibald - the retired director of the Royal Ballet - was away, or she would have introduced him to Kath and Rob. Kath was in awe of her mother-in-law's dazzling acquaintances, but was pleased to be having Tilly on her own territory for a change. Tilly might realise then how hard she and Rob had worked! Kath felt stupid to have dumped the ten pound cheque in the bin in a fit of pique. Ten pounds was ten pounds and who were they to turn their noses up at that!

Rob said to forget the whole incident and refused talk about it again.

To Kath's surprise - or more to her credit for being so thorough in her planning - Tilly's few days with them was a success, apart from the blow-up bed being irreparably punctured on the second night, and Tilly having to put up with the hard floor. Plus, the car had broken down in the middle of Tower Bridge, resulting in Tilly having to push it to the other side, before it would kick up again.

Despite all of this, Tilly was impressed with the couple's antique collection: several Victorian prints in hand-carved frames, a brass inkwell, a tortoiseshell tea caddy, a set of Art Deco silver spoons in a silk lined case. She also complimented Kath on her cooking: grilled salmon, continental salad, baked potatoes, lamb chops, mint sauce and green beans. The jaunt to the Antiques markets resulted in some good buys for Tilly, too; including a collection of fans. Kath fancied the ostrich feather and tortoiseshell one, which nineteenth Century muses in Paris used in the famous fan dances. The tiny, hand-painted silk one, like the ladies of Versailles used in courtship, was too fussy for Kath's taste, though.

Kath didn't buy anything, but concentrated on making Tilly comfortable. She believed she had, but wasn't convinced, until Blodwyn wrote and confirmed it. Tilly had written glowingly to Blodwyn, saying how well Kath was looking after Rob and what a good team they were !

Over that weekend, Tilly had spoken a lot about the state of affairs in Somerset, but made light of Leo's situation, saying he would grow out of his depression one day. He just needed a good woman to fall for him and did Kath know anyone who might take him on! Kath had already decided she wouldn't wish him on her worse enemy, not even Jenny, who had given her hell on the gym floor; Leo would have to find his own lady loves.

Tilly bemoaned the fact that Jeannie hardly visited and Sam was getting senile, but she cheered up when she talked about the many important customers at the shop. Lady Mildred Rainer, the sophisticated doll expert, who had already had several books published on the subject, was a frequent buyer. Sam, loved her visits when she went with one, two or even three of her lovely daughters. Willowy things with wispy, long, blonde hair and bright blue eyes, Sam had captured them on paper and given the Lady his sketches.

Nancy Downe, the contemporary writer, a petite lady, but

surprisingly, rather too Bohemian for Tilly's approval, was down from London once or twice a month, usually accompanied by her 'boy friend', Jack. He was a man of striking beauty, as if he had strayed from a band of angels in a Quattrocento painting, Tilly said, after taking a shine to him. Jack had been a 'knocker' during the years when many of London's grand town houses were being converted into tiny flats. He knocked on doors, charming furniture out of the owners, which he then sold to the trade at a great profit. Now, he was exporting antiques to Switzerland from his up-market antiques emporium, in the King's Road. He was greedy for quality restorable furniture and Tilly had tons of it.

Kath smiled and told Tilly that they had two-hundred pounds saved up for their house, but that they would need at least five hundred. She was hoping Tilly would take the hint and lend them the shortfall.

"But you don't want to get a noose round your necks with a mortgage." Tilly said. "Tie you down, it would."

Kath stared hard at the floor and clenched her fists, when Tilly went on about how she was going to have to borrow money to be able to buy the shop next door. Kath brought the conversation to an end with port and lemons all round and feet up to watch *Great Civilizations*, a new series on the BBC. It was Tilly's last night in London.

Rob took Kath to the pictures and a meal out the next day, to celebrate Tilly's departure. They saw *Sunflower,* starring Sophia Loren, and had a curry in an Indian curry house afterwards.

"Spending all our savings?" Kath questioned Rob. "At this rate, we'll never get a house." Rob remained silent. "Tilly says we shouldn't get a mortgage," Kath went on, but Rob would still not comment.

Kath was vomiting again on her return to school after half-term. *It's nerves now,* she thought, as it had been two weeks since she finished the antibiotics for the infected finger. She was feeling panicky about going back into the den of sixty children. It wasn't the hard work of it all, it was the chaos and the feeling of letting the children down. Kath knew instinctively that this school, with its idiotic team-teaching system, was not doing anything for the children's education. Far from it, it was a disgusting experimental exercise, which would have catastrophic effects on these young people for years to come. But, in her position, she felt impotent. In fact, all that really mattered to her was to pass the Teaching Practice assessment, but that was a bigger challenge than expected. Distressed at the thought, she contemplated abandoning her teacher training altogether. On seeing an advert in her local Barclays Bank for trainees, requiring only seven 'O' Levels, including Maths and English, Kath applied and attended an interview.

She was offered a job there and then - but was given a few days to make up her mind.

In the end, she decided to carry on with teaching. As much as she was finding the course grinding, she liked teaching and the thought of the holidays with Rob and their future family, was a powerful force. Also, after nearly two years of studying, it would be silly to give up now. And, what about Nelly and Arthur? How disappointed would they be?

Arthur's words, *We Tyler's don't give up* prayed on her mind. She finally rejected the bank's offer.

Being offered a job at the bank should have given her back her self-esteem, but she felt even more worthless; the empty feeling just wouldn't shift. Not even a solitary swim made her feel better.

Another month dragged on. She missed more days of TP's – never before had she been so down. She saw the doctor and was prescribed amphetamines, for depression. There would be a review in four weeks. Kath's shame was a secret, which she kept from her mother and father, whom she was visiting now every weekend, driving home on the Friday and returning early Sunday with just enough time to sort out a few lessons. There was no time for Rob… no time for love.

In her solitude in the flat after school, she spoke to her reflection in the mirror, " I am a mess. I am fat, I am a useless lump. I should die." She suffered migraine after migraine, vertigo and spent hours in bed. With only one more week to go, Kath was convinced she would fail TP. Rob had taken to staying on at work late more often, and going in on Saturdays. Kath could hear the words in her head, "Told you so," words she imagined Tilly saying to Rob. She could see Tilly's full face, smirking in triumph, as the degree nisi divorce papers were read out. It was all too much. Kath stood sweating and shivering in the bathroom; she snatched a bottle of amphetamine pills from the bathroom windowsill and swallowed them all at once. As their effect took hold, she staggered onto the landing to the top of the stairs. She wobbled, then passed out, tumbled down the stairs and lay in a heap, until Rob found her later, freezing cold and lying in her own vomit. She was still clutching the empty bottle of pills. Semi-conscious, Kath's head was bursting with pain. Rob lifted her into bed, and, in between her sobbing and shaking, helped her drink water. There was nothing else he could do.

"Cry it out. Sleep and wait. Let tomorrow come," Rob said, soothing her hair from her face. He always knew best.

-25-

Rob took time off from work, citing a sore throat. Kath remained in bed, head buzzing and feeling bloated like a beached whale. Robert sanded down a table, their latest purchase, in the dining room, "You are not to mention this to anyone," he repeated as he brought Kath a hot drink. "Not even the doctor. We don't want you being thought of as deranged".

"You must think I am, though ?" Kath pulled the bed covers up to her chin and rolled away from him.

"Well," Robert hesitated, then cleared his throat. "No, I don't, but others might not understand that you have been under a lot of strain lately. I just don't want you to be stigmatised. You'd have trouble finding work." Kath rolled back and reached out for Robert's hand after he had lain the mug of chocolate down, on the bedside table. "You do still love me, don't you ?" she said, as she guided his fingertips to her lips and kissed them.

"You know I do, but you must be brave."

Kath returned to her teaching practice four days after her 'fall'. Three weeks later, she went to the doctors.

"When did you last menstruate ?" Dr. Smith asked.

"But, I can't be pregnant " Kath spluttered. " I had a period at the end of February. I am due on now." Kath thought again. *The bleeding in February, and in January, had been light.* "But there wasn't much blood." The doctor swivelled round in his chair towards an open doorway.

" Nurse," he called. "See to a pregnancy test for Mrs Llewellyn..."

Kath was three months gone. She must have conceived on that New Year 's Eve, that *noche de locura* (night of madness). She recalled how on January third, Robert's twenty-seventh birthday, she had fainted in the supermarket. She assumed now that was the moment of conception. *A New Year's creation, just like me, and could be born on Sept 28th my birthday.* Kath warmed to the idea secretly. *A baby, a real baby, my very own baby* - but then reality clicked in. Babies were not allowed in the Litchken's flat. *Who would want to put a baby in that horrible place, anyway? And they couldn't afford to rent a bigger flat or buy a house. How would they manage ? How could she finish her College course? She really shouldn't be having a baby:* This would have to be kept a secret, until they found a way out of the dilemma.

Rob accepted Jeannie's invitation to Oxford for a few days, during the Easter holidays. They hadn't made other plans. Facing Tilly, in her state, Kath thought, would be unbearable, and she wouldn't have been able to keep her pregnancy a secret from Nelly. It wouldn't be difficult with Jeannie; they were yet to develop a close relationship. *If ever,* Kath had doubts, but still a break-in at the old cottage again would take Kath's mind off the baby.

Jeannie was working nights an old folks home again, after her part-time teaching job had mysteriously ended, but she had arranged a few days off to be with her brother and his wife.

It was a bright spring day when the couple set off, in the *Austin*, for Abingdon. Rob drove. Travelling west, Kath soaked up the sun through the open window. The breeze caressed her cheeks and filtered through her long, loose hair. Morning sickness was now an uncomfortable memory. Daffodil heads, along the roadside, nodded playfully. The trees were sprouting new leaves. Kath raised her head to the deep blue sky and, for the first time in months, sang. *Jesu joy of man's desiring* rolled off her tongue. Robert smiled to see his wife happy and reached out his hand to hold hers.

Kath's feelings, that all was good in the world, soon evaporated though, when they arrived at Bellows Cottage and nobody bothered to greet them. Robert rapped on the living room lattice window, only to have Jeannie jump up from where she had been sitting reading. Slapping the book down (*Ghosts,* by the infamous Henry Price,) she made for the front door. “Martin has gone out for bread,” Jeannie said as she ushered the couple into the hall, “I’m making parsnip and turnip soup.” The abode, which had smelled musty and damp that previous autumn, still felt cold. Spring hadn’t worked its magic here. Jeannie was wearing a winter tweed jacket and Kath bristled at the sight of the stuffed badger, in the hall, now carrying a whip in its mouth.

Jeannie laughed, saying that she had found the riding crop at the bottom of a box of junk, along with a Victorian policeman’s cloak, a set of hand cuffs, a wooden truncheon and a leather-bound copy of *The Marquis De Sade.*

A taxidermist’s moth-eaten, cross-eyed baby fox in a glass case, sat on the hearth, a two-foot tall heron stood by its side. Kath shuddered and was glad when she was ushered into the kitchen.

Inevitably, when Martin returned with two loaves, the conversation turned to teaching. Jeannie shrugged when her teaching experience was mentioned. It was obvious that Martin was not enjoying his job. Copies of the *Times Educational Supplement* had to be cleared from the kitchen table before they could eat. Kath attended to that. She had regained her appetite and, after the long drive, she was hungry; that was until she read what was on a slip of purple paper that slid out from amongst the papers:

THE SPELL FOR PASSION- Anointing a suitably coloured candle with patchouli oil and using it to cast a spell is an age old-way to restore passion in the loins of a flagging lover…

Kath wondered, unkindly, if Martin had ever had passion in his loins… but she was more shocked to think that Jeannie was resorting to witchcraft to find a solution. Skilfully, Kath disguised her unease, and forced the vegetable soup down.

Kath didn’t tell Rob about the *Spell for Passion* ‘till they were on their way back to London. She felt that the cottage had ears and even thought the couple’s cat, with the cranky name, might be a secret spy and could, somehow, communicate what visitors said during their sojourns at *Bellows.*

Kath was glad to be back in her own flat. Even though it was plain, small and slightly chaotic, it wasn’t spooky. Robert was so down-to-earth and solid; Kath wondered again how strange it was for him to have such odd siblings.

Still, having to return to College, embarrassingly pregnant, Kath had more to worry about than Rob's family. The prospect of them being thrown out of their flat was daunting too. Kath went over their accounts again. Their savings stood at two-hundred-and-fifty pounds. If only Tilly would lend them another two-hundred-and-fifty, they would have enough to put down on a house. Rob said he wouldn't ask anyone at all.

"We'll get our own deposit - buying a house will have to wait."

Kath got house particulars from local agents anyway and miraculously persuaded Rob to view three terraces, but he still wouldn't ask for help with the deposit.

Kath, again submerged herself in work to stave off self-pity and comforted herself that she had at least scraped a pass on teaching practice. And now if she couldn't be playing netball, tennis and doing athletics, she was going to make sure she would be a good coach, and umpire. Gym and dance out of bounds too, she would watch from the side and learn. None of the PE girls or tutors mentioned the baby. Only Pat, when they met at break times, had a kind word to say. Kath had had such hopes for new friendships, when they moved to the flat in Lewisham, but now there weren't going to be any.

Rob coped by working more and watching TV: *Till Death do us Part*, *Steptoe and Son* and the *Kenny Everett* shows, kept Kath's blues at bay, too. She read true-life stories like *Beyond Belief (*the story of Myra Hindley and Ian Brady, the moor's murderers) and *In True Blood (*a whole family murdered in their home just for the hell of it). Stories like this put her own troubles in perspective.

Kath didn't go to Stoke, citing work and the cost of petrol. She told Nelly and Arthur not to visit; they were renovating furniture and there was no room. But, as Kath's bump was beginning to show, so did her anxiety. She was seriously contemplating running away, when, at the beginning of May, Rob returned from school, waving a letter and smiling. He was confident they stood a good chance of a council flat. To retain teachers, The Inner London Authority, was offering fifty homes to teachers who fulfilled certain criteria. First and foremost, the teacher applying had to be working in certain designated areas, deprived areas like Stepney Green, where Rob worked. The selection process was to be decided on a points system. Points were awarded, depending on how many years of service the teacher had given, more points for a married man and even more if there were children. More points if the current property the teacher was living in was substandard. After a social worker had seen their flat and a doctor's report proved that Kath was pregnant, the couple were allocated a two-bedroom, tenth storey flat. They were to move at the end of the Whit break, after the painters and decorators had finished.

Kath wrote to Nelly with the good news and announced her pregnancy at the same time. She then sat up three nights making maternity shift dresses. Only when she knew for sure that Nelly and Arthur had received her news, did Kath write to Tilly, Sam and Leo. Kath was always careful to address her letters to all three of them. She left Tilly to tell Jeannie.

The new flat, in Lewisham, had electric under floor heating, and Robert insisted on buying a king size bed. Nelly wondered how the bedroom windows could be cleaned. *Trust Nelly to think of that,* Kath smiled, as she wrote back and explained that two square windows swivelled round on hinges, so both sides could be cleaned from the inside. *Oh Life is good,* thought Kath, as she slipped a list of essentials in with her letter to Nelly, saying, "If you can get hold of any of these things cheap... beg, steal or borrow them, we will collect at Whit, along with our wedding presents. I know Dad will be glad to get his parlour clear again."

Kath wasn't disappointed. After a few days in Stoke, that school break, the couple filled up the back of the old van with the household goods Kath had asked for: An Axminster red floral carpet was the last to go on. One of Aunty May's cast offs, it had sat in her show parlour for six years and never been trodden on with more than a woman's slipper. Kath put the box of her childhood memorabilia, which she herself had packed up on leaving home to go to Barry, on the front seat of the van - by her side.

It was a hot summer, seventy degrees Fahrenheit nearly every day. Wearing her favourite maternity dress - the blue sailor cloth one she had made - white Jackie Onassis style sunglasses and straw sun hat, Kath sat down at the little table on the balcony of their new flat to write letters.

First, as always, she wrote to her parents. *When could they visit?* Next, she wrote to the Old Parsonage, now renamed *The Tilly Llewellyn Pram*

Museum and reminded Tilly they had room now for the antique furniture she had promised as a wedding present. They specifically needed a dining table, sofa, armchairs and a sideboard - or cupboard - along with a nice bureau. She signed off with a P.S. *We would like some pictures, too.*

Tilly took so long to reply that Kath fretted. *Didn't she like the idea of being a grandmother or was she perturbed about having to give some of her stock away!* Rob dismissed his mother's silence and spent a weekend scouring second hand shops. He found a table, four dining chairs, and two Edwardian armchairs. The oak refectory-style table needed sanding off and refurbishing and the armchairs needed reseating and reupholstering. Kath would do that.

Arthur approved; he always stuck to his idea that too much study and not enough physical work addled the brain.

Tilly eventually sent a card congratulating the couple on the news of the baby. She said that she hoped it would be a girl, as girls were less trouble than boys. As for furniture, that would be decided when the couple next visited; but, in any case, she didn't deal in furniture any more, only in toys, dolls and prams... but then Leo might let them have a nice clock. (That would have to be bought of course!) Kath wasn't enamoured with the tone of the correspondence, Rob accepted it as par for the course. He knew his mother!

It wasn't until the third week in June, and Kath's exams were over, that a visit to Somerset was arranged. Kath, at six-months pregnant was radiant. Jeannie had written once to offer her and Martin's best wishes and with the promise to visit in the school holidays. Kath hoped they would, she thought she would like Jeannie better, once she had the chance of being with her on her own territory.

On arrival in the West Country for the four-day visit, it was evident why Tilly had not found the time to write to her and Robert properly. Business was booming. After devaluation of the pound by the Wilson Government in 1967 and a booming stock market, Sotheby's efforts in opening up the global market for art and antiques was succeeding. Every Joe Bloggs was investing in the commodity. The ever-increasing popularity of TV programmes like *Collecting Now* was doing much to fuel the mania for collecting too.

The Old Parsonage was stuffed to the ceilings with exhibits. The drawing room had been laid out as a Victorian nursery, complete with an enormous wooden rocking horse, a host of *Stief* teddy bears, a doll's pram, dolls, a Russian sledge and a sealskin pair of ice skates. Another room was solely for automaton toys; like the circus monkey, which clanged symbols when he was wound up and the elephant doing a turn on one leg on a wooden barrel. Dolls screamed 'Mama' and rocked, when picked up and colourful jumping Jacks sprang out of boxes at the turn of a handle.

The atmosphere was both beguiling and bizarre - but Kath was glad she didn't have to share a home with such strange objects. She preferred uncluttered houses. Tilly scoffed, but boasted about the ever-increasing number of celebrities beating a path to her door. These included the affable presenter of *Going for a Song* - who had been entertained at the Museum, prior to Tilly being invited to appear in his show.

Conversation inevitably centred around antiques and Rob was marshalled into first knocking a doorway from the Old House into the shop they had just bought next door. Then, he was used as a pick-up and delivery service for the rest of his visit.

Sam reported on the headline grabbing stories from the Daily *Mail*, of antiques being bought for next to nothing, then being sold for record prices: a Chinese Ming bowl having been used as a water bowl for the pet dog was sold at Sotheby's for sixteen thousand pounds; and a first edition of Isaac Williams' *The Complete Philosopher 1653,* bought at a Jumble sale, was sold for five thousand. Paintings by old masters like Turner, Titian and Velasquez were fetching millions.

Tilly lamented at her lost opportunities, like the time she sold a seventeenth Century embroidered lady's cap for ten pounds, only for the new owner to promptly sell it at a London auction house for two thousand! Tilly said she wouldn't have minded, but the woman, Shirley, was a fellow antique dealer, who never failed to remind her about her faux pas every time she passed by.

Leo's jibes didn't help either and he reminded everyone of how much of her stock, Tilly had lost through rough handling. Tilly bemoaned the fact that the house transaction had taken longer than expected. After selling the old shop, she still needed a hefty mortgage on the new one and the bank was not prepared to lend the money, without more of a guarantee. The couple's income, Sam's pensions and her declared profits for the business, was not enough to secure the loan. The income would have to be a good few thousand pounds more! Mr. Hassel, Tilly's accountant, soon dealt with that. Of course Tilly's profits were higher than she had declared. Most of the dealing was in cash. "In one hand, out the other," Tilly laughed. But this time it seemed to have backfired, until Mr Hassel rewrote the accounts, showing a healthier profit and Tilly got her loan.

She would, of course, have to pay more income tax, and this irked, but not as much as it would have if she had been denied her mortgage. So, with another property, Tilly was on top form again. Sam was set on painting and decorating again and hauling furniture around.

Kath couldn't help; she spent time playing with Peaches. He was getting bony with old age and slept most of his days on a chair in the kitchen, when he wasn't called to sit on Tilly's lap. Sam usually worked in the garden after lunch, while Kath sat reading. She coaxed him into conversation sometimes and was spellbound by his stories of his art and life as a single man.

Sam's mother had articled him into training as an architect on leaving the grammar school in Monmouth at sixteen, but it was not what Sam had wanted. After two years of suffering the job, (by his own admission he was a dud at trigonometry and geometry) he gave that up and - much to his family's disgust - enrolled at the art school in Chepstow 'You'll never earn your living at that', they had said. But Sam was a born artist. He recalled how, as a three-year-old he had sketched the town castle At primary school he had drawn on the blackboard for the teacher - to help her with her lessons.

He went on about how he liked to copy the illustrations in the weekly comics of the day, like *The Boys' Own* and *Chums*. They had brilliant illustrators like Gordon Brown and Stanley Woodville. He reminisced about how his mother had taken him, as a little boy, to the Chepstow Museum where there was a painting exhibition on and he had revelled in the beauty of the great paintings by J. F. Bullock, the famous Welsh Victorian landscape artist. "When I went to art school myself in the town I spent all my free time in the art gallery there, just walking round looking at the pictures," Sam said, teary-eyed.

It had taken Sam three years of study to get a scholarship to the Royal College of Art, after failing the year before. He knew he shouldn't have even tried after just two years of study, but his family were short of money and anxious for him to get out and work. Sam was not one to shirk. He loved his mother and so wanted to prove he was a man; a gentleman. Sam admired good behaviour, the stiff upper lip, the traditional, the conventional. *Quite a staggering paradox*, thought Kath, when he now dressed like a dandy fallen on hard times and looked like a tramp, with his odd socks and hole in his waistcoat! But yet it was amazing. Sam had been the young man about town.

He lit up when he described the paddle steamer cruises he took girls on across the Bristol Channel from Newport to Weston. He recalled the antiques room in the College with gusto and marvelled at the array of classical Greek and Roman statues they had on display for drawing. "Exact copies of the originals they were, Michelangelo's *David*, The *Discobalis*, The Belvedere Torso…so many… so many."

"But, tell me more about the Royal College," Kath implored.

"Oh, dear, yes. I often wonder what would have happened to my career if I had stayed on in London!" Sam's eyes welled up again. "Ah, well that was all a long time ago. Must get on with my garden now, Tilly wants some carrots pulling up for dinner."

Kath wandered around the house on her own, studying Sam's paintings again. She stopped to study *The Welsh Cowshed:* a painting of cows and Tilly pushing a wheelbarrow, Leo holding the pet cat.

"That was my motorbike battery," Rob shouted over Kath's shoulder, as he was passing through the house. She looked again at the painting and noticed the little black box battery looking lost on the window ledge.

"Of all the places to leave it Rob!" Kath turned round. " You never do keep things in their rightful places. But you will never change, will you," she chided. "You're chaotic - like your parents." She lowered her voice. Rob grimaced, but patted her bump and kissed Kath on the lips, secure in the knowledge that Kath would forgive him anything!

It was almost dinner time when she was contemplating the lopsided breasts of the nude woman oil painting, relegated to hanging over the cellar door, when Leo got up and joined her in the hall. "Pretty lady…pity about the tits."

Taken aback, but ignoring the vulgarity, Kath responded. "Yes beautiful face, and lovely hair."

"Bet your tits are better than hers..."

Kath's cheeks burned, but she ignored the comment and went on looking at the painting, noticing the way the girl was posed and the bob hat so innocently included in the composition. "I expect she was a proper nude model at the art school. Very natural."

"Nah," Leo pulled a face and looked like Popeye. "Old slapper, I bet. Anyway, it looks like the nude picture Augustus John did of Tallulah Bankhead. The old man's just copied that!"

Kath felt her stomach drop, her ignorance was crippling.

Robert explained that Tallulah Bankhead was an 1940s American starlet, a bonne vivant, who was linked with the "racy set" that included Greta Garbo, Joan Crawford and even Wallis Simpson and the Duke of Windsor. Her liberal sexual exploits had led to VD.

Leo might be right then, Kath thought *but VD, ghastly stuff, I don't want to know any more about that !*

Kath was glad to be getting back to London. Jeannie and Martin had not shown up at the Old Parsonage as promised, Leo was an irritant, Tilly was waylaid by the business, Sam was always in the garden and Rob had been kept busy with work on the new property next door.

It was only on mustering the suitcases together, that Tilly gave the couple anything for their new flat. Robert took charge of the Victorian dark wood, highly-polished mantle clock with a porcelain face and Roman numerals - and Sam was relegated to carrying a white wicker cot on castors to the van, for the new baby.

"Very good clock that, French it is," Tilly stressed. "Worth thirty pounds of anybody's money that."

Kath was more concerned about the cot... it only had three legs. Robert would have to fix it. Detecting a frown, Tilly shouted as the couple drove out of the drive. "Mend anything, he can! Cheer up gal!" and she laughed as she turned her back and rushed back to her toys.

"Can you mend it?" Kath asked Rob, doubtfully.

"Bah. It will be like new when I have finished." Rob relished the challenge.

-26-

True to his word, Robert mended the Lloyd Loom wicker crib. Freshly painted, in white, it was installed in the second bedroom that was to be the nursery. Kath bought a *Mothercare* mattress and made the bed linen. When she finally tied the last bow of blue ribbon of the cot lining, the baby moved violently. It felt like a punch. *A hooray punch for joy* thought Kath. Morning sunshine streamed in through the windows and filled the flat with life. Kath padded around barefoot. The antique clock, from Tilly, on the mantelpiece, chimed at each hour precisely, the pendulum swung back and forth, the tick-tock soothing.

Sitting at the refractory style dining table by the south-facing patio doors, Kath wrote copious letters inviting friends to visit before the baby's birth. Those in Stoke declined, saying they had to work. Pat wasn't leaving Hampshire. Jeannie and Martin were tied up with Martin's family. Tilly and Sam were too involved with their business - and Kath didn't want Leo coming on his own.

It was a long summer and the clock didn't need winding up for thirty days. Anticipating the need for more money, Rob sold his Velocette motorbike, and spent a few days delivering it to the buyer in Cornwall. Still reeling from yet another sceptic finger, Kath was too delicate to travel with him. Apart from being guests at Alun and Silvia's wedding, the couple's social life had come to a standstill. Rob took on more removal jobs and Kath retreated into her own world of impending motherhood and study. She started using the municipal library, having at last found the courage to join. She had felt awkward before at having such a noticeable Northern accent, as they called it. No matter how many times she corrected that to a Midland accent, no one cared. Anywhere north of the Watford Gap was labelled The North by the Southerners!

Kath liked DH Lawrence and devoured his novels. She was thrilled when *The Virgin and the Gypsy* was released as a film. She got through Somerset Maugham's, *The Moon and Sixpence* and *Cakes and Ale,* and revelled in Oscar Wilde's, *A Portrait of Dorian Grey*.

Only Nelly and Arthur punctuated the solitude and put a halt to Kath's daily readings, when they arrived for a two-week stay at the end of August. Kath was eight months gone and a picture of health. She had never missed a check-up at the pre-natal clinic

Kath walked to the park, to the shops, went swimming, and didn't touch alcohol. Nelly did all the cooking and helped Kath 'bottom' the flat. They wiped down the woodwork and doors and cleaned the windows, polished all the furniture, and degreased the cooker. Arthur went for pints at the pub with Rob. Nelly talked much of babies. Kath's cousin, Elle, had just had a baby girl on the same day, in the same hospital as Gill Bowley had a boy. The two mothers became friends. Mick's wife had had a baby boy a few days later and cousin Lynne was eight months pregnant too. Kath was now keen to join "the baby club". She was sailing through calm seas at last.

From the tenth floor, the South London suburbs stretched into the distance silently. That was a different world. She was of another.

When Nelly and Arthur left, Kath delved into her box of treasures, which she had brought down from Stoke that Whit and hadn't had chance to unpack. Lovingly, she handled the Doulton figures, a 1940s *Pearly Girl* and *Pearly Boy,* a legacy from her grandmother, then placed them on the mantelpiece by the splendid clock.

Next to her swimming certificates and medals, lay a bundle of postcards. She had received one every week for almost a year from what she had thought of then as a real boyfriend. She had met the twenty-year-old German student at Trentham Gardens outdoor swimming pool, just before her sixteenth birthday. He had wooed her with love letters after his return to Berlin, but turned nasty when he failed to steal her virginity after returning to Stoke the following year. Kath looked through the post cards and letters, wondering what the point was of keeping them was. She had taken off the stamps to give to Billy for his collection; the cards would never be worth anything now. Still, they were a reminder of the big world that she hoped she would experience one day. The ski slopes of St. Moritz, Nuremberg at night, Hamburg city centre, Escala Opera House in Milan, Vienna.

Kath put the cards back in the box next to a packet of rose petals, remnants of the red roses received from this brute on her sixteenth birthday. She clutched her stomach and was glad she was having Rob's baby, shuddering at the thought that her first child could have been half-Hun. Then, instinctively, she pulled out the faded pink envelope containing the dried up rose petals and, as if in a trance, slipped through balcony door and moved to the railings. Crushing the envelope in both hands - twisting it at the same time - pulverising the contents, she thought about the violation. Weeks of verbal abuse, exposing himself and jibes of "Frigid little girl, fat belly" had left Kath traumatised. When he tried to pull her knickers off, she kicked him, bit his hand and punched him on the chin. He had gripped her upper arms hard, leaving finger length bruises, and slapped her legs.

Kath tipped the petal powder over the balcony rail. She watched the particles drift down, out of sight. Satisfied, she threw the empty pink envelope into the kitchen bin. Now, she felt cleansed and free.

Kath breathed in the summer air deeply, held her belly and dreamed of a bright future. She was happy now. She sang, "Que sera sera…" until she realised it was teatime and Rob would be back soon, and starving.

Rob had just bought a *Leyland Beaver* lorry, ripe for renovation. Reckoning that now they were living in a council flat, at a very reasonable rent, they would be in no hurry to buy their own house. Rob spent the couple's entire savings on his 'project' as he called his latest acquisition. His aim was to do it up and make a profit. Kath made no objection. Rob claimed as Kath would be busy with a baby, he needed something to keep himself busy too, and preferably something profitable. Rob reminded her all too often that she wouldn't be working very much now and that he would have to compensate. Kath accepted her husband's lack of paternal instinct, but insisted he start thinking about names. Kath liked: Sally, Natasha, Natalie, and Lisa. Robert suggested: Caroline, Hilary, Dawn and Judith - which put Kath in a huff, as these were the names of his ex-girlfriends! Robert wasn't bothered. Thinking about names for a baby was the last thing on his mind. He had to go to Birmingham, sometime soon, to pick up spares for his new love, his lorry.

Sensing Kath's unease at being left alone again, Rob took her to the West End that Saturday. The event was a free talk on Vintage Lorries at the VCC in Battersea. Not much of a thrill for Kath, but nonetheless, she would enjoy the drive out and it would be a change from Lewisham.

The talk wasn't as boring as she first thought it would be and she was pleased that Rob was enthralled. But at ten-thirty, when they were about to leave, Kath could hardly stand up. Looking down past her big belly, her legs had swelled up; they looked liked tree trunks. *Toxemia,* Kath deduced, could be a killer. She urged Rob to call the doctor. He was reluctant. It was Saturday night, and Rob wasn't one to fuss. Kath insisted and while she sat and waited, he dashed off to find a phone box.

"Doctor Smith says it's nothing to worry about, puffiness in the legs is common, you just need to go home and rest and he will see you at his clinic on Wednesday."

Kath's legs were not just puffy, they were bloated, tight to bursting point. *Perhaps Rob had not sounded urgent or described the symptoms convincingly enough.* Kath wondered. Still, she could wait till Wednesday.

She walked to the surgery on Blackheath Common for the pre-natal appointment that day. It was still sunny. After four days with her feet up, she needed the fresh air and exercise and the swelling in her legs had gone down.

"Sorry... but Dr Smith is away today, no pre-natal clinic now until next Wednesday." The receptionist informed sweaty Kath as she threw herself into the waiting room after her lengthy walk.

"But, he told my husband on Saturday that he would see me today," Kath protested.

"Well, he can't, he is away, like I told you already..." The young woman was not sympathetic.

"My legs have been swelling up, like elephant legs they were on Saturday night!" Kath spluttered.

The girl looked over the counter and down at Kath's legs, but then came out from behind the wooden contraption to get a proper look.

"Well, they seem perfectly normal to me now," she said, returning to her post and giving attention to the next patient in the queue. Kath stood shocked to the bones, speechless. She turned and walked home slowly. Robert returned to find her in bed, sobbing.

Kath, from her supine position on the bed, wrote to Nelly. She didn't mention her legs. She was looking forward to her parents coming again, when the baby was born. Nelly was not to forget to bring all the baby things Pauline had promised to send down, things which she had used for Kerry and no longer needed, knowing well she needed never to remind Nelly of such things; she worked on instinct and love.

Kath revelled in the intimacy of their flat. No sharing front doors or bathrooms any more. She walked around in stocking feet, enjoying the full effect of the electric under floor heating which they had only just begun to use, as the nights were drawing in. The brown soft wooden floor, the texture of *Weetabix* sprinkled with brown sugar and softened by warm milk, evoked safety and contentment. Only the TV broke the spell: Alan Whicker with his *Whicker's World* dominated the travel scene. She wrote to him at the BBC to suggest that he go and interview Henri Charrière, the author of the true story, *Papillon*, which had just been published.

Kath had marvelled at the French fugitive's exploits. Her struggle too was becoming a case of defend or die, kill or be killed, sink or swim, or so it seemed. Kath reprimanded herself for getting carried away and reminded herself of how lucky she was to be with Rob.

Kath drove to the doctor's surgery for her appointment, the following week and was kept waiting for two hours. No apologies were offered and none for not being attended to the week before.

"Yes, you do seem to be a bit swollen around the ankles," the old doctor casually stated, as he glanced down, while taking her blood pressure. "...and your blood pressure is up." Kath was given a glass bell jar and instructed to fill it with her urine - produced from the following Friday night to Sunday night. She was then to take it to the Lewisham General Hospital Laboratory for testing and would need to see the consultant obstetrician there on the following Wednesday for the results and a check-up. The doctor didn't feel her belly.

Leaving the surgery, she felt like a lost teddy bear: alone, unloved, forgotten.

Rob was coming home late from school again, a new term and lots to prepare: the lorry, the traffic. Still, he was always back for his dinner and rarely went out after. He often did the washing-up and of course mended everything that ever broke. Having a second hand washing machine, fridge, TV and radio, car and van there was always something or other needing attention. Nelly complained that she only ever saw Rob's back as he always bending over something, putting screws into something, or sawing.

Kath didn't worry Rob too much about the bell jar and urine. Just routine, she told him. Rob believed it and went to Birmingham that weekend to collect his lorry parts. He would be spending one night in Stoke with the Bowley's and would be back Sunday night. Kath filled the bell jar, as instructed, but insisted Rob drive it into the hospital laboratory that Monday morning with her, before he went to school.

Post arrived the following week in profusion. The College timetable and a dispensation for Kath for teaching practice. She could start after the October half-term and then complete it the following year after exams in June. Another letter detailed prospective child minders near the college and there was also a letter from Trinidad! *Wow,* thought Kath as she fingered the red and white stamp. A personal letter from her hero, Mr Alan Whicker. He was already in the Caribbean on a motor launch with a camera crew and they were about to sail to British Guiana to interview and film some of the old cons in the Devil's Island Penal Colony, with *Papillon*.

It was with a spring in her step, (thanks to Mr. Whicker, *Sir Whicker* as Kath labelled him, even then,) that Kath almost sprinted down to the hospital to see the consultant obstetrician that Wednesday morning.

"Well," the lady consultant started. "Your urine is full of albumen. Let's see what your blood pressure reads. "High." The consultant tried not to sound alarming, but Kath knew this was bad news.

"You will have to come into hospital today. Go home now, collect your nightdress and ablution requirements – but be back here as soon as you can."

Kath, desperate to tell Robert the news, cursed as she passed one phone box, then another, all of them out of order. Finally, she found one with a queue and had to wait half an hour for her turn. She got through to the school secretary, who promised faithfully to pass a message on. That done, Kath went home, tidied up, prepared a plate of salad for Rob to have when he got in, then had a bath. It was a hot day and not too far to walk, but she didn't get back to the reception 'til three o'clock when she was promptly put to bed and given a sleeping pill. She would see Robert the next day.

Kath woke at eight o'clock the next morning. Robert had been to the hospital the night before and would visit again that night. It was a pity he had to be at work. A junior nurse monitored the baby's heart with a trumpet. Having difficulty with the instrument, the little nurse called a staff nurse with a stethoscope. There was still no sound. The nurse called the sister, the sister called the matron, the matron summoned the consultant. Wires were fixed in gel onto Kath's bulge and then the obstetrician spoke.

"I am so sorry… but we are going to have to induce you. We cannot guarantee the result!"

"You… you mean the baby's dead, don't you?"

"Yes."

Kath's wails reached beyond the ward doors and out through the walls, like a haunted being, and into the big uncaring world. They ceased after a shot of morphine. As the drug worked to silence her, she heard the doctor saying, "…You won't feel, or remember anything."

After the inducement, Kath's labour was short, apparently. She was out cold and felt no pain, until she was about to give birth. The force of the baby's head in the birth canal and the need to push was so strong she sat up and screamed helplessly. Kath in her stupor cried out, "Quick… I am shitting myself." Nobody, not even Nelly, had described the act of birth like this.

With the overhead spotlights so bright that they were blinding, even with closed eyes, Kath was dragged from her bed to the birthing table. Two black nurses pushed her feet up to her bottom and held her knees out. Three pushes and the dead baby slithered out. As one nurse whisked the baby away, Kath sat up. The other nurse pushed her back. Kath resisted and sprang back up. "Boy or girl" she asked as she glimpsed her child, thick black hair and yellow skin.

"You don't need to know," the nurse carrying her child said.

"I do, I do," yelled Kath.

"Boy." The nurse bellowed from across the room.

Kath collapsed as another morphine jab pricked her thigh.

Rob was holding her hand when she awoke the next morning, Kath didn't speak until he had felt her empty belly and understood that she really had lost the baby, and it wasn't just a bad dream. "A boy," she said.

"Yes, only four pounds and four ounces," Rob went on. "He must have starved to death in your womb."

The fiasco of the last three weeks, from the night her legs first swelled, to the bell jar and the inevitable hospital ambulance, flashed through Kath's mind. She didn't speak. She couldn't cry and she couldn't even look Rob in the eye. She turned her cheek when he tried to kiss her on the lips. "Sorry," she finally said, as Rob left her side, crying and blowing his nose into his handkerchief. Grief had taken hold of her and her heart ached.

For four more nights, Kath languished in a private room. She was discharged from the hospital on September 28th - her twenty-first birthday. She was relieved to be going back to her flat. Her birthday cards which had been sent to the hospital, had been mistaken for baby congratulation cards by far too many people coming in and out: the cleaner, the tea lady, the dinner lady, the junior nurses, and the odd porter. Nobody said they were sorry. Not even Rob. True, he had cried, but he never said *sorry we lost the baby*. It was like he felt relief. It had not been a planned child. Finding himself rushed into fatherhood must have troubled him, but he had never said it did. He hadn't really wanted that baby, like Kath had, but then *perhaps men never do*, Kath rationalised.

Nelly, too, didn't seem too sad about it all either, and told Kath she was young enough to have more. Tilly wrote and said it was probably for the best as now Kath could get on with her studies without worry of a child in tow.

Kath didn't know what to think. She felt numb and as though one of her arms was missing. She did wonder if she could ever have another baby. She had heard the nurses whispering just as she had given birth, "What a pity, a lovely girl... she'll probably never have more children now..." Toxemia was a killer and if it strikes once it would mostly likely strike again.

Rob was on compassionate leave for a few days, when Nelly and Arthur arrived at the flat, for a week. Kath cried. Cousin Lynne had had a baby boy, David, on the very same day of her unnamed stillborn.

Robert collected his parents from Paddington for a day visit; their first visit to the flat. Tilly arrived in a buoyant mood, obviously having enjoyed the train journey, and the break from Leo. After a quick handshake with Nelly and Arthur and a pat on the back for Rob and Kath, Tilly took centre stage.

"Jenny and Martin send their condolences. They are too busy with work to pay a visit, but a letter, or a card, will be forthcoming." Leo was not mentioned. Sam spent most of his time on the balcony, sketching the view beyond.

"I've bought you a birthday cake," Tilly said, as she produced a tiny, round, ice-covered thing. It was no bigger than the young Queen Victoria's coronation crown, so admired amongst the Crown Jewels at the Tower of London.

"There, isn't it pretty?" Tilly enthused, holding the cellophane cake up high on the palm of her outstretched hand, towards the sunlight.

"Yes," Kath answered. She noticed the purple ribbon and lilac-coloured iced flower decorations.

"I thought you didn't like purple, Tilly?"

"Oh, I don't remember saying that! Now come on, let's all have a piece."

Kath was in no mood for birthday cakes, especially as she remembered Tilly being so adamant once that purple represented death and no young girl should wear it! Still, buying a purple cake was probably thoughtlessness on Tilly's part. Kath was just glad she wasn't pressed to eat any and was even more relieved to find she wasn't requested to blow out any candles. At least her in-laws were not staying overnight.

Nelly and Arthur drove home the next day and took back the baby stuff they had brought down that summer. It would now do for all the other babies just born in the family. Kath cried as she handed the bags to Nelly.

"Just the pram and cot to sell on now and we can have this room as a study again." Robert stated, matter of fact.

It was heartless of him to talk like this about the nursery only a few days after Kath's discharge from the hospital. But, sensible Rob was right; Rob always knew best. Arthur had called him solid - in the same breath as he called, Kath, scatty.

"You are going to need a desk, all that work you have to catch up with," Rob painfully reminded Kath. "Tilly says she has a nice one we can have, if we go and fetch it. I told her we will go at half-term," Rob shouted from the almost empty room across the corridor to the bathroom where Kath was now examining herself in the mirror.

Her breasts were still heavy with milk. With no child to suckle, milk was painfully bursting out of the nipples in streams and she had to wear breast pads to mop it up! Nelly had mentioned that medication was available to dry to up the milk, but the doctor, on his one and only house visit since the birth, had said that there was no need for such drastic measures. Kath was a big, strong girl - she should cope naturally!

Kath didn't feel strong, but had no option but to pretend to be.

"Okay, we'll go to Beckton at half-term," she shouted back at Robert.

Kath's mind froze when she contemplated having to go on teaching practice after that. She was sore after the birth and still rubbing oil into her breasts and belly to offset the effects of stretch marks. Besides, her mind was full of "what ifs". *What if she had insisted on going to hospital immediately - would the baby have lived? What if she hadn't had all that stress of moving house and taking amphetamines?* It seemed like guilt ruled her thinking and blocked her future. *And what had happened to her baby boy? Had he been disposed of in a hospital incinerator with all the other dead flesh, body parts chopped off, just meat*! Kath howled inwardly and had nightmares about her child being pushed through a hole into a wall and sliding down a chute, screaming to oblivion in a big melting pot at the bottom. Images of dead, naked bodies, like those being scooped up by bulldozers at Belsen after the war, pervaded her thoughts.

Two weeks after the birth, a bill for ten pounds arrived from the undertakers in town for supplying a coffin for a baby, and arranging for a burial. Her child was to be buried within the coffin of an unknown individual. Luckily, the social worker, who incidentally had only called on orders of the police, to see if Kath had stolen the baby that had gone missing that day in Lewisham, was with Kath when she opened the envelope. Rob was at school.

The thought that she was even suspected of having stolen someone else's baby and was now being charged for a burial neither she nor Rob had authorised, was enough to send anyone crazy. But, Kath held her nerve and waited for Rob.

As indignant as they were, he said, they would pay the undertaker and that would be that. "No use making enemies of local businessmen," he reasoned, "...and you can't bring the dead back." With that, Kath solemnly went with a cheque to pay the bill. She noticed again Barclay's Bank were advertising for staff and was tempted to apply. She had already suffered enough at keeping up with her studies. Surely, she would stand a chance as a cashier, after all - she had applied before and been accepted.

Kath discussed the prospects with Rob. In the end, the thought of teachers' holidays and spending time with Rob won again. She gritted her teeth and carried on.

She rarely mentioned her lost baby again.

Arriving on that Monday morning, mid-October, at the designated primary school for her teaching practice in Catford, Kath braced herself, and just got on with it. Although spending a few days in Stoke had been therapeutic, the trip to Somerset had not gone well. After handing Tilly the cane cot, for safekeeping (Kath envisaged it being on display with a doll in it, as part of Tilly's growing antique pram and doll collection) she offered the couple an Edwardian leather-topped desk. It meant having to buy it, for seventeen pounds. Rob paid reluctantly. Kath speculated that Tilly was short of money. Leo was wearing a brand new leather coat and *Clarke's* new shoes. Then, as they were manoeuvring the desk into the lift, to get it up to their flat, they noticed the underside was riddled with woodworm.

"...and it's alive," screeched Kath, in disgust, as live flies emerged from the little holes.

"Drat that woman! Tilly must have known about this! Look at all the bloody wood powder falling off!"

Kath remained silent, but shook her head in solidarity with her husband as they returned the desk to the back of the van. "We'll dump it tomorrow - I don't want it contaminating our flat."

Rob slammed the van back shut.

Rob got Kath two kittens after the desk fiasco and Kath complained of being lonely, as Rob was always on his lorry. He was determined to run it in the London to Brighton Rally the following year.

The kittens, Catherine and Henry, fulfilled Kath's need to nurture. She named them after Henry the Eighth and his first wife, Catherine of Aragon. The engaging *Henry the Eighth and his Six Wives* TV programme was running on the BBC at the time and Kath was a big fan; TV and caring for cats took her mind off things.

Kath and Robert didn't see Tilly and Sam again 'til Christmas when they spent a night at the Old Parsonage, before going to Stoke. Kath left Rob to deal with his mother and the woodworm desk. "We couldn't afford to have all our own furniture being infected," Rob explained. "We had to throw it away. Seventeen pounds we paid." Rob went on, almost believing that he would never get a reply, let alone a refund.

"Well, that will teach you to look carefully at something you buy in the future. Turn the things upside down, inside out - if you have to."

Kath was listening from the doorway, already red in the face after discovering her cane cot rotting away. It had been drenched in rainwater, which had poured through a broken pane in the glass roof of the outhouse where the thing was stored. Broken glass lay across the mattress.

Kath, sobbing, told Rob later that night as they lay in bed about the cot .She thought about their own nursery still empty, except for a hand-me-down rug and some cushions. She was using the dining table to write on and now, with no reimbursement of the seventeen pounds for the desk and no other offered in its place, that's how things would remain. Robert simply repeated "Well you should know what Tilly is like by now…" and he promptly went to sleep.

Sensing discontent the next morning, Tilly made some effort to atone. Two single beds were dragged down from the attic and loaded into the van, with Tilly yelling, "Well there you are, not a bad Xmas present eh?"

Tilly was too busy to attend to her son and his wife any more. She had provided a roast chicken dinner, mince pies and a glass of sherry and chatted with them for two hours and thought that was enough. Leo was unusually quiet when he joined them after lunch

Tilly did all the taking mainly about all the famous people passing through her antique shop; Peter Ball, the actor, looking for Teddy Bears, Lady Mildred Rainer, again wanting bisque-headed dolls. Archibald Pasquall, the avid antique collector of children's memorabilia liked silver rattles and old ceramic feeding bottles.The book, *Nurseery Needs,* he and the Llewlyns were collaborating on was coming on well.

Tilly and Sam had become so chummy with the grandiose chap that they had started calling him, Archy. Sam had already completed over a dozen sketches to be used in the publication. A sketch of Tilly's American baby carriage was to be used on the book's cover. Kath sighed when she saw a drawing of *Silver Cross* pram, like the one she'd had for their baby.

Sam told her to forget about that, "Imagine it all happened a long time ago. As far back as when Caesar first arrived in Dover," Kath couldn't fail to be amused, but then she concentrated on the next drawing, a pushchair in the shape of a scallop shell. Sam explained it was called a buggy and was one of the earliest baby carriages ever made. After being commissioned by the Duke of Devonshire in 1770, it could still be seen in Chatsworth House in Derbyshire. Sam had drawn it from a good black-and-white photograph.

"We expect to have the book published in the spring," Sam said, "…to coincide with the official opening of Tilly's Museum.

Robert had heard enough and he made an excuse to leave early, "Well, it looks like snow is on the way, we'd better get off before dark."

Kath was ready to leave too. As she waved, she took Rob's arm and reminded her in-laws that she had left presents for them on the hall table.

"They don't deserve presents," Rob said, in a whisper.

"Well… just chocolates, wine and jerseys for Leo and Sam. Can't be mean at Christmas."

Rob didn't answer that, but just turned the van's radio up high, as they sped from the village, up the trunk road towards Bath.

Troika was playing and the snowflakes started falling.

"Tilly never mentioned Jeannie and Martin," Kath remarked.

Rob remained silent.

-27-

Christmas in Stoke was thwarted with pointless commotion and palaver. Arthur couldn't open his mouth without causing an argument with Billy.

"Thee looks stupid in that 'ere David Crocket's 'at," Arthur chided on Xmas Eve. "Ashamed I am of thee."

"A man with two kids and you are going about like a …"

"Give over, Arthur," Nelly slammed a plate down as she was setting the dining table. "On bloody Christmas Eve."

"Yeh, give over, Dad. Look how you made Mum swear."

"Swear? I'll bloody swear! All you lot ganging up on me. Jesus bloody Christ!"

Billy slouched off to the parlour. Rob joined the family again after clearing the snow from the back yard.

"Now our Rob, he's a worker, man after my own heart," Arthur went on.

"It's nice you say that, Dad, but don't keep running Billy down," Kath's stomach churned to think of the number of times she had heard her father call Billy a 'numbskull', a 'fat rot' or a 'bloody liar'.

Kath wondered if all fathers were ashamed of their sons, after all, Sam didn't seem to think much of Rob. Kath felt confused.

Nelly had new made-to-measure *Playtex* corsets for Christmas and Arthur, a new pipe. He had cut down on cigarettes after they were being blamed for lung cancer. Kath got her longed-for camera, three colour films, and a pair of winter hush puppies. Rob had a book on motorbikes and three polo neck sweaters.

On Boxing Day, Aunty Evlyn held the extended family of fourteen spell bound with her tales of local folklore. She swore she had seen the Victorian Lady ghost dressing in a black cloak and leaving a trail of lavender scent in her wake as she crossed the courtyard of the castle at Alton Towers, just a few nights before while the park was open for the Christmas fortnight. Kath didn't believe her of course, but didn't let on. Her ghoulish description of Molly Leigh - the Burslem of the Five Towns seventeenth Century witch - who was accused of turning milk sour, was riveting. The spell binding tales of the Black Death witch 'Agnes' burned at the stake in 1349 for "will full misdoings" in the nearby village of Caverswall, left Kath shuddering in disbelief. She felt shame to think that her country had not repealed the satanic witchcraft laws until 1951 and sickened to think how people in this day and age could even think Witchcraft had any credence at all. Her insides prickled at the thought that her sister-in-law might be dabbling in the Dark Arts.

Her suspicions were compounded on New Year's Eve, when she and Rob returned to London and checked their mail box. A Christmas card, depicting a devil, was accompanied by a letter:

Sorry we haven't been in touch for so long but we have been busy and as you know Martin hated his job (his boss is a devil) in Abingdon and so he has now

got another one in Somerset ! We are going to live in Tilly's flat over the new shop and will be moving in on January third. See you sometime in the New Year.
Jeannie and Martin

"Wow, and Tilly never said a word when we were there! And they are moving to your mothers on your birthday!" shrieked Kath. "Get on the phone to Tilly now and see what's what."
Rob hastily went down to the phone box outside their block.

"Yes it's true, they are having the flat. Martin is going to teach art at a prep school for boys aged seven to twelve." Rob reported back.
"Which prep school?" Kath enquired.
"What does it matter? What's it to you?"
Kath wrinkled her nose and grimaced at Robert, tilting her head to one side. "You always get on your high horse with me after speaking to your mother," she said. "You go all high brow. It's as if this arrogance is catching, like a disease."
Robert coughed then spoke, "Oh, Tilly said something about the school being in an old manor house, and there being an ancient skull, one of the Lord of the Manor's, from the 1600's, being kept polished and stored in a cupboard. Brought out on only certain nights of the year for cantillations - and it is heard to scream!"
"What a load of bollocks, but I bet Jeannie will believe all that and I bet she can't wait to see it." Kath laughed out loud and added, "I expect Jeannie will get a teaching job too?
"No, Tilly says she will be helping her in the new shop and museum, full-time."
"Well I can't see that lasting, can you? She was supposed to be helping in the shop at weekends for the past year, but how many weekends has she actually done? Not more than five!"
"Oh well, time will tell."
Rob left for school to 'get cracking again' on his lorry restoration. Kath then thought about college again.
It came as no surprise to her, to learn that she had failed teaching practice. The crying, the being late, the lack of sympathy that she had lost a child, it had all been too much. She would have to do another TP after the June exams. Kath forced the six-week's torturous TP before

Christmas out of her mind and June was too far ahead to worry about. She was looking forward now to doing gym, dance and chasing around the netball courts again. She had regained her figure. Only ugly stretch marks reminded her of what her body had been through; studying would cure her mental sorrow.

The books listed for subsidiary English were a start: children's classics like Beatrix Potter and Enid Blyton. Kath was thankful of the winter and the dark nights when it was too squally to think about going out. It was head down and burn the midnight oil. Only letters were her link with their world outside London. However, when the postal strike in January went on for weeks, and the stimulating input came to a halt, Kath succumbed to depression. She hadn't realised how much it meant to be corresponding with her old school friends in Stoke and her Australian penfriend, Kerrie, in Sydney.

Kath and Rob had talked about how one day they would emigrate to Australia; Kath honed in on any news about the driest continent on earth: the outdoor life, the open spaces, no traffic jams. One day all that would be theirs, Rob assured Kath, but he would make no plans. He had a lorry to restore and Kath had a teaching certificate to gain. Kath sang along to Stevie Wonder's *We Can Work it Out* and *It Don't Come Easy,* as well as Paul McCartney's *Just My Imagination* and *Just Another Day*. Songs made life bearable.

After the postal strike ended, and the country was no longer using pounds, shillings and pence, but decimal coinage, letters for Kath started arriving again. The first one was from Jeannie: she and Martin were not happy in Tilly's flat.

Tilly had originally said they could live there flat rent-free in exchange for work, but now she was now demanding rent, along with an exorbitant contribution to the fuel bill. Leo had been admitted to the Royal Bath Hospital, after overdosing on paracetamol and gin and was now undergoing therapy.

Rob was more concerned over *Rolls Royce* going bankrupt. He argued that whatever he said or did regarding Leo, no one ever listened. Kath wrote back and said that they couldn't visit till the end of term.

She empathised with Robert. He had been left to deal with Leo after his arrest at Goldsmith's college, when he had smashed the common room up some years before.

Demonstrations in America against the nation's military involvement in Vietnam were hitting world headlines when Rob and Kath finally drove down to Somerset in the van for a two-night stay with the Llewellyns, at Easter, as promised. Kath had acquired an antique fireguard, an American nursery rocking chair and ten Victorian prints, of religious scenes, in carved oak frames. She anticipated selling them to Tilly, who had said to be on the look out for anything useful for the shop and museum. Kath was beginning to get her eye in for buying and was thrilled when Tilly gave her almost double for the chair and the semi-circular nursery fireguard. Tilly didn't want the pictures though, but Jeannie agreed to take them, to sell on a ten percent commission.

Jeannie sat wrapped up in her winter furs in front of a two bar electric fire in their flat over the shop, when Kath and Robert joined her on the Sunday morning. Kath was wearing jeans and a short sleeve T-shirt. "Got a viral infection," Jeannie explained, as she blew her nose and disposed of the paper tissue in a wastepaper basket by her side, already full to the brim with *Kleenex*. "Got to keep warm," she went on as she pulled the woolly headscarf tightly around her head with her fingerless, gloved hands. For a moment, she looked like the face in the Edvard Munch painting, *The Scream*.

"Not very happy with things here, then?" Kath ventured, looking around the room for an empty chair. Robert leaned on the doorjamb.

"No, we are trying to get away. But... don't say a word to Tilly."

"Not what you expected then?"

"No, Tilly's always short of money, wants us to pay for this, that and the other, says we should help with Leo more. We just can't do enough. She's always out. Sam's always drawing. Leo's always in bed." Jeannie complained, while handing Kath a pre-publication leaflet pertaining to Tilly and Sam's new book, *Nursery Needs*.

"*The book opens up a new field of study, the archaeology of the nursery*." Kath read the blurb out loud. She felt proud that with her fireguard and rocking chair, she was contributing to the excitement of this new venture. It was a pity that Jeannie didn't feel the same.

"Tilly is getting rather arrogant with all this attention," Jeannie grumbled on. "She called Martin a Jabbernowl, this week, and a Runnion."

Kath tutted. "Yes, she went on at me this morning about me not calling the sitting room 'the withdrawing room' as she wanted.

"Well, at least they are not calling it the ballroom!" laughed Rob and then said if everyone at the Old Parsonage was going to be carrying on like they were, they would all end up in Queer Street and he was just glad he lived in London.

"And, you should see her boudoir, as she is calling her bedroom now." Jeannie was in full flight with her list of things to be disgruntled about. "Antique Louis VI style four-poster bed. Pink velvet curtains, swags and all. Marble statues of Venus up there too, gold candelabras and what she says is called a girardole. She talks about having no money, no wonder!"

Kath didn't comment on Tilly's extravagances. "Don't you get out much then, Jeannie?" Kath went on as she removed a pile of papers from a stool and sat down.

"No, not much, but I am taking on a night class after the holidays in Frome, just 'til July. I am doing textiles with a group of old women. I have decided to make patchwork quilts with them." Jeannie pulled out a plastic bag of old rags from behind her chair. The Maid of Honour dress, the unmistakable petrol blue shantung silk that Jeannie had worn at her and Rob's wedding, lay on top of the pile, its sleeves already cut off and the back and fronts pulled apart. Choking back the emotion, Kath left the room. Any sympathy she may have had for Jeannie before, was now truly dead.

A walk around the garden, with Peaches at her heels, focusing on the tulips, revived her spirit. Tilly then called her in.

Kath was obliged to sit by Tilly on the sofa, while Sam was up in the attic sorting out some of his wartime drawings. He was going to show them to the many distinguished visitors they were now getting, many of whom had served in the Forces. He needed to put them in some chronological order and make a few notes on each one. "A mammoth task, do you follow?" he said, as he joined the couple later.

Kath listened with a mixture of fascination and tedium to Tilly's account of their antique seeking visitors. Along with Sirs, often merchant bankers, chairmen of Blue Chip companies, there were non–executive directors of hospitals, trustees for Dukes, not to mention High Sheriffs, too. Inevitably they had sons, with names like Randal, Basil, Peregrine or Walter, who went off to Kathmandu to climb Everest, went trekking over the artic wastes, or overland on camels, or through the Sahara to prove their manhood. Their daughters, with names like Lucinda, Sibella, Charlotte and Divinia were either in Florence studying Italian Renaissance, Art in London, fashion design in Paris or learning to be cordon bleu cooks.

Kath was amazed she had sat still for over an hour, not getting a word in, when Rob poked his head round the corner of the door and joined the pair.

"Just rescued a bit of my stuff from the garage." He had already loaded a tool box full of chisels and tenant saws onto the van, along with a pile of old car magazines. Tilly only half-heartedly objected, saying that she had thought they were Leo's and better to check with him before carting anything off.

"And that old motor bike frame is mine too. Can't take it now, as I have nowhere to put it, but make sure you let Leo know not to touch it."

Tilly nodded in agreement, but then added, "You tell Leo yourself, you know he won't listen to me."

"Yeh, yeh." Rob would do as he pleased and he wasn't about to consult Leo on anything. "Got some quality stuff for sale now, Tilly," he said, fingering the exquisite marquetry what-not in the corner of the newly christened drawing room.

"That's called an étagère," Tilly corrected.

Kath said she thought that was French for shelves. No one disagreed, after all, it was time for lunch and they were all hungry.

"I'll set the table," Kath offered. "For seven, I presume, in the kitchen?"

And, for once, Tilly said "Yes" and nothing more until they all sat down to the roast chicken dinner and all the trimmings. Jeannie had bathed and washed her hair since Kath had seen her earlier and was now pristine in a summery floral top and lightweight pencil skirt, her hair in bunches and with a whiff of make-up on her oval face. Martin, the school master as ever, sat up straight as a Corsican pine at the table and spoke in short sentences. Only Leo acted silly by making clucking noises as he ate the chicken and belched a few times, after sipping the bubbly white wine. He and Rob sat at opposite ends of the table and didn't exchange a word. Tilly hogged the conversation and concentrated on relating the visits from her Australian gentleman friend: car mad Douglas. A right yonker she called him, prompting Kath to ask what a yonker meant. "Handsome Knight," Tilly informed her, causing Sam to flinch.

"Gave my painting to him, she did, my landscape of *Weymouth Harbour*." Sam nodded at Kath.

"Sold, sold," Tilly rallied.

"For a pittance."

"The market price."

"No, too cheap!"

"We needed the money, you–"

"Now, now." Rob interrupted. Acting like a boxing referee, he raised his arms and put a stop to the bickering. "No use crying over spilt milk," he said, then added, "...but just how much of Sam's work has this Douglas filched?"

"Now don't say filch, the man has paid for what he has had. You mustn't call Douglas a thief. He's a real gent. He's bought a Georgian farmhouse up in Powys which he is going to restore!"

Leo's eyes rolled in disgust and he rose from the table, saying he had had enough and was off to bed. His querulous disposition, was quelled by the gargantuan amount of valium he was taking, no doubt.

Rob picked up the folder of some of Sam's war sketches he had brought into the kitchen. Kath had a quick look, but sketches of rifles and barracks and Nissan huts didn't appeal to her. She sat silently, while the two men talked about Sam's wartime commission. He'd been ordered by the colonel in charge of the regiment, to paint a picture of men undertaking the morning maintenance of their biggest search light. "Finished it in three months flat, I did, and where is it now? Gone disappeared, look! Only my preparatory sketches remain." Sam's arms were flaying in anger and disbelief that his painting had never been put on public display and had completely vanished from the regiment's headquarters. He only calmed down when Rob asked what had happened to Mr. Jones - the man in the ARP uniform. Kath got up from her chair. She wasn't interested in the war.

"I don't know, all dead now, I expect." Sam was lamenting, as Kath withdrew from the kitchen, saying she would wash the dishes later.

She hurried up to the Catherine of Aragon room to look again at the array of prams, dolls and old toys sitting there regally in front of Sam's now completed *Saint James Park* Mural. Kath must have lingered longer than she thought, for when she went back to the kitchen, Tilly told her Jeannie had cleared up and had gone off to bed to nurse her cold. Kath didn't see her again, until she waved goodbye the next day, when she and Rob set off for Stoke.

Kath was bursting to tell Nelly about the dolls and toys Tilly had so elegantly arranged in the big room with the mural. There was even a toy canon, which actually worked, an authentic, full-sized Punch and Judy puppet set, and a large tin train, manufactured in 1880, sitting alongside the ubiquitous prams and wax-faced dolls. But Kath's mum was in too much pain to listen to Kath going on about Antiques. Only the week before, when Arthur was driving his *Corsair* a car had jumped the traffic lights. Nelly had been left with three cracked ribs. She could neither laugh nor cry and found it hard to sleep lying down, so had been propped up downstairs in an armchair. She already had black rims round her eyes.

Capable Kath, as Arthur had recently started calling her, took on the household duties. The first one to rise, most days, she raked out the grate and laid the fire. Mesmerised by the silver fish darting for cover as she shovelled the spent ashes into the metal bucket, memories of her childhood combined with the lost love of her stillborn son, filled Kath's head. Often Rob caught her crying. Kath had so wanted to pour her heart out to her parents but just couldn't, not now, especially as Nelly was in so much need. They had planned to do so much together; going to the church bazaar in the Town Hall - Kath and Nelly had always run the White Elephant stall together, until Kath had left for College in Barry. They also wanted to view houses for sale, were going to have a day in Hanley shopping for clothes - but all this was now out of the question. Kath stayed in with Nelly and made tea for the visitors, mainly Aunty May with the marcel-waved, red hair and Aunty Anne with the husband, who stuttered.

Arthur shook his head and repeated, “It upsets me for to think about it.” Kath thought he was not only feeling sorry for Nelly but he couldn't bear to think about Kath and his lost grandchild. It wasn't a happy visit, but Kath tried her best and talked about the future - hers and Rob's future - and as far as Kath was concerned, that would include Nelly and Arthur.

Kath and Rob had already discussed emigrating to Australia, but Kath said she wouldn't go, unless Nelly and Arthur could come too and neither would she go unless they had some money to go with! Kath had it all worked out. She told Nelly, "Now we are in a council flat, we are saving money. I will get a good job in September, and don't forget it's equal pay for women now. After a few years, we will have a few thousand pounds in the bank. Dad will be retired in nine years and then, yes, you sell this house and we all go to Australia. Billy can come if he wants," Kath added as an almost inaudible afterthought as Arthur had already interrupted the conversation and called a halt to what he termed, 'her mithering and belly aching and building castles in the air'.

Kath, knowing Arthur and his ways, was undeterred, but thought best to let her plans rest. Australia was not mentioned again for a while.

Loaded up with yet another van full of Blue Band Staffordshire Potteryware to sell off in London, Kath and Rob drove off from Bluegates Street just as it was going dark. Arthur called from the front door, "Just thee keep dipping ye bread in thee gravy and dunna werrit thee head about nowt."

Nelly had already said "ta-ra" from her armchair, still too sore to get up.

Kath breathed deeply as she sank into her seat next to Rob. It was a long drive to Lewisham. Kath pondered, her heart heavy in her breast; she knew now she no longer belonged in Stoke - but neither did she feel at home in London. Being 'stateless' was crippling.

-28-

Kath scooped up her cats, clutched them to her chest and buried her head into their warm fur. Their purring reassured her that she had been missed. Sighing at the thought of being grounded in SE London for the next few months, she tuned into the radio; Ringo Starr's hit, *It Don't Come Easy*, gave her the strength to press on with her college work.

Robert returned to school and stayed over most nights to finish the restoration on his beloved *Leyland Beaver*. He had applied to take part in the London to Brighton Vintage Vehicle Rally in June. Kath listened to Leonard Cohen songs, and played the *South Pacific* LP over and over again. She watched TV and honed in on *Panorama,* and News programmes. She admired Robin Day in full flight against the likes of Michael Muggeridge and Mary Whitehouse. Joan Bakewell, christened by Frank Muir, 'the thinking man's crumpet' held sway. Kath secretly wondered if she had done 'A' Levels, she would have gone to university and would perhaps be training now to be a journalist. Brushing regrets aside, Kath steeled herself for the last term of teacher training. Stevie Wonder's, *We Can Work it Out*, George Harrison's, *My Sweet Lord* and Bob Dylan's folk songs spurred her on and kept Arthur's mantra 'Not for the likes of us' out of her head.

It was a weekday in mid-May, the radio was blasting out Bob Dylan's, *Times, They are A-changing,* when Kath picked up three distinguished-looking envelopes from the mail box. She had been sitting in the sun in her bra and pants on the balcony of their flat, swotting up on Piaget and cognitive development theory. Putting aside her notes, Kath fingered the quality stationery: two postmarks from London, one from Bath. She opened the letter from Bath first, assuming it was from Tilly. Kath was both pleased and disappointed. The gold-edged envelope contained a cordial invitation to Mr and Mrs R. C. Llewellyn to attend the official opening of the *Tilda Llewellyn Pram Museum* on Wednesday the 23rd of June at three o'clock, but there was no letter. The next envelope contained Robert's pass for the London to Brighton Rally and the last a job offer.

"Just like Tilly, she knows I'm at school mid-week and will have a job to get the time off - and no letter!" Rob fumed when he came in from school later that night.

Kath was too excited about the news from the Ministry of Overseas Development to carry on a conversation about Rob's mother and her museum. Her Rob had been offered a job in the Cayman Islands!

"You will take it, of course?" Kath looked into Robert's eyes. He was in no doubt. And Kath burst into a rendition of *Times, They are A-changing,* 'til Robert said, "Pack it up, we aren't home and dry yet. I'll need a medical and police clearance."

But Kath was confident all that would be just a formality and the two-year contract to teach technical subjects at the new comprehensive school on the Island of Grand Cayman, BWI, would indeed be Rob's.

Duties were to commence early September but until contracts were signed, the couple thought it best to keep the good news a secret.

However, Kath couldn't stop dreaming of flying in an aeroplane, sunbathing on white sandy beaches under palm trees, floating in an azure sea, snorkelling among coral reefs, swigging rum punches and swaying to calypso music. Wow! Taking part in the London to Brighton run in a lorry paled and Kath only mentioned Somerset again the next day.

"And what about your mother and the Museum? What shall I tell her?"

"Don't tell her anything... yet. I'll see if I can get the day off first. See what I can do."

Kath wrote to Tilly, accepting the invitation, just a few days before the ceremony, by which time she and Rob had passed the medicals and Rob had signed the contract for the Cayman job. Kath had agonised over how she was going to tell her parents that they would be leaving the country. Nelly would take it hard. Kath had told her at Easter that she wouldn't visit Stoke till after the exams, but hell, this was important. Leaving Rob a note and a dinner ready to warm up in the oven, and after posting the letter to Tilly, Kath hot-footed out of London and zoomed up the M1 in her *Austin A35*.

"I just had to come..." Kath fell into Nelly's arms, exhausted. Nelly and Arthur took it for granted that Kath and Rob would go far, and didn't flinch when Kath said they would be gone for two years. "We knew you had the wonder lust in ye," Arthur said. "Knew you wouldn't stick it 'ere. Just good luck to you. Ter the both of ye," he said with a tear in his eye as Kath prepared to head back to the metropolis after just fifteen hours at home.

Shouting through the open driver's side window, Kath promised to be home again in July. Knowing Billy and his family lived nearby, eased the sadness she felt for her mother, who she knew would miss her dearly.

Kath fired on four cylinders, according to Rob, after a dose of love from home. Her adrenalin was pumping day and night, until all final performances for practical work in dance, gym and games had been done and the theory papers sat. Kath was confident she had written enough to pass, but only the results out in August would reveal whether this was so. But, Kath wasn't too worried now that Rob had this job in the Caribbean. Teaching was gruelling work and she still wasn't sure she really wanted it. Still, it would be nice to have the qualification and the choice. *Such a pity to fail now, after nearly three years of slog*, she thought while getting ready for the final hurdle, six weeks teaching practice.

After some prompting, Robert phoned his mother to check that she had received Kath's letter. She had. Tilly stressed that they shouldn't be late for the ceremony. She didn't mention her son's new job in the Cayman Islands, nor his lorry. Robert slammed the receiver down and threatened not to go to Somerset. "Just think of the cost of the petrol… for two bloody hours of boredom."

"It's your duty to go," Kath said, putting her arm round his shoulders. "We'll go in the car, if you're bothered about the fuel."

"Tilly won't like that, she'll have something ready for me to shift in the van for sure."

"Well, not this time. I won't have it. I insist we take the car."

The couple drove the *Austin* onto the Old Parsonage car park, which furthermore was to be know as THE TILLY LEWIS PRAM MUSEUM, at quarter to two. After re-powdering her face and applying more lipstick, Kath carried the antique clock that Tilly had given them as a belated wedding present, to the house and deposited it on the sideboard in the hall. Tilly had promised to sell it for them in her shop.

Other guests were already assembled in the rearranged dining room, which now, having been decluttered, was no longer like the inside of a wardrobe, but looked its proper size, eighteen foot square.

The oak panelling had been polished and the brown, velvet drapes pulled back. The mullioned window now let in ample light. The wind-out antique walnut table was extended to its full length and a cream damask ivy leaf patterned table cloth was the perfect backdrop for the grande buffet including: caviar, charlotte ruses, pate fois gras and smoked salmon.

Tilly appeared at the dining room door, wearing a black silk embroidered kimono, looking like a Geisha girl. Kath enquired if it was a fancy dress occasion.

Tilly's stern look assured Kath it was not and snapped, "But you look like a *Liquorice All Sort*."

"Well… good enough to eat then," Kath quipped back and pulling her shoulders back to show off her white, pink and black geometric patterned dress to perfection, she added, "This dress is a Mary Quant original!"

Tilly smiled, said,"Touchez " then moved on quickly with the tray of sherry glasses she was carrying. Robert followed in her wake.

"This is Robert, my eldest son," Tilly beamed at her guests as they each took a glass." And, er… er… this is Kath.

"The wife," Kath interjected as she took a sherry from Tilly's tray then sat down on the nearest chair; she felt a migraine coming on. Robert helped himself to the filo pastry cream cheese and walnut canapés, while Samuel complained that copies of their *Nursery Needs* books, which had been faithfully promised for the museum opening, had failed to materialise from the publishers, and lamented they had only a few of the dust jackets to give away to their honoured, top drawer, blue stocking attendees.

Jeannie, in a frilly apron, hair in twirly pigtails drooping from high up on her head and hanging down like cocker spaniel ears, bobbed in and out with yet more food. Leo said she looked like a French Maid relishing her role as a happy hooker.

Kath blushed at the comparison, but sipped her wine as if she hadn't heard, then commented on her brother-in-law's clothing, a plum-coloured, velvet, heavily brocaded, eighteenth Century gentleman's frock coat. "You only need a mask, a three cornered hat and a gun and you could pass as Dick Turpin!" she told him as she helped herself to a vol au vent from the table.

"Good for you I haven't got a pistol, if I had, my first bullet would be for you," Leo said as he shoved his hand in her back. Kath, stewing, turned and Leo fled from the room, pushing several of the ladies present to one side to make way for his exit.

Kath sat down, and fanned her face with her bare hands as if to shoo away Leo's bad manners; then smiled apologetically at the offended women, one of whom was muttering something like what a terrible cross Tilly and Sam had to bear.

The ladies, dressed in empire line dresses with short puffed sleeves, spangled headbands and Roman ringlets, looked as if they had just stepped out of a Jane Austen novel. The gentlemen too were from the *beau monde*; men of letters, ancient lineages, impeccable pedigrees, sons of Royal Russian émigrés, painted peacocks with names like Peyton and

Sheridan and dressed in the finest cloth. In contrast, Aunty Gladys, in her brown crimplene two-piece, strutted about like a mother hen, collecting up the empty plates and glasses.

As Kath munched her way through the buffet delicacies, she listened to the conversations of the *Belle Assemblée*. Naturally, the talk was on antiques and country houses, London "pieds de terre", the arts and ballet. The older men mentioned their inflammatory gout, Coutts Bank, and reminisced about their travels to Cannes and Biarritz. Women complained about the failings of their offsprings' public schools.

When Staffordshire was mentioned, on account of the Portrait of Mrs Fitzherbert now hung in the dining room and the lady's connection with Swynerton Hall in North Staffordshire, Kath said she was from Stoke-on Trent; she was met with interest, until she went on about the city being famous for Diana Dors, who had just had her first baby, a son they called Jason.

Tilly glared at her daughter-in-law and coughed loudly from the other side of the table. Kath stuttered, turned beetroot red and was about to bolt, when Leo advanced through the crowd and scrambled about the room as if he was playing football. "And what about Stanley Matthews," he yelled " He's another Clayhead!"

The party looked aghast at Kath, who having been relieved from one predicament, found herself cringing that she was in another! The arrival of the most honoured guest, the famous ballerina, Anya Morova, saved Kath from further scrutiny and real agony. The great "dama" of ballet had been delivered to the front door of the Old Parsonage directly from London. She stepped out of the white limousine like a princess, but was to stay just one-hour to deliver her speech, have photographs taken, look around the museum and then be on her way back to London.

Archibald and Veronica Pasqual were the first to greet her and never left her side. Even the most arrogant of the guests melted in her wake. Dressed in a pale-green, lightweight, long-sleeved jacket and matching knee-length skirt, she was a paragon of grace and beauty. Samuel took out his sketch book and captured her from several angles; the long, swan-like neck, the full bouffant of thick black hair.

Huw and Lianne Royce, two writers from South Wales and friends of the Llewellyns, wrote a poem and an article for the occasion, which were later published in the *Bath Standard*.

The event was over by 5.30pm. After the champagne was all drunk, the guests drifted off quickly. Only Gladys remained to clear up. Leo had already disappeared, and at six o' clock, Robert suggested they go too - but Tilly had other plans and Robert was set on taking suitcases upstairs and moving furniture from the outhouse to the garage. Kath helped out with the dishes.

It was nearly eight o clock when Robert reminded Tilly that Kath needed to get organised for her teaching practice the next day. Kath's stomach lurched at the thought. "But we'll be down again in August to get the money for the clock and perhaps some money off Jeannie for the pictures, we gave her at Easter, which she says she still hasn't sold yet?"

"By the way, bring your lorry then. You can leave it on our car park while you are abroad. Daft to be taking it all the way up to Stoke ," Tilly said, as she waved goodbye.

"Okay, thanks," Rob spluttered.

-29-

Kath was assigned to a good school this time for teaching practice, only two miles from Lewisham. Having agreed on the theme of water, again, her lessons almost wrote themselves, after all, Kath was going to Grand Cayman soon. She had already set her sights on doing sub aqua diving, sailing and water skiing.

Robert participated in the London to Brighton Rally. Kath accompanied him in the driver's cab and daydreamed about the West Indies. Restored to its original red and blue, the lorry never stood a chance of winning a prize, but at least the sun was out. They finished on time and the *Beaver* was parked up for the rest of the day on Brighton Promenade, alongside the other seventy entries. Robert mixed with other vehicle enthusiasts, while Kath absconded to the beach.

Kath, basking in the sun in her bikini, meticulously planned out the rest of the summer. Teaching practice would finish on July the 23rd. Robert would take the lorry to Somerset that weekend. Kath would follow in the car with the cats, which were going to their new home on

Alun's cousin's farm in Cardiganshire. Kath and Robert would then return to the Old Parsonage for a few days. They would then return to London to attend an orientation meeting for new recruits of the British Overseas Development Agency, at Farnham Castle in Surrey. After that they would sell the car. Finally, they would pack up their van and say " Good bye, and Thank God " to their London life. They would take the van up to Stoke with the remnants of their belongings to be stored with Nelly and Arthur. Then, on September 6th, they'd be flying to Miami!

It was still hot that Sunday morning when Kath and Rob arrived at the Old Parsonage to park up the *Leyland* for the next two years. Jeannie and Martin weren't there. "They are at Martin's parents, again," Tilly complained bitterly.

Sam carried on attending to his Laburnum and Rowan trees, while Leo helped Rob to batten down the lorry with tarpaulins and then manoeuvre the old Romany caravan, which Tilly had just bought, into place by the car park gates.

"We've bought another house, in Frome." Tilly told Kath. "Wisteria Cottage, it's a riverside gem," she said. "Ripe for renovation. Only only fifteen-hundred pounds. Come and see it with me this afternoon."

"Yes I would love to," Kath quelled the bad feeling she felt in her heart, thinking about Tilly's meanness with her and Rob.

It was dark when Jeannie and Martin returned to Beckton, and learned Kath had been out with Tilly. "She never takes me out!" Jeannie scowled, then flustered when she confessed that she hadn't sold any of the pictures Kath had asked her to sell. Martin still hadn't secured a job away from Somerset either. "Looks like we will be stuck it this village forever..." Jeannie moaned, but then, after a pause said, almost inaudibly, "You are so lucky to be going abroad," It was the first time she had mentioned Robert and Kath's good fortune.

"But you will come out for a holiday, surely?" Kath reached out to touch Jeannie's hand.

"Yeh, maybe," Jeannie shrugged and moved up on the sofa. She then folded her arms and sat glumly, while Martin went on about Leo. He called him Ludwig, the mad king of Bavaria and related how he had been expelled from college some months before, for not attending lectures and being abusive to staff. Since then, he had been lounging around. "Furthermore, according to Tilly, Leo had put some kind of explosive in Sam's Cohiba cigars, which had nearly blown his father's head off."

Tilly hadn't breathed a word of this to Robert, who sat aghast. Jeannie then added that Sam had now 'pulled strings ' to get Leo into Leicester Art School and that they were going to buy him a house to live in while he studied there. Rob's eyes rolled over yet again remembering, no doubt, that Sam hadn't pulled any strings for him when he wanted a job in South Wales.

Kath said nothing, *let sleeping dogs lie,* she thought! Blodwyn, the only one in the family to speak Welsh, often said, "Leo mae gair drg iddo" (Leo had a bad reputation) in her town and he wasn't welcome there anymore.

Tilly was adamant that she would never be able to leave the Pram Museum to visit her son and daughter-in-law in Grand Cayman. She didn't fancy tropical islands anyway. Sam said he only went where Tilly sent him. Kath understood. It was true, they had their lives together. They wanted, nor needed anything else. Tilly had her antiques, her gallivanting, her flamboyance. Samuel had his art, his garden, his war memories and his cigars. Still, Kath made the invitations and left it at that.

Tilly was busy signing the *Nursery Needs* books, which she had just received from the publishers, and was muttering about the fact that the book hadn't received glittering reviews. *Infelicitous*, one account had strangely described the contents! *Cursory style,* observed another. Kath wasn't sure what all that meant, but realised it wasn't complimentary. Kath said she thought the book was fantastic. Tilly smirked as if to say, *What you think doesn't matter,* and that was the end of that conversation. Tilly offered to give Kath and Rob a copy of the book, once it had been signed by all three of the authors. That would probably mean having to wait for some time - as Archie hardly ever visited them anymore.

Kath sighed with pleasure at the thought of two years in paradise, then sighed again, this time with sorrow, at the thought of missing Nelly and her family. Tilly didn't notice. She now had a first edition of Beatrix Potter's *Peter Rabbit* in her hands. With a price tag of hundreds of pounds, that was more important. Tilly was still feeling proud that she had only paid a quarter of the asking price. She had also acquired a rare, pristine example of a 1930s bisque head doll, which was a depiction of the Scandinavian Olympic ice skating star, Sonja Hense. It was up for sale at two-hundred pounds, Tilly boasted. *Business was brisk and with prices like that*, Kath thought privately, *no wonder Tilly could afford to buy another house for herself and yet another one for Leo.*

Rob wasn't pleased about any of it either, but he didn't let it show. He was more concerned about his lorry and sorting out his own things in the garage. He warned Leo not to touch his old *Rudge* motorbike which still lay in pieces in a box in one corner.

When Robert had finished in the garage, he wandered into the kitchen where he found Sam reading an old leather-bound book, volume two, part of a set of three about the 18th Century Lord Bute. *Burying his misery in history*, Robert thought. Sam talked endlessly about the two World Wars he had lived through.

Sam often repeated the story of when he and Tilly, newly married in 1939, had an Anderson shelter installed in their garden. One night, Sam painted caricatures of Hitler and Mussolini over its roof and scared all the neighbours so much he was ordered to clear it off by the Air Raid Warden. He then elaborated on the *War* mural he was commissioned to paint for the Chepstow Council. The fifteen-foot-by-eight-foot masterpiece depicting the town's efforts during the war was never finished. "I had to go to the war, you see," Sam lamented.

"But what happened to the canvas, Sam?" Kath said, as she put the kettle on to make her and Tilly a cup of tea.

"I took it home, I did, tore it down from the wall. It was up in the big room, you see. It was tacked up on the wall. I pulled it down, rolled it up and took it home. Carried it all the way on my shoulder, I did. If they had given me just three more months, I would have finished it." Sam banged his fist on the table. "Tilly's still got her tin hat. And her gas mask. She likes wearing them now and again. Frightens the visitors, she does. We have no end of visitors now." Sam's shoulders drooped like a bar-tailed godwit. "I am up and down, non-stop, answering that doorbell, making cups of tea. Good Lord!"

"Anybody would think you won the war single handed, the way you go on," Leo snorted. "He never set foot out of Prestatyn, he didn't. He was a battery clerk." Leo looked at Kath and shook his head. "Never fired a shot."

Sam left the room as if he were dodging gun fire.

"Gone to brew up his brimstone and sulphur for his bad back," Leo laughed. "Or gone to dig round his potato plants. Looks like he is still on rations. But he's a strong bugger, I'll give him that. He's still going up ladders and riding his bike."

"Yes, he'll need his bike even more now Tilly's buying that cottage in Frome by the river. It certainly needs some doing up. Sam's job, eh what!" Robert jeered.

Desperate to stop the insults, Kath attempted to change the subject.

"My grandfather, Gordon Tyler, was in the Welsh Guards, he was born in Birmingham, but he had Welsh parents."

"Oh, Tyler, hmm," said Tilly, who had come into the kitchen to see why Kath was taking so long to get the drinks. "We had a few Tyler's in Glamorgan, bad lot they were." But then she added, "I don't suppose they had anything to do with you though?"

"No, no, my grandfather's parents were from North Wales, mining people, or so it's been said."

Tilly's nose curled as if she had just detected a bad smell.

Kath changed tack. "But my mother was a Brereton, there's a Brereton Hall near us and a Lord Brereton, though I don't suppose we are anything to do with them, either."

"No," Tilly's definitive answer, put an end to that conversation and they drank their teas in silence, then Tilly went upstairs.

Kath was sitting in front of the TV when she came back and threw a plastic bag onto Kath's lap. "There you are," Tilly said. "Don't say I never give you anything now." Kath fumbled with the packet and finally pulled out the black silk kimono that Tilly had worn at the museum opening. Choked on emotion, Kath was lost for words, but managed a hug.

Rob and Kath left Somerset a few days later and returned to their flat in London. Kath had mixed feelings about Tilly now. Although she had been generous with the antique kimono, she had only given Robert three pounds for the antique clock. Just a few months previously, she had said it was worth thirty pounds. Kath was also perturbed that Jeannie and Martin were so miserable. "It's their own fault," Robert said. He pointed out how Jeannie had declined to go to the cinema in Bath to see *The Tales of Beatrix Potter* with Tilly and Kath one afternoon. "And look what her and Martin went to see instead – *The Devils* – that awful thing with Oliver Reed and Vanessa Redgrave. And did you see her face when you told her Tilly had given you that kimono! Ranting

"*Oh she never gives me anything!*"

"Yes, Jeannie has got a big problem and really I don't think Martin is the one to cure it."

Kath wore the silky black kimono again and again and revelled in its softness and exquisite embroidery, but she was still cross over the measly three pounds for the clock. Kath even dragged up the incident of the woodwormed desk and the three-legged wicker cot, until Rob called a halt. Robert was right. There was too much to do before they left London. The future was more important. Kath stopped fretting and concentrated on selling off their possessions; 'asset stripping' she liked to call it. "Fifty pounds for the car." Kath beamed, later that week. "The same as you paid for it two years ago." She held the pound notes she had just received up to the light to make sure they weren't fakes. "Ten pounds for the rocking chair, doubled me money," she went on. They certainly would have enough in the bank to buy a decent car in Grand Cayman.

"And we won't even need to touch the silver coins in the dimple bottle neither," Rob calculated. "They can only go up in value."

Kath's delight to be sweeping away the past was compounded by receiving news that she had passed her teaching course and a certificate would follow. It crossed her mind to tell her College that she was moving, but, in the end, she didn't bother. She was in no hurry to work in a classroom. The Cayman Islands were developing fast into a major tax haven; there would be office jobs on offer to women like herself. *One-eyed beings in a blind man's country*, as the ODA called the expatriates they sent abroad.

The television was the last thing to be bundled out of the flat. There would be no TV where they were going. TV had been her godsend in London, *how would she fare without it?* She had no idea, but made the most of viewing while she still could. *Top of Pops* was a favourite. *Spanish Harlem* was the song of that summer. John Lennon was belting out *Imagine.* Peter Ustinov, Dora Bryan and Thora Hird were still making the nation laugh, while Eve Pollard was banging on about women's rights.

Oh well. Got to be more to life than telly, Kath thought, as a neighbour carried 'the box' away !

-30-

The Transit van containing the couple's entire possessions, (apart from the lorry, and a box of motorbike bits at Tilly's), reached Stoke in record time. "Progress," laughed Kath, as they put their possessions, just three cardboard boxes of them, into Arthur's parlour. " We only had one box when I moved to London."

Kath was 'demob' happy. She revelled in Billy's children and bought them *Mr Men* Books at twenty pence each. She had at last come to terms with having had a stillborn child.

Shopping for the Caribbean, and nights at the cinema with Rob, to see: Glenda Jackson and Judi Dench in *Mary Queen of Scots;* Hitchcock's *The Birds*, and Sarah Mills in *Ryan's Daughter* - filled their time left in the UK serenely. However, the few days in North Wales with Nelly and Arthur in an uncle's caravan left Kath sickeningly sad. She thought about how her dad had had his own caravan ordered off the site and let it go to a farmer for £5 for a hen coop.

The memories flooded back: *She had spent half her childhood in this caravan that Arthur, and his friend, had built when she was three-years-old. Arthur romantically described how he had only done it for her sake, as she had been a weakly child who couldn't keep food down. She only weighed ten pounds when she was a year-old. Congestion on the lungs, bad Potteries air, the doctors had said. "She won't live long if she isn't moved to a cleaner place." Having half a caravan by the sea had been the answer. Going to Wales for weekends and school holidays had made Kath grow strong.*

There had only been three caravans on the site, a farmer's field that they shared with the cows, and the cow pats, when she started going there. The toilet, an Elsan contraption which had to be emptied periodically, was housed in a wooden shed that Arthur had built. It stank of creosote and Jeyes fluid. Jugs of water were collected from a communal tap in the corner of the field. Kath had made daisy chains, progressed to climbing trees, train spotting, flying kites, making campfires on the beach and finally learning to swim in the river that wound its way around the caravan camp. The Whit weeks (over six consecutive years) were extra special, when Kath holidayed with Aunty Evelyn, Uncle Dan, Cousin Jimmy and their pet dog, Tina - a perky Welsh terrier. Jimmy taught Kath to fish for trout. Jimmy was gone too now, and had been for four years. Her heart ached as she remembered the motorcycle accident which killed him.

“Tilly and Sam don’t like caravans,” Kath remarked as she sat down to play knock out whist that night with her parents, after their trip to Wales. Robert had just popped out to the toilet. “Tilly says they are too working class, too pokey and uncomfortable.”

“Well she bloody would, lady la di da. Well ye can tell ’er we have friends ere who ‘ave caravans and who are bank managers and publicans. Er’s got some egg on her chin.” Arthur went on. “You can tell her that…” Then he reflected. “Well, tell ‘er about the bank managers, but don’t mention the egg bit. Best to keep your trap shut, our Kath. But, you do worry me. Getting in with that lot, they’re more than mad. Oh you do worry me, you do. What ‘ast thee got thee sen into!”

“Parky tonight,” Rob said as he rejoined the group, rubbing his hands. It was always cold in the Tyler’s bathroom. “I think it’s going to rain again.”

“Yes, been bloody awful all week 'ant it?” Arthur said gloomily.

“Wales is always wet,” Rob stated.

“Yes, I'm glad we’re back in Stoke, aren’t you?” Nelly agreed, as they revelled in the heat and convenience of the new four bar gas fire in the kitchen. Nelly said they’d have to be quick with the cards as Eric Sykes and Hattie Jacques would be on TV soon and she didn't want to miss it. Nelly was getting more and more addicted to ‘televising’. “We’ve missed you, Kath, these past three years away, and we will miss you even more, now you are going abroad.” Nelly’s eyes, red and bloodshot, sank further into their dark sockets. Kath winced to think how many tears she had shed.

“But you will come to see us next year, won’t you, Mum?" You can fly out for a holiday for a couple of weeks, can’t you ?”

Nelly and Arthur had never flown and neither of them had even seen the sea, until they were married and had a tandem. Then they were able to cycle to North Wales and fell in love with it. Arthur, out of tune, sang out, “*Daisy Daisy*” and Nelly burst out crying, “We anna used to this globetrotting.”

Arthur went on. “All this jet setting is not for the…”

Kath cut in. “Now don’t say it, don’t you dare say *not for the likes of us* again. What did I tell you when I was younger? Don’t say that again. Remember what I told you I would do if you did? I said I would… well you know what. I won't say that now. You will come to Cayman - and that's that."

"Now where will we get the money from?"

"Don't kid me, Dad, just pack up a few fags and cut down on the beer and you'll get the air fares. And, if you don't, we'll help you, won't we, Rob?"

Rob, hummed, looked away and pretended he hadn't heard. Kath nudged him and he automatically mouthed, "Yes" without further discussion.

Arthur had made the packing cases that the couple had needed for shipping their stuff to the West Indies, in his work's workshop in lunch breaks. The boxes, slightly larger than tea chests, but still not too big to go through the front door, sat in the parlour next to the boxes brought up from London. Kath did the packing, finally ramming in two pairs of fins, (Kath called them flippers) snorkels and masks, then Rob and Arthur delivered the boxes to Tilbury Docks.

While they were gone, Nelly and Kath had their hair permed, and their eyebrows plucked. Mrs Cliff had converted the front room of her corner terraced house - two doors up from the Tyler's - into a salon and she did a steady trade. Nelly liked the gossip and always arrived early for her appointment, so that she could flick through the pile of glossy magazines stacked up in the waiting room, which she said she would never waste her money on buying. Kath wasn't too keen on having her long hair cut and bobbed, but had let Nelly talk her into it, on account of it being hot in the tropics. Still, it would always grow back if she wanted it to, so she let Nelly dictate. Nelly didn't like Kath wearing hot pants, the latest fashion, either. Kath didn't quibble, but privately thought that she would be able to do as she liked in the Cayman Islands.

For now, Kath kept her skirts to just a few inches above the knee. The leather mini skirt she had paraded around in before she became pregnant had already been relegated to one of the cardboard boxes, brought up from London, which would be stored in Kath's old bedroom.

With all the hard work done and just a few days left in England, Kath and Rob relaxed. John Peel, the DJ, was popular and Tom Jones was still singing his way to stardom with songs like *Delilah* and *What's New Pussycat*. The nation was intrigued by the 'romance'– was it or wasn't it? of Fonteyn and Nureyev. Jane Fonda and Raquel Welch had replaced Brigitte Bardot and Sophia Lauren as the country's favourite "babes". Marianne Faithful was beginning to lose popularity and Mick Jagger was getting a bad reputation as a womaniser.

Kath and Robert drove to Keddleston Hall in Derbyshire, in Arthur's car. The Transit van had already been sold and the money banked.

Tilly had often mentioned the old Hall, designed by Robert Adam the brilliant Scottish architect, who Robert had been named after. But Kath didn't like the house. Even the hot summer's day failed to lift the austerity of the façade or humanise the Doric columns and the sea of veined marble. Built in the Roman style, the grandeur echoed the power of Rome. Designed to subdue and suppress, Kath felt indignant on behalf of so many poor people, who would have worked like ants to build such a monstrosity. Confronted by the portraits of the owners, Lord and Lady Curzon, painted in the early twentieth Century, Kath shied away from their air of arrogance. Rob argued that at least the building would have given employment; a job creation scheme, in fact, and the workers would have been a lot better off doing that than being sent to war.

Rob was right, of course, but Kath was glad when they left the confines of the lofty Hall and found a quiet, pretty spot by the river where the water cascaded from a weir by the Adam Bridge. That was much better.

-31-

Neighbours in Bluegates Street lined up to say goodbye when Kath and Rob stepped out from the terraced house, struggling with two big suitcases and bulging hand luggage. Only half of it fitted into Arthur's car boot, the rest sat on the back seat with Kath. Rob sat with Arthur in the front. There was no room for Nelly, though. She stood on the front door step crying; one hand wiping the tears from her eyes with the edge of her apron and the other meekly waving. Kath blew kisses as the car edged away from the pavement, then she slumped into a stupor across the bag by her side.

Glancing across to Robert, Arthur said, "Cheer up lad. Thee at'ne going to prison!" Rob's hangdog look had Arthur worried. "What thee werreting about? Ye should thank ye lucky stars ye getting this opportunity of a lifetime to get on in the world. I wish I had gone to New Zealand years ago, but Nelly wouldn't leave her mother!"

"Give over, Dad," Kath chimed in. "Mum always said it was you who wouldn't leave your ruddy mother. And how many times have I heard that? Give over. Let's talk about more exciting things, or say nothing at all."

"See what I mean, Rob? 'Er's always going to have the last word! How you put up with 'er I dunno, you're a bloody saint, that's all I can say."

Rob chuckled and reminded Arthur to grease the tools now and again, the ones that he had left in the outside shed in the yard. That pleased Arthur.

Getting to Grand Cayman entailed three flights: Manchester to Heathrow, Heathrow to Miami and then from Miami to Owen's Airport, the only airstrip in George Town, the Island's capital.

Finding the take-offs exhilarating, Kath went goose pimply all over. She grabbed Rob's hand hard each time, and, once airborne, kissed him passionately for making all this possible. Watching the land, the trees, the buildings, and then the sea getting smaller each time as the plane soared upwards and over the clouds was surreal, uplifting, reassuring. Flying put her life into perspective and freed her mind.

By the time they reached Grand Cayman, after a sixteen-hour journey, Kath had finished the book she had picked up at Manchester Airport, *Black Like Me* by John Howard Griffin. She felt profoundly moved by the author's exposé of racism and the need for equality. It wasn't that she had ever thought any differently, it was just that she had never thought about it that much before. She would have to now she was about to enter the world of the Caribbean.

As a working class British subject, Kath had shouldered class distinction without realising just how oppressive it really was. Like a snail or turtle having a shell, carrying a burden, was just the way nature intended and that was that. *Experience, travel, these are an education in themselves.* Kath reminded herself of Euripides words as she began her life abroad. *A traveller without observation is a bird without wings.*

Without the yoke of class prejudice, Kath found she was accepted immediately by the friendly islanders; more racially mixed people than

Kath had ever witnessed before. They had frizzy brown hair, green eyes and dark skin, and all shook her hand warmly. The manageress at the hotel, where she and Rob stayed - until their government-provided house was ready - was Filipino. The deputy headmaster of the school where Rob was to take up his post was blue-black like the darkest of Africans from the Congo.

Within a week, Kath had been offered jobs as a hotel receptionist, manageress of a book shop, and a primary school teacher. Kath declined all offers. Like a pauper winning millions on the Pools, it was just too mind-blowing to handle. Kath needed time. There was a car to buy, a home to organise, a husband to love, friends to make and a new world to explore.

Rob had the support of his headmaster and staff and the company of half a dozen newly recruited teachers from the UK, as well as another half-dozen established ones. They worked twelve hours a day to get the new school up and running.

Kath had yet to find her place. She wrote to Nelly and Arthur every day, expounding the wonders of their paradise: afternoon naps in a hammock, snorkelling over coral reefs teaming with parrot fish, and dining on lobster thermador, conch chowder and turtle steaks. Kath hoped to find a quiet clerical job, licking stamps, addressing letters and running down to the post office now and again would do.

She was offered a job as sub-editor on the island's only newspaper, *The Caymanian Weekly*, just a few weeks after her twenty-second birthday. Kath could only assume that as she was White and British, she had been attributed with a status, a level of competence, knowledge, skills way beyond her abilities. Had Kath been a fully qualified black woman, she would have had a much frostier reception! Kath shuddered at the thought but brazenly said she would consider the offer. Rob was adamant she should take the job. Even though she couldn't type, she could learn. "It will improve your spelling, too," Robert sniped. Kath knew he was right.

Within weeks, armed with a *Polaroid* camera, a note book and a pencil, she paraded the streets to find news. Dressed in hot pants, *Clark's* Caribbean blue leather sandals, her black Jackie Onassis style sun glasses (and with a mug full of *Sanatogen* in her stomach each morning, which Nelly had insisted she take from home to keep up her strength), Kath trawled the streets as the *Voice of the Turtle,* the name of her column. "Under every stone is a story," She also reported from both the court and the police station. Encouraged by an American colleague, a forty-five year-old divorcee, who had worked on the *Miami Herald,* Kath's storytelling talent emerged.

So engrossed was she in her newfound vocation, she hadn't noticed that it was nearly Christmas, when they had their first letter from Tilly. The letter, written on the back of the Christmas card, started off amicably, apart from having a minor complaint about the cost of sending anything by air mail. They were doing well with the antiques, there were plenty of Lords and Ladies buying. Leo had been apple picking and earning twenty-five pounds per day. Archibald Pasqual had relocated from London to Bath and was now a regular visitor again to the Old Parsonage. Then came the bombshell. Rob's lorry was in the way. There was no room for Tilly's customers to park and children were climbing on it at night. *The lorry would have to be sold.* Tilly had already commandeered Martin to place an advert in an appropriate vintage vehicle magazine and she was hoping it would be gone by the New Year.

Rob was livid. Kath reproached him with a "Told you so, you should have taken it up to Stoke and left it at Dad's works."

"Bitch," he fumed. "Didn't even ask me."

Kath understood. "Just tell Martin to get a good price. How much would you say that was?" Kath asked.

"Five hundred pounds,"

Kath worked out that that would amply pay for airfares for Nelly and Arthur. Rob agreed that selling the lorry was the best thing as they were already thinking they would never live in the UK again; assuming they would be emigrating to Australia.

Rob accepted the imminent loss of his lorry and immersed himself in work. He had a technical block to design and machinery to requisition. He had been directed to order it all from Buck and Hickman suppliers in Britain, but because of strikes and a backlog of orders, made the necessary purchases in the USA. Kath accompanied him on shopping trips to Florida.

One week before school broke up, news arrived that Martin had let the lorry go for two-hundred-and-fifty-pounds. "You paid two-hundred pounds for it," Kath screamed. "Think of all that work you did on it, oh, this is not right! It's bloody awful." If Martin had been near, she would have rammed the pound notes down his throat.

Rob took the bad news like he always did and sighed quietly. He blamed himself for ever letting his mother talk him into leaving it with her in the first place. "Now you really know what I have had to put up with all my life!" He said no more on the matter. Kath consoled him.

They both had jobs and Rob was doing extra work at weekends, mending *Land Rovers* for the *Cable and Wireless* Company. He even got called out at times to fix the Governor's car when his Lordship's regular mechanic was not around. As a reward, as Rob couldn't be paid directly, the couple were invited to Government House on Seven Mile Beach for drinks and snacks with the Governor and his wife.

Arriving on New Year's Eve, Nelly's letter shocked Kath to the core: Billy, Pauline and the children were emigrating to Australia. They had already sold their house and they were all to leave on a ship from Liverpool on the twelfth of January, Billy's twenty-eighth birthday. Kath was adamant that Nelly and Arthur must get out to Cayman as soon as possible, but that they should avoid the hurricane season. May or June would therefore be best. The money from the lorry sale would pay for their airfares. Kath reminded Rob of her parent's kindness. They had paid for the wedding, they had provided free board and lodgings for weeks on end, Dad was always the taxi.

"OK. OK, don't rub it in, Kath." Rob begged Kath to stop. She had hit her mark like Diana the Grecian Goddess striking a deer through the heart with an arrow.

Kath cried bitterly for the mother she could not hug and comfort. Poor Nelly without her son and wife and two adorable grandchildren, forever! Kath in disbelief, felt she was suspended in time, so wrote home copiously. Nelly hid her pain and always ended her letters with '...and just look after YOURSELVES.'

Kath loved her even more for the brave, quiet lady she was. *How could God let this happen to my Mum?* Kath was losing her faith. She fumed silently at Billy. *How could he even think of doing this to our Mum? When he had never, ever in his whole life, even opened an atlas*!

Nelly explained; some six-months before, Pauline's cousin had been to the UK on a visit from Sydney, where she had emigrated to five years previously. That did it. Billy and his family were eligible for a ten pounds sea passage if they were able to go within the next six-months. Billy had to act quickly. The *Ten Pound Poms Scheme,* was soon to end.

Kath reasoned that perhaps one day they would all be together in Australia, when Arthur was retired. Nelly said not to be so sure as Billy had never said anything about her or his father joining them. It was as if he wasn't bothered.

Arthur resigned himself to the situation; he wrote that he and Nelly had taken on more dancing classes, and he was looking forward to visiting Cayman. He enthused about flying for the first time and a good dip in the sea. Nelly was burying her head in novels.

Naturally, Rob expected the money from the sale of the lorry to be deposited into his and Kath's joint UK bank account, but it wasn't. He was reluctant to write to Jeannie and Martin directly; he was still angry with Martin for selling his lorry off too cheaply. He asked Tilly to remind her daughter of the delay, but when there was no sign of the money by the end of January, Rob rang his mother again.

Sam answered the phone. With a different hearing aid he was able to converse. *Jeannie and Martin had left the flat over their shop! Martin had secured a teaching job in London. Jeannie was still looking for a job. They were temporarily renting a flat over a dentists' surgery and it was expensive. Jeannie would give Rob his two-hundred-and-fifty pounds when she could. Jeannie had sent a letter explaining all this and was annoyed that Rob hadn't replied.*

Rob related the tale to Kath. "What bloody letter ? There's been no letter. And she's angry at you!" Kath had never been so mad. "And to think, I have sent them postcards inviting them over to Cayman for a free holiday." Kath felt like giving herself a slap for being too thoughtful. The words of her mother resounded again in her brain. "Proffered offers stink, Kath, don't keep doing it. You anna better thought of." Yes, Kath needed a kick up the backside to stop her being so gullible!

Robert rang his mother the next day to complain and mentioned the subject of the ten Victorian prints that Kath had given to Jeannie to sell in the shop in Beckton. Tilly claimed to know nothing about the pictures or the agreement; Jeannie would sell them on a ten percent commission and bank the rest of the money in the same account as the money for the lorry. Tilly was adamant the pictures were not still in the Old Parsonage but she would pass the message on to Jeannie in good time. As yet, Tilly still hadn't got a phone number or new address for her.

Kath huffed and puffed at Jeannie's brass cheek but didn't dwell too long on that. Her priority was getting flights booked for Nelly and Arthur. The couple were due to fly from Heathrow to Cayman via Jamaica for a three-week holiday in June.

With a pending visit from her parents, Kath's work at the newspaper showed new vigour. She interviewed the island's extraordinary population, from Cuban refugees to bank managers, lawyers, sea captains, deep-sea divers, artists and politicians. Her life in Stoke, South Wales, London, Somerset, were now history. Kath was alive at last.

Nelly and Arthur had the holiday of their dreams; Arthur tried water skiing and Nelly got swept of her feet doing the samba with a local chap on the dance floor in the *Galleon Beach Hotel*.

Their departure coincided with Kath's American ally and mentor at the *Caymanian Weekly* handing in her resignation. Jane was replaced by ageing Margaret from the Bronx, but the two didn't gel and Kath left after a tiff. The spectre of Kath "ending upon her arse" as Arthur had always prophesied, was even more threatening when Kath found herself driving around the island in a mini-moke, delivering milk at six every morning. She doubted she would ever be paid to write again. But luck struck. A new newspaper was to start up in George Town and *would Kath like to be a reporter again*? So off to the *Cayman Compass* it was.

Beaming like a sweepstake winner, Kath buckled down. It was mornings only again, so there was plenty of time for reading, cycling, taking up scuba diving and water skiing. Rob was building a *Fireball* sailing boat too. Sailing would be their next hobby, Rob, at the tiller and Kath on the trapeze!

Letters from Tilly, which she tended to sign off, 'from we three' were scant. When they did arrive there was always an apology for taking so long to reply and then the news was inevitably depressing. Bad weather, Leo's out of control spending, Sam's failing health and his arthritis, cataract removals, mortgage rates and price of petrol going up. The antique business was doing well though, or so Kath thought. Tilly enthused about the number of important buyers she had beating the drum to her door since the Museum had opened. And now they were going to buy another house.

Rob snorted at the news like an old walrus. " She must be made of money.. and couldn't even lend us two-hundred pounds to get on the property ladder in London."

"Perhaps Tilly has had one of those rare finds you sometimes hear about amongst Antique dealers and she is not letting on about it," Kath surmised. "You know, like when it was on the news a couple of years ago about a man buying an old painting in the Rastro, Madrid for about a pounds worth of pesetas, and it turned out to be a Rubens worth nearly a million! And that time a first edition of Don Quixote, in Portuguese mind, fetched three-thousand pounds at auction after being bought in a second hand bookshop for a couple of quid!"

"Well, if Tilly has come into money, you can be sure she won't tell us. Don't suppose she would even tell Jeannie. So devious, she is. No wonder she's nicknamed, Tiger!"

Kath had mixed feeling about Tilly and Sam not visiting them. The lorry business had left a bad taste. She couldn't forget about the other dirty tricks Tilly had played on them either, like the woodworm desk and the wicker cot, and the measly three pounds for the clock, but she kept her thoughts to herself. She knew his mother's meanness pained Rob.

Without any more visitors, Kath's time was hers and Rob's only. They lived simply and quietly. Having discovered that they could save substantially, they set themselves the task of accumulating enough funds to put down a big deposit on a house near Nelly and Arthur on their first leave, due at the end of Rob's contact. They resisted a temptation to buy land on the island, as they reckoned it would be safer to invest at home. In the event that they were to go to Australia, it would be easier to sell. Also, Arthur would be on hand to attend to the property while they were away.

Already, after a year into the contract, Rob was intending to renew it for another two years. When other teachers went on cruises and stayed at five star hotels in Miami and Jamaica, Rob and Kath counted the pennies. They saved by not indulging, but with wise budgeting, they still managed trips to Jamaica, Mexico and Costa Rica. Kath learned a bit of "Espanol" for the trip to Central America and took up French again with a French expatriate lady she had met on the beach. Kath became fitter than she had ever been, so it was natural to find she was pregnant again. She had already decided not to believe what she had heard the nurses saying when she had her stillborn: that she would get toxemia again.

Baby Llewellyn would be born late August, 1973, perfect timing. Kath would go to England alone in late June, find and buy a house. Rob would arrive home late July, and they would move into the new house together. The baby would be born, Rob would return to Grand Cayman early September and Kath would stay home, till late September, even late October.

The pregnancy went well. After the first three months of morning sickness, Kath's energy levels soared and she revelled in her bump. The only disappointment was that she could no longer ski or sail on the Fireball. So, while Rob sailed (on Sundays) she lay on a sun lounger on Seven Mile Beach, listening to the strumming on the guitar and the songs of the Island's principal entertainer, *The Barefoot Man*.

Kath boarded the LACSA Plane for the flight to Miami in June. Miraculously, everything went according to plan. A three-story Edwardian semi, in a leafy avenue in Newcastle-under-Lyme, only three miles from Nelly and Arthur, was bought and furnished with pieces bought from the local auctions. Bonny baby Christian was born on time, on August 24th; Nelly and Kath arranged the christening. Rob left for Cayman in early September.

Rob had visited his parents overnight just one day after the birth, while Kath was still in hospital. He came back to Kath in a fury. Jeannie and Martin still hadn't paid him for the lorry. Leo had been expelled from Leicester Art College and was again living at the Old Parsonage. He had set himself up as a Vintage Car Dealer! Douglas Brady, the car magazine magnate, Tilly's 'friend', was running a free advert for Leo in his magazine:

THE ANTIQUE SPORTING CARRIAGE COMPANY – offering for sale. *1936 Rudge Rapide 250 motorcycle, in pieces but well worth getting together – a bloody quick bike for only two-hundred and eighty pounds.*

That was Rob's Rudge motorbike, the one he had placed in the garage when he left the lorry, and specifically asked not to be touched. Leo was trying to flog it off. Luckily, Rob had rescued the bike as soon as he had found out, and was able to store it in the garage of their new house in Newcastle.

Needless to say, Leo wasn't invited to the christening and although Jeannie and Martin were, only Tilly attended and she insisted on having her photograph taken with baby Christian, holding a five-pound note she had given him as a present. She also wanted a photo with the baby holding a copy of her book, *Nursery Needs,* the signed copy that she had promised Kath and Rob some two years before.

Jeannie's congratulations card arrived the day after the christening. Luckily it had been forwarded on from the hospital after Kath's discharge; the envelope contained a cheque for two-hundred-and-fifty pounds, exactly the money owed to Rob for his lorry. There was no apology, just a meagre explanation: "We used the money as a deposit to buy our house in London."

Kath left it to Rob to reply and never even bothered to check if he had. Sam stayed in Somerset, citing his bad eyes for not travelling by car. As for the Victorian prints, left in Jeannie's care to sell, Kath left that to Rob to sort out - but he never did.

Although the Indian summer in September had been glorious, by October, Kath wanted to be back in the Tropics, but she wasn't in a hurry to go back to work. She had fallen in love with her baby and she just wanted to be his mum. Motherhood suited her.

Nelly and Arthur agreed with Kath that the Llewellyn's had treated their daughter shockingly, but advised Kath to stay calm. "Stay in touch, send them letters, don't argue, but dunna get involved. Ye dunna need em. Live your own life. Don't worry your little head about 'em." Arthur took on the role of caretaker to the new house, as if he was born to it.

Kath got a part-time job, when Christian was six-months old, selling advertising space, and writing copy in Cayman with The *Northwester Company*, which published a monthly magazine of the same name, as well as tourist and business information booklets. She left her son with a Jamaican nanny, who came to their house every day. With Kath's commission earnings and Rob's two jobs, their savings mounted. Then, when Christian was two, Rob was offered a job in New Guinea.

With a new sense of adventure and a step in the right direction to the couple's ultimate goal of going to live in Australia, they packed up and flew out. Kath shed a tear, but didn't look back. Cayman had been good… but an even brighter future beckoned.

-32-

Late July 1975 - after a three-week tour of Florida - Kath, Robert and Christian arrived in the UK; taking up residence in their house in Newcastle.

The country was in a state of foreboding. Harold Wilson's Labour government was fighting a losing battle with the trade unions over excessive pay demands. Strikes were common. Even stable boys were out for a nineteen percent pay increase. With employment at over one million and inflation running at twenty-six percent, Denis Healey, Chancellor of the Exchequer, did a lot of head scratching. By November, the money had run out to prop up major manufacturing companies, like *Norton Villiers* motorcycles, so they passed into foreign ownership. *British Leyland* was nationalised, other companies simply disappeared. Britain asked for a thousand million pounds loan from the IMF. The country breathed deeply, and staggered on.

Kath sensed leaving their island haven was a mistake when the IRA bombed the *Hilton* hotel and two were killed outright. She drew comfort from Nelly and Arthur and retreated into a world of comedy and drama. TV programmes, like the hilarious *Fawlty Towers* and costume period pieces like *Upstairs and Downstairs,* were entertaining the nation. In any case, she would be going to New Guinea soon.

Tilly moaned, on the phone; trade was slow, Leo was bad. He had given up the wildly extravagant idea of the vintage car company after six-months of failure and was now enrolled in Maidstone Art College. Living in a ménage a trois with an older couple, who Tilly surmised were keeping him, as he was no longer entitled to more government grants, Tilly swore she would never have him home again. Kath bet she would, Arthur did too. 'Er's a wily old bugger, that Tilly," Arthur said.

"But Kath, just keep own your counsel; dunna worry ye little head about them."

When Tilly went on about *Wisteria Cottage,* the riverside dwelling they had bought to renovate and sell on, Kath just listened. The house had flooded when the river burst its banks. The clean-up operation had been costly. Now there was talk of road widening and, if it went ahead, the cottage would be demolished. Tilly was raving mad about that and had joined the local resident's campaign to object, but moaned that no one in the family cared. Jeannie, had moved again, and was now living in an isolated cottage in the middle of a Norfolk cornfield, which, according to Tilly, looked in the photographs like a wedge of cheese on a cheese board!

Even with a strong early September sun outside, the *Old Parsonage* still felt like a cold storage unit. Kath thought her blood must still be thin after living in the Caribbean, but Tilly was wearing a fur coat indoors after confessing that the central heating had broken down and she couldn't afford to get it repaired.

Since buying *The Old Parsonage,* the traffic through the village had increased fourfold. There were movements to get a by-pass built, but Tilly was impatient. The Parsonage was discreetly up for sale. She didn't want a sale board outside; that would affect trade. The museum-come-antique shop was attracting customers, and Tilly said that she would carry on regardless, until they bought a grander place! Then she revealed that she *had* bought yet another property, an old ruin, to do up and sell. Tilly, Sam, Kath and Robert walked around the block to view the latest acquisition. It had been a bakery, part of the Old Parsonage, but then got walled off when it was sold. Sam looked glum again at the thought of more DIY and less time for his art. He went on about Andy Warhol's *Campbell Soup Cans* and *Coca Cola* bottle paintings being an affront to proper artists. He rambled on about the state of British politics being a national disgrace. The Government couldn't keep up with inflation, the trade unions were in league with the Communists - and the IRA was more evil than Qin Shi Huang, the tyrannical emperor of China, who in 206BC had his labourers on the Great Wall of China holed up in the wall.

"It doesn't make sense," Kath said to Rob later. "Tilly going on about trade being bad and having trouble selling the cottage in Frome, then buying a ruin and contemplating buying an even bigger house than *The Old Parsonage.*"

"Bah. She thinks she is going to make money buying and selling property, well let her!"

Sam's efforts to catalogue and store his work properly, which he had told Kath he was planning to do two years previously, had not materialised. Huge folders, bulging at the seams with sketches of all sizes, were still cluttering up any space where the museum visitors wouldn't see them. Although he wasn't painting much these days, Sam was never without his sketch book. Kath fingered through his latest and commented on a drawing of a baby, then asked him to draw year-old Christian.

"Sit him on that cushion and I'll see what I can do," but Christian wouldn't stay still. In the end, Kath gave Sam a photo of the little lad and asked for a portrait from that, never thinking he would draw it; he had never found the time, (or inspiration) to sketch her or Rob. Sam admitted he liked drawing children and after rummaging around in his folders, showed Kath a few of his favourite ones. "This one, drawn in 1930, is *Boy of Croes*, and this is *Girl of Croes.* I went to infants' school there – it's a village near Chepstow. I was always drawing, you see, always had a pencil in my hand, and could draw before I could walk. The teachers used to get me to go to the board to draw whatever it was they needed to illustrate. Most of them couldn't draw for toffee. I even had to draw things in the teachers' report books! A duck, a fish, whatever… you follow. Yes… I was always drawing."

Rob was anxious to get back to Stoke. He was, after all, using Arthur's car. The couple hadn't bought one as they thought they were only going to be in the mother country for a few weeks, before setting off again to New Guinea. Rob had been assured, by phone from Australia House, the day after they had landed at Heathrow, that the job offer at Port Moresby in New Guinea was watertight and the official forms would be forthcoming in the post. However, by mid-September, and after several phone calls, Rob was worried. The last call, from Stoke was devastating. "Awfully sorry, old chap. Jolly bad luck. All aid to the protectorate has been suspended, until further notice. You can blame Gough Whitlam for that."

Kath cried in disappointment. Mr Whitlam, Australia's Labour Prime Minister, had so mismanaged the country's finances and there was just not enough in the kitty to fund aid to New Guinea - at least for another financial year. Rob threw recriminations at Kath and a shouting match ensued. "We had it made," he lamented. "And you blew it, got bored, wanted a different adventure."

"Well you didn't go against me at the time. Just like you to shut the stable door when the horse has bolted!"

"Would have got residency in Cayman if we had stayed just another two years. And you bloody well threw all that away."

"Come on, you said you needed a change and you know we want to get to Australia one day anyway. Can't we apply directly now?"

"We could, but, that Gough Whitlam has put me off. Things are obviously not so rosy there anymore. No more ten pound POME passages. They are only taking highly skilled workers too. I don't fit that category."

Kath winced.

"Anyway, just can't think about that now. I'll have to get work here. Can't live on our savings or we will all go down the swanny!"

Kath didn't argue and suggested Rob went back to college, to night school, to do 'A' Level maths and physics, so he could do an engineering degree. "It's what you have always said you regretted not doing, "Kath reminded him.

"And... what will we live on in the meantime?"

"Well, I can find something, and with you working in the day and studying at night, we'll manage. Or, failing that, maybe the Overseas Development Agency has a job for you somewhere else?"

Robert made a cursory call to the ODA, but there were no more jobs in the pipeline, so he bought a *Ford Transit*. With a van, he figured, there was always work to be had, moving this and that.

It was like the old times in London. Kath enjoyed shifting stuff. Christian, a smiling two-year-old with a sparkle in his big brown eyes, sat between her and Rob on the bench seat at the front.

Rob tried enrolling at the college for 'A' Levels, but had second thoughts when a snooty receptionist cold-shouldered him. Still, he found a job as a car mechanic. Kath took in a two-year-old girl for child minding. Rob's name was next on the list for an overseas posting with ODA, and Kath was happy that Rob hadn't pushed for emigration to

Australia. It would mean more time with Nelly. Kath had pined with Nelly over Billy's absence and had railed against his insensitivity: so few letters, only the odd photograph. Nelly and Arthur had only a vague idea of where Billy was and knew they had docked at Fremantle, after a six-week voyage from Liverpool, via *The Cape of Good Hope.* The family had lived in a state run hostel for migrant workers for six weeks, until Billy had found a job labouring on a building site, but then had moved on.

It was late November when an overseas job offer came for Rob. A two-year contract in Malawi, Central Africa. Kath let out a long rendition of *Born Free*, when Rob read out the letter. He was going to be a technical teacher at a secondary school in the capital, *Lilongwe*. Kath cried and laughed in equal measure. She was happy to be on the move again, but it would mean another two years away from Nelly and Arthur.

"Africa," Nelly mused. "I expect we'll come and see you."

"Of course, you will," Kath told her lack of funds was no obstacle now that Kath and Rob owned their own home. Nelly was proud.

Rob followed the news from Rhodesia. Ian Smith, the white rebel leader there for the past eleven years had announced a two-year plan for a transition from white minority rule to black majority rule. Rob wasn't convinced it would transpire without bloodshed and that trouble in Rhodesia would have implications for them in Malawi.

Kath couldn't grasp the bigger picture. " But we won't be in Africa once your contract is up, and Rhodesia is not Malawi..." Kath argued naively.

"But don't you see, Kath, we may never leave Africa; after Malawi we might go to South Africa and then, if there's bloodshed in Rhodesia, just think how much reason for fighting there is in South Africa, there's more reason to hate the white man there."

"But we are going to Australia, aren't we? In two years time? Dad will nearly have finished work and Mum will already be retired."

Kath told her parents of their plans over Sunday tea.

"You'll come to Australia when we emigrate, after our stint in Malawi won't you, Mum? We will go first, set up home, and buy a house with a granny flat. You can both come over as soon as Dad has retired and you have sold this house."

Nelly nodded, half-heartedly "Oh, our Kath, you make it all sound so simple."

Arthur said, "well, 'ers 'ere agin, running everybody's life, but I reckon we will come to Australia with you, Duck. I reckon we will. There's nowt here for the young 'uns anymore."

"Well, you never can tell, life is a funny thing," Robert interjected.

Kath kissed Rob on the lips and Arthur on the forehead. "Now now, don't let's all get our eyes off the ball, we are all going to Australia and that's that. You wait and see. Now let's sit down and watch *Dixon of Dock Green*, shall we? It's the last episode ever tonight, Mum."

"Is it? Oh what a shame." Nelly's shoulders drooped and she shuffled to the kitchen to make a cup of tea before the episode started.

It wasn't till mid-February of 1976 that Rob finally had clearance to travel to Africa. The Malawian government were strict on receiving only "TP'ed" personnel in their establishments: (only people who had been approved of as not being Communists, political activists, criminals or other undesirables, could be given work permits). Government approval took time.

Kath and Christian stayed home. They were to follow some four weeks later. Kath packed up, re-let the house and moved in with her parents. Loving thoughts of that Christmas sustained her through her last icy month in the UK.

Chestnuts by log fires ,friends and family visits and two-hundred Christmas cards.

The last envelope was addressed to Kath in Sam's hand with a warning, *DO NOT BEND – OPEN CAREFULLY.*

It had slipped through the letterbox the day after Boxing Day. Along with the card was a pencil sketch of Christian. Kath revelled in the drawing on white paper, Christian sitting with a vintage toy car in his chubby hands, smiling coyly. Kath had phoned her father-in-law straight away, but he told her that none of the Llewellyn's would be visiting them for some time. *Tilly wasn't going to drive in bad weather and was too busy anyway. Jeannie was still mourning over the death of her pet rabbit. Leo was in Kent.*

Robert hadn't seen his parents' prior his departure. Kath did the letter writing and made the phone calls. When she did manage to catch Tilly, it never seemed convenient: either they had visitors, someone was at the door, the roof was leaking or there were mice in the attic. In the end, Kath stopped phoning, except to say goodbye the night before she and Christian flew. Unexpectedly, she was rewarded with a most interesting conversation. Sam was anxious to try out his new hearing aids in both ears; the Tories were gaining seats in Parliament after several by-elections and would soon oust that Labour. But then, Sam's chat turned to Art. A certain fraudster, Tom Keates, had finally admitted to the art world that it was he who had been faking masters and fooling them all over the past twenty-five years. Sam admired the fellow's nerve and audacity. Kath pictured him, doubled up with laughter at the thought of the old rogue and she let out a shriek of delight herself. Tilly then took the receiver and ordered Sam to make her a cup of tea while she wished Kath a safe journey and a fruitful couple of years in Malawi. Her last dramatic words were: "To *march on and never be daunted*".

She cited something she had seen in the Press recently about a young MP who had resigned after becoming bankrupt, but had risen again to great heights after penning a best-selling novel.

"How is *your* novel coming on?"

"Still at it," Tilly replied, and offered no more.

–33–

Rob was living on his own in the headmaster's house on the school site in the capital. The Head had been removed from his post, the day before Robert's arrival, by the President's personal police squad. The unfortunate was a dissenter and had been 'disappeared' to a prison in the south. Kath's heart sank, as she read Robert's letter, at the thought of having to live under the Fascist dictator, Dr. Banda, but rallied when she remembered the warning from the Overseas Development Office: *You must always remember you are only in Malawi as a guest. Do not get involved in politics. You are there to impart knowledge. It is not your country, do not overstep your welcome and remember you are a one-eyed man in a blind man's country.*

Kath finally flew to Malawi, with Christian, in late March - the end of autumn in the Southern hemisphere. During the nineteen-hour flight, Kath thought about the ODA advice again, the same as when she and Robert had left the UK to work in the Caribbean.

"Keep your noses clean," were Arthur's last words, as he and Nelly left her and her son at Manchester airport. Kath was in no doubt she was a 'one-eyed man'.

The plane landed at the country's most southerly airport, in Blantyre. The sub-tropical rains were now less frequent than they had been in the summer but the lush green vegetation, sprouting dazzling brightly coloured flowers, was still thriving under the hot sun. Hibiscus, jasmine and frangipani perfume filled the air, until the car reached the sparser, drier, timeless landscape of the central region. The horizon shimmered in the dry heat. Rustling insects, screeching wildlife and bird song inhabited the vast plains. Goatherd bells tinkled. Tribal chanting and drumming emanated from the 'rondavals' (round huts), clustered in villages here and there. Sturdy Baobab trees stood mighty along the red, dusty roads. Groups of barefoot women, swathed in ankle length, brightly patterned cloth and matching headscarves, balanced clay pots and woven baskets on their heads. Most carried children bundled up on their backs. Those hoeing in the fields, stopped only to wave and smile, at the foreign folks gliding past in the white *Ford Anglia* that Robert had just bought.

The autumn faded into winter gracefully but the days were still warm. A log fire in the evening and only ever one blanket on the bed was needed.

By September, the couple were ensconced in a detached, three-bedroom bungalow, surrounded by citrus fruit trees. Their new home was only half a mile from Robert's school and the city centre. Two small rooms built on the back of the house served as the servants' quarters, (a '*kyre*' in Chichewa, the local native language). With a houseboy, cook and gardener, Kath organised what work was to be done and left them to it, while she was supply teaching at the nearby expatriate primary school.

Letters from Nelly and Arthur arrived every week. Kath replied promptly. They soon started supplementing the letters with cassette tapes for each other and exchanging Super 8 home movies. Nelly sent a tea chest full of the English things Kath missed: *HP* sauce, mint sauce, horseradish sauce, marmalade and lemon curd.

Nelly's care and attention contrasted with Rob's parents' lack of it. Tilly took three months to reply to Kath's first letter from Africa, but at least she said she fancied a trip to Malawi more than Cayman. The thought of sharks in the sea, after seeing the film *Jaws*, had put her off the West Indies.

Kath replied post haste that they would of course be delighted to receive, but that they might have to put up with crocodiles in the rivers, mosquitoes, scorpions, cobras and black mambas, not to mention eight-inch daddy-long-legs. Kath heard no more about a visit. Further letters complained about bills, arthritic knees, Samuel's prostate and Jeannie's lack of communication. But she did rejoice in Leo's absence.

Since appearing on TV's *Going for a Song,* some months before, (the reason she had given for not having had the time to write any earlier), Tilly was adding more celebrities to her list of clients wishing to buy antique dolls. The National Theatre was paying her to loan them prams for a long run of Chekov's *Cherry Orchard* and there were plans in the making for her to appear on *Cash in the Attic.*

"With coach-loads of visitors to the Museum, a ruin to renovate, part of a defunct convent to sell and The Old Parsonage on the market, I don't think Tiger will be coming to see us," Rob assured Kath, who couldn't decide whether she was pleased or disappointed. Anyway, she was too enthralled with her and Rob's new life to think further, especially as she was pregnant again. Rob liked to boast that she had conceived as soon as she had stepped off the plane; William was born in the February of 1977.

More parcels arrived. Gifts for the baby, books, newspapers and LPs like Rod Stewart's latest, Queen and the Motown groups. Local radio was idiotically bland; fearful of subversion, the Malawian regime blocked foreign stations. Any International newspaper of repute, like *The Times,* was censored too. The pages were inspected and any suspect article was either torn out of the paper altogether or blacked out with thick black felt tip pens. Rob discovered though that this ink could be removed easily with nail polish remover. The couple got pleasure getting one over on the dotty authorities!

Only once did the customs officials pry open one of Nelly's tea chests, but they still failed to spot the article in *The Times*, slating Dr. Banda for his seemingly oblique response to South Africa's apartheid and his high-handed rule in Malawi.

For some strange reason though, Kath never feared for her life in this little country. Other expatriates had been frog-marched out of the country at a twenty-four hours notice, banished from the land for such minor indiscretions as owning a copy of *Playboy* magazine, the men for having long hair, the women wearing trousers in public, or criticising the President. It all seemed so arbitrary to Kath, but, nonetheless, she wouldn't flout the rules, well, not openly, of course.

Rob felt charmed and invincible too; his engineering skills were called upon more than once and way beyond the terms of his contract. He ended up mending the local primary school's swimming pool pump equipment and servicing the General Attorney's car.

When William was nearly a year-old, Kath, now a well-respected member of the local community, started a shop, by chance. She was asked to sell masks, snorkels and swim fins, for a teacher friend who lived miles out of town. Kath put up an advert in a shop window and within a week everything was gone. Other expats, gave her things to sell, too. Within a month, their third bedroom was full of fridges, radios, record players etc. Kath got her ten percent. But it wasn't to last. Nelly and Arthur were due out for three weeks in July (1978) and a third baby was due at the end of that month. Kath finally stopped trading in late June and the *Jeep* she had been using to cart all the stuff about was sold and replaced with a black *Plymouth Limousine*, which sat six people.

Tilly's letters had become chattier after the birth of William. She wrote: *Wouldn't it be wonderful to have a sister for the two boys, how about Lucinda, Prunella or Annabella for a name?* She said they had no money, no time to visit. Again they had to pay out fortunes for solicitors to deal with planning objections from neighbours in the village who were opposing their proposals to convert the old bakery ruin into a two-storey house. Local council rates on all their properties were now double what they were some two years before and Leo had had an accident in his *Aston Martin*; they'd had to bail him out as he didn't have insurance. Besides that, Jeannie and Martin had only visited once since Christmas, when they made a detour on their way to West Wales for a weekend where they were to study *The Dyfeyd Enigma*. Tilly wrote, '*Jeannie was a nice kind girl before she married, not the least bit spiteful or hurtful. Now they are thinking of emigrating to Canada!.'* She closed with the news that Britain was having a heat wave and how horrible it was, and on second thoughts, she didn't like the idea of going to a hot county.

Kath kept up her copious correspondence. She learned a bit of Chichewa too, always said "Zikomo", instead of thank you in the shops, and greeted the people with a "Mulibwange Dilibweno?", (*good morning, how are you?*).

Medicine was *mankwala* and the veranda around the house was called the *khonde*. *Kutundoo* was the word for 'stuff' and was in fact what the servants called all their possessions as they moved from one 'madam', one 'bwana' to another. African servants usually only worked for a white family for a few months of the year, then they would head off back to their villages with their *Kutundoo* and their wages, only to reappear in town again some months later. Kath felt honoured that her contingent of house staff stayed with them for the full two years of their contract.

It was a sad day when they left Lilongwe for good. Joyce, the nanny, cried as she handed Kath a six-inch high soapstone carving of an eagle, a token of her appreciation.

But this wasn't to be the end of life in Africa for the Llewellyns. Just before Rob's teaching contract ended, he secured a job on a tea estate south of the country, only three miles from the border with Mozambique. He was to be manager of the vehicle workshop, in charge of keeping a fleet of fifty tractors, ten company cars and six company vans on the road. It would mean three more years in Malawi with paid leave back in the UK mid-way, free accommodation in a company house with two acres of garden, free electricity and a company car. The Golf Club, where there was a swimming pool, was only seventeen miles away and, in any case, they were told they could build their own pool in their garden. Robert signed the contract before going back on leave to the UK.

Kath accompanied Robert back to England with their three sons. Carl was just three weeks old and had been born in Lilongwe's new hospital, *The Kamuzu Central* - named after the President - just two days after Nelly and Arthur left Africa.

Robert left Kath and the children in the UK, after three weeks, to start his new job. Kath relied on Nelly and Arthur to look after her and the boys in Tunstall, as their own house in Newcastle was let out. Christian attended infants' school, but Kath struggled with the younger ones at home. Kath pondered... *If two children were three times the work of one, how much more work is three children*? She didn't complain to Robert. Getting to grip with his new job was not easy.

It would be nearly three months before Kath saw him again.

The bitter winter frosts bit into Kath's well-being; the lack of space, in the tiny terrace made her feel like she was suffocating, the dark nights and dank mornings were like being drowned.

Bad news, bombs in Belfast and boat people arriving from Vietnam sapped her soul. Margaret Thatcher, the new Tory leader, was warning of racial problems. The atrocities of the PLO and Israel made headlines and the sordid episode of the kidnapping of a Paris baron, during which the poor man had his fingers cut off by his captors, was splashed across the TV screens.

Only films and music, like *Saturday Night Fever*, with John Travolta's disco dancing, kept Kath buoyant enough to ask Tilly and Sam to visit. But that was a miserable affair. Nelly, obviously, couldn't offer them anywhere to sleep and suggested a hotel, but Tilly baulked at the idea. They visited their grandchildren for just one day, but Kath wished they hadn't. Nelly offered to cook lunch, but they went off and had pie and chips in the Tiko café in town. *They didn't want to impose*, Tilly said. Kath fumed; they could have at least all gone out together somewhere, a country pub, for example.

Still, Sam sketched a portrait of baby Carl in his pushchair and Tilly pressed a fifty-pound note into Kath's hand, before Arthur drove them to Crewe Station that night. Nobody had mentioned Leo or Jeannie - Kath thought it best not say anything about them either.

-34-

By the time Arthur had bundled the luggage, the children and his daughter into his car, all Kath's negative thoughts about the Llewellyns had been dispelled by luxurious thoughts of life to come on the tea estate. Kath blew kisses and waved goodbye to a tearful Nelly. Arthur put the car into first gear and pulled away from the curb.

It was after sunset when the plane landed in Blantyre. Robert gathered up his exhausted family and ushered them into the *Black Plymouth*. The car slid silently along the newly laid tarmac of the main road. Only the flickering flames, here and there, of village fires lit up the black sky. In seventy miles, they passed only one truck and no one overtook them. When they turned onto a dirt track, the red earth sparkled under the glare of the headlights. The car wove its way up hill like a snake. They passed a forest of blue gum trees, eerily tall and still, then a lake, a little bigger than the Serpentine. They bumped over a narrow, cobblestoned bridge, which just cleared the bubbling waters below, spewing rocks downstream at a thunderous rate. Then, in first gear, they went round bend after bend, each time climbing higher and higher. Then, suddenly, their house was there. Lit up by a string of garden lamps and the lights inside.

Wide-eyed, Kath took in the glory of the one-storey white building and the wide veranda; a roof cascading with bougainvillea, amidst an oasis of tropical fruit trees, lawns and a vegetable plot. This jewel of a home stood timeless in the middle of a sea of tea trees. Mulanje Mountain, three-thousand feet high, rose majestically to the east; waterfalls cascaded down its steep sides.

Just a tinge of the fine water and a whisper of its sound reached Kath's senses that night as she wandered around the garden, the air vibrating a little to the cracking sounds of the cricket's calls. The moon flowers' perfume reached deep into her soul like a magic potion.

Rob had underestimated Lujeri's charms. He hadn't conveyed the beauty, colour, light; the surrealism of it all. Still, Kath had time to savour all that.

In a country where only two percent of the population had electricity,

Kath thanked fate.

Again, with a contingent of servants: a cook, houseboy, nanny and two garden boys, plus the "launder" (the night watch-man who came at dusk, when the other staff went home, and left at dawn when they came back), Kath was free to indulge her pastimes. Swimming took priority. Kath used the pool at the Golf Club, until their own pool had been installed. Jams, jellies and drinks were made from the fruit harvested from their garden: guava, mulberries, oranges, lemons, strawberries. Cakes and puddings were made from the bananas. Chickens, rabbits and ducks were acquired, reared - and eaten. Kath made clothes for her sons, the servants and their children. She also read novels and kept a diary; writing at least one letter every day.

The Llewellyns' correspondence, like their lives, was chaotic. They lurched from one house, one DIY project to another, swore they would come to Malawi in one letter then, in the next, said they couldn't; no time, no money. But then Tilly would say how excited she was to be going to Turkey to buy carpets! Rob guessed rightly that she would be going this time with Douglas *the Parvenu*, as he called him, after he had ditched his long-standing girlfriend, Tina, to go off with a bank heiress, Sarah Richie.

Sarah had injected money into his Georgian Mansion project and, being important within a National Heritage Society, she had guaranteed him a trouble-free passage through both local and national planning regulations. Leo had spared no detail in relating how Tilly drooled over the man some fifteen years her junior. Rob scorched at the thought of the greasy cad buttering up his mother and father for more of Sam's artwork at knockdown prices.

Kath tried not to think too much about the in-laws, but couldn't help feeling for Leo when, Vicky, his lovely landlady and friend, in Maidstone, died of a brain haemorrhage. Leo was back in Somerset. *The boy is inconsolable,* wrote Sam later, and even though he had got his Degree was *utterly unemployable*. He described how Leo had taken to his bed and was popping pills, lithium and gallium, and then had gone blind.

Then suddenly, after a flash of lightning during a thunderstorm, Leo's sight returned. He ran out into the rain, swearing that he had heard the word of God telling him he had been chosen to save the world. He took his car, untaxed and uninsured, out of the garage and drove through the night to Jeannie and Martin's. Jeannie refused to let him in. He was ranting and raving, "I thought he would kill us," Jeannie told us. The police took Leo away under a restraining order. He's still in a psychiatric hospital in Devizes.

Tilly wrote: *Death would be kinder for him.*

Robert wept.

With Leo's absence yet again from the Old Parsonage, Tilly tried to get her affairs in order: Wisteria Cottage was finally sold for a slight profit, after plans were shelved to widen the road into town.

The old house that had been part of a monastery went under the hammer for cash, as it was too riddled with dry rot to attract a mortgage. The Bakery was finally finished and she and Sam moved in. Tilly was happy in her new dwelling, with two bedrooms and all mod cons. Rob said it was about time she showed some common sense.

The Pram Museum was still a curiosity and visitors trickled through the door. Tilly described her more colourful visitors in detail: Old Etonian and Charter House scholars, Burkes Peerage persons. The "Noblesse Oblige," she called them. She complained they didn't buy much though; business was in the doldrums.

Once their old friend, Archibald Pasqual, collaborator with them on their book, *Nursery Needs*, had died, Sam lost interest altogether in the Museum. He even stopped drawing for a month, so hurt was he by the loss of such a dear friend. Archie had raised the Llewellyn's profile to new heights. He had even been instrumental in getting Lord Villette to buy Sam's oil painting, *The Village Blacksmiths*. They would never ever be able to repay Archie, they said.

Rob was sceptical and presumed Sam had probably sold his work too cheaply to this so-called Lord. Kath reminded him it was really none of his business. Tilly complained bitterly in one letter that, with Archie gone, only Douglas could cheer her up.

After three months in the mental hospital, Leo was installed again at the Old Parsonage, but he longed even more to get away. *He's more petulant than George Best,* Tilly wrote, which Kath thought was strange, since Tilly had no interest in football.

"Probably read about him in *The Sun*," Rob said, as he read the letter out aloud.

Kath suggested again that her in-laws should come for a holiday in Malawi, but the reply was swift this time; too far and, in any case, they were going to France with Douglas to buy antiques in the Dordogne!

Rob was hospitalised for a fortnight with cerebral malaria. The week before he had told Tilly she was a fool for letting Douglas persuade her to go to France and letting him buy Sam's oil landscape painting of Weymouth Harbour for one-hundred-and-fifty pounds.

Kath cited it as divine justice. "They can do what they want with their own things," Kath argued. But she agreed with Rob that his mother was besotted with Douglas.

"Yes, he's got her just where he wants her, the swine!" Rob concluded.

Kath's assimilation into tea estate life was exceptionally easy; the MD's wife remarked, with a tad of envy at how adaptable she was. Within weeks of arriving in Lujeri, she got herself a bicycle for touring the plantation and had taken up squash in the makeshift court that had been converted from a barn. After trying her hand at golf, but deciding it was not for her, she ended up secretary at the Golf Club, being partly responsible for organising social evenings and activities for the members' children. Jaunts into the local villages once a week to buy wild boar, ground nuts, cassava and river fish, were an education and so was the monthly drive to Blantyre for shopping and to have a meal at one of the smart hotel restaurants. Kath was so adept at buying right, she was offered the job on the estate of setting up a staff-only store: employees purchased goods on account and the monthly tab was taken from their wages. Even Christian used the shop: a ball here, a toy car there, a bit of chocolate.

Eighteen months into Rob's contract with Lujeri Tea Estate, the couple were eligible for leave. By then, Nelly and Arthur had moved house. It had been decided that once Rob had got the job on the tea estate, they would lend Kath's parents the money to buy a semi-detached house in Newcastle.

Their terraced house in Tunstall was sold and the new house purchased in their four names. Nelly and Arthur would live in the new house as long as they wanted, but of course they would sell it and go to

Australia with Kath and Rob once that was going to be a reality. Kath had spotted the bijoux 1930's red brick dwelling not far from their own house, in Wolstanton. The back garden sloped down to a stream. Now she knew that Nelly and Arthur were settled in, Kath wanted to be with them again.

Packing up their belongings, but leaving enough out for Rob to survive a month alone (she and the children would be home for three months, Robert just one), Kath locked the family's most treasured possessions in one of the bedrooms of their tea estate house. She informed the servants that it was not to be opened during her departure, adding for good measure that she had had the witch doctor in to spread the magic potion, the "mangotomec", just to make sure nobody dared to break in. Kath could never understand anyone believing in such hocus-pocus, but there it was; the Malawians did so, *when in Rome*!

With reggae blasting out on the car radio and the chiperoni wind in their favour, Rob got to the airport in record time. "Make sure you keep the panga (machete) by the bed, make sure you eat what's left in the freezer and make sure you eat plenty of fruit," Kath said, as she kissed Rob goodbye.

This time, Kath had made sure the ground floor flat in their own house in Newcastle was free for her and the children, for the whole three months. Getting used to life in England, Christian was bewildered when he realised that one just couldn't go into a shop and take what one wanted and that money had to change hands first!

The weather was perfect. Kath decided on a dual christening for both Carl, now eighteen-months-old and William, three. As Christian had been baptised in the Anglican Church - to please Arthur - Kath decided on a Methodist ceremony to please Nelly. The family gathering after the chapel ceremony was in Arthur's garden.

Jeannie and Martin, having recently relocated to the outskirts of Manchester, came to the 'do' in their *Mini*. Tilly brought Sam, and Leo arrived in his sports car. He was still ill, but now safely in receipt of social security benefits, and handouts from Tilly and Sam.

Although they all only stayed the day, as Tilly, Sam and Leo would be going to Manchester afterwards for a few nights, the occasion was pleasant. The morning service was short. Kath and Nelly had prepared the buffet lunch and they sat on the lawn in the back garden. Everyone admired the brickwork terracing and steps that Arthur had built down to the stream, and complimented him on the pond he had built on the lower terrace for goldfish. Tilly's seal of approval was obvious when she stated that she could easily live in their house. Arthur puffed up with pride.

Evelyn sang *All Things Bright and Beautiful* and Uncle Dan sang Paul Robeson's *Old Man River,* while William and Carl splashed about in the inflatable paddling pool and Christian ran around squirting everyone with his water pistol. Jeannie pointed out how expensive the two engraved christening mugs she had presented had cost, but respectably managed to give her nephews a cuddle and kiss or two. She sat on Martin's lap afterwards and gave him a tickle in the ribs. Leo joined in with the water pistol battles and Sam speculated on his grandson's growing up to be artists. As he left, he handed Kath a copy of the latest handbook from the Tate Gallery. "To teach the boys," he said. He also gave her a sketch of Carl, which he had started some two years before, when he had last seen his grandsons. "To commemorate the birth of Carl," it said on the back of the drawing, now mounted on card.

"To commemorate the birth?" Arthur questioned, "...that was eighteen months ago! I think Sam must be bonkers!"

Kath opened *The Tate Gallery Illustrated Companion*, when the boys finally fell asleep during their flight back to Africa. Scanning the pages, she mused that Sam thought her three muscular lads would become artists. Heaven forbid they did, Kath was not impressed with any of the artists she knew; they were self-possessed, neurotic, unstable and fussy. Still, if that was their talent, so be it. She reprimanded herself for her thoughts on the subject, not being talented herself in that department. However, she liked looking at pictures and she did want to learn more about Art, if only to please Sam.

Gauguin had captured her imagination. She thought Rossetti divine, Dali sublime, Constable and Gainsborough too prissy, Goya and Hogarth too shocking. Turner was tempestuous. Modern art in general, she thought too obscure to even contemplate.

As the plane descended, Kath's thoughts returned to Rob, who would be waiting at Arrivals in Blantyre Airport, and she thought how lucky she was to have such a marvellous husband and excellent father for her children. *Fortes fortuna juvat* – fortune favours the brave, and a *gens du monde*. It was a good feeling.

Life on the tea estate resumed its perfect pace. Kath was 'Madam' and Rob 'Bwana', to the African servants. They were living history. The last of the colonials, a drama to be lived through and to be cherished: Kath was under no illusion that this life would end soon. There would be no more lucrative contracts. A directive from the Malawi government was pushing the large companies like theirs to Africanise its personnel. Rob would be replaced in just over a year's time. Now was the time to apply for emigration to Australia. Kath pained at the thought of uprooting Nelly and Arthur from their newly-found paradise in North Staffordshire, but at least that wouldn't be for at least three years, well, not until Kath and Rob had sold their house in England and bought another one in Australia. Kath convinced herself that settling in Australia would be easy and let the matter rest, once their emigration application papers had been filled in and returned.

There was still the possibility of Tilly and Sam visiting; Kath made the prospect seem attractive: a trip to Lake Malawi; a few days in the lakeside cottage, where she and Rob and the boys had already been several times; a drive up to the Zomba plateau, with a stay in a log cabin overnight and a flight in a private six-seater plane over the Victoria Falls, taking a *Land Rover* on safari up North.

Tilly waxed lyrical in her letters back to Kath and Rob over the thought, but that was all; she was too busy. She wrote that The Old Parsonage was finally being sold, along with the old bakery - which they had modernised - and they were to move to a great mansion, in Rode, which needed a little attention.

Tilly's descriptions of the massive Georgian mansion, Northfield House, didn't impress Rob. If Tilly said it needed a little work on it, the property was falling down! When she marvelled at the size of the five-foot wide marble sweeping staircase, leading to a galleried landing, Robert commented on how cold it would be. When she mentioned the height of the sash windows, he said that they would be in need of a thorough overhaul. When she said a bit of damp was coming through the ceilings, Rob predicted a new roof would be required. When she described the garden with a stream passing right past the back door,

Rob envisaged flooding.

Kath made no comment and wrote back wishing them luck in their move, and hoping Sam would send a sketch of their new dog. Peaches had died of old age and had been replaced by Rufus, a white standard poodle. The new home, in the main street, included an attached, stone, three-storey building, which had been used as a grocers shop in the past, but which Tilly was now going to set up as an antiques outlet. Leo was to be given the few rooms upstairs and he was to turn it into a flat for himself. Rob had doubts he ever would.

Tilly later wrote how it had taken their belongings over a week to shift to the new home. She described how livid she was when the removal men broke several of her precious dolls and her four-poster bed fell off the back of one lorry and smashed to smithereens.

The move had been orchestrated in March, during college term time. Much to the annoyance of Tilly, Jeannie and Martin didn't help out then and didn't even visit at the Easter break. Martin had cited too much exam marking and Jeannie had gone off gliding on Saddleworth Moor, to relax. She was finding her new teaching job taxing, as she was teaching Art full-time in a secondary school in Oldham. In truth, Martin was still smarting over Sam's recalcitrant behaviour when he was asked to speak up for him, after his application for the director's job at Sam's old Art School in Wales some months before. The Head, immediately following Sam, in 1968, had been removed from his post after rumours of embezzling. Both Sam and Tilly scoffed at the idea that their son-in-law should even get a look-in as a Director of the Art school and raised an eyebrow when Martin was eventually given the deputy director's job at an Art school in Greater Manchester.

Tilly drooled over the daffodils in the new garden, the kingfishers, the stream, the red brick walled secret garden and – joy of all joys – her finding a ruined cottage under the mass of brambles that they had cleared along the boundary with the neighbouring farm... *And the cottage wasn't even on the deeds,* Tilly wrote.

"A likely story," Rob chortled.

"And they are going to do it up," Kath read from the letter. "Poor Sam, more work for him..."

Kath cried when she heard how it was impossible to get the paintings Sam had done on bare plaster in the Old Parsonage, off the walls in one piece. There was no alternative, the *Saint James Park in the 1880s* mural in the Catherine of Aragon room and the Beatrix Potter figures in the smaller display room remained in situ. Kath sobbed again when she heard the new owners had whitewashed over the murals and ruined them forever.

However, moving house didn't put an end to Tilly's financial troubles: the Inland Revenue were demanding capital gains tax on the various properties she had bought and sold, since arriving in Somerset. Leo's social security benefits were not stretching to the lifestyle he was assuming for himself: gadding about buying clocks, at exorbitant prices, failing to resell them for a profit. Tilly was starving herself to death, scrimping and saving to keep them afloat. Rob only shook his head and said he had heard it all before.

At the little school for expatriate children in Mulanje, Kath took on the teacher's job, while the regular teacher was on long leave. With only twelve pupils, aged three to eight, there were two classes: she taught the older group, including Christian, and one of the planters' wives took the nursery class, which included three-year-old William. Eighteen-month-old Carl stayed with the nanny. Kath loved the job. Her letters home spilled over with the joy.

Music filled the house and Kath sang the latest pop songs from the LPs which Nelly had sent over to her: Abba's *Super Trouper,* Blondie's hit, *Call Me* and The Polices' *Don't Stand So Close To Me.*

Back in the UK, Margaret Thatcher was 'Not for Turning' and was pressing for painful economic reforms and massive privatisations. Reagan in the US was on the move towards the Presidency. Mugabe's rule in Zimbabwe was one of bloodshed. John Lennon's brutal death in New York was still stunning the world until Prince Charles announced his engagement to Diana, but that didn't concern Kath. For now, she only had thoughts for Malawi and their next move, to Australia.

Billy and Pauline were settled in Mandurah, south of Perth, in a bungalow they had built themselves, after buying a block of land only metres from the Indian Ocean. Billy had a permanent and pensionable job with ALCAN, as a plant fitter. Pauline was still a housewife, having produced another son, Ben, in the same month as Kath had had Carl. Kath looked forward to staying with them, for a few weeks on their arrival in Australia, just long enough for Rob to secure a job. Billy assured him good mechanics were in demand and Kath no doubt would find work teaching too. Rob, however, wasn't convinced. He always had a sixth sense when it came to sniffing out trouble ahead. He wasn't sure they would even get past the emigration officials who were coming to Blantyre to interview him. He didn't feel his paper qualifications would stand up to scrutiny. " '*Australian labour legislation demands union approved qualifications for each job,'*" he quoted. Rob's qualifications were all in Art, apart from a short course at Massey Ferguson on tractor maintenance, which he had done in Coventry - when he was on leave in the UK that previous year. He had nothing major to prove he was an engineer and most certainly he wouldn't be accepted, no strings attached, on teaching skills. Rob always had an eye for the bigger picture of world politics and economics and how it could impact on his life. Having been thwarted once by the Australian government, he wasn't about to place his trust in them again.

Rob was right. Although the interview went well and the whole family had passed their medicals, the official letter stated that residential status would only be considered if /when Mr Llewellyn could prove he had a definite job offer. A job offer wasn't a guarantee of entry, but, nonetheless, Robert agreed with Kath that their best tactic would be for them all to go to Australia for a long holiday on completion of the contract at Lujeri. They would stay with Billy, until Rob had secured work. Kath would then return to the UK and sell their house.

"Kath, you make it all sound so simple," Rob admonished. "Just don't count on it."

Kath scowled but knew that Rob was right. There was always some snag or other, best to just take each day as it came.

By mid-April and without the prospect of having any visitors at all from England, Kath started the job of sorting out their belongings. Only the bare minimum was earmarked to go back to the UK, by sea, in a packing crate. A suitcase each was put to one side for the flight to Australia and filled gradually with suitable clothes and necessities. Many of their belongings were sold off, toys Rob had made for the children: a wooden slide, a metal sea saw, a plywood garage, a wooden truck. Everything else: carpets and curtains, towels, bedding, excessive clothes, pots and pans, crockery, the sewing machine and bicycle -

were left for the servants.

By the beginning of July, all that was left was for the flights to be booked to Perth. Kath had that planned for the day after the end of term, July 12th, when she would go to go Blantyre. Rob's contract with Lujeri was to finish in the middle of August.

On the morning of July 8th, Kath was teaching, when Rob phoned the school. Nelly had collapsed with a brain haemorrhage and was in intensive care, but not expected to live. Kath's world stopped dead. The phone dropped from her hands. She staggered to the "khonde" and collapsed on the wicker settee in the shade. Time turned black. Rob arrived with tranquillisers and William and Christian left with the nursery teacher for the night. The servants looked after Carl.

It wasn't until Kath flew home, sedated enough to travel, with her children, some two days later, that she was able to cry.

Kath fell into her Uncle Eric's arms as he met her and the boys at Manchester airport. Aunty Hilda, was at home comforting Arthur, her brother. She took charge of the children and Eric drove Kath to the hospital. It was 2pm. Nelly was still in the intensive care ward, but her life support machine was turned off. Only her face and arms were visible above the white sheet. Nelly's face, eyes closed, was white, flat and expressionless, except for her mouth. The lips, were stretched tight and drooped slightly at the corners. Kath took hold of her mother's left hand. It was going cold. She stroked the fingers, and touched her mother's wedding ring, remembering that her parents had been married for over forty years. Tears streamed down Kath's cheeks. Nelly had died of a broken heart, she reckoned. At sixty-four, she had not seen her son Billy, or his children, for almost ten years. Kath felt hurt for her mother's loss, and for her own. She stood by the bed shaking, staring at her mother's face, thinking how cruel fate was and how life would never be the same again. She left the room with the cold of death lingering on her palms and a knot of pain in her gut.

-35-

UK, 1981

Carl's third birthday (the same day as Prince Charles and Lady Diana's wedding: July 29th 1981) forced Kath to put aside her grief and throw a tea party. Arthur rallied too, blew up a few balloons and acted the fool.

Tilly declined the invitation, and the offer of few days in Newcastle; Leo was not making a go of his antique shop and unpaid bills were piling up. Only restoring the cottage (the one rescued from under the brambles) and selling it would 'save their bacon', she said.

Tilly was in France with Douglas for a fortnight, when Robert got back to England. "No money indeed!" He poo pooed. "Gadding about Normandy buying antiques is not cheap; she's nothing but a charlatan, a fraudster, and a fake."

Robert phoned his father. Sam was resigned to Tilly's wanderings; he was more upset that his wife had forced him to sell yet another of his paintings.

"He knocked me down to two-hundred pounds, that Douglas did." Sam complained. "*The Welsh Farm Hand,* one of my best paintings. She said she needed the money. You know how it is, big houses, Leo ... you follow?"

Kath shook her head in disgust, but was more concerned about Rob getting a job; with unemployment over two-and-a-half million, and on the rise, it was a worry. Thoughts of Australia had evaporated like the morning dew and Arthur had lost the will to live. Kath survived on mogadon and they moved to the ground floor flat of their own house in September.

Rob started teaching after Christmas in a comprehensive school, five miles away. At Easter they took over the whole of their house and started putting in a new bathroom and a fitted kitchen.

As the summer approached, Tilly started dropping in, on her drive up North to see Jeannie and Martin, recently moved to a village west of Manchester. She regularly stayed a night or two with Arthur. She adored his little house and swore she missed her little grandsons. Kath was at last beginning to wonder if Tilly was going to be a good grandmother, after all. Arthur looked forward to her company and was taken in by her newfound charms. He was in awe of the woman, who made herself out to be an angel and the parish priest, the devil incarnate. Kath was both amused and relieved. at last there was hope of a warmer relationship between her and Tilly *and maybe with time, there would be a little love,* Kath crossed her fingers and wished.

Eventually, Jeannie and Martin invited her brother and his family, to their art deco style semi. The white, flat-roofed dwelling stood incongruous against its moorland setting. Three-foot tall stone eagles, topped the stone pillars at the entrance to the drive. A print of Goya's *The Witches' Sabbath* hung in the hall. Kath's spine quivered and she broke out into a cold sweat, thinking Jeannie might still be doing witchcraft.

If Tilly was aware that her daughter was in league with the devil, then she never let on. Blustering over Martin's behaviour was *de rigor*; he was too effeminate, juvenile, namby-pamby, a mummy's boy - but criticising Jeannie was off piste. Nonetheless, when Tilly talked of her daughter, her eyes spelled out sadness. *What was it that pained her so? Jeannie having no children, perhaps?* Kath wondered.

Tilly complained endlessly about a lack of money. Dry rot had destroyed all the wooden floors in the big house in Rode, and was going to cost over thirty thousand pounds to put right. Rob had been right about the windows, but Tilly said they would just have to stay put, along with the leaky roof, which was patched up for the fourth time since they had moved in. Still, she remained firm that her decision to move had been a sound one. She poetically praised the house's picturesque and spiritual qualities: the tranquillity; the weeping willows; the *fleur-de-lis* design on the wrought iron railings across the arched bridge over the bubbling stream; the nightingales' song; the honeysuckle; their walled "secret garden"; the perfect arbour outside the kitchen door - the perfect place for her to write.

Having abandoned her novel on the Rebecca Riots, 'too disturbing' she said, she had taken up writing children's stories again and was about to complete *The Harvest Mice.* Sam had already produced pen and ink drawings for it and the book was to be dedicated to Carl, the youngest grandson.

Kath and Rob went to Somerset on completion of the cottage's restoration. "Totally unmortgageable," was Rob's verdict.

"Just the sort of comment I would expect from you!" but, Tilly, ensconced in a wicker chair under a wide parasol, was in no mood for confrontation. She ordered Sam to bring extra chairs and cooled champagne from the fridge, and made the couple sit down. With a glass of bubbly in hand, she told the tale of the bloody murder, in their village in the nineteenth Century: Constance Kent, a teenager had slit the throat of her three-year-old bother, and dumped his body in the family's latrine outside their mansion. "Jealousy, they say. I'll take you to see the house where it all happened, tomorrow, Kath. "

"Yes... jealousy is a powerful emotion," Kath said, thinking of Jeannie.

In between more stories, Tilly played the accordion with gusto, and swigged more wine. Kath was dispatched four times to the fridge to replenish stocks of the stuff! She fell off her chair laughing at Tilly's tale of the time she delivered an antique doll to a client in the Royal Crescent in Bath:

I arrived a few minutes before four o' clock, after parking away from the house, beyond the yellow lines, expecting to have to get help to collect the doll from the car later. Anyway, a tidy gentleman, a retired colonel, opened the front door and showed me into the drawing room. "Everything is in hand," he said calmly and then brought me one glass of Champagne, then another. I drank half the bottle in the course of the next half an hour! The man told me I had good dress sense and said he liked tall women of mature stature, especially blondes! Then he told me he was financially stable and had been a widower for a respectable eighteen months.

Of course I was confused, but then amused, so I told him he had exquisite taste in antique furniture and oil paintings. He then told me he had a country house in France and that he liked the finer things of life and had good contacts in London, where he enjoyed attending the ballet and opera. Well, I was wondering where this was all leading, so I mentioned the doll in the car and said we ought to go and collect it.

"Doll, doll," the Colonel spluttered. "You are delivering a doll which Mrs. Goldencrab has bought from you! Why, the lady lives next door, at Number 22. Do forgive me Mrs... Erm, I didn't catch your name...?"

"Tilly Llewellyn, but just call me Tilly," she laughed. "I've come to the wrong

house then?"

"Well, you certainly must have, Tilly." The old chap soldiered on. "I thought you were the lady they were sending round from the dating agency!"

Just then, as I was enjoying the little faux pas, the doorbell rang, twice. The colonel then peered around the curtain and strained to see who was at the door. "This must be the woman from the agency," he stated, sheepishly. "She's not like you," he said, "I won't let her in." I was intrigued, but embarrassed, of course, I left half a glass of champagne on the table, and insisted on leaving. The little lady from the agency was still on the pavement, looking up at the tall thin three-storey house, squinting at each window for a sign of life, when I slipped past her and winked. "He's very deaf that old colonel, better give the door a good bang as well as a ring. He's slow on his feet too, so give him some time to get to the door, and don't forget your handkerchief, he's full of cold today, you could catch something."

When I glanced back the little woman had walked off.

But you know... what a pity I am tied up in Rode. Didn't seem a bad chap, this Philip Michael Hunt.

Sam puffed on his cigar and expelled the smoke slowly. He'd obviously heard it all before.

"I'm too old for taking on another man now," Tilly sighed.

At sixty-three, and weighing over fourteen stone, old age was beginning to show. Sleepless nights had left her with black rims under her eyes and her knees were creaking with arthritis.

Sam never stopped stripping old vanish off old doors and skirting boards or whitewashing walls. It was a credit to him that he had already filled several sketchbooks with drawings of the old house, including Rufus the dog, some of the houses and people in the village and now, the Llewellyn children.

Jeannie and Martin visited Somerset only once that year, staying in Bramble Cottage after Rob and Kath left. Tilly rang Rob after their visit and spoke of her concern for her daughter's sanity, "Not another one round the bend," Tilly bluntly expressed her pain. "She's up to something that one. She keeps going to London, something about a Hell Fire Club and visiting haunted houses. I hope to God she isn't involved with drugs."

Kath heard Leo quoting the Bible in the background, "Leviticus: A man or wizard shall be put to death. They shall stone them with stones". Kath could only say she was sorry and refused to be drawn into speculation. Life was tough enough without cluttering her brain about Jeannie and Martin's pastimes.

By 1983 there were three million unemployed. Race riots had ripped through the country and Michael Heseltine had got the go-ahead to rejuvenate the inner cities with millions of government money; at least Rob had a permanent and pensionable job now. Moira Stuart, the first black woman to be a newsreader on TV, was making a dash. Torville and Dean were thrilling the nation with their dance performances on ice. British pop music and films were bringing in foreign currency and establishing the UK as the creative centre of the world. Kath, like everyone else, used culture to cure and turned up Radio One to revel in latest music from Culture Club, Michael Jackson and David Bowie. She also saw the new films, like *Ghandi* and *Educating Rita*.

Tilly had no trouble selling her cottage, to a fellow antique dealer, for a good price and had no compunction in telling Rob, to prove him wrong. The lady needed only a small mortgage to complete the sale and she and her husband moved in, spring of 1984.

Sheila and Tilly were not only friendly rivals in the antique trade, but sparred over who was the best writer and who had the most success with their submittals - Tilly with her children's stories or Sheila with her tales of cats, the supernatural and ghosts.

Neither of them got published until they succumbed to the vanity press, but they seemed content to have gone down that road. Kath thought Sheila, a little younger than Tilly, was having a good influence on Leo. They often went buying together at the auctions in Wales and to the South Midland flea markets. Tilly was only too glad to get Leo off her back and sang Sheila's praises to everyone. She was a godsend to Tilly too, now that Douglas was not paying her visits like he used to. It seemed that Sarah, his new wife, was keeping the gentleman on a tight leash in Wales. Tilly felt ditched but not finished and she battled on.

The year after the cottage was sold, she got Douglas - much to his new wife's annoyance - to get her and Douglas's old girlfriend Tina, tickets to the Chelsea Flower Show. Kath winced at how Tilly had rejected her offer to take her to the Garden Festival in Stoke some years before, stating that Chelsea couldn't be beaten and she would never bother to go anywhere else.

Kath was therefore surprised when Tilly asked about buying Arthur's little house in Newcastle. Since Nelly's death, Arthur had complained that he couldn't afford to run the semi alone on his small pension and was planning to move. Kath wasn't so sure she would want her in-laws so close. Kath couldn't forgive Leo completely for calling her a Clay Head, either. Leo said Tilly had hated the idea of Kath living near them in Somerset - when Kath and Rob finally had to settle in England after leaving the tea estate in Malawi. Kath had tentatively broached the subject of renting the flat over her antique shop next to Northfield field House. Tilly said emphatically that she couldn't help. The rejection still stung.

When after months of contemplation, Tilly wrote, "We have decided that we couldn't live in your little house. We couldn't live in Stoke, either." Kath was relieved, but wondered if Tilly still thought her to be a Clay Head!

Jeannie remarked to Kath. "Thank God. We couldn't bear them living so near to us!" Jeannie still hadn't forgiven her mother for the bad experience she and Martin had living in her flat over the antique shop. Furthermore, they were fuming at the money Leo was leeching from Tilly for regular weekend trips to South Wales and jaunts to London to buy antiques, which always included a two-night stay in a Mayfair hotel.

However, the desperate financial situation of the Llewellyns was evident by autumn, 1985.

Leo was hospitalised again at the Royal Bath. He had been Sectioned and sedated after throwing himself into the hospital swimming pool and nearly drowning. After a brief visit, Robert suggested Leo change his identity and live away from his parents. Kath chastised Robert, for what she thought was impractical, idiotic advice, but he stuck firmly to his beliefs and blamed the eccentricity of his parents for all Leo's troubles.

While Leo was incarcerated, they heard nothing from Tilly: she didn't reply to Kath's letters or phone calls. It was only after three months and a phone call to the local police station, that Kath began to think that Leo might be right and his parents wrong.

"My in-laws live in the Rode High Street - they have a mentally ill son, a manic depressive, schizophrenic–" Kath told a policeman on the phone.

"You're talking about the Llewellyns?" The policeman interrupted.

"You know about Leo?" Kath asked in disbelief, but then she was reassured at least to learn that he hadn't escaped from the secure unit at the Royal and murdered his parents in their beds.

Robert finally spoke to Tilly who told him not to worry; and he didn't. There was more than enough to deal with in Newcastle. Rob with his teaching, getting Arthur's house cleaned up to sell, looking after the children. Kath was teaching swimming five nights a week at the local baths, and now she was learning Spanish.

After deciding England was a terrible place to be in the winter and after hosting adorable teenage Spanish students that summer, Kath had enrolled at night school for beginners Spanish.

Fifteen more years work and the couple worked out they could finish teaching and retire to Spain. After ten years of having no winters (while they lived abroad) Kath was sick of the ice and snow of her homeland. She was still sore too at the way Canberra had thwarted their chances to emigrate; but her thoughts were now set on Southern Europe; the cheapest sun on earth. With this in mind, she set to learning Spanish with gusto – and celebrated with a night out in the newly opened Spanish restaurant in town.

Tilly and Sam's plans to be in Newcastle that Christmas and at Jeannie's for the New Year were scuppered, when just a few days before the festive season, the stream in their garden bursts its banks. Over a metre of water swilled into the house. By candlelight, Tilly and Sam watched in horror from the top of the stone staircase, as their furniture got shoved around by the swell on the ground floor. The water subsided as quickly as it had arrived, but the aftermath was inevitable devastation. Thousands of pounds worth of antiques were destroyed in a flash and relegated to a skip, along with carpets and books. Many of Sam's drawings had got soaked, too. Sam dealt with those first, hanging them up on a makeshift clothes line upstairs by a south-facing window for a few weeks, until they dried out. Tilly was dumbstruck, yet again they were not insured! By spring - and after a modest clear up - the 'For Sale' sign went up.

Leo, whose friendship with Sheila, in the cottage, had blossomed, was so overcome by anguish of the pending separation, he went into a psychotic rage, smashing up dining chairs and breaking one over Sam's head. He was removed from the house in a Black Mariah. Sam quaked when the policeman came to the door. He begged him, against Tilly's wishes, to go away, but Tilly won the tussle and Leo was dispatched to the Royal Hospital in Bath, again. Constrained by a straight jacket and in a padded cell, he was plied with a cocktail of pills. Tilly spared Rob and Kath the horrific details of his initial detainment and subsequent confinement, and left it to them to decide whether to visit or not. Jeannie didn't bother and Rob never could find the time, either.

Once Tilly had turned her back on the idea of buying Arthur's house, Rob lost interest in his parent's plans, but Kath still phoned and suggested they look for a house in Shropshire. Market Drayton, the market town, was only twenty miles from Stoke. There were beautiful and inexpensive black-and-white timbered houses... but when Tilly showed little enthusiasm, even Kath gave up trying.

Months of silence ensued, followed by a letter from mid-Wales. Northfield House and the shop, in Somerset had been sold and all the contents moved to their new home, *The Winery,* in Presteign. The border town in Powys was only four miles from where Douglas was living in splendour with his London born wife, Sarah, and now their two young children.

Rob reckoned it was still a good three hours drive to Presteign from Newcastle, and on winding country lanes, the driving would be more troublesome than driving to Somerset.

Leo was still confined to the mental hospital in Bath, when they moved, and Tilly hoped he would be kept in care permanently. She hadn't even informed Leo or the hospital of their departure from Somerset. When Leo was discharged and found new owners in 'his' house in Rode - and no sign of his parents - he went into shock and was hospitalised yet again. After heart-wrenching negotiation and a guarantee that Leo would get the higher social security benefit rate for serious mental illness, Tilly was eventually persuaded to take Leo back and quoted Margaret Thatcher, her heroine, 'Life Goes On'.

They had cheered when Maggie won the Falklands War for Britain, survived an IRA bomb blast in a Brighton hotel and been re-elected Prime Minister again in 1983. They slated the Unions and took delight in mocking Arthur Scargill. Sam took up caricaturing the Union leader. He thought the spending of millions on upgrading these hot beds of unrest, where inner city rioting had taken place, was a waste of public money. Sam's enthusiasm for Thatcherism bordered on Fascism. Sam relived his summer of 1932, which he spent in Berlin. "Those Aryans looked so smart and clean..." he told a horrified Kath; she hadn't seen so much of Sam's dark side before, he wasn't the gentle lamb, the humble servant, after all.

Perhaps Rob was right in thinking that Leo had been driven round the bend by his parents. Kath wrestled with her thoughts but realised, whatever the truth, she would never know it. Her in-laws' lives had become so complicated, so entwined like a ball of string where the end was lost, and there would be no hope of ever unravelling it.

Kath put the Llewellyns to the back of her mind, and filled her life with what was good: children, work, study, cinema, and pop music. The Pet Shop Boys, Simply Red, Madonna, and Lionel Richie were all topping the charts. Films like *Jean de Florette* and *Manon de Source* filled her hours, along with doses of *Bergerac*, *Spitting Image*, *The Antiques Roadshow* and Philip Marlow in *Private Eye* on TV.

But, Kath still found time to pursue her Spanish.

-36-

Just as Tilly and Sam relocated to mid-Wales, Kath and Rob found a buyer for their Edwardian semi and moved to a modern detached house with a large double integral garage in the same area, so that Christian could continue attending his secondary school. Jeannie left Martin and set up home, on her own, in a dilapidated end terrace in the middle of Oldham. Money from the sale of the semi, would fund its renovations.

At forty-two and with a full-time teaching job, Jeannie found the confidence to divorce Martin: the relationship was stale, she said. She wanted to 'live', which meant having an affair with one of her colleagues at the art school. However, the married man, well known as a sower of 'wild oats', soon abandoned his latest conquest and, at five months gone, Jeannie miscarried. Kath empathised. She too knew the pain of what it was to lose a child. Jeannie swore her to silence; Tilly must never know, and Kath was true to her word.

It was spring when the two women met again. Jeannie had survived the loss but it had cost her job: the art school Head was her ex-lover's buddy – so, Jeannie moved to another college, an inconvenient hour's drive from where she lived, but Jeannie remained unnervingly cheerful.

She had at last embarked on giving her new home a facelift. Hilary Hardwood was in charge of the project; the finest master builder, plumber and electrician for a hundred miles, according to Jeannie. She was in awe of the little man, with a balding head and short neck. He reminded her of Humpty Dumpty, and she towered over him, she even had the urge to pick him up and put him on a wall!

Local man, Hilary, had such a strong Mancunian accent, that Rob wasn't even sure he was speaking English… but felt he must have had something, as, by that summer, restorations were completed – and the fellow moved in.

Jeannie made it sound so natural… he had left his wife and two children to live with her. Kath felt her soul groan. She knew the liaison would spell disaster.

The coarse man spat in the street, swore at the end of every sentence, and he had a beer belly. But, Tilly, (uncharacteristically, thought, Kath) only praised the man's achievements. "He's a fine craftsman," she said, on inspecting Jeannie's house shortly after all the work had been signed off. "Excellent business brain," she went on, after learning that he had declared himself bankrupt to avoid paying maintenance to his wife, but had somehow cleverly engineered to keep a flat in Tenerife. Kath was intrigued and suggested that they all go and stay in Spain together. "I'm learning Spanish," she told Jeannie, again.

"Yeh, yeh…" Jeannie wasn't listening. Kath's blood ran cold.

Tilly and Sam had bought the medieval house, *The Winery,* because it was the only one of the big houses they saw that they could afford and had a barn, that could be a studio for Sam. The old fellow whitewashed the walls and used long ladders to get to the ceiling. "I feel like Michelangelo painting the Sistine Chapel when I am up there," he beamed. Eventually he nailed up some of his large canvases. Kath was staggered at the sight. Twice as big as real life, the murals depicted Welsh early nineteenth Century, farming families, nude women - reminiscent of Picasso's *Les Demoiselles d'Avignon* - characters from Greek Mythology and children at play.

As Kath poked at a hole in one of the canvases and lamented the frayed edges and the peeling paint, Sam thumped the wall next to her. "Second place in the Prix de Rome 1928..." he said. A tear came to his eye. "By one mark, one mark, Augustus John was mad about that. By God he was angry! He thumped the table, he did, when he knew I hadn't got the scholarship." Kath had heard him complain about that before.

Kath patted her father-in-law on the back, "And this one?"

"Jason and the Argonauts," Sam explained, but when Kath said she didn't care much for the ancient Greek stories, Sam tutted. Kath mused; that here she was being made to feel like an ignoramus 'cause she didn't take to Greek mythology and there Hilary was, who had never read a book in his life, being feted as the great creator because he could put a few electricity cables in! She tried hard not to feel offended for her and Robert.

"Don't fret your head about Hilary and Jeannie, Tilly and Sam or Leo," Rob argued back." They won't thank you for it!"

Tilly made new contacts in Powys and carried on with her antique dealings. She took to standing at antique fairs in Ludlow, Leominster and Bombard, and built up a trade from the house. Sam took on commissions for portraits. He did sketches for the local church magazine and a series of drawings, at the behest of Tilly - for free - of Douglas's children. Tilly's pram, doll and toy collection, being diminished by the day, was now housed on the first floor of the three-storey, black-and-white, timber-framed home, but still attracted attention. The couple, along with their antiques and interesting anecdotes, were often featured in local magazines. Efforts to set Leo up again in an antique shop in the village, with his very own flat over the shop, failed miserably. After buying the premises, it was sold again after six-months to a Chinese couple who turned it into a take-away and Leo returned to *The Winery*.

Tilly made no secret of the fact that she hated having Leo living with them, but it wasn't until 1992 that an opportunity arose to get him out. A red brick, three-storey, Queen Anne house, in the village square, was up for sale. It was going cheap as it had a sitting tenant and needed extensive repairs. Already divided into three flats, the ground floor flat housed an old bachelor, on a fixed rent, but Leo could live on the second floor and let the top one out. Tilly secured a mortgage on the new property on the strength of owning *The Winery* and Leo was installed forthwith.

Jeannie had already moved from her terraced house, with Hilary, to a hillside cottage, with two acres of land, on the Lancashire side of Saddleworth Moor. She and Hilary were too busy now to be visiting Wales and spending weekends doing odd jobs for her parents - they said. The truth was that Jeannie was peeved that Leo was yet again sponging off his parents, something she nor Rob ever did. By boycotting her parents in Wales, Jeannie, with all the subtlety she could muster, thought Tilly might change her behaviour. Kath agreed with Jeannie, so she and Rob kept a cool distance too. Tilly meanwhile, was oblivious to the boycott.

Tilly now talked about Kathleen, in endearing terms. Her and Rob's wedding photograph was displayed on the mantelpiece in the main living room, which Tilly insisted on calling the withdrawing room, just like at the Old Parsonage. Photographs of the grandchildren: Christian, William and Carl, stood on the sideboard. There weren't any of Jeannie or Leo.

After five years studying Spanish, Kath was capable of studying it at degree level. Finding she loved the language and with the prospect of being able to live in Spain becoming more and more likely, the motivation to work hard was easy. However, it wasn't until she was faced with the possibility of having to use her skills to work, as a language teacher, she decided she would definitely have to take her study to the higher level. Rob, who was approaching fifty, was having a mid-life crisis. He hated his job and was threatening to resign. Kath told him to make his own mind up, assuring him that if he did finish with teaching, he could always find work as a mechanic. He could have his own business perhaps and in any case she would now get qualified and get a job teaching languages in schools.

Kath gulped at committing herself so much. Still she 'girded her loins,' and she got on with the necessary. She studied French again and did it 'A' Level, after which she was accepted at Wolverhampton University. As she already had a Certificate in Education, she needed only to study two years part-time, spend a year abroad to perfect one of the languages, and then spend a further year in full-time study. Kath suffered anxiety at the prospect, experiencing all the doubts and fears of a mountaineer trying to conquer Everest. But Robert stopped complaining of schoolwork and, in fact, never did give up his teaching post. The lure of the teacher's pension at the end of it all one day was too much to lose.

As Kath went off to Wolverhampton, Christian, now eighteen, went off to Cambridge. Tilly sent a handsome cheque after Robert phoned to invite her and Sam to celebrate, and she declined to travel up north. Jeannie was informed, but never responded. Leo said he could have gone to Oxbridge, if his stupid father hadn't insisted he did art. Rob said he wasn't listening to any of it.

Kath's endeavour and hard work contrasted sharply with Leo's lazy lifestyle, but no one ever commented on that. Rob broiled at the thought of Leo lying in bed, day after day. He received social benefits and got the rents in from the flats. Robert exploded when he found out that Tilly had been channelled into transferring the deeds of the Red House to Leo, when it was found that, as a Grade II listed building, a grant to repair the place would only be forthcoming if the property were owner-occupied. It was a fete accompli. Tilly smarted, along with the rest of the family, but there was nothing more to do, than accept the situation.

Rob dealt with injustice in his usual fashion: more work and more self-sufficiency. It was the most sensible thing to do.

Kath was more vociferous. When Tilly let it slip that Leo, although he still had his flat in the Red House, was actually living in Bath from Monday to Friday, in a rented flat and *she* was paying, Kath told her "Kow-towing to Leo's blackmail, and his delusions of grandeur, is affront to the likes of us, hard working people, who pay their taxes to pay benefits to him, and other miscreants like him!"

Kath henceforth was branded a troublemaker. The impasse lasted a few years. Kath was only partially sorry. Her patience had run out. But at least now, she had time in her life to grow. It was only when Kath succeeded in gaining a BA Honours Degree that Tilly made a move for reconciliation; their relationship was resumed and life went on.

Sam still groaned about missing out on a Rome Scholarship *The Prix de Rome* and since Andy Warhol had died, he now never failed to ridicule Damien Hirst for his success in modern Art. "They should put him in a tank of formaldehyde," he said in reference to the artist's infamy for putting dead animals in glass tanks of preservatives. Kath agreed with him. The art world was cockeyed. Well, the whole world was, wasn't it? Nothing made sense. No justice, no rewards for the workers, just crazy. Visiting her in-laws, was still depressing. The only thing she liked there was sitting in their garden. Sam had a used his green fingers to turn out a paradise of flowering shrubs, cascading climbers, a flower for very season, a trompe l'oeil here and there. At ninety, he was a miracle, a picture of strength and living proof that hard work never killed anyone. If Rob had half his genes, which of course he did, then Rob too would live a long life. Kath assumed she wouldn't live that long. Nelly had gone at sixty-four, Arthur at seventy-five; he had died instantly of a heart attack. Kath at forty-seven began to wonder about her own mortality.

After finishing her Degree, she was elated to find that she wouldn't need to take a full-time teaching post. Rob had ridden out the storm of his mid- life crisis and was content to stay put in his school, until they made him redundant or pensioned him off. Kath got part-time work teaching English as a foreign language. She had already qualified as a TEFLA teacher after a five-month short course, just prior to starting on her Degree and had run summer schools for foreign teenagers in the summers - for the past four years. She had also spent eight months in Northern Spain, teaching English in a school, as part of her Degree. The part-time job in Stoke now would do nicely, until they got to live in Spain!

The day Kath started work at the university, their first grandson was born. William, their middle son, had become father to Damien, and it was with a mixture of joy and fear that the new baby was welcomed by his grandparents. William, after all, at eighteen, was only a boy himself. Still, the baby was healthy and would be loved, unconditionally. Kath and Rob would see to that.

Tilly and Sam responded to the birth with a card and a ten pound note. Jeannie sent a fiver. Leo didn't do anything.

Now, as a granny, working and saving up to go to Spain, Kath had even less time to go to Wales.

Tilly was getting bad on her legs. Arthritis was eating away at her knees and she had stopped driving, even as far as Ludlow. She had also developed a stomach ulcer and was on strong medication. Leo was getting into pub fights. After being set upon on one night by gang of men he was left with a detached retina in one eye and a smashed cheekbone. Months of visits to Moorfields Eye Hospital in London followed, but he never recovered the full sight in his right eye. After being wrongly prescribed eye drops, his face now was scared with a port wine stain. His hair had thinned out and was greying. He had lost weight and he looked like Worzel Gummidge.

Sam, for all his moaning, seemed the only fit one of the trio. He put it down to being skinny and always active. Nobody argued about that, but he never did get round to putting paint to canvas again in the old barn. The light was not good enough, he complained. In the summer it was always too hot and stuffy to be inside. The autumn rains seeped through the wooden beams, making it too damp to work and the winter chills brought frost through the cracks in the wattle-and-daub walls.

One year, the March winds blew the roof off the barn and part of the north wall of the house collapsed. In the light of the house insurance company not paying out sufficiently, Tilly was left with thousands of pounds worth of debt to pay for the repairs from her own funds. So, the house was put on the market.

Sam took a deep breath and resigned himself yet again to the task of packing up, but was secretly pleased they would be moving away from Leo. His son's daily visits were an annoyance; when he left, there was always something missing. Leo, it seemed, had made off with almost half their possessions since he had moved into the Red House some seven years before. Tilly swore to Sam that she had sold off the missing items: the Paul Nash print, which Sam had purchased from a street vendor in Bayswater Road when he was studying at the Royal College; a Victorian ebony and ivory carved screen and a 1930's hand-painted single bed. Some of Sam's sketches had gone astray too, but since he never kept track of what he had drawn, he couldn't be sure.

Tilly talked about being fed up with Wales, and how it was a mistake to have ever gone back over the border. This time they moved to Kinsley Hereford.

Tilly could hardly contain herself, "Just think how grand that sounds, *The Castle,* High Street, Kingsley," she said as she filled in the form to send off for an order of stick-on address labels. The Castle, a defunct pub, was big and cheap. Tilly pocketed a few thousand pounds as a result of the move – that was, until she stocked up again on antique furniture. She had given up on dolls and prams by then, as she had too much trouble trying not to damage them as she moved about the house. No, this time her money went on a robust Georgian mahogany dining table and eight chairs, a late nineteenth Century Belgian Orchestrum with dazzling, cut glass, mirrored doors, huge, gold-framed oil portraits of the famous and infamous, a large contingent of stuffed animals and waxed flowers under glass domes. The three-storey premises housed their books and boxes of antique sundries. Some boxes - from the Sixties onwards - had never been opened and were still tied up with string. Old leather, well-worn, brown suitcases with rusty fastenings held the couple's clothes and a large wicker hamper was full of old shoes.

Sam's art work was again relegated to 'The Barn': a large room over the double garage, which stood apart from the main house, a short walk across the garden from the kitchen door. This 'barn' had been used as the billiard room when the pub was at its Zenith. A full-sized slate billiard table stood in the middle of the space, left intentionally, no doubt, as the green baize was beyond repair and the wood was riddled with woodworm. The floor was strewn with green faded wallpaper, which had peeled off the walls over time as the damp penetrated the plaster. Only a little light wormed its way into the room, through the small dusty windows.

It was amazing that six-months of Sam beavering away, had resulted in a studio. His murals were out again, hung up in the 'barn', with nails like before, "Look at this..." Sam picked up a magazine from a pile of papers he was sorting from an old chest in the living room and handed it to Kath, who was sat by the log fire. She read from *The Times, 1937.* A photo of Queen Elizabeth, the Queen mother, inspecting army troops, graced the front page.

"Open it at page twenty..." Sam said. The painting of, '*The Welsh Rat Catche*r', took Kath's breath away "My picture was the most popular painting at the Royal Academy that summer."

Kath listened hard. She had heard much of the picture but this was the first time she seen a photograph of it.

"Wish I hadn't sold it, but I needed the money to get married, you see." Sam continued. "...and that Chepstow lot, they never even put it on display. Well, not after the war they didn't. Stayed put in the cellars, I bet..."

"Who was the man in the picture? A farm labourer with bad legs?" Kath enquired.

Sam laughed. "Not bad legs, no, that cloth around his legs is not a bandage, khaki puttees they are, what the soldiers in the First World War used to strengthen their legs. Henry was just a poor soldier in India once. That's his old army coat. Did a bit on the farms now and again to make a bit of extra cash."

"And, what did he think of his portrait being so famous?"

"Oh, nothing, didn't bother, you know, just a poor fellow, never saw him again after he left Llanyron. That was a long time ago. Oh well... I'd better get this trunk up to my room or Tilly will be complaining.

Sam dragged the box across the room to the foot of the stairs and left Kath reading the article. Kath decided then she would seek out *The Welsh Rat Catcher* painting. She would phone the art gallery in Chepstow as soon as she got back to Newcastle, the next day.

She was pleased to be getting away from the Old Castle – it was even colder and dirtier than any of all the other houses they had ever lived in.

Kath felt miserable at the thought of Sam's new bedroom at the back of the house. On the top floor, facing north, the tiny window was covered by ivy too high up to cut back and the room stank of beer and tobacco – as if it were still an alehouse.

"Good morning.... John Jones, Museum and Art Gallery, how may I help you?"

Kath was pleased she had got through to the civic building without too much fuss, but was disappointed to find the keeper of art not in his office.

"Mr Cookson will be in at eleven, he is the only person who can help you. If you would like to leave a message, I am sure he will call you when he can."

Kath left her number and was rewarded some two hours later with a call from Rodney Cookson. "We most certainly do have the *Welsh Rat Catcher* painting in stock. Actually, we have two oil paintings here by

Samuel Llewellyn, your father-in-law, was it, you said?"

"Yes, my husband's father." Kath was excited. "And, of course, we can come to the art gallery to see them?"

"Any time you like, my dear, just say when. I may not be on hand myself, but there are any number of staff here who would only be too willing to help you."

Kath already had a date in mind, October half-term, only four weeks away. She gave Rodney the dates of their proposed visit, there and then.

Kath related to Sam and Tilly how she and Rob had been to Chepstow, just before visiting them that half-term. Sam's paintings had been taken out of storage for Kath to photograph, too. Copies for Sam and Tilly would be forthcoming and there was an assurance that the paintings would now go on display in the main gallery. Rodney was delighted to hear that Sam, now ninety-two, was still living and working and was not even that far from Chepstow. He would definitely be paying Sam a visit.

After a good bath, a haircut and a new set of clothes, in preparation for Mr Cookson's visit, Sam appeared ten years younger. With a spring in his step, Sam showed Mr Cookson and his companion from the Museum, around The Castle, and particularly Sam's barn where he had hung up all his murals again. *Saint James Park in the 1920s* sat side by side with a fifteen-foot high depiction of *Chepstow in the War, 1940*. The oil on canvas was half finished and held up by only three rusty nails. The canvas sagged, exaggerating the three gaping tears across the middle. The German aeroplane depicted attacking, was only pencilled in. The outline of the bomb blast was only a mere suggestion of the devastation on the ground and contrasted dolefully with the busy figures of the rescue team, which were already painted.

"I never had time to finish it," Sam explained to Mr Cookson. "If only they had given me three more months, I would have done it. But no that, that–" Sam couldn't bring himself to say the director's name; the head of the Art School, who had Sam sent off to the Army.

"I had to go to the war, you see," Sam went on to Rodney. "I couldn't bear it, you see. I didn't want anyone else at the Art School mucking about with my picture. So, I took it down, that's when it got torn, you follow. I took it down, I did. I rolled it up and carried it off on my shoulder."

"That, that fellow… sent me off to the war. He never forgave me for marrying Tilly. Tilly was my student when she was eighteen. I was thirty-two then. That fellow told me I shouldn't be mucking about with my students. He said I would lose my job if I didn't give her up. Before we married, I looked him right in the eye and said, "Mr Blunder, Mr Blunder, you can come to our wedding!" That did it. I had to go into the Army then. I wish I'd had just three more months on the painting, just three months."

Mr Cookson looked distraught at the thought of Sam's removal from the art school to the Army, but was more interested in the mural.

After research, he discovered that Sam had been commissioned by the Chepstow Council in 1940 to paint the mural showing the town's war efforts on the Home Front. Sam had been summoned to do the painting in school's time and the canvas had been set up in the Antique room. With the removal of Sam, and the closing of the art school for some time, the mural, in effect, had disappeared!

Rob laughed at the fact that the mural had been rolled up, sat on by children, dogs, cats and even chickens. How they had tossed it onto the back of lorries and removal vans, as they changed from one house to another. It was a miracle it had ever survived at all.

Sam still had the pencil drawings he had done in preparation for the mural, and together with the big canvas, he proudly handed them over to Mr Cookson for restoration and eventual display in Chepstow. For good measure, *Mr Pugh* - a head and shoulders painting of an ARP warden, which Sam had painted in his own time - was donated to the Council too!

Rodney was thrilled with Sam's generosity and likened it to finding the crown jewels.

There was an article in the local press. Jeannie said it was a cheek that Sam had had to give the mural back. Tilly thought it was wise to let Mr Cookson deal with things and Kath just enjoyed watching Sam revel in the attention.

Events developed quickly. Sam was interviewed at home, talking about his wartime mural and appeared on Welsh prime time television. Other paintings were taken from the house, on loan, to be part of a

Millennium Exhibition to be held at the Art Gallery in Chepstow and the mural was sent off to be restored.

After attending the Exhibition in January, where Sam's paintings were on display - along with paintings by Ceri Richards and other well-known Welsh artists - Kath and Rob stopped in at *the Castle* to report back to Sam and Tilly, who said they were too old to travel to see it for themselves.

On leaving Kinsley, Sam pressed a black-and-white photograph into Kath's hands., "This is my bottle kiln painting; don't suppose it's still around?"

Kath understood. This was a photograph of the painting Sam had done when he was visiting his fiancé, Miriam, in Stoke all those years ago. They had met when they were students at the Royal College.

"I sold it to Gwyneth Jones, my best teacher in Neath," Sam continued. "A long time ago."

Kath promised to try to find the painting and, within three month's she had. An article in the Western Mail, along with a photograph of the painting, brought results, an email from the current owner's nephew. Kath now had the name of this aunty and was told she lived on the Gower, but still had no address or phone number. However, after research, Kath got what she wanted, and after a brief telephone conversation with this lady, Kath and Rob set off to Wales.

The Bottle Kiln painting was still in pristine condition. It had been given to the lady and her husband as a wedding present and although they agreed to let the painting be photographed, they were not interested in selling it. Still, Kath was thrilled that she had good news for Sam.

Champagne was ordered and celebrations were held at the Castle. Rob was finally given his portrait, the one Sam had painted of him in 1947, when Rob was three-years-old, and Kath got *Rocio,* Sam's painting of their Italian au pair in the 1950's. It was the best Christmas present she ever had.

After a thirty thousand pound facelift, taking over a year, and reframing, the *Chepstow War* mural was unveiled in by the Lord Mayor on Armistice Day, 2002. Dignitaries at the ceremony included a famous South Wales author - who described Sam as a great artist. Unfortunately, neither Sam nor Tilly attended. Sam had the 'flu and Tilly was bedridden. Jeannie and Hilary failed to show up, citing bad weather and work commitments. Leo wasn't even invited.

Life in the new Century was going well for the Llewellyns: Sam was rejoicing in his newfound fame. Kath and Rob, after Rob retired early, had at last bought their dream home in Southern Spain, a house with panoramic sea views and just two minutes walk from the beach.

Jeannie and Hilary were gutting their moorland cottage and driving around in a brand new *Land Rover,* but Jeannie failed to hide her chagrin over Rob and Kath's *casa en Andalucía*. It rankled that she and Hilary had lost their flat in Tenerife, some years before when an unscrupulous agent had let it out and not banked the rent. With the mortgage unpaid, the bank foreclosed and that was the end of their Spanish dream. Jeannie had, however, made some effort at being a good aunty when Hilary's mother died. Hilary, being an only child, inherited everything. Kath reckoned Hilary must have been left over fifty-thousand pounds, as that coincided with huge building projects at their cottage. The boys were invited up for weekends and weeks at a time over the school holidays and for three years received lavish Christmas presents. But it seemed once the money ran out and the boys grew up, Jeannie lost interest and retreated into her shell-like world again, only to come out when there was more money to be inherited.

Robert reckoned that Jeannie was having her old Aunty Blodwyn, in South Wales, over to stay in her moorland cottage for what she could get out of her. It came as no surprise therefore to find childless Blodwyn had left Jeannie half of everything in her estate, when she finally died.

After the New Year in 2003, Sam was still enjoying the attention from the art world. He attended a ceremonial luncheon, in his honour, in the Lord Mayor's parlour; Chepstow Twelve people sat at the table, including the Lord and Lady Mayors, Rodney Cookson and his colleague from the museum.

Sam was chauffeured from Kinsley to Chepstow in the Lord Mayor's limousine, along with his Carer, Mr Pim, who owned the care home from where Tilly and Sam had been receiving help. Kath joked to the Lord Mayor that perhaps his favours could stretch to having Mr Llewellyn chauffeured up to Newcastle to visit her and Robert, as he hadn't been their for some time!

A television crew recorded the day and Sam signed the visitors' book, chuckling to note that the previous signature had been the Queen's!

At 5pm, after a wonderful day in the Lord Mayor's Parlour, Kath and Rob set off towards Portsmouth, in their van. They had the evening ferry to Bilbao to catch for their three month wintering in Spain.

And… Sam was chauffeured back to Tilly.

-37-

Hardly had Kath and Robert arrived at their villa in Spain, when the phone rang: Tilly had died in her sleep, William informed his father. "You have to phone Aunty Jeannie."

"Heart just gave out," Jeannie told her brother.

Robert, still stunned, couldn't speak.

Jeannie went on as if she were reciting lines in a school play. "I was with her the night before. We had a great night together; singing away we were, at the top of our voices, enjoying a few Alcopops. Then I gave her the pills, and got her into to bed. Sam found her the next morning. We were in Oldham by then. Drove home all through the night, we did." Jeannie paused, Robert crippled with disbelief only sighed. Jeannie carried on. "We had to be at work the next morning, you see. Now listen Rob, the funeral is next Wednesday. I hope you can make it."

"Of course, but how is, Sa…?"

Jeannie butt in, before Robert could finish asking how his father was. "Now, just remember. Kath is not to come to the funeral. Do you understand? You know how much she hated her…"

Kath, who had been listening to the conversation on the upstairs phone, tingled with indignation and confusion. *How much she hated her*, the words seared through Kath's brain like a sharp knife slicing ham. *Did Tilly hate her that much?*

Jeannie continued, still unaware that Kath was listening." Okay, see you next week, Wednesday, and just remember Rob… NO Kath. Tilly would jump out of her coffin if she knew Kath was anywhere near Kingsley."

Kath spoke up, "Jeannie, Jeannie…" she said, as if she were trying to calm a child. "I heard what you said, every word, and I just want to say this - whatever your mother thought of me, I never hated her…"

But Jeannie cut in, "Rob, get that woman off the phone, I can't talk to her." The venom was palpable; Jeannie was the only one doing the hating.

Kath stayed in Spain, and unloaded the van; Rob flew to the UK for the funeral. Jeannie had already installed herself in *The Castle* with her father.

Kath might have gone to Tilly's funeral, had Jeannie not spoken so harshly, but now was glad she hadn't. In truth, she had very little to thank her mother-in-law for: Tilly made her feel like a fly being swatted and she seemed to enjoy seeing her own children squabbling with each other. When Kath had been banned from ever setting foot on Jeannie's land again, after a minor tiff, some years before, and had asked Tilly for help, she was told then that Jeannie didn't forgive. Kath was falsely accused of calling Jeannie's cat scruffy, saying Jeannie was a bad cook and describing Hilary as a horrible fellow.

Although Kath had lived in hope that her sister-in-law would relent, she knew that she probably wouldn't now. After the funeral, ninety-seven-year-old Sam went to live with Jeannie on Saddleworth Moor; Robert returned to Spain.

Jeannie had the space, the time; it was inevitable that she would become her father's carer. She gave up her part-time teaching job and Sam… *paid her well for his keep*.

Before Tilly was even cold in her grave, Jeannie had the locks changed at *The Castle.* Leo protested. When he tried to 'break in', to get his belongings. Jeannie rang the police and the Mental Health authorities, suggesting he should be Sectioned for aggressive behaviour.

Sam said he was to too old to deal with any palaver and left Jeannie to deal with all that. In less than one month, half the furniture from *The Castle* was sent to the auctions, the rest was transported to Jeannie's house and Sam was installed, along with his artwork, in the biggest room in Old Oak cottage.

To please her mother, Jeannie had named the farm house, *Old Oak Cottage* after the house in which Tilly had grown up in, in South Wales. Kath thought it odd, especially as on the moorlands there wasn't an oak tree in sight.

Sam's room looked out over the bleak landscape from picture windows on three sides of the square space, but Sam never saw any of it. The curtains were drawn. "Sun light is bad for his eyes," Jeannie said.

Sam spent the last years of his life entombed in this room, where the door was always shut and the curtains, which hung like sheets of steel, never stirred. With whisky and soda and a box of *Tom Thumb* cigars at hand Sam received visitors.

Robert, sat with him once a month. Kath didn't. She would have visited, but Sam only said that it was Jeannie's house and there was nothing he could do.

Jeannie wouldn't say who else visited Sam, but Rob learned from Sam that Rodney Cookson, still the keeper of Art in Chepstow had called by and had put Sam's name forward for an MBE for Welsh Art.

With all the excitement of talk of an accolade from the Queen and the media exposure of Sam's work - following events in Chepstow that January - Jeannie believed she was on to a good thing and ratcheted up the publicity on her artist father. More articles about the "Welsh Artist", appeared in the local newspapers, as well as national magazines. Jeannie hired a film company to record her father, in his new surroundings. The hype machine was working hard and Jeannie was the ringleader.

Leo, however, was not one to be ignored lightly. Having removed all the contents of *The Castle* to her house, Jeannie brushed aside Leo's claim that three of the grandfather clocks were his. Leo took her to court, where Jeannie argued that they were her father's clocks and that she had only taken them to her house on his instructions.

Jeannie implicated her Father even further, by getting him to say that Leo had *stolen* Sam's painting of *Saint James Park* and that her father wanted it back.

The ensuing court case was bitter and costly, but Leo won. He got his clocks back and the *Park* painting remained in his possession, after the judge believed his father had in fact given it to his son as a gift. (There was evidence that Leo had actually paid for its restoration and framing, too.)

Jeannie had a minor breakdown, after the clock court case; only the thought of her father's work being worth a small fortune one day - *if she kept at the publicity* - kept her going.

The Dylan Thomas book, which Tilly and Sam had produced in the early '60s, was reprinted with further drawings and more footnotes. All of Tilly's stories for children were put together in one book. How profitable these ventures were was debatable. Robert seemed to think they had been a disaster when Jeannie complained of having to pay for storage for the thousands of Laugharne books she still had unsold.

Rodney, who had been invited to the book's re-launch at Brown's Hotel in Laugharne, spoke of how insipid the affair was. Jeannie arrived late and the press didn't turn up. At least Sam hadn't witnessed the ignominy of it all; he was confined to his room. Jeannie lied to him that the book was selling well. *How many more lies was Jeannie spinning him,* Rob wondered.

Hilary was spending more time than was respectable out of the house. It was rumoured he was seeing his former wife. His two sons, grown men now, were doing guard duty at the Old Oak Cottage from time to time. Rob reported seeing two shotguns in the kitchen and wondered about Jeannie, her husband and their true motives for taking on his father. Rob was constantly battling with her to see Sam. When he rang up to say he would like to visit, he was often told not to go as father was ill, or they couldn't cope with an extra visit.

Once, when Rob had arrived unannounced, Jeannie said it wasn't convenient and he would have to go away for a couple of hours. She was about to go off to her computer class and explained that no one was allowed in her house if she wasn't there.

"What if he drops his cigar and starts a fire?" Robert quizzed, feeling sorry that Sam was left alone. Jeannie only shrugged.

However, Sam put on weight. After a year, Jeannie got power of attorney, she now had the upper hand over her father's affairs. She let Rob visit more, but meetings were strictly limited to two hours, and either she or Hilary was always present. Rob found it inhibiting and he never did find a moment to talk to Sam alone. It wasn't till that first Christmas with the Hardwoods that Sam, having spent three weeks in hospital with a serious chest infection that made him think he was going to die, told Robert that he had signed a will and Robert would have his fair share.

Sam lived on for another five years, though. He received his MBE for services to Art but, as he was too infirm to go to London to receive his medal, he was presented with it at a private party at The Old Oak Cottage. The Lord Lieutenant of Manchester attended but Robert didn't; Jeannie hadn't invited him.

Sam said he hadn't known about it all, until the very day it happened. "What can I do? I'm an old man." He looked at Rob in resignation, then slumped into his winged armchair and lit up another *Tom Thumb* cigar.

Kath phoned Chepstow Art Gallery and was floored to learn that Rodney too had not been invited to the celebration. It was sacrilegious, unforgivable, that he who had instigated the whole honour idea was then ignored. Rodney accepted the slight with as much dignity as his position commanded, but asked for his feelings to be made known to Mrs Hardwood, as he always referred to Jeannie.

"After all, if it hadn't been for Kath meeting Rodney at the gallery in Chepstow in 1997, none of all this would have happened." Robert reported to Jeannie, some weeks later. The sister scowled and dismissed Robert with a flick of the hand. She didn't want to be reminded of her guilt. She was in charge now of her father's history and she would write it as she chose, and that evidently wasn't going to include Kath or Rodney, she said. She added that Mr Cookson had been sacked from the museum for embezzlement!

Kath rang Chepstow Gallery.

"I am afraid Mr. Cookson no longer works here," came the reply.

"Could you give me his home phone number?"

"Sorry, we can't do that."

"Err, no of course not - but can I leave a message with my phone number for him to contact me?"

"You can - but we can't guarantee that he will reply.

"Sounds ominous," Kath told Rob.

As time went by and Mr Cookson didn't ring back, they believed Jeannie... Rodney had really disappeared under a cloud!

By the spring of 2008, Jeannie had catalogued most of Sam's artwork. Several paintings had been sold at a Fine Art auction house in Cambridge. The results were positive. Five hundred pounds for a twelve-inch high, signed sketch of a lady's head.

A chance meeting, later that year, with Paul Fritz, the owner of a prestigious art gallery in London, ended with Jeannie signing a contract on her father's behalf for the Fritz Company to stage a grand exhibition of Sam's work. It was to run at the Civic Art Gallery in Luton for three months - from June to September, 2010. Sam was to be heralded as the, 'Welsh Artist'.

Jeannie signed away over one hundred thousand pounds of Sam's money and fervent preparations went ahead for the exhibition. Sam talked of nothing else. His murals were taken away for major restoration to a chateau in France; the second home of the esteemed, Paul Fritz.

Mr Cookson, unknown to Robert, had warned Jeannie, when he was still in favour with her, about parting with her father's artwork, without the safeguards of such things as receipts. But Jeannie was in awe of the dark, handsome, French-born Mr. Fritz. Just as Tilly had been enchanted by the enigmatic Douglas from Tasmania, years before. Sam too was swept up with the excitement of it all. Jeannie directed operations, just as her mother had done and even sounded more like Tilly every day as she barked out orders. "Samuel!" she would shout. "Be careful with that ash, we don't all want to go up in smoke just yet!" Jeannie was even wearing her mother's old clothes. Now she had acquired a middle-age spread, the old fur coats fitted her like a glove. Sam approved, smiled and did as he was told.

"He thinks Jeannie *is* Tilly," Rob told Kath. "He's going senile, he is."

Neither Jeannie, nor anyone else agreed, by all accounts, Sam had a mind like an encyclopaedia, "There wasn't a memory like it for miles." They said. "Mr Llewellyn, at one hundred-and-two years-old is a marvel."

Leo was drafted in, after Jeannie realised she was going to need some help with Sam's exhibition. The bitterness of the court case over the clocks and Sam's *Park* painting, Jeannie said, was forgiven. She needed hard facts; a list of details about Sam's life, in chronological order, for the exhibition. For all Sam's mind being as sharp as a needle, he couldn't remember things in the right order and had the habit of distorting things. Leo had the facts at his fingertips, and after falling out with Kath when she failed to buy the *Park* painting off him - because he upped the price at the last minute - he was only too pleased to be hauled in from the cold by Jeannie.

The ageing sister steered Leo into her camp with relish, aiming to 'nail the coffin' for Robert and Kath.

Leo worked for months with Jeannie, who blackened Rob's name even more. "He only comes here to see what he can wheedle out of Father," Jeannie told Leo. "But I've put a stop to him giving him any more drawings, thank God. Do you know how much they are fetching now?" She boasted to Leo.

Leo thought he was on to a good thing and believed Jeannie had truly forgiven him for taking her to court over the clocks. Little did he know, she hadn't. Still, Rob wasn't in a position to tell him and, in any case, Rob was more concerned with his own family: Carl, William, his partner, and their two children: Damien, now in his teens and a little girl Lizzie; Christian, his wife and two-year-old Poppy - and a new baby, Nicholas.

Jeannie received them cordially, but made no move to encourage any further involvement with Rob's family.

2009 saw an Indian summer. Kath was preparing for her and Robert's Ruby wedding (September 20th) a weekend in Anglesey, with their sons and families. She and Robert would then drive to Spain for a few weeks.

Rob was anxious to see his father before he went to Wales. He rang his sister on September 8th, "No you can't come " Hilary answered the phone. "We all have bronchitis and Jeannie is in bed."

Robert rang again the following week and was told yet again they were all too ill for visitors. Kath begged Rob to go anyway, as it would be his last chance before going to Spain, but Rob didn't visit. He never saw his father alive again.

-38-

Samuel died at nine o'clock on the morning of September 9th, 2009. After having spent his last hours coughing and gasping, in his bed at Old Oak Cottage, he was certified, by the family doctor, as having suffered pneumonia. It was a traumatic end to a talented artist.

Rob was not informed, though. On September 24th, when he left the UK for Spain, he was still under the impression that Sam was just poorly.

The bad news didn't reach Rob till the end of that month; Jeannie used William to pass on the news.

Rob called his sister and Hilary answered the phone. Sam was indeed dead, the funeral had been held in Chepstow on the 17th of September and he had been buried in the same grave as their mother.

"But why wasn't I told before !" Robert was livid.

Hilary replaced the receiver.

"Sam was dead when I spoke to Hilary on September 14th, and he said he was just poorly!" Robert ranted at Kath.

A phone call to Leo revealed that he too had not been informed of Sam's death till September 21st as he was away in Ireland. He didn't offer an explanation as to why he hadn't himself informed Rob and, on the subject of the will, he simply said that the old man had left everything to Jeannie and that was all right !

The audacity of the woman not to tell him his father had died, the wickedness of Hilary to dismiss his phone call - his own father disinheriting him. Rob seethed and swore, then phoned his sister again, only for the call to be interceded by Hilary. "I don't know why you are phoning. Sam left everything to Jeannie, but there's nothing left anyway, so don't phone again." This time, Hilary slammed down the receiver.

Rob sulked and sighed for three weeks; there was nothing he could do till he got back to England.

Kath *Googled* will contesting, but came to a blank when every piece of information ended with the statement to '*...consult your legal representative about this*'.

If Rob were to contest his father's will, it was going to be costly. Rob wondered why Leo didn't seem bothered about being left out of the will. *I bet Jeannie told Sam that if he left everything to her, she would share it all out fairly. She had Sam round her little finger; Lady Bountiful, he thought she was, the lady with the lamp, kind to everyone and all that.* Jeannie has got a lot to answer for.

Kath agreed that was a feasible explanation and added, "I suppose Leo thinks because he was roped in to do work on the catalogue for the Luton exhibition, he's well in with Jeannie. I can't see why he's not suspicious about Sam's death, though, or the fact that he was away at the time of the burial, with money that Jeannie had sent him!"

"Just give him time, let it all sink in," Rob continued. "Allow him to come his own conclusions. He knows now about Hilary telling me my father was alive, when he was dead, and he knows that there were only four people at the funeral."

Kath had established this when she contacted the vicar of the church presiding over the funeral service. Beside Jeannie and Hilary, Kath deduced the other two people were Mavis, Rob's cousin and her husband, Don. Sure enough, a phone call to Mavis revealed that they had only found out about Sam's demise by pure accident. Don was a burial board member of the local cemetery, where Sam was to be buried, and had noticed Sam's name on the burial application list. Mavis had then phoned Jeannie, who confirmed that it was indeed her father, but then warned Mavis she was not to tell anyone at all about the funeral.

Rob continued, "...time will tell if Jeannie shares any of her ill-gotten gains with him or not. I reckon she won't, but we'll see."

Rob's pain about the secrecy of his father's death and funeral was fuelled even more, when, at the end of October, he returned to the UK to find a one-line letter from Jeannie stating, '*I wish to inform you that your father died at 9am on 9th September, 2009.*'

"9/9/9/9," Kath pointed out. "That's a witch's number," she said as she did a *Google* search. "Money and fortune, that's what four nines means, wow! What the hell do you make of that then, Mr Llewellyn?"

Rob had already drawn his own conclusions.

Kath nodded. "Yes, I can see you are thinking what I am – a mercy killing? But who would object to that. He was one-hundred-and-three."

"You are bang on there, babe. You know he had just started being incontinent. My hair went on end when Jeannie told me in July he was pissing his pants and it was getting her down. I wouldn't be surprised if they did him in. But you had better not say that to anyone else though, you could be had up for slander !"

"I reckon they must have suffocated him," Kath offered. "And I can't get over Jeannie having a secret funeral. Rodney Cookson, for one, should have been told. Pity we have lost touch with him. I can't take it in he had the sack! Nice chap he was. Avuncular."

"Well, let's just leave it at that, Kath. It's better to put our mind to seeing what we can do about contesting the will. By the way, 'avuncular'? How come you're using such big words these days?"

"Tell you later," Kath wasn't one to talk about what she was doing, till she had done it!

Kath sought advice on how to contest a will, from Citizens' Advice. She was told that Robert must enter a caveat. Kath immediately arranged that by phoning the Probate Office in Birmingham.

The lady at CAB also suggested this saga would make a good novel... Kath warmed to the idea.

Not many solicitors in Newcastle and District dealt with contentious wills, but Kath found one she thought might be suitable, a Mr Renrut.

"Not without merit," he concluded, on having read the five-page document Kath had prepared, outlining Rob's case. "A lot of what you say will have to be substantiated, witnesses and all that, but I'll make a start. You may, of course, be covered for your legal fees on your household insurance policy," Mr Renrut proffered. "Many people are, these days."

The couple had never considered that money would be available from such a source, but Kath made the necessary calls to the Insurance Company. *No chance,* Kath thought, as she waited in a queue for someone in the right department to answer her call. She had changed insurance companies just some weeks before, to a cheaper offer. She was bowled over when a company clerk informed her that, yes, they had up to a hundred thousand pounds worth of cover for such a legal case, but it was up to a solicitor to make the claim.

"Manna from heaven," Kath lifted her arms to the skies and rejoiced. "We're off, let's go."

Sam was not of unsound mind, Mr Renrut, was reminded, so the case would rest on his sister being proved to have had undue influence over her father. Having him hospitalised for three weeks, prior to him changing his will in her favour, after nine months of living with her, would certainly look bad for Jeannie.

The will itself, although it had been witnessed by a solicitor - Hilary's Freemason hard drinking buddy - appeared to have been written with little thought. It consisted of two paragraphs only. The first stated that all Sam's worldly goods were to be left to Jeannie. Paragraph two said that he wanted to be buried in Chepstow with his wife. No mention had been made of Robert or Leonard.

However, two years after the will was made, and following the court case concerning Leo's long case clocks and the *Saint James Park* painting, Samuel signed a codicil to his will, stating categorically that Leo was not to profit in any way from his will as Leo had been a drain on him and his wife all their lives. Rob was not mentioned in this codicil and Sam had misspelled his signature.

After two months in the hands of Mr Renrut, Leo, of his own accord, defected to Robert's side. Jeannie had shown her true self and was now ignoring Leo's phone calls. What's more, she had not given him a penny since her father died. Jeannie had also failed to fulfil her promise to take him to Luton to attend the opening of the 'Welsh Artist Exhibition'. At the Exhibition, the famous former MP and author, Lord Fletcher, purchased two oil paintings for nearly one hundred thousand pounds!

Leo contracted his own solicitor in Ross-on-Wye, a vociferous Welsh woman who took up the case with great zeal. After Mr Renrut's feeble efforts, and the fact he had already spent two thousand pounds' worth of the pot of money trying to prove Sam was of unsound mind, Robert decided to hand the whole case over to, Myfanwy Forrester.

While Kath and Leo were thrilled that Godfrey Fletcher was a fan of Sam's work, Robert remained indifferent, and speculated how much the great mural really had been sold to the famous writer for. No doubt less than the asking price of sixty-five thousand pounds! Still, it was a feather in Sam's cap to have such illustrious patronage. It was pity Sam had not lived long enough to see the Exhibition.

Kath and Rob went to Luton incognito - after Jeannie said she was going to get them barred. They now knew just how much was at stake.

Sam's entire works, most of which were in the care of Jeannie, could now be worth millions.

Mrs Forrester's line of attack was direct. A sharp letter was sent to Jeannie's solicitor, citing his client's bizarre behaviour on her father's death. There were affectionate letters that Sam had sent to both Leo and Rob, which were at odds with the fact that he had seen fit to disinherit them in his will. Of course, Myfanwy Forrester concluded, in her letter to Jeannie's solicitor, that any out-of-court settlement on her two brothers would be the best course of action for all concerned. Rob and Leo thought that their sister would never agree to that.

"Well, not after you called her Myra Hindley..." Leo, who of course had recently been in his sister's confidence, said that she may have thought about giving something to her brothers at one time, after being advised to do so by her solicitor, but when Hilary thumped the solicitor's desk and shouted "Over my dead body", Jeannie had succumbed to her husband's wishes.

When Jeannie's reply to Mrs Forrester's initial letter arrived, some three months later, the contents were as expected. Mrs Heywood would not settle out-of-court. What was surprising though was the fact that Mr Thornton, Jeannie's original solicitor, was no longer acting for her; Jeannie now was using a Mr. King, from a different practice.

Kath's hunch that Mr Thornton didn't want to be implicated in such dirty business, where client's husbands go thumping tables in his office, had paid off. "He knows what Jeannie and Hilary were up to, that's why he's backed off," Kath reported to Rob, after getting Mr Thornton to talk to her on the phone. The lawyer had said that Sam had fretted about signing a will where his sons were not provided for, and he thought that was the reason for his delay in signing. He also said Sam was under the impression that Rob was a millionaire and didn't need any money, but he couldn't state why Sam had failed to give any reason in writing as to why he would disinherit his sons. Mr Thornton concluded the conversation with, "I do sympathise with you and your husband, Mrs Llewellyn, but what I have said is strictly off the record, you do understand?"

"There you are Rob, what more evidence do you need that Jeannie, and Hilary, knew exactly what they were doing with your father and for exactly one thing - his money.

"Yeah, but remember what Thornton said was off the record and there it will stay. The rotten buggers," Rob said. "Still, we have more to go on, let's see what tomorrow brings."

Kath was working on the case again, one rainy Sunday, when Robert ran upstairs to her study and pushed a Vintage motorbike magazine under her nose.

"Look at that advert," he ordered. "Look who is selling that bike."

"Rodney Cookson." Kath yelled." It's *our* Rodney, look the advert says the bike can be seen in Gwent. That's got to be our man."

One phone call and contact with the former Chepstow Art Gallery Keeper was established again.

"Sacked, my Aunt Fanny." Rodney was aghast at the lies that Jeannie had put out that he had been fired. "I retired, simple as that. My time had come and I just retired. I am very annoyed with Mrs Hardwood if she has been putting this awful rumour around. But thank you for telling me and, what's more, thank you for your news about Samuel. I am sorry and, yes, annoyed too that I wasn't informed about Sam's death. A lot of other people in South Wales will be very angry with Mrs Hardwood, We would have liked the chance to go the funeral. It's disgusting that such a talented artist had such a paltry send off."

The phone call lasted over an hour. Kath spared no details of recent events. Rodney told her that Jeannie had even contacted the new keeper of art, incidentally a friend of Rodney's, just before Sam died and had requested that all the artwork that Samuel had donated to the gallery be returned to her father. The request was refused, of course, but Rodney was disgusted that Jeannie had even asked.

The pair agreed to keep in touch. Rodney's revelations only hardened Kath and Robert's resolve to expose Jeannie's dirty tricks and bring her to justice.

Kath dug for more information and contacted prospective witnesses. They would need every scrap of evidence if they were to get the case before a barrister and then, hopefully, to court. To get more money from the Insurance Company, the solicitor would have to give the opinion that there was more than a fifty percent chance of winning the case. As it stood, it was just fifty/fifty. Not quite enough to get going. Kath scratched her head.

Leo ran round in circles but produced even more intimate letters written by his father which provided evidence that Sam had been sending him money, now and again.

Some friends of Rob's, who had visited Sam with Rob, provided photos of a time when they had visited together, to prove Rob had not cut himself off from his family - as Jeannie had been telling everyone. One such chap, who had been Sam's pupil in Neath, said Jeannie had told him several times that Rob was *persona non grata* in the family, that he had gone off to live in Spain and they didn't know where he was. Gareth was dumbfounded when he learned of Jeannie's deception. Kath scoured the magazine and newspaper articles featuring Sam, looking for the names of anyone she could contact for information. She needed to know about anything Sam might have said, anything that might have happened, that would throw light on Jeannie's manipulations. Her search for the truth and for willing witnesses stretched from Manchester to South Wales, but the pace was slow. Still, they had six years to bring the matter to court, if ever they did. Kath began to lose heart when Mrs Forrester had Robert, Leo and Kath into her office for a discussion.

"Just look at you three," she said, peering over her gold-rimmed spectacles, which were held on more by resting on top of her rosy red fat cheeks than her nose.

Kath looked at Leo, who looked like Rasputin with his scruffy black hair and unshaved face, then she looked at the fat solicitor again, who by now was wagging a finger at Kath and saying, "I can't put you before the judge, I just can't. You make it up as you go along." Then, pointing at Leo, she went on. "And look at 'im…" then looking at Rob, she said "…and 'e's got dementia!"

Mrs Forrester, was letting them all down.

Rob, as usual, stayed calm for the next three months when nothing happened, although Kath continued to send Mrs Forrester relevant information, by email. Kath however doubted that the case would ever get to court. People who had been supportive in the beginning, now spoke of how difficult it was to prove undue influence. Mrs. Forrester finally sent details of a few successful cases, and pointed out that there was much stronger evidence than the Llewellyns could muster. She proclaimed her gut feeling that Jeannie was guilty without doubt, but said by God it was going to be nearly impossible to prove. The woman had covered her tracks so well, it would take a miracle to prove her guilt. Still, Kath clung to the fact that *Vincit Omnia veritas (truth conquers all)* and faith drove her on.

Leo fretted and cussed, but admitted he had no more evidence to offer. He was more worried now about losing his house. David Cameron and the newly elected Conservative/Liberal Democrat Alliance Government had just brought in new legislation stopping social benefits for mortgage interest relief. Leo was receiving the maximum amount for his mortgage and, if he lost this, he would face the eventuality of having to sell up. In the economic crisis of 2011, property prices were dropping and the prospect looked grim. Leo's mortgage stood at over two hundred thousand pounds.

When Tilly died, house prices had been at their Zenith. Leo had cashed in on the property boom and sold his Queen Anne House for three-hundred-and-seventy-five pounds and bought a three-storey Georgian Vicarage, in Whatey-on-Wye, for four-hundred-and-fifty thousand. He was living well for a man on social benefits, but now the gravy train was about to end.

So distressed was he that he lost weight. Also, the authorities had, due to his bad eyesight, told him he was not fit to drive and that they would be rescinding his driving license. Leo withdrew more into his own world.

His only social interaction was with three social workers who worked on a rota to take him out one day a week, and Kath, who spoke to him on the phone on Sundays. But that was becoming unbearable for her. Leo's rantings and ravings were wearing her down. His vitriolic for viperous Jeannie and Hilary, Sam and his mother and every other living creature, was an attack on her nerves. She tried to limit the calls to half an hour, but they always went on longer. She tried avoiding the calls the odd week, but then thought about the common cause. Jeannie was the enemy, and must be defeated at all costs.

It was the middle of May when, one Sunday, Kath didn't get a call from Leo, and she felt that something was amiss.

"I'll call him in the morning," she told Rob that Monday night. "You know how stressed I get when he goes on. I'll have more fortitude in the morning."

Tuesday came and, before Kath was even dressed, she took a call.

“Good morning, this is the Coroner’s Office, Hereford. I have some bad news for you. Leo Llewellyn is dead.”

-39-

“Leo was found dead by his bed this morning at 11.30 am.” Kath relayed the phone message from the Coroner, to Rob.

“Dead?” Rob slumped against the doorjamb. Kath put an arm round his shoulder and guided him to the sofa in the living room..

“The coroner will ring tomorrow with the results of the post-mortem. In the meantime, you are to contact your solicitor, Myfanwy Forrester; he has already given orders for the police to give her your brother’s house keys.”

“Police ?” Robert jumped up.

“Yes, the police broke into Leo’s house. They were called when the social worker couldn’t rouse him at eleven. They found him flat on the floor in his bedroom. He must have had a heart attack...”

“Or, been murdered?” Robert put his head in his hands. “Jeannie would want him dead, for one.”

“Yeah, but I don’t think she would go that far! Really, Rob.”

“No, but Hilary, that joke of a man, would.”

“You’re getting a bit off kilter now, Rob, give over. But you know what, it’s Jeannie’s birthday today. I bet when she knows Leo died on her birthday, that will spook her out, especially as it's her sixty-sixth. You know what sixty-six means to witches, don’t you?” Robert's mouth opened wide, but no sound came out. Kath carried on. “The Devil’s work.” Kath cringed as she said it and she felt a chill down her spine as if a malevolent spirit had walked over her grave. She picked up the phone again, after giving Robert another hug.

Mrs Forrester answered Kath’s call, instantly. “If you come down tomorrow, I’ll let you have the keys. We don’t hold Mr. Llewellyn’s will. I expect it’s in his house, unless, of course, you have a copy?”

Kath explained that although Robert and her were in league with Leo, as far as contesting his father’s will went, they knew little of his private life and nothing about his possible will. Rob doubted there would even be a will. Leo was not the kind to think of his own mortality, well not at sixty-four, anyway.

"Well, in that case," the solicitor was treading her way carefully. "Perhaps I had better come to his house with you. Let's discuss matters further tomorrow. In the meantime, I will get my staff to ring around the solicitors in the area to see if by chance there is a will held with any of them."

"Just one more word before you go." Kath was curious. "Just why did the coroner entrust you with Leo's house keys, even before he rang us?"

"Good question, my dear, you have a discerning mind. The police couldn't find a phone book with names of contacts. There were letters by the bed from my office to your brother-in-law, and of course, Mr. Jenkins, the coroner knows me very well. He rang me straight away. I told him I would deal with everything, but of course he has the duty to inform the next of kin personally of any death in a family, and so I gave him your phone number. I didn't mention Mrs Hardwood, naturally. I warn you though that she will have to be told - later rather than sooner," Myfanwy laughed at her little joke, then went on, "But we'll discuss that tomorrow at 9am in my office, if that is in order?" Then she added blithely, as if she were telling a maid to take a suit to the dry cleaners, "You can go ahead with a funeral, of course. The coroner will put you in touch with local undertakers - if you wish."

Kath had never had to deal directly with a family death before and she found the responsibility of making funeral arrangements paralysing. She thought that if there was a will, perhaps she and Rob wouldn't have to be involved at all; thinking about sorting out Leo's affairs was even more daunting .If there was no will, her brother-in-law's worldly goods would be divided equally between Rob and Jeannie. Kath broke out into a sweat at the thought of helping Robert to deal with Jeannie.

Mrs. Forrester made it quite clear that if there wasn't a will, she would get Rob the letters of administration, to deal with Leo's affairs, at the exclusion of his sister. However, she was duty bound to wait at least a week to see if a will appeared.

Leo had sworn he had a will and had even told the girl in the solicitor's accounts office that he had it hidden in a hidey-hole, eighteen inches square, in his house. Armed with this information and the bunch of keys to Wardle House, Rob and Kath set off to search.

Mrs. Forrester had said she would send Jeannie a letter. She would address it to her via her "old" solicitor's office, at the end of the week. Hopefully, she explained, that would delay things and give her time to have either got the will, or if not, she would be well ahead of the game to be able to secure the letters of Administration for Robert. Even though Mrs Forrester seemed confident, Kath worried that the solicitor might not be around for long enough to finish the job, after all, she was now over eight months pregnant and could give birth at any time. She had already forgotten she had suggested going to Leo's house with them, only yesterday, but Kath was glad she wasn't. *The woman never stopped talking.*

The next day, as the couple stepped out of her office, Mrs Forrester, said, "Just drop the keys back this evening, before 5pm - I will be here. By the way, if I am indisposed. you can depend on my staff, Rita and Sian, to do my work."

Rita nodded, then smiled doubtfully. Sian, looking like a sixth-former, giggled. Kath was not reassured.

Rob just said, "What will be, will be."

Already, the post was piling up inside the front door of Leo's house when Kath and Robert let themselves in. There were demands for unpaid bills: one-thousand pounds for central heating oil and five hundred pounds to a local building company for a fence around the back of the house.

Payments were due on more than ten credit cards, several outstanding loans were being called in and there was an unpaid mortgage indicating an imminent foreclosure. With debts like these, Rob wondered if Leo's assets would be enough to repay them. The house, which he had paid over four-hundred-and-fifty-thousand pounds for, would now surely only fetch three-hundred-and-fifty-thousand, *if they were lucky*. If it didn't sell before winter, then, more than likely, it would drop even more. Even now, due to lack of ventilation for just a few days, the house was beginning to smell. Mould, and even a piece of fungi the size of a baby's head, was starting to spread up the stairwell.

Kath removed wet towels, and Leo's dirty clothes from the first floor bathroom, threw out the kitchen rubbish, turned the fridge and freezer off and emptied the food cupboards, while Rob looked for the hidden place Leo purported to have kept his will. He took up floorboards and backs of wardrobes. He looked behind paintings on walls, but there was no sign of a safe or hidey-hole.

It was already past midday when they returned to scrutinising the mail; an appointment for Leo at Moorfields Eye Hospital, an invitation to a Bonham's champagne supper party and a long letter from the DHSS stating that they were to carry out a full review of Leo's benefit payments. Kath smiled at the absurdity of the situation. Here was a man who had never worked in his life, living in a substantial period property, furnished with fine antiques, and yet the state was paying his council tax bill of two thousand pounds a year, not to mention his living expenses.

At three o' clock and still no sign of a will, and with only a tenth of the piles of papers sorted through, Rob decided it was best to pile the rest of the papers in the car and check through them at home. Every room upstairs was full of cardboard boxes, which were full of files, newspapers magazines and unopened mail. It looked like Leo had kept every scrap of paper since he had left Somerset, some years before. Kath heaved and hauled the packed boxes, as well as Leo's artwork portfolios, to their *Saab*. Rob baulked at the lack of space and reckoned at least another trip would be needed.

Kath fretted about the possibility of a break-in at the house. Rob thought it highly unlikely. He had already contacted the burglar alarm company and had the alarm at the house reset to ring his own mobile. He had nailed up windows and put more locks on the front gates. However, Kath still walked up to the church next door and spoke to the vicar about Leo's death and the house being left unoccupied. The chap said he would put the word out amongst the churchwardens and told her that, rest assured, nothing untoward would happen to Leo's belongings. After all, this was a quiet country English village, full of good honest people.

Kath remarked as they left the village on their way back to Ross-on Wye, how unusual it was that there were no more house keys to be found, no wristwatch either, and she vaguely wondered if someone else had been on the premises between Leo's death and their arrival. *Perhaps Leo had died a few days before he had been found?*

The coroner said they couldn't be sure of the exact time of death and admitted that he could have died some days previously. *Someone could have been in then, but who and why? If a watch was missing, what else could be... but why not Leo's wallet?*

It was pure speculation, but it bothered Kath. Rob didn't dwell on that; he was more concerned about getting home, then returning with tools and a five-gallon tin of anti- dry rot liquid to tackle the mould and rot on the staircase. Kath was thinking about organising the funeral.

It was just five to five in the evening, when the couple parked up outside the solicitor's office in the main road of Ross and dashed in to see Mrs. Forrester.

"No will," Kath reported, handing Mrs Forrester a plastic bag and the house keys. "Just these papers, mortgage demands, credit card debts, bills," Kath wiped her forehead. "We will have to go in again, there are still four rooms full of boxes of papers we haven't checked yet."

Myfanwy sat at her desk, arms across her big belly, one hand gripping the other hand's wrist, constantly checking the time on her wristwatch. Kath and Robert hovered by the office door.

"What about payment for you, Mrs. Forrester, for doing all this work?" Kath was to the point.

Immediately, sitting up straight and rubbing her hands together, she spoke. "Oh, of course you don't have to worry about that. I will deal with it all." She emphasised the word, 'all '. "...and of course I will take my fee from the estate. There is no need for you to worry about anything at all. Nothing at all. There is plenty of money there." Kath focused on Mrs Forrester's hands, she was wringing them dry with expectation. "There's plenty of money there," she repeated. "The house is stuffed full of antiques - the coroner told me."

Kath's thoughts turned to the one-hundred-and-fifty-thousand pounds worth of antiques they had left behind in Wardle House and she wondered if they would really be safe from thieves.

As they drove back to Newcastle, she found it laughable that they had entrusted a vicar to watch over the property and Mrs Forrester's staff to check on it every morning! Rob thought that was a perfectly satisfactory arrangement; after all, he didn't want to go into any expense having Leo's possessions, that he might not be entitled to, removed. Kath reminded him that if he felt he shouldn't be moving furniture that he was not entitled to, why was he bothering to treat dry rot in a house that he might not be entitled to? Rob didn't see the stupidity of that and she implored him again to get the antiques moved to a safe place.

Two days later, when they returned to Ross to collect the house keys from the solicitor and check again through Leo's House, Kath broached the subject of the vulnerability of the valuables left there. Speaking to Myfanwy, she said, "You know, we should get the stuff moved, otherwise, if Jeannie gets to know about Leo, she will be down here with a seven-ton lorry, emptying the place." Kath recounted how her sister-in-law had stripped her parent's house bare in a week when her mother died and then whisked Sam up to her house on the moors.

Myfanwy only laughed and the office juniors joined in, politely. "You and your imagination, Mrs. Llewellyn!" Myfanwy tried to end the conversation, but Kath went on.

"Well, at least I've made an inventory. I will have it all typed up, with photographs for you by the weekend. There were more than two-hundred items of value listed, including twelve long case clocks, a Bavarian, 19th Century two-foot tall cuckoo clock, a four-poster bed, a Georgian bureau, a Victorian ivory and ebony screen, a Persian carpet, a polyphone, a gramophone, several Ottomans, Chinese and Japanese vases and English Majolica pots, oil lamps and oil paintings.

It's quite an impressive and unique collection, Kath thought. *I suppose if anyone were to steal anything, then it would be easily detected.*

After another day scouring the house, there still wasn't a will, so at 4 pm., after filling up the car again with the rest of Leo's papers, Robert made sure the alarm was set and the house locked up. Reading lamps, one left on each floor, had been set up to come on and off with the three timer switches that Robert had brought with him that morning. Kath reassured him that she had good photographs of all the valuables and enough notes to produce a substantial inventory.

They arrived in Ross exhausted, but satisfied they had done their best. Kath was adamant Leo must have a dignified ending and her thoughts turned to his funeral again.

At the Solicitors office, Rita greeted them with a glum face, as she was leaving. "We've done a few calculations," she said. " It looks like even with the proceeds from the antiques you say would bring in a hundred thousand pounds, and that's only a rough estimate, with all the debts your brother incurred, we can't even see there will be enough money left to pay for his funeral."

"So… we might even end up with the bill for that?" Kath's spirits sank.

"Just typical of Leo, to leave a bloody mess like this." Rob wasn't fazed. "We'll just have to bugger on, that's what I say."

The undertaker from Four Cocks, a Mr James, wasn't too thrilled when they heard Forrester's and Forrester's were dealing with Leo's estate and would therefore be responsible for paying out the funeral costs. "They haven't paid us yet for burials we did three years ago," they said.

Kath sympathised, nonetheless, she was worried that Leo's liabilities would gobble up any assets and she repeated her assertion that they should at least get the antiques to a place of safety, ready for selling. Rob said he just wished a will would turn up and he could just walk away from the bloody lot of it. Kath said she had already invested too much time and effort to stop now and believed that there never would be a will so, maybe, just maybe, if the house could be sold for a good price and the antiques too, there would be something worth hanging about for. In any case, Leo must have a decent funeral and she put all her energies into that.

She arranged for a humanist speaker, as Leo had given up on religion. She had deduced this on finding a Bible, torn to shreds by his bed, just a few days before.

Leo was cremated on June 8th after Rob and Kath had checked that Wardle House was still undisturbed. Kath relaxed a little once the funeral was over. Only she, Rob, and Leo's three social workers, had attended. A précis of Leo's troubled and complicated life had been read out, along with two poems, *This be the Verse* by Philip Larkin and *Don't go Gentle into the Good Night* by Dylan Thomas. Adagio in G Minor and Fur Elise in A minor were played. Leo had no known friends and, in any case, Kath and Robert thought it better not to publicise Leo's death. It was imperative that Jeannie wasn't to find out about Leo, until *after* the funeral, until it was clear about a possible will. Mrs Forrester assured Rob she had applied for the letters of administration for him, but until the application was approved, he was not to touch the antiques or make plans to sell the house.

Kath wept on the way home to think of how Leo's last words to her were, when he thought his creditors were moving in on him and his lifestyle was about to end, “That's it. My life is fucked.”

She sobbed more at the thought of the hand-written statement he had left by his bed:

‘I had a promising career in art but due to unremitting pressure put on me by my parents and my tutors, I broke under the strain.’

Kath saddened even more to think he had kept his christening certificate on his bedside table, too. On it was a photograph of his mother holding him as a baby. Next to this was a paper showing that he had changed his name by deed poll. From 1994, he wished to be known as James Llewellyn. He had discarded the Leonard and his middle name of Wight, his mother’s maiden name. It was always a mystery why Leo had been given his mother’s maiden name, to make a double-barrelled name - and Robert and Jean had not. Whatever the reason, Leo hated his real names, but the family had refused to use the new one he had chosen. To them, the new James would always be Leo. Only *Classic FM* on the car radio, provided balm for Kath’s over-stretched nervous system and a broken heart.

Kath flew to Spain alone on June 12th for a holiday, to recuperate. Robert was to join her ten days later. She left Robert at Birmingham airport with a plea for him to get Mrs Forrester to hurry up with finalising the letters of administration and to, most certainly, get the antiques in Wardle House moved to a safer place as Kath feared Jeannie, would do something radical.

-40-

A Mephistophelean air hung over Old Oak cottage like a winter fog. Jeannie still wasn't using the room her father had died in, some eighteen months previously. The furniture was arranged as it was on the morning he died: the dark wooden commode stood by the bed; Sam's drawings and oil paintings hung on the walls; the heavy steel coloured curtains were drawn. The room, only ever opened now to inspect Sam's portfolios, harboured the smell of death.

Jeannie felt a shiver down her spine every time she slipped through the dark oak door into this space. How she had sat by her father's bed, wiping the sweat from his brow, as he lay struggling for his last breath, was still sharp in her mind. Hilary's harsh words, which he wrongly thought he had uttered in solitude, were engraved on her senses.

"At last, at bloody last. Six years, listening to him droning on about the damn war, his art, London and the Royal College. It had better pay off."

Since then, Jeannie had found herself alone most nights. She had anxiety and panic attacks. Sipping herbal teas had become her remedy for insomnia. Sleeping pills were downed when she found herself tossing and turning in bed. Sam's apparition haunted her. In her dreams, he called out, again and again the very last words he'd ever uttered. "Look after, Leo!"

Jeannie hadn't complied with her father's request and the guilt was beginning to bite. She sat for hours in front of her dressing table, staring blankly at her ageing face, combing and plaiting her long, dyed red hair. On this day, she had wound the long plait around her head, like a Cossack woman. Then she surprised herself. As it was a hot, sunny day, she had put on her long *Millais* brown velvet dress. It had been Tilly's, her favourite one - the one she had worn when she'd had important guests to *The Castle.* Leo loved that dress and used to stroke it across the back and shoulders, whenever his mother had worn it.

Jeannie's movements became sacerdotal, almost regal. She got up from the dressing table stool and opened the window. She felt uncomfortably aware of her younger brother's existence and bristled.

Trying to quell the unpleasant feeling, she gulped in fresh air from the Spartan moorland beyond and damned the fact she should feel so disturbed. Leo, the enemy along with Robert, the two of them, were haranguing her for a share of their father's will. "How dare they?" she shouted out to the gathering clouds, before going back to the mirror. She spat at the glass. "I, who looked after my father for six-and-a-half years, I deserve everything." She scrutinised her sixty-six year-old face again. The skin, stretched tight across her bony cheeks, once eggshell white, was now the colour of a peeled onion, but she didn't flinch. In her mind's eye, she still had the 1980's, New Age, carefree look of the hippy that she had once aspired to be. Her mind flashed back further, to Rose Mansion, the Georgian house where she had lived as an infant. She thought of the ghost she had seen, taunting her and screaming she would never have *Silverkrin* shampoo or *Camay* soap.

All three Llewellyn children complained later on in life that their mother was too mean to buy shampoo and they had to make do with Lifebuoy or carbolic.

Jeannie recalled how, while she had scrubbed and skivvied for hours in the kitchen, the boys had played with their guns, knives, and bikes, outside with their friends. They had spent rainy days reading comics indoors, while she was at the beck and call of her mother. She writhed at the thought that she had never had a pretty doll, real friends or even a new pair of pyjamas. At thirteen, when she needed a bra and begged for *Gardiner* scented bath salts, Tilly only laughed. *There wasn't money for luxuries*, she said. Jeannie seethed: there had always been enough for fur coats and an *Austin Princess* for Tilly. No, Jeannie was now determined to hold out for what she deemed her birthright. All Sam's worldly goods - and that was that.

Composed now, she descended the stairs with the air of a sad Tudor Princess, her small, almond-shaped eyes narrowed as she concentrated on beating her two brothers to their father's fortune. Six years she would have to wait to get the caveat lifted. Then, the money in the bank, and everything else would be hers. It had been three months since she'd had the last letter from her brothers' solicitor in Ross-on-Wye. Jeannie was feeling confident that there would be no more. She assumed that her brothers had given up their fight. She was now more concerned that Sam's drawings at the art gallery in London were not selling well. The economic recession was hitting hard, and with the agent taking fifty percent of all sales, Jeannie was hunting around for new outlets. Now Sam's pensions were not going into her bank account anymore, she needed hard cash. Hilary hadn't done a decent days work since Sam had gone to live with them. He first claimed he had broken an arm after falling off a ladder. Then, he said he had a sprained ankle after jumping off a wall. After that, he said he couldn't see as a splinter had gone in his eye, when he was stripping oak beams in their attic. The list of accidents was endless.

Robert had wondered if he really had injured himself or if it was a ploy to gain sympathy with his father and get even more money out of him; Hilary was a big spender. Their two-acre garden had been professionally landscaped. Diggers had been brought in to form a fishpond, twenty metres long. Stonewall terraces, waterfalls, flagged patios, life-sized marble statues - reminiscent of Versailles - graced the lawns. A two-storey extension and a deluxe model conservatory all added to the opulence of the stone cottage. A new *Range Rover* was parked in the drive, alongside a classic *Aston Martin*. All of this shouted out the couple's access to a fountain of wealth.

It was almost lunchtime. Chicken giblet broth was on a slow boil on the AGA cooker. Jeannie phoned Paul Fritz, manager of the art gallery in London, who was handling the sale of Sam's art work She had entrusted him, on behalf of her father, with a large mural, *Jason and the Three Goddesses*, some years before, for full restoration, but had heard nothing of the painting since. She admonished herself for not having even had a receipt for it. Without an apology, Mr. Fritz said they were having trouble completing the work as the only person available to undertake the job had died and it was taking time to recruit someone else. He cited the freak weather in France, where the work was being done, as a factor in the delay too. The whole area, usually famed for its hot, dry climate, so necessary for such artistic restoration, had experienced floods and, therefore, high humidity.

Jeannie hung up prematurely, feeling exasperated in the face of Mr. Fritz' excuses. She flopped down, cross-legged onto the floor of the downstairs living room and meditated, amongst the glass-domed, Victorian wax flower arrangements and the copper bowls of ruby crystals, placed there to sap up bad energy. She had studied Jung and psychoanalysis and believed in Anima Id. A stuffed barn owl, which she had taken to the taxidermist herself, after finding it dead at the gates of their cottage, looked down from its case in the corner. Jeannie breathed deeply, savouring the smell of beeswax and turpentine, used to preserve her antique furniture.

"The land belongs to those who till it," Jeannie reminded herself. "I have Sam's things and they are mine." The Bible was a useful reference.

She was sitting up at the dining table, spreading out the Tarot cards, when Hilary joined her. He'd been out with his eldest son in Oldham, looking to buy a car. Jeannie scowled. Buying cars for Kevin was not on her agenda, but she remained silent, the cards were more compelling.

"Death," Jeannie blurted out. "The cards say Death."

Hilary lifted his chin, sniffed and commented, " Dinner smells good."

Jeannie dutifully followed him into the kitchen and ladled out two bowls of the bubbling chicken broth, without a word. She was preoccupied with the Tarot card reading and the portent of death.

Hilary talked excitedly about his Freemason activities and the forthcoming Feast of John the Baptist, which would be held on June 24th, in just eleven days time. He wanted a new suit. He also wanted Jeannie to chauffeur him that night, so he could have his fill of all the free booze on offer. Jeannie reminded him it wasn't *free* - that his exorbitant membership fees were paying for all that alcohol. Now that Hilary was a Grand Master of his Lodge, his monthly dues were beginning to grind. Jeannie was in charge of their company accounts, but for now she would remain silent on the subject of monthly dues.

Hilary had a gun. He was also spending far too much time out of the house. Jeannie worried his drinking was getting out of hand, too. Spending afternoons with his Brotherhood pals and then being deposited home, blind drunk after dark, was becoming a nasty habit. She was sick of his *Boy Scout* activities, but didn't dare call for him to put an end to it. Freemasons didn't take lightly to being dumped, and Jeannie was afraid of them. How many times had she heard Hilary chanting away in what he thought was the sanctity of the bathroom, and felt ice run through her blood?

May my throat be cut across, my tongue torn out by its roots, and my body be buried in the rough sands of the seas at low water mark, should obligations be violated. My breast be torn open and heart plucked out and given over to wild beasts of the fields and fowls of the air, if I reveal the secrets of the sect. May my body be cut in two, my bowels removed and burned to ashes then scattered to the four winds. My punishment for betrayal.

Jeannie thought of the Seventh Marquis of Bath, the Lord of Longleat, and wondered if he was a Freemason. She amused herself thinking of him and his seventy wife-lets and his bizarre wall paintings - including his most famous one, a take on the Kama Sutra.

"Art's a bloody good way of laundering money," Jeannie mused.

Reading an article about Francis King in one of the back issues of the monthly magazine, *Man, Myth and Magic,* Jeannie honed in on the author's novel, *Voices in an Empty Room,* and made a mental note to get it from the library. Dealing with Spiritualism, she envisaged, would help her come to terms with death.

It was three o' clock. She was dozing off on the chaise longue in the conservatory when the phone rang. As always, she listened for the caller to identify themselves on the answering machine, before responding.

Jeannie snatched the receiver up at once. She knew from the tone of the man's voice, she was to hear some shocking news.

"There's a rumour that Leo is dead," the antique dealer from mid-Wales said. "You know, Eric…? He used to be the gardener for your parents, then he did a bit for Leo. Well, he called round to Leo's house today - he noticed the lawn was looking overgrown, so he went round the back and saw Leo's kitchen window had been forced open, then boarded up. The neighbours said they hadn't seen Leo about, and now I come to think of it, he hasn't been around here for some weeks now. He used to come every couple of weeks to browse in my shop window."

"Well, thank you for that, David. I'm stunned, but I will make enquiries from here and keep you informed. I'll phone Eric first. I still have his phone number."

Jeannie pondered about phoning Robert, but thought again about that. It had been nearly two years since they had communicated verbally. Robert had called her a bitch then and she hadn't forgiven him. She phoned the police, instead.

"Yes, I can tell you that Mr. Llewellyn of Wardle House was found dead at his home on May 25th and was removed from the premises by our Police Force. The Coroner in Hereford will give you more information."

"I can't tell you much. The coroner is off today," the Registry Office receptionist informed Jeannie, "...but Forrester and Forrester's Solicitors in Ross-on-Wye are dealing with Mr. Llewellyn's affairs. Do you require their number?"

"No thank you, I have it," the receiver, dropping from Jeannie's trembling hands, knocked a coffee cup off the desk.

"So... Robert knows," she screamed. "And, he died on my birthday, nearly three weeks ago. On my birthday!" Downing a tranquilliser pill, Jeannie picked up the phone again.

"Good afternoon, Forrester and Forrester's Solicitors."

"Put me through to Mrs Forrester, please," Jeannie said.

"Whom may I say is calling?"

"Mrs Hardwood. It's in connection with Leonard Llewellyn."

"Just one moment. I will try to put you through." After an uncomfortable and overly long silence, the receptionist spoke again. "I am awfully sorry, Mrs Hardwood, but Mrs Forrester is not in the office at the moment. Can I put you through to someone else?"

"No, that's quite all right. I will call again later." Jeannie sensed it would be futile to persist. Instead, she called her solicitor.

After attempting to speak to Mrs Forrester on the phone, Mr King reported that he believed there was a deliberate attempt by the Welsh solicitors to avoid communication. He advised Jeannie to go to Leo's house herself. If there was anything in Leo's house, she was to remove it, 'for safe keeping '. In the meantime, he would try to contact Ms Forrester again.

Jeannie had envisaged that Leo's antiques would have already been removed by whoever was beneficiary of his will, or worse by Robert, who she presumed wouldn't be in Leo's will. Even though her brothers were collaborating against her, Jeannie knew there was no love lost between the two of them. Leo had always stated he would will his entire goods to the National Trust. She had no reason to think he hadn't.

It was a revelation for Jeannie to discover that the contents of Wardle House were apparently undisturbed. Jeannie had contacted Eric Par, to go and take another look at Leo's house, peer through windows, even get into the house again, through the broken back kitchen window.

Eric reported back that the gates to the drive were securely locked and there was no evidence of the house contents being removed.

-41-

Kath rang Rob four nights on the trot from Spain. He hadn't been able to speak to Mrs. Forrester on the phone; she was on maternity leave. He spoke to the younger members of staff instead. There was still no sign of Leo's will, so everything was going through for Robert to get the letters of Grant of Administration.

On Wednesday June the 15th, Myfanwy Forrester, who was about to give birth, called Rob from her hospital bed. Jeannie's solicitor, Mr. King, had telephoned her office about the rumours that Leo Llewellyn was dead. Her staff had told Mr. King she was off work, and they knew nothing about Leo. But, in any case, Rob was to go to her office immediately to sign papers. Rob assumed they were the Grant of Administration forms, required to take charge of Leo's estate. In that case, Jeannie would have no dominion over the house or its contents.

Kath prayed that there would be enough assets to leave the estate solvent.

"You would think Jeannie would have phoned you, if she had thought that Leo might be dead, wouldn't you?" Kath said to Robert that night. "Do you think she hasn't, because she feels guilty over your father's Will?

Rob didn't speculate. He just knew he should get Leo's estate settled, without his sister's interference; the sooner the better. Jeannie was the last person on earth Leo would have wanted privy to his affairs. Kath begged him to drive to the solicitor's office the very next day, but Robert said he needed to check the car over first, before undertaking the long journey.

On Friday June the 17th at 6 a.m., Rob left Newcastle for Ross-on-Wye. With the hood down on the *Saab* and the sun out, the drive was divine. It was Robert's intention to check Wardle House first, then get to the Forresters' Office, a little after nine o clock, where Sian, the young assistant, was to meet him.

It was 8:40 am as he passed the double, wrought iron gates to Leo's grand house. They were wide open. His heart missed a beat as he feared there had been a break-in. His thoughts were confirmed when he saw a white removal van parked up in the drive and three men loading Leo's possessions into the back.

"What the hell do you think you are doing?" Robert bellowed at the men, as he screeched the car to a halt in front of the van.

"Orders from Mrs Hardwood to fill her up," the gaffer of the group curtly answered, without looking up. With a wave of his hand, he indicated to his men to carry on.

Rob whirled the car round in four seconds flat, shouting out that he was going to call the police. He arrived at the solicitors' office in Ross out of breath, but with just about enough strength to phone 999. Sian phoned Myfanwy, who was in the first stages of labour, and passed the phone to Robert. "That's it, we've got them now. Breaking and entering is a crime, hey, what a scoop," she shrieked.

Robert smiled as he envisaged the woman spitting out the words, then he returned to Wardle House with Sian, only to find Jeannie and Hilary orchestrating the removals. Their *Land Rover* was parked by the white van.

"You can't do this," but Sian struggled to be heard over the clamour of furniture being banged and bumped, the grunts and groans of removal men and pop music blaring out from the van's radio.

"It's against the law! These items have not been granted probate. They are not yours to remove, Mrs. Hardwood."

"Carry on, lads," Hilary commanded, pushing Sian to one side, when she resorted to taking photographs on her mobile phone. But, much of the 'booty' was covered in blankets, Leo's bedding! Rob looked at his watch and estimated it was over half an hour since he had dialled 999 and there was still no sign of a copper.

Sian said that the police would put a halt to this blatant act of theft. Not only had the Hardwoods' cut through the front door locks with an angle grinder, they had smashed the alarm system and forced locks to the other outside doors. Antiques were streaming past them as fast as a trail of ants.

After engaging with Hilary, who shouted and hissed, the conversation amounted to nothing, so Rob turned round to speak to Jeannie. As he moved, he felt a heavy hand on his left shoulder. Startled, he spun round and lashed out like a lion, giving Hilary a hard slap on the cheek. The little man staggered backwards, some five metres, then fell to his knees. Tottering, as he regained his footage, he glared into Rob's eyes, but didn't dare advance again. The gaffer moved forward, as if to strike, but one look from Rob and the geezer backed off. The other two men never moved. Jeannie stood unmoved, but then retreated into the shadows, before stealthily manoeuvring herself around to her husband's side, where she spirited them both into the house.

Robert and Sian retreated to the *Saab*.

PC Tardy arrived an hour later, and coughed before he made apologies.

"Sorry, I am a bit late; we had a firearms incident in Kingsley… I understand there's been an assault?"

Robert realised then that the Hardwoods' must have called the police. "A family affair, is it?" The policeman grinned. Robert knew then whose side he was on. "Robert Llewellyn, I believe," PC Tardy said, as he eyed up Robert. "I will have to arrest you, Mr Llewellyn. You will have to come with me to the station."

Robert seized up for a moment. Then, Sian spoke, "It was not an assault officer, I can assure you. I am Mr. Llewellyn's solicitor's assistant and I vouch for his integrity. He will make a statement of course, but there is no need for arrests."

Rob's faith in the legal profession took a turn for the better when the petite Sian negotiated for Rob to make a statement at a later date in his own hometown.

Feeling sick, reeling from the trauma of hitting Hilary, and the shock of the policeman's stance, Rob left Sian to handle the situation.

"Of course, Mrs Hardwood, you cannot leave all these valuables in the house. Yes, you have to remove them to a safe place, I understand… make an inventory, then take the keys of the lock-up to Forresters'," the policeman said to Jeannie.

Rob lost the will to protest, now Sian had given in to Jeannie as well –

so the removal van was allowed to drive off. Robert accompanied Sian back to her office in silence, but there were no Grant of Administration papers to be signed, as promised, only a customer care contract waiting for his signature. Rob wasn't prepared for that. Without signing, he drove home.

Kath reassured Robert on the phone that night that she expected Jeannie would do as the policeman had ordered and deposit the antiques into safe storage, then hand the keys to Mrs Forrester.

Rob was not so confident. "I'll put a bet on it, she doesn't. Why should she trust Forresters'? After all, they are fighting her over Sam's will? They didn't tell her Leo was dead, then they gave her the run around when she got King to phone up to check out the rumours about that. Hmm."

"But… she would be disobeying a police officer if she didn't carry out his instructions - wouldn't she? Isn't that a serious offence?"

"I am not so sure about that now," Rob said, "Looks to me like Hilary's got friends in the Police Force, through his Freemason connections, no doubt. Who else would blatantly dare break into a house like he did? "

Robert boarded the plane for Almeria a very troubled man.

-42-

Frantic phone calls from Spain to Forresters and Forresters left Rob and Kath perplexed. Myfanwy Forrester was still on maternity leave; she was not to be disturbed. Her minions were unprepared. The police refused further communication as they said the break-in at Wardle House was a civil matter.

Kath and Robert went over the facts:

PC Tardy had given the impression that he had the authority over what was to be done with the antiques and non-compliance would have severe consequences for Mrs Hardwood. Now the police wanted no more to do with it! It was evident that when PC Tardy arrived, he was fully aware of the family dispute over removing antiques, and the altercation. But why had he so readily allowed

Jeannie to remove the entire contents of Leo's house ? Rob believed Hilary had used his Freemason contacts.

Kath urged Rob to make a formal complaint to the IPCC, and drafted the salient points, then sent for the official complaint forms. She clung naively to the hope that Jeannie had taken the antiques to the safe storage unit, in Ross, as ordered by the PC, and that at least they would all be there, as per their inventory. No doubt the items would be a little worse for having been being 'thrown' into the back of a removal van. Robert described seeing clocks with smashed faces, a chest of drawers with handles knocked off and boxes of crockery being rattled about!

Kath tried to make light of Rob whopping Hilary, the so-called assault, and revelled in Rob's account of the action. "It was like slapping a side of cold bacon," Rob grimaced. "The greasy man fell like a cold-blooded toad. I wish I had given him another one, the other side." Rob swished his hand through the air, relishing the moment he had struck his brother-in-law.

Kath inwardly thanked fate. The way events were turning out would certainly add spice to her story: she was well into her novel, that had seeded itself when Sam had died. Writing every day in Spain kept her sane.

Robert spent the mornings restoring his Vintage motorbike, the Rudge he'd rescued from Leo's *Stable of vintage motors* at the Old Parsonage in Beckton all those years ago, but had never found the time to put together before. With three children, lives on three continents, study, full- time and part-time jobs, there was never enough hours in the day. It was different now they were retired, and living half the year in Spain. Forcing negative thoughts about Jeannie out of their minds, they now enjoyed each other and revelled again in their love life. Siestas on sun loungers in the shade of the awning on the terrace, cold beers for Robert, summer wine with ice and lemon for Kath. The afternoons stretched into the nights.

It was a week before Rob received written communication from Forresters and Forresters. An email, (a copy of the letter sent to their home address in Newcastle,) outlined details of a letter sent to them from Jeannie, following the heist on June 17th at Wardle House.

Mrs. Forrester finished with:

In these circumstances, and in the light of my current absence from the office, it would be in your interests to instruct a local firm with your brother's estate. I trust you find my bill for a thousand pounds reasonable - for work carried out so far.

P.S. I will arrange for the papers concerning the case to be returned to you by Registered mail. Please confirm your postal address.

Jeannie had threatened to report the Forresters' legal practice to the Law Society. She said she had tried to deposit the storage keys (a lock-up in Ross) with Forresters and Forresters that Friday evening, after taking off with the antiques, but the staff at the solicitor's office had refused to take them.

Rob fumed at Forresters' bill. "For what? A bungle if ever I saw one. No, I won't pay it."

"But you might have to, remember Myfanwy has the file on contesting your father's will? She won't release that, if you decide not to pay..."

"She can't do that, it's against the law," Rob protested. "You can't put a hold on one case 'cause another one hasn't been paid for!"

"A lot of things are against the law, but people do them, and get away with it. But, you are right, she shouldn't be levering money out of you for one thing with the threat of endangering another, but she will make the contesting difficult for you if you don't cough up."

"Bah, never."

"What a cheek that Jeannie has in demanding expenses for hiring that removal van and the storage costs of the lock-up!"

"I've just about had enough!" Robert, with a cold beer in one hand, stood relishing the panoramic sea view from the terrace of their villa. "Let's say nothing more on the matter until we get home?"

"Good idea," Kath replied, sipping a brandy and joining her husband in the sunshine. She raised her glass. "I'll drink to that!"

With lips sealed and a steely determination, what could have been a fiery two weeks in Spain, like boiling in a witches' cauldron, turned out to be a useful interlude.

Kath emailed the solicitors, but discreetly omitted the matter of the bill. She said she and Robert would collect the papers mentioned, in person, as soon as they got home to the UK.

By then, Jeannie should have provided them with a set of new house keys, for Wardle House, and they could check on that.

Kath was being overly optimistic again; keys never materialised, but still Robert and Kath went to Ross. A sad looking receptionist at Foresters' handed over the papers sheepishly. Awkwardly, she told the couple they wouldn't be allowed to see Mrs. Forester or any of her staff personally; any communication would have to be by email only.

Without keys to Wardle House and with an air of despair, the couple peeped through the windows of Leo's empty house. A mop and bucket sat in the corner of the kitchen. An upturned cardboard box lay on bare floorboards in the living room. The Hardwoods, it seemed, had cleared the house out: lock, stock and barrel.

A phone call to Jeannie later resulted in Robert having to leave a message on her answerphone. As expected, a reply was not forthcoming, but a phone call to her solicitor, Mr. King, revealed that all communication with Jeannie Hardwood was to be through him - by email.

The priority now was for Robert to engage another solicitor to deal with Leo's estate. Jeannie wouldn't know that Forresters' had backed out, but Kath felt sure King would have advised putting a caveat on Leo's estate, therefore blocking any attempts for Rob to obtain the Letters of Administration. King might even have applied for Jeannie to be the sole administrator? Rob reckoned he wouldn't have had the necessary information regarding Leo's financial state. Kath poured over the figures of Leo's assets and liabilities again, then drew up a balance sheet.

Assets: House, three-hundred-and-fifty-thousand pounds, antiques/household goods, seventy-five thousand.

Liabilities: Mortgage, two-hundred-and-fifty thousand.

Loans: seventy-five thousand.

Credit card debts: fifty thousand.

Bills outstanding: five thousand.

That left fifty thousand pounds in credit. However, if the loans were not paid quickly and interest accrued, that figure would soon diminish.

The mortgage, loan and credit card companies assured Kath that, on production of a Death Certificate, no more interest would accrue from the day Leo had died. That was a relief. Kath had purchased several copies of the Certificate before the funeral. Robert was still doubtful the debts would be cleared; the house might not fetch even three-hundred-and-fifty thousand because, after the flood some two years before, the house might have been unmortgageable. Papers in Leo's house pertaining to the flooding, showed that the house was below the water level of The River Wye, just across the road. Should the water level ever rise over its banks again, Wardle House was in line for the overspill. The dry rot was going to cost over ten thousand pounds to treat, according to Rob, and when the auctioneers' commission had been taken off the sale of the antiques, well, they would be lucky to clear fifty thousand pounds. But still, with a bit of luck, then the estate might be solvent and any effort now surely should pay off.

Mr. Flowers listened to Rob's story and took up his cause. A jolly fellow, he had been the family's solicitor as a young man, taking his articles at the local solicitor's office in their village, in the Borough of Newcastle. He explained that he now worked freelance. Kath joked, "Don't you mean 'fancy free,' when she saw this sixty-year-old man was whizzing about in a *Madza* sports car like a twenty year-old. Mr Flowers wanted five hundred pounds up front and a contract of care signed there and then. Robert complied and Mr. Flowers set to work.

Jeannie apparently had not applied to the court for letters of administration. Mr. Flowers would do that for Robert, after he provided a signed oath. Robert was staggered. Myfanwy Forrester had never mentioned the fact that a signed oath was a pre-requisite of applying for the Grant of Administration." My God," he thought. "She really did spin me a yarn, that one. What a rat of a woman. "

Kath calmed Robert down and Mr Flowers demanded that Jeannie declare what she had done with the antiques. She was to present an inventory of the goods she held and that they must coincide with the inventory that Kath had prepared.

Two weeks later, and still with no word from Jeannie, Steve Flowers, relayed the bad news, he had made a mistake and Jeannie had in fact put a caveat on the estate. Robert just had to accept that Jeannie and he were to have joint administration. Mr. Flowers pressed again for Jeannie to produce an inventory of the goods she held as part of her brother's estate, disclose their whereabouts, and produce an undertaking not to dispose of any of the items without specific consent of her brother, Robert. Jeannie had a week to comply, failing this, a high court injunction order would be issued and she would end up in court at a cost to her of two thousand pounds.

Jeannie's response came just one day before she was to appear in court. Could she have a stay of execution, as she had been ill?

"The mystery virus again!" Rob and Kath wailed in unison as they laughed. Every time Jeannie had ever had to do anything important, she was always infected by mystery virus!

Mr. Fowler kindly gave Jeannie another week to comply.

Jeannie finally explained: *After having the antiques in store in Ross for a month, she had had them moved to a fine art auction house in Cambridge. The inventory and probate valuations clearly showed that the items were due to be sold at the end of August, just a few days hence.*

Kath immediately rang the auction house. "The items you hold for Mrs Hardwood, that she delivered to your establishment on July 19th are to be withheld. She took those things illegally, from her deceased brother's house and you have to put a hold on their disposal. You will get a solicitor's letter in the morning to confirm what I have told you." Kath prided herself on how she had handled the auction house staff and was delighted at the thought of the office gossip going round about how Jeannie was a thief.

But, there were more obstacles to clear before things could get moving again. After painstaking hours of scrutinising the inventories from the auction house and comparing them with their own inventory - over two-hundred items - it was evident that the two didn't match. Whereas Kath had labelled each individual pottery item, the auctioneers had lumped several together under the heading, 'Box of pottery.' How would they know for sure that the ten items they had listed were the same ten items in that box? How would they know even if there *were* ten items? Even if Kath were to dispute the amount of pottery, well how would they prove it ? They couldn't - so that was that.

What was blatant though, was the fact that three very expensive clocks were missing. Jeannie was informed, but denied all knowledge and swore she had moved everything to the auction house and taken nothing for herself at all.

When asked about the washing machine, the fridge, the top of the range sit-on lawn mower, and a set of brand new, triple extending aluminium ladders, Jeannie said they had all been scrapped! She also said, as joint administrator with Robert, she was not prepared to let Mr. Flowers deal with Leo's estate: an independent solicitor would have to be hired!

Robert, exasperated yet again, swore vengeance - but Kath skilfully crafted an email, outlining the case for allowing Mr Flowers to carry on. He, after all, knew the background and had all the information on file. A new solicitor would have to cover old ground, and, in the long run, cost more.

Jeannie finally conceded, but was still loathe to proceed, until other issues had been resolved. Her compliance with the settling of the estate was dependent on Robert lifting the caveat he had put on their father's will and the promise that, '*Predatory Kath*' was banned absolutely from any dealings with the case.

Mr Flowers pointed out how unethical all this was and would land her in court if she persisted with such defamation of character.

Next, she wanted a cast-iron guarantee that she would get all her expenses back, for: hiring a removal van, paying for storage and getting Wardle House cleaned up. Robert was advised to agree, if he didn't want the whole thing to drag on. Kath chuckled at the thought of being called 'predatory' but henceforth, any correspondence she sent regarding the matter was signed: Robert Samuel Llewellyn - and Kath was only the scribe.

It was another month before the caveat Jeannie had put on Leo's estate was lifted and she'd signed the oath to make it legitimate for both her and Rob to be administrators of Leo's estate. Robert had already paid Mr Flowers three-thousand pounds to get this far. Robert fumed at the impudence of his sister, but was again impotent to do anything about it. Even when Jeannie was asked to send in a signed oath, it arrived damaged, torn in two and stuck together with Sellotape; useless. Getting another one meant a week's delay. Until the oaths were signed, neither the antiques nor the house could be sold.

The estate agents' valuation for Wardle House came in at between five hundred and five hundred-and-fifty thousand pounds. Robert thought that was over optimistic, but nevertheless, trusted the agent knew best. The valuation depended on having the dry rot treated first and that would cost less than five thousand pounds; half as much as first thought.

Robert pointed out that there was no money in the estate to pay for that work, but there could be, if Jeannie would give permission for Robert to purchase a few things from the probate list of Leo's antiques still in Cambridge. Some weeks previously, Jeannie was insisting peevishly that everything should be sold at auction and that neither she nor Rob should be allowed to buy anything. Now, she was having second thoughts. Robert would pay the probate estimate for the few items he wanted, and that would amount to over five thousand pounds. Jeannie finally saw sense, when she realised she could be reimbursed immediately for her outgoings, the cleaning and the house insurance.

Robert and Kath collected the desired antiques from Cambridge in their van: a red lacquer long case clock, an ebony and ivory Victorian screen, a large oil painting of a French Battleship, an oil painting of Loch Lomond, and a French enamelled ormolu clock. Celebrating their victory over Jeannie's maniacal obstinacy, the couple bought fish and chips and sat in the sun by the River Cam. It was fun to see Cambridge again. It was twenty years since their eldest son, Christian, had graduated from Trinity College. Nothing seemed to have changed.

The antiques remaining in Cambridge were sold over the course of several months and the money used immediately to pay off credit cards and some of Leo's loans.

Robert's complaint to the IPCC, about the police's treatment of the break-in at Wardle House, amounted to nothing. Rob's verdict was that the IPCC should be taken to court for Trade Description violations, as it was no more independent from the police force, as the church was independent from the State.

But, at least Robert had been cleared of all assault charges. Six-months after the altercation with his brother-in-law, the Crown Prosecution Service, stated that Mr Llewellyn had acted in self-defence. With another battle won, Christmas was bearable that year.

In the New Year, Kath typed up an appeal for Rob to the odious verdict of the IPCC, but the response was swift and emphatic; the police had no case to answer and any further action on the matter would have to be taken up with an independent solicitor. Robert wasn't prepared to go down that road. Already, the legal wrangling had taken up far too much of his money and worse - his time. However with a house sale in the spring expected, Robert was now confident that Leo's estate would be solvent and there would be a few thousand pounds left for him.

It was mid-January, 2013, when the heavy frosts were starting, that Robert thought the central heating system at Leo's house would need draining and it would do no harm to go there and meet the estate agent face to face. A weekend away from Newcastle would be welcome and, after being in Ross, they were going to Wales - where they would meet possible witnesses for carrying on with contesting Samuel's will.

Robert was in no doubt that once Leo's estate was settled, he would notch up activity again on that. Jeannie's manner, being so awkward over proceedings regarding Leo's affairs, would not go down well with the will contesting judge, Robert imagined.

It was the day before Robert and Kath were due in Ross that Mr Jones, from the estate agents called. "There has been an accident at Wardle House." Kath envisaged a flood, Rob a fire. "No, no nothing so disastrous, it's just that the neighbour's barn wall has collapsed onto the front lawn of the house. The whole gable end of Farmer William's barn, you know, the Farm shop building, well, it's strewn all across the front, knocked two big trees down at the front as well. Terrible mess it is."

Robert surveyed the scene; "It looks like a battle field!" Stones, scattered to every corner of the garden lay embedded in the muddy lawn, churned to pulp by tractor tyres.

A JCB must have been driven in through a gap made in the front fence. Five tall Leylandii trees had been sawn down and removed: this wasn't the work of a falling wall. Mr Williams would have to explain.

The farmer said of course he would tidy up the mess, replace the broken fence and make good his own barn wall, but that wasn't the point. Trees had been removed without permission and privacy at the property compromised. Robert didn't like it, neither did Jeannie. There was talk about litigation against the farmer, when he refused to compensate for the lost trees, but Mr Flowers argued against that.

More delays and expense. Better to accept the situation and get on with selling the house as it was. The cheek of the farmer was yet another example of blatant law breaking and not being called to heel. "Just how do these people get away with it ?" Kath cried.

Robert wondered if Williams had deliberately engineered his barn wall collapsing onto Leo's land. After all, the farmer had put in a ridiculously low offer to buy Wardle House, just the week before. "Just to get the monstrosity of your hands," he'd said. Robert had sent him packing - but at least he did tidy up the garden, as expected.

By March, the remaining trees were sprouting leaves and the garden didn't look as forlorn as it had in January. The asking price had been reduced to four-hundred-and-fifty thousand pounds. By the end of the month, a businessman from Birmingham had made an offer of four hundred thousand pounds. Robert pushed for more. In the end, four hundred-and-five thousand was agreed and the waiting game began.

One week had passed when another frantic phone call from the estate agent revealed that huge hoardings, advertising the farm shop next door, had been put up in front of the house. Farmer Williams was responsible. The billboards were out of character, but their removal was dependent on the council planning department's say-so. Any attempt to have them removed would be seen as an act of aggression and, in any case, if Robert or Jeannie were to have them removed, the farmer would soon have them replaced.

"Another example of bureaucracy gone mad," Kath wailed at the injustice.

Naturally, the businessman from Birmingham was reluctant to sign for the house when problems with nasty neighbours were looming. He tried to lower the price, but the estate agent and Mr Flowers recommended holding out. It paid off. Williams offered four-hundred-and-twenty thousand. The businessman was then given three weeks to sign at his original price, but didn't. Whether he didn't believe there was a better offer in the pipeline, no one will ever know, but Farmer Williams had his wicked way. He paid on the day, the gentleman from Birmingham failed to sign.

The money, from the sale went straight to Mr Flowers, to pay off

Leo's remaining debts, the solicitor's fees and the residue, a nice tidy sum, went equally to Robert and Jeannie.

Robert and Kath's Christmas 2012, was one certainly to be remembered. With money in the bank, they finally put an end to thinking about the trouble Leo's death had caused. They would start thinking about contesting Sam's will again in the New Year.

-43-

Robert emailed Jeannie on New Year's Eve expressing relief, and joy, that at last Leo's estate was settled. *Now would she make an out-of-court settlement on their father's will?*

The immediate reply was, "Happy New Year from Jeannie and Hilary".

"That's a 'two fingers up yours, if ever there was one," Kath said.

A week later, Kath and Rob drove off to Spain for their three month winter, vowing not speak to about Jeannie and the will contesting business, until they got back to the UK in March.

Kath buried her head in words and completed six more chapters of her novel. Robert finished restoring the Rudge and began working on his Gillera motorbike. They lived the life of young lovers. With a casa in the village, three kilometres from their flat on the beach, they moved between their two homes. Cycling up and down became a way of life. They reflected on their time in Grand Cayman, the birth of Christian, the wonder at being parents and now grandparents to two boys and two girls. They also reminisced about Africa where their two youngest sons were born and revelled in their good fortune to have good health and wealth; the will business was just an inconvenience.

Why hadn't they just accepted the fact that Sam had willed everything to Jeannie, and then got on with their already busy and interesting lives? *Had they just accepted the fact that the past three and half years, since Sam's death, would not have been so hard going, but then not quite so interesting*, Kath thought.

She had enjoyed delving into her past and committing it to the printed word.

On the ferry crossing from Santander to Portsmouth, at the end of their time in the sun and, after finally finishing reading the *Fifty Shades of Grey* trilogy, Kath revised the six-page rational on Robert's claim of his sister's undue influence on their father and added details of two new witnesses and their testimonies. She felt apprehensive that a new solicitor would have to be contracted. It was inevitable that Forrester, after her negligence over the handling of Leo's estate, would no longer be trusted to carry on with the contesting case.

Kath downed a gin and tonic in the ship's piano bar and held up her glass to Robert's beer pint glass. "Third time lucky, eh?"

Rob looked perplexed. "Well, Myfanwy won't be carrying on with the contesting anymore, that's for sure, so you'll have to engage another solicitor."

"A third one!" Robert's eyes rolled. "We said we wouldn't think about the will till we got back to the UK."

"Well, come off it! We are only two hours from docking, and I'm in the mood for battle," Kath replied.

The first letter Kath opened, on arriving home, was from the solicitor, Mrs Forrester, who was no longer on maternity leave.

The content was a body blow; but not fatal - Kath had foreseen something like this. She said that as Robert had concealed the death of his brother from Jeannie she could no longer use the fact that Jeannie had concealed the death of her father from Robert. Myfanwy was being spiteful and revengeful.

Kath penned Robert's response to the injustice (after all, it was Mrs Forrester herself who had insisted that Jeannie not be told of Leo's death straight away.) As for demanding nearly one-thousand pounds, yet again, for the measly, and messy, bit of work she had done pertaining to Leo's estate, Robert was furious.

Mrs. Forrester was not giving up:

Now that Wardle House is sold, and I believe for a very good price, I assume you will settle my bill.

Robert, like he did with everything else that was unpleasant, said he would ignore the demand. Kath reminded him he couldn't, as the woman still held the file notes on the contesting case and she was sure to withhold them. A quick phone call, there and then, confirmed Kath's gut feelings. The file would only be released on payment of the money owing to the company for the work carried out on Leonard Llewellyn's estate - but a copy could be provided on request. The copy duly arrived, but was of such poor quality, Kath assumed it had been done deliberately. Still, the copy would have to suffice for now. There was no time to lose.

With vim and vigour, Kath set about looking for another advocate and plumped, after two weeks of disappointing responses from local firms, for an energetic old lady practising in Macclesfield - not too far from Newcastle. An Oxford graduate, her communications were prompt and concise.

"It unlawful for Mrs. Forrester to withhold the file. She has been paid for the work and it was her choice to resign from the case. Mrs Forrester is being pertinent in trying to extract money from you Robert..." Thelma Sanders said, but thankfully, the copy would just about suffice for her to proceed. "There is no point in arguing with Forrester's." The solicitor oozed grace and common sense.

Leo's death would certainly weaken the case, Mrs. Forrester's resignation and her reasons given wouldn't help either, but Mrs Sanders thought, like Kath did, that they were born of malice and she was convinced she could surmount their impact on getting further funding from the Insurance pot. Once the matter got to court, how many solicitors had dealt with it previously would not even be mentioned.

Perusing over the six-page rationale and with a list of points to discuss, Mrs. Sanders sat facing Robert and Kath across the heavy oak board table in the solicitor's room. The sun streamed through the mullioned windows of the Georgian office suite in the centre of the ancient market town. Kath, dressed in a short-sleeved striped shirt and denim jeans, fanned herself discreetly with her latest Spanish fan; she had one to match every occasion. Robert sat transfixed, unbelieving that this solicitor, nearing pension age, but who looked like a slip of a girl to him, could be so in command of the situation.

"So... Modus operandi," she said, then noticing their blank faces explained the way forward. "Just to clarify, had your father, Sam Llewellyn, not made a new will in 2003, the old one would have been in vigour, when he died. Robert, you would have had a third share in his estate."

Robert nodded.

"Your father, was living in your sister's house for nine months before he made the new will. Hmm… and visitors to see your father were told by your sister, that you never visited…?"

"All correct," Robert nodded again.

"And… she told everyone that you had cut yourself off from your family and had gone to live in Spain?" Robert shook his head at his sister's behaviour.

"Your father's dubious internment in hospital for three weeks, prior to making the will - and his subsequent letter to you – is a very good point. The evidence is stacking up." She looked up. "The Judges report, on the court case in Oldham against your brother… *Mrs Hardwood, I find you a congenital liar…* that's excellent!" and she clapped her hands. "And… I like this one: *…promised your father that she would not sell any of his artwork. Would buy a chapel on the moors, turn it into an art gallery to display all Sam's work. Have it as a centre of excellence for art, a shrine to his memory.* We just need the evidence for that. You say your grandson will testify he heard his aunty say this to his mother, just after Sam died?"

"Yes, and our grandson will be eighteen in September. He will be able to sign an affidavit then. His mother won't let him at the moment."

"Right. Then we have the evidence of your sister's inadmissible – and not far from criminal behaviour – when your brother died. Breaking into his house, telling you she would not cooperate, unless you lifted the caveat on your father's will. All very compelling evidence of your sister's mal-intent."

"So you think we have enough evidence to get to court?" Robert wanted more reassurance.

"Well, it's not my job to say so, unequivocally. I will have to submit all this to a barrister and, only then, if he feels there is more than a fifty percent chance of winning, will I be able to ask for more funding from your insurance company. There is no guarantee that they will pay, but we can ask."

"But, they say they *will* pay if new evidence is produced, and you can convince them that Forrester's reasoning for dropping the case is spurious." Kath went red in the face from delivering her comments so vociferously.

"It will cost about seven hundred pounds to consult a barrister, but should we get the go-ahead for court and when *or if* we get the funding from the Insurance company, I can arrange for this cost to be absorbed into the final bill."

"How long will it take to get the report?"

"No more than six-months, maybe only three."

The fact a barrister's opinion was needed came as no revelation. The legal profession certainly knew how to 'make firewood from a fallen tree'. Kath thought about the analogy. It was a direct translation of a Spanish saying.

"Well let's celebrate clearing that hurdle," Robert suggested as they stepped onto the pavement, after leaving the solicitors office.

"How?" Kath responded.

"You say."

"No, you choose. I always do the organising. You think of something for a change."

"Ok, curry at *Wetherspoons* in Biddulph. It's Thursday, they always do a good curry on a Thursday."

Kath didn't argue, even though she thought it was a daft suggestion. *Curry on a hot summers day! Just like Rob to come up with that idea. If it had been a freezing cold January, he probably would have suggested a buying a sandwich and a can of Coke at M&S and gone for a picnic in a forest.* "Okay, then, so long as I can have an ice cream for afters."

They set off in their *Saab*, with the hood down, for the six-mile drive to the next town.

"You know what, Rob?" Kath turned to Rob later on in bed that night. "I don't care if this thing gets to court or not, or if you win or lose. What's important is that I tell the story of how we got even this far. I just want everyone who cares a jot to know what a hell of a bitch your sister has been. Right from the first. That's all that matters to me now. The money, the art, well, so what. I grant you it would be great if you did beat your sister in court, but really, if you don't, well, I feel like we have beaten Jeannie anyway. I've written our story and that's all. When I get it published, who knows who will read it. I should get it out within a year and that will be before you even get to court. That's if you do go to court. They may be someone reading it who might lend a hand with a bit of evidence. I see my book like the instrument that drills a hole through a thick dam. One tough job to get the hole right through then, once the dam is breached, well, you know what happens… the waters come flooding through, the hole gets bigger and bigger, till the whole bloody damn wall falls down. My story will breach that dam."

"Oh, you're so dramatic, Kath, but by God, you're right. What are we waiting for then? Come on, let's breach the dam. By the way, what will you call your book? *The Dam Busters?*"

"Don't be daft… I'll think about a title tomorrow…"

ABOUT THE AUTHOR

Mary Mae Lewis has been writing all of her life; she has kept a diary since she was sixteen and it is from the pages of her memoirs that her fiction is born.

Mary Mae has had articles published in the Press, including *The Telegraph*, and is also a published poet.

The Author has always been a prolific letter writer, too, and prides herself on having kept most correspondence ever sent to her… in fact, her dream is to write forever!

The Stoke-on-Trent born Mary Mae, always had a yearning to live in foreign climes and, together with husband, Chris, and their first son, lived in Grand Cayman for four years and then Malawi for five, where two other sons were born. Mary is now a frequent visitor to The United States, where one son and his and family live and has also visited Australia where both her brother, and a long standing pen-friend reside.

In Grand Cayman, Mary Mae worked as a reporter for the Island's weekly newspaper and as a copy writer/account executive for the monthly magazine, *The Northwester*. In Malawi, she was Secretary of the local Golf Club and produced a monthly newsletter with all the local Expat news.

Mary Mae excelled in sports and as a teacher helped others to fulfil their potential (she loved netball and was a champion swimmer). She taught English as a foreign language for the last ten years of her working life, after completing a degree in Combined Studies, with Spanish and French as her main subjects.

The Author, now spends her time equally between Southern Spain - where she does most of her writing - and Newcastle-under-Lyme, where she enjoys buying and selling antiques, and delving into local history.

Acknowledgements

With love and thanks to :

Christopher, my husband, without whose unstinting support I would not have achieved anything.

Jacki Jackson, my first reader/editor, who taught me a lot.

Wenda Dyer, an old school friend, my second reader, who had the patience to read the whole novel, and whose praise spurred me on.

And to all my other friends, too numerous to mention, who found the time to read a few odd chapters and tell me they liked my style!

To the members of the Newcastle-u-Lyme writing group, who meet in the town's public library every other Saturday and where I have been going for the past few years, for their generosity of spirit and camaraderie.

Finally, to Tania Cheslaw (www.in-scribe.co.uk), my Editor/literary consultant, whose expertise and brilliance, combined with compassion and intuition, is incomparable. She has been an angel!

Printed in Great Britain
by Amazon